Trouble Is Pili

The door opened, and the rain grew even louder. Lightning flashed, silhouetting someone who didn't need that kind of theatricality to get her point across. It was Pilar O'Heaven, all fifty feet of her. She was dripping from the swim from Catalina Island to the mainland, her blonde hair hanging loose around her shoulders. She was in her famous leopard-print bikini, and I am a little ashamed to admit looking at her more closely than I might have otherwise. She was a well-built woman, with a body sculpted by her daily swim. As she pulled a giant towel from a hook in the foyer, she looked strangely vulnerable, not something I would have expected to see in a giantess.

I had to remind myself of a very simple fact: she was fifty feet tall. She came into the living room, wrapping her towel around herself to end the show, and looked down at me with a pair of brown eyes so warm I no longer needed that fire.

Yeah, I was in trouble all right...

Praise for Fifty Feet of Trouble

"Told with irresistible charm, *50 Feet of Trouble* blends a '50s monster-film setting with a Raymond Chandleresque sensibility to tell a noir tale, often with tongue firmly in cheek."

—John F.D. Taff, Bram Stoker Award-nominated author of *The End in All Beginnings* and *I Can Taste the Blood*

City of Devils series:

City of Devils
Fifty Feet of Trouble

Other Candlemark & Gleam books by Justin Robinson:

Mr Blank
Get Blank

Fifty Feet of Trouble

Justin Robinson

First edition published 2016.

Or possibly that's just what they want you to think.

For information, address
Candlemark & Gleam LLC,
38 Rice St., #2, Cambridge, MA 02140
eloi@candlemarkandgleam.com

Library of Congress Cataloging-in-Publication Data
In Progress

ISBN: 978-1-936460-71-7
eBook ISBN: 978-1-936460-70-0

Cover art and design by Kate Sullivan

Book design and composition by Kate Sullivan
Typeface: Marion

Illustrations by Fernando Caire
www.artofernando.com

Advertising design by Alan Caum

Editors: Kate Sullivan and Athena Andreadis

www.candlemarkandgleam.com

For Lauri.

ONE

The pitcher was melting in the late August heat. Standing on the mound in the center of Gilmore Field, his right arm hung loosely just past his knobby knees, the ball imprisoned behind six-inch yellow claws. The bluish fur popping out of his collar and at his wrists was actually steaming. He mopped his brow with the back of his glove, a giant web of leather that looked like it could comfortably palm a bowling ball.

Wendigo were not built for the heat.

Even his name, Snow, written on the back of his jersey over a lucky seven, was a bad joke. I don't know what possessed him to come to Los Angeles—ghost, vampire hypnosis, or mummy's curse—but he was clearly regretting it now. Despite that, it was the top of the fourth and he had only given up one hit (and that on an ogre bunt no one could have seen coming), so maybe the big yellow California sun wasn't doing *that* much to slow him down.

The wendigo swept his fuzzy head to the left and I could just make out his beady amber eyes checking on the ogre at first. No way he was stealing second, not with that plodding run of his. Snow turned away, shook off a signal from the catcher's translucent pink pseudopod, shook off a second, then gave a grim nod at the third. He checked on the ogre again, found the monster industriously picking his nose, and wound up. Watching the wendigo gather up his spindly limbs, kick out the throw, and swing that catapult of an arm in a brutal arc was like watching a knot get yanked from a coil of rope. There was no whipcrack, though my mind supplied it, and the speed at which the ball hurtled toward the plate made me think that even if the batter made contact, his bat would just explode into wood shavings.

These things happen in the Monster League.

The batter, a beefy martian wearing a surgical mask over his lipless face, narrowed his goggle eyes, choked the bat with his tentacles, and swung.

The crack, now *that* was loud. And say what you will about life in America after the Night War, the crack of a bat against a ball hasn't changed. It's gotten a little louder, sure, depending on who's doing the throwing and who's doing the hitting, but that pop of leather off ash echoing through the stands on a summer day, that's the same as it ever was. Took me back to when I was little, watching these same Hollywood Stars—though back then they played at Wrigley Field in South LA and all of them had the normal amount of arms and legs—with my dad.

The ball miraculously stayed intact, and I pictured the stitches holding on for dear life as the ball streaked for the left field bleachers. The martian hit the jets. He ran with this slithering, hopping gait, his tentacles grabbing the earth and flinging him at first base. The ogre reacted several seconds later, thundering to second, leaving huge footprints the groundskeepers must have loved.

The hit was a line drive between second and third and I already knew it didn't have a prayer. That's because of the large gray wolf that had been prowling the infield the whole game. He didn't wear a cap, mostly because no one knew how to keep it on his head, and instead of a jersey, he had a blue kerchief knotted around his neck with LUPUS and the number 4 in red. Lupus dug into the turf, took a few quick strides, and was airborne, snatching the ball right out of the air with his teeth. He was already changing, and I swear the ball left his hand before he was totally human, right into the mitt of the second baseman.

Double play.

Lupus was a wolf again by the time he hit the ground. The crowd popped up, even us humans way out in the right field bleachers. "Yeah, Looper!" Gary Hammond called out, his little voice swallowed up in the roar. Lupus tilted his head up skyward and let them have a howl, and the crowd howled it right back at him. Even, I saw with some dismay, little Gary and Phil.

I sat back down while the Stars headed into the dugout and the Haunts took the field.

"That Lupus," Will Hammond said, shaking his head. "When he hits the majors, it's a Gold Glove for him for sure."

"Doesn't wear a glove. Think they'll call it a Gold Mouth?"

Will stifled a laugh as he looked around. No monsters in the right field bleachers, most of the time, but there might be a couple zombies who couldn't afford any better. This was the human section of Gilmore Field, and from the way the seats were in danger of falling apart, you could tell maybe the team wasn't too fond of their human patrons.

It's not like we were really fans. The Hollywood Stars were a Minor League club in the Pacific Coast League, farming out their best players to the majors. Not "our" players. The Stars were under the larger umbrella of the Monster League, and I was still enough of a loyalist that the Human League Angels were my team. We were there because Will's boys wanted to see a Stars game, and it was Sunday afternoon and no amount of species pride was going to keep me from a day knocking back some suds with my friend and taking in a game.

Gary, the elder of the boys, was sucking down his second Bebop cola, and Phil was on his third. The stuff was bright pink and powder blue in swirls that never mixed, and supposedly tasted like cotton candy. I tried a sip of Gary's and it tasted like a rocket of pure sugar trying to blow my brains out of the back of my head. It was made for clowns and gremlins, but human kids loved it too, proving there wasn't much difference. I used to like Coca-Cola in the old days, but there was scarcely a market for it anymore. I didn't envy how crazy the boys would be later when all that sugar hit them, but they were Will's problem. Besides, it was nice having them around. They took my mind off the last time I had been to Gilmore Field.

The Haunts threw the ball around as the Stars' organist played a happy little tune. It almost immediately turned into something dark and gothic, the notes giving the impression of surrounding all of us very closely, ready to carry us off at the slightest provocation. It drifted off into solo after solo—impressive that the organist could even convey the sense of playing a purposeful solo when she was the only one playing the whole time anyway, but she did. The song seemed passionate and angry, the kind of song that might follow you home and furiously demand why you hadn't returned its call.

Such were the dangers of hiring a phantom organist. That, and developing unhealthy fixations on random players and fans.

The bottom of the fourth kicked in, and since the Stars were already up two runs to none, I leaned back. Across the park, beyond the first baseline on an advertisement, Miss Hollywood Star offered a wink and a come-hither look, inviting all of us to SEE THE STARS IN HOLLYWOOD! She was Jayne Doe, a doppelganger who'd earned her fame as the in-house model at *Twilight Visitor* magazine. It was a little unseemly if you ask me, even if she was dressed like a normal, albeit shapely, housewife. That wasn't the kind of magazine you wanted to show kids—but then, most of my dislike was because it was a monster magazine. If it were just something wholesome like half-naked women, I'd have a lot less of a problem.

I watched a killer clown hit a double and zoom through the bases, his shoes honking. He slipped on a banana peel and slid into second. I couldn't help but wonder if he would have made it to third if he didn't have the urge to make everything funny.

I laughed.

"What?" Will asked. "Never met a man who thought clowns were funny."

"No, it's not that. I was just thinking. How much has changed, you know. Time was, we'd be watching men play this game."

"White men," Will said.

"Well, yeah."

"Not *that* much has changed, Nick." He surveyed the players. Will and I were friends, but the truth of the matter is, before the Night War, I would never have met the man. Or if I had, I probably wouldn't have paid him no never mind. I certainly never would have gone to a baseball game with him and his kids. "Look out, boys. Lupus is up."

The werewolf approached home plate. He was almost naked, except for a blue loincloth and the kerchief on his neck. He was a big fella, hairy and strapping like most werewolves. When he got the hit—and he *would* get the hit—the loincloth would explode off of him and he'd run the bases like furry gray lightning. The crowd was already cheering, clapping in a rhythmic thump as flesh, tentacle, metal, chitin all slammed together for the Looper. When I heard the crack, I thought for sure he'd skinned the ball. Then I saw the catcher lob it back to the pitcher. It wasn't the crack of a bat.

I'd never seen clouds move so fast. Big, glowering ones coming in from the west, flashing and growling. The thunder was so close, it was starting to sound like artillery and I flinched a little. The rushing sound, almost like applause, was the rain, getting closer and closer until it dumped out over Gilmore Field in a deluge that was so biblical I expected an ark to float through the outfield.

It happened in a matter of seconds. The crowd and the players were so stunned we all just looked upward into the rain like turkeys, like maybe our collective confusion would get the greasy black clouds to boom, "Oops! Sorry about that. We were looking for monsoon season and took a wrong turn."

The rain, of course, did not give a lick that it had just spoiled a perfect day at the park. It came down in fat stinging drops that felt like getting slapped by a drunken leprechaun. The crowd finally responded with a groan and the P.A. crackled, barely audible over the rattle of the rain, that the game was called.

"For what?" some wit a couple rows back demanded, but no one took the bait. We were already getting up, our programs or newspapers held up over our heads because no one thought to wear rain gear on a clear August day in Los Angeles, and heading for the exit.

"What's gonna happen?" Phil asked. "What's gonna happen?"

"They reschedule the game," his father said. "That's why I told you to hold onto your ticket stub. We can trade it for another game."

"But I want *this* game. Looper was gonna homer. You just know it!"

I smirked. "Looper's gonna go find a young human woman to... " I noticed Will was giving me the stink eye. "... share a soda with! At the, uh, at the fountain."

We filed out, and my program wasn't doing much more than turning into mush in my hands while the raindrops took turns kicking me in the eye. We were all soaked to the skin, and against all odds, I was actually shivering. I didn't even know it was possible to be cold at this time of year. The wendigo was probably loving it.

I looked up. The sky had totally closed in. Might as well be night for the amount of sun that was around; those big blue-black clouds blotted out everything. I wondered if the monsters realized it only *looked* like night and the Fair Game Law was still in effect. Not that that sort of thing stopped them all the time.

Can't even go to a baseball game in the goddamn City of Devils.

We piled into Will Hammond's Packard and drove away from the park. At the corner of Beverly and Fairfax, it was right on the edge of Hollywood and technically not part of Los Angeles. I'd had a little trouble with the Hollywood Sheriff's Department about two months back, and though I hadn't been linked to any crimes, I wasn't keen on another run-in with them. I felt a little better when we rolled into Watts, and then better still when we arrived on Juniper Street, where both Will and I lived.

The monsters were only just beginning to arrive, in lumbering Studebakers and sparking carts and in one case, a tripod striding from street to street. They had been caught just as unawares by the sudden storm as we had and were making certain they wouldn't miss nightfall. Will pulled into the driveway of his one-story house and we all got out.

"Place is going to be crazy tonight," Will said, looking up

as the tripod walked over us, momentarily sheltering us from the rain.

"You can say that again." Tomorrow was Monday, and chances are, I would get hired in the morning to find someone who would disappear tonight. I sighed. "See you later, boys."

They stopped shoving each other long enough to say, "Goodnight, Mr. Moss!"

I shrugged at Will. "In the grips of the Bebop."

"You have no idea."

I jogged across the street, ignoring a vampire brooding under his blackout umbrella. I'd seen the ads for that. There was a big billboard on Flower, up the street from my office. Para-Sol, some new kind of thing to block the sun for those monsters who preferred the dark. Down the street, Sam Haine, a pumpkinhead who used to harass me nightly, was pointedly ignoring me, camped out instead on Mrs. O'Herlihy's lawn. Sam looked like a skinny, dapper man with a jack-o-lantern for a head. He probably heard about Mrs. O'Herlihy's award-winning rhubarb pie, figured that translated into a working knowledge of jams and jellies, and thought he could just teach her the whole "vengeance" part of being a pumpkinhead. Still. his heart didn't seem to be in it. I might have cared had he not spent the previous several months trying to replace my head with a pumpkin.

I let myself into my house. My cat glared at me sullenly from the couch and went back to sleep. It seemed to be implying that if I disturbed it again, I would be hunted for sport. I grabbed a few things off my spice rack and checked outside. All the wards—the evil eye charms, the feathers, the crosses, the wind chimes, and so on—those were just fine. But the powdered deterrents, the sand, the salt, the allward, they were washing away into the gutter. I swore, since that stuff was more expensive than I'd like, and wondered what I was going to do. I felt the hungry gaze of several monsters waiting for the moment they could call it night and descend on the lot of us.

I sprinkled the allward on my windowsills and hoped that would be enough. If they broke down a wall, I had bigger problems anyway. I cursed the amount of windows I had in the place: the big one in front, the one in my bedroom, the two in the kitchen, and even a small one in the bathroom. At least it was only a four-room house. As I finished up at the kitchen window, a nosferatu hopped up on the fence separating my house from the alley behind it and squeaked.

"It's four o'clock," I called out to him through the closed window. With those ears, he could hear me just fine. "And if you try anything, I have a cross in my jacket and more bat guano than I know what to do with."

He hissed and dropped back into the alley.

"Like I know what to do with bat guano otherwise."

I watched the fence, waiting for him to bob back up, but he must have taken my warning to heart. Good. I moved along, sprinkling a bit of the stuff along the gap below the window on the door and hoping enough clung on. Then I put a little on the threadbare rug at the doorway to my bedroom for all the good it would do. With everything as secure as I could make it, I locked up tight and settled in with a paperback.

About an hour later, things started up. The sun wasn't down. I knew it and they knew it. But with the sun completely blocked, no one would stop them. After dark, all humans were Fair Game as per the law, and the monsters weren't going to let a little something like it not being night-based darkness stop them.

Around six, I started to make myself a sad bachelor dinner. Outside, a crawling eye slithered over my fence. No way he was getting past the lines of sand, even in the rain, and good thing, too. The same time I had trouble with the Hollywood Sheriff, I had tangled with a crawling eye, and once was enough for a lifetime. I settled into the living room with my bologna sandwich and my potato chips and listened to the sounds on Juniper Street, wondering if she was going to come.

Of course she was going to come. Never the right *she*, either.

In fact, I was three bites in when the knock came, barely audible over the hammering rain, booming thunder, and the cacophony of monsters outside.

Cacophony. Hate that word.

I set aside my food and went to the peephole, even though I didn't need to. I knew who it was, though I wondered what she'd look like this time. I was annoyed to find out she'd decided to look like Imogen Verity, the star of the silver screen and an incomparable beauty—when she had her face on—and my former client. Six feet of ice queen, platinum blonde hair, and eyes blue enough to have been yanked out of a mine in the Orient. Not to mention a face so perfect and curves so elegant, she was almost too pretty to look at. You'd probably need special gloves if you ever tried to handle her.

"Hello, Mira," I said through the door.

Because it wasn't Imogen Verity, it was another doppelganger entirely. Mira Mirra, a bit player with a contract over at RKO, who I had met a couple months earlier under embarrassing circumstances.

"Hey, Nick. Whaddya know?"

"Does Miss Verity know you're wandering around with her face? Or is that even a concern with doppelgangers?"

"Why don't you let me in, Nick? We can talk all about this face if you want."

"Um... no. No, I don't think that's such a good idea."

"Come on, don't be like that. I just want to talk."

"No, you want to turn me!"

"Don't be rude," she scolded.

I sighed. "Mira, look, I'm flattered and all, but I'm not interested. You're not my type."

"My mother used to say 'How do you know you won't like it unless you try it?'"

"You can spit out broccoli. You can't spit out being a monster."

"Nick! I expected better of you. Is it the face? Because I can change."

And she did, right there, the flesh running off her skull like melting wax, reforming and moving around to give me a look at the options. The blue eyes turned green, then brown, then hazel, then some color I didn't know the word for and hurt a little to look at, then back to blue. Her hair went through the paces, darkening to black, then bringing it back up through brown and red before completely going off into the woods with green and blue and gingham checks. Her cheeks got fuller, her body rounder, then slimmer and younger.

"The answer's still no."

"Now you're just being mean," she pouted. "I think I deserve an apology."

"I'm sorry, Mira."

She brightened. "How about a little kiss before I go?"

"Goodnight, Mira."

She continued to wheedle, but I was past listening. I picked up the paperback, knowing good old Zane Grey wouldn't hector me until I let him make me a cowboy, and went into my bedroom. When sleep came, I dreamed about the rain washing the monsters away.

Serendipity Sargasso

Two

Not a single monster was washed away, so at least the Almighty was keeping up His track record when it came to my prayers. I know no one actually expected that to be the case, but I thought I should mention it. So when I woke up—right before the sun, a habit ever since daylight had become precious—I checked out the front windows. Habit, you know. There were still a few monsters out front, notably a headless horseman urging a spectral Porsche Spyder up and down Juniper Street in a drag race against his own imagination.

Not only had it stopped raining sometime during the night, there was barely any evidence that it had rained at all. The sky was perfectly clear, steadily brightening to a clean, flat blue.

I went into the bathroom and cleaned up. I shaved, for all the good it would do; by the end of the day, I'd already have the beginnings of a beard. I always left a mustache, mostly because I went through a solid decade where shaving was unpleasant, rare, and difficult, and I still liked the novelty. It wasn't like I was going to make myself better looking. Back in the service they started calling me Weasel, and it's not like I didn't see the resemblance. By the end of the war it was Sergeant Weasel, so at least there was that. I got dressed in one of my cheap suits, tied on the matching bowtie, and checked the jacket.

Sewn into the lining were small pockets. Special job my dry cleaner did for me, but I hear a couple human clothiers will actually sell them this way now. In the pockets were the tools I needed to be the last human detective in a city of monsters. First were the vials arranged like cartridges in a bandolier: sand, salt, holy water, chicken blood, powdered potassium, among others. Then were the slightly larger objects, still within easy reach: a flashlight, a Spanish piece-of-eight, a jar of speckled mushrooms, a handkerchief I sneezed my last summer cold into, some makeup remover, a whistle, a cross, and so on. And then the holsters: one for a cold iron dagger and the other for my .32 revolver loaded with silver bullets. The revolver wasn't there.

I went into my closet and pulled out my footlocker. I'd bought it after the Night War, since in those days I never owned anything I couldn't carry on my back, but it felt like the one I'd had in Basic, back when the world made more sense and the monsters walked around looking like humans. Guess things got more honest since then. I opened it up and found my revolver waiting next to a box of silver bullets. I tended to put it into the footlocker whenever I was feeling maudlin. A sad way to try to reconnect with my days in the service, back before... well, now. I checked the load and holstered the weapon under my left armpit. I should have put the footlocker away, but I didn't.

Memories have a way of sneaking up on you, and the locker was where I kept mine. It was full of my old things, the trophies I'd taken from the two wars I'd fought back to back. The things I'd kept from my time in Europe, and the few mementos I'd dragged through the long night of the eight years that followed.

I'd held onto my Purple Heart and my Bronze Star, a swatch of the chute I'd used in France, my jump wings, and of course, the pride and joy of the collection, my old Luger. I'd taken it off a Kraut officer and had been the envy of my unit for a while after that. Everyone wanted a Luger. The ironic thing was that gun had come home with me and ended up seeing more use in the Night War than it ever had in Europe. More than one werewolf had met his end thanks to that weapon.

The other stuff in that footlocker could have gotten me killed if anyone ever found it. I'd kept the glowing core of the tripod we'd taken down over Sepulveda. The thing was only fist-sized and looked something like an hourglass filled with glowing green goo. I'd kept the Egyptian scarab off a mummy who tried to punch my ticket on the old *Intolerance* set that was still rotting on Sunset. He was a bit surprised when I'd lit the end of one of his bandages, something that never would have happened if Pharaoh brand had existed back then—it was in all their commercials. I'd kept a tooth from the nosferatu we took out near the tar pits. He had learned firsthand the danger of making his home near a bunch of trees.

I had no contact with my friends from the Army, the real army, and no idea if they were still alive or even human. The chances of surviving both wars seemed like such a long shot to me, especially considering how many times I almost got bumped. They lived in my head now, where no one could touch them. My friends from the Night War? I still talked to them—the ones who stayed human, anyway. I haven't seen Mickey in years, but Izzy Rangel and I see each other once every few months and make the same promise to go fishing. Will and I are neighbors, and I still get my meat from Janina Rakoczy's shop.

I shut the footlocker and slid it back into the closet. With a final check, I saw that the sun was up, and even the horseman had gotten tired of his one-man race and was zooming from Juniper Street, his tires leaving streaks of fire that shortly guttered and died.

I locked up the house, got into my old Ford Coupe, and drove north to the office. It was garbage day in Watts, so a blob was coming up the street, dipping its translucent pink mass into the cans and eating what it found. Every so often it would swallow the can, too, which would then dissolve into nothing. A pair of zombies followed it, each with a backpack full of powdered potassium feeding down into a hose and a gun, almost like a flamethrower. Whenever the blob got too big, they'd hose its extremities down, which would hiss and evaporate into acrid smoke.

My office was over a dry cleaner, and an external staircase led up to the two small rooms that are home to Moss Investigations. I probably should have thought the name through a little more, since it sounded like I exclusively investigated swamp plants.

Maybe that's why I hadn't had a case in a week.

I parked on the street and went upstairs, hoping my secretary would tell me about a couple of new cases. Felt guilty about that for a moment, since a case for me usually means someone got turned into a monster, but a man has to eat. And pay his secretary.

Who had her head stuck in the aquarium she kept behind her desk.

"Oh, come on. We're open."

She pulled her head out of the tank and grinned sheepishly, which for her meant the baring of hundreds of needle-like teeth. "Sorry, Nick. I caught a nice-looking halibut this weekend and I couldn't stop thinking about it."

So the aquarium *was* filled with things she had pulled out of the Pacific. I'd always had my suspicions. "Cheating on your diet?"

She pouted. "So you *do* think I need one."

"I never, ah... that is, I've always thought you were, you know. Just fine. The cat's meow. Or the fish's... whatever sound they make."

"It doesn't translate on land."

I shook my head, wondering what possessed me to hire a siren in the first place. Oh, that's right, because Ser was a hell of a deterrent against getting turned myself, and she worked for cheap so long as I gave her copious time off to be discovered. Ser, that was short for Serendipity Sargasso. She was what polite people called a siren and what rude people called a sea hag. Siren was a better word anyway, since even at her most frightening, Ser was no hag. Sure, she had blue skin with thick, wavy yellow stripes like a clownfish. Sure, she always smelled a little like the ocean, and her eyes looked ridiculous behind her goggles, and she was always getting saltwater everywhere. Sure, she had those teeth, and fins for eyebrows, and webbed fingers with little claws, and gills that frilled out like a bright red Elizabethan collar during her frequent moments of embarrassment. She was all these things, but she was also a loyal employee, and one of only a handful of monsters I could trust.

"Ser... I need to talk to you about... uh... "

"What?"

"Your roommate. Mira Mirra."

She rolled her eyes, which were huge behind her goggles, producing such a theatrical look of contempt I nearly laughed. "What did she do now?"

"What does she always do?"

"It was only because she caught you watching those stag films in our apartment."

"They weren't... ! Well, they were, but they're not the kind of stag films I like... er, you know, if I had ever seen a stag film. Which I haven't."

"She won't stop talking about it. Acting horrified, but you know she's not."

"I know that because she's harassing me at home, which you told her how to get to."

"I thought she wanted to date you, and I figured since you liked doppelgangers, I don't know, it might work out."

"I don't like doppelgangers!" I paused. "Um, I mean... I don't like or dislike doppelgangers. Someone's status as a doppelganger does not make them a more or less attractive, um... you know."

"What about ghosts?"

"Stop trying to fix me up with your roommates."

"Suit yourself. You could use a woman around your place."

I sighed. "Any cases?"

"The phone hasn't rung all morning."

"All week."

"I got doughnuts," she said.

"Thanks, Ser. You're sticking around at least until lunch."

"At least," she said, this time smiling with just her lips as she picked up an issue of *Look*. I investigated the doughnuts, and was grateful her diet meant she hadn't picked up the ones they made for sirens and gill-men that were topped with bits of raw fish. Just good old-fashioned fried and frosted dough.

My office was a cramped little thing, and by nine I had to turn on the rickety fan, ineffectually blowing swampy air through the small room. I hung up my hat and jacket and plopped behind my overflowing desk, then spent most of my time staring out through my open blinds over Flower Street. The day looked like it would be a hot one, with no trace of the deluge from yesterday. Not a cloud in the sky and the kind of still, punishing air that made summer in Los Angeles a test of one's mettle. The rainstorm had probably been one of those freak showers that swept through the desert, dumped a year's rainfall in a couple hours, and moved inland, past the two mountain ranges hemming the city in.

It was getting on toward lunch and I was beginning to think I should just let Serendipity go for the day. She was still dead set on being in pictures, and I swear her autographed photo of Imogen Verity that hung on the wall behind her desk had become her equivalent of Mother Mary. Outside, a gargoyle flapped lazily in the direction of the taller buildings downtown, losing several feet of altitude between every clumsy beat of his wings. Probably off to his security job guarding a building that didn't need much guarding. *I know how you feel, pal.*

I straightened up, and even opened my mouth to tell Serendipity to go to the Brown Derby or wherever it was she had decided on this time, when I heard the creak of the door.

"Can I help you?" Serendipity asked.

There was a response, but it was too whisper-quiet to hear. Serendipity poked her head into my office a second later. "Mr. Moss? You have a walk-in." In front of clients, it was always Mr. Moss and Miss Sargasso.

"Send him in."

She nodded, and I couldn't miss the look of distress on her face.

A moment later, a slender silhouette eclipsed the frosted glass on my door, putting my name into shadow. The door swung open, hitting one of the chairs set out for clients, and I saw who it was.

Hexene Candlemas. Maiden in the Candlemas Coven, and one of the more powerful witches in the city. She was a hex-slinger and had helped out on my last big case. She was thin as always, wrapped up in a dress that looked like an old quilt.

I smiled as soon as I saw her. It had been two months, and she had been on my mind more and more lately, even though I understood how silly that really was. But that smile died soon after. Her skin was always pale, but now it was sickly. Her bright green eyes had dulled. Even her mass of wavy red hair hung lank around her shoulders.

I popped out of my chair. “Hexene? Are you all right?”

“No,” she whispered. “You find people. Do you find toads too?”

THREE

Escuerzo?" I asked. It was a dumb question, especially if you knew who Escuerzo was. It wasn't like Hexene was concerned for toads at large; she was concerned with one particular toad. *Her* toad. Her familiar.

She nodded, and seemed on the verge of collapse. I ran around the side of my desk, slamming my knee into it. "Ow... okay. Let me help you."

Hexene used to smell like a cabinet full of fresh herbs. She still did, only now they were all dead and beginning to rot. I helped her into the chair and suddenly knew the full extent of her distress. She would have hexed anyone who tried to help her on any other day.

Serendipity was hovering in the door, her gills frilling and relaxing against her neck. "Ser? Can you get Miss Candlemas some coffee please?"

"I like tea," Hexene mumbled.

"Do we have tea?"

Serendipity shook her head helplessly and even glanced at

her aquarium, where the halibut she still hadn't eaten stared balefully back.

"Could you bring me some water?" Hexene asked.

Serendipity ran to the coffee pot, poured it out, and took it outside to fill from the drinking fountain.

I didn't know quite where to sit. Getting to the other chair would involve squeezing past Hexene, the office door, and the filing cabinet in the corner, and going back behind my desk seemed far too formal for a friend.

I settled for leaning on my desk, pushing a tower of papers back and settling down. They promptly collapsed in an unplanned demolition and scattered across my floor. "Sorry about that," I grumbled.

Hexene barely seemed to notice. She was slumped in the chair, her leather satchel cradled in her lap. She kept herbs and hexes and what-have-you in there for her spells, but more importantly, it was where her toad usually rode. She stared through me, and even ignored the silvery flying disc that momentarily eclipsed the morning sun through the window.

Serendipity had come back into the reception room; she poured some water into a mug and pressed it into Hexene's trembling hands. Hexene reached into her satchel, removed a handful of what looked like dried thistles, threw them into the mug, and spoke a magic word. It came out like someone telling a dirty joke at a child's birthday party: nothing happened.

Hexene started to cry.

"Oh. No. No no. Please don't... don't do that."

Hexene wiped her nose and kicked the desk. That was a little closer to the Hexene I knew. "I'm sorry. But not even that works. Nothing works."

"Why don't you tell me everything?"

She swallowed, her throat clicking, and nodded. "All right."

"When did you see him last?"

"Yesterday. San Pedro." She pronounced it in a flawless Spanish accent, which was not how natives said it at all. "A client called me down there for a... " She finally looked up at me, and that was almost worse. She gave me the ghost of her former defiant sneer. "Hex deal."

"What time?"

"I was around there about four in the afternoon."

I had been at the game and the sky was just about to open up.

"What happened?"

"He wanted to meet at Royal Palms Beach." That was a rocky stretch of coastline just off the suburban neighborhood of San Pedro. Mostly vampires, sirens, and gill-men, if memory served. "He wasn't there. I landed, waited, and Escuerzo tried to warn me. He ribbited—his danger ribbit, you understand—but it was too late. Something jammed a hood over my head and wrapped me up in these strong arms. Very strong. They stank, too, almost like a skunk, and I felt fur or hair or something. I tried to fight, tried to hex whoever it was, but something hit me on the head and I blacked out. And when I woke up... " She sniffed, and I could tell she was fighting her damnedest to keep from crying, "Escuerzo was missing."

"I thought witches could see through the eyes of their familiars?" That was something Lily Salem, a previous client of mine, had told me. She had a petite red robin, a far cry from Hexene's corpulent toad.

"We can, but all I see is darkness. I can hear these booms and hollow clanking. And I can feel his fear, but... "

She was getting ready to crumble, so I swept in. "The monster holding you... was it your client?"

She shook her head. "No. Paolo's a gill-man. He has scales, not fur."

"He was the one who called you, right?"

"Yes. It was his voice on the phone. He asked to meet at that beach specifically."

"And that's unusual?"

"Normally I go to his house."

"Which is in San Pedro?"

"Watts. Not far from your place."

I frowned. "Strange place for a gill-man to live." We didn't have many monsters in the neighborhood. To my knowledge, there had just been a zombie or two, which are really only barely a step up from humans in the eyes of most monsters. Gill-men generally like to live on the coast, or at least next to artificial bodies of water. Of course, sirens are the same, and Serendipity lived in Torrance with her two roommates.

"He wanted to be close to his... well, he calls her his beloved."

"Oh. Right. Yeah."

In the world of monsters, gill-men were romantics. Not like vampires, who did a whole metaphor for eating that only got more disturbing the more you thought about it. And not like phantoms, who developed an unhealthy obsession with their crushes that inevitably led to arson and death traps. No, gill-men seemed to be prone to pure and incorruptible swanning over any number of humans and monsters. It wasn't always about turning them—though with humans it tended to go in that direction—more that the gill-man wanted to be with the person. It was almost normal. Well, as normal as anything could be when one was dealing with a super-strong green monster who spent most of his time underwater.

"This beloved have a name?"

"Corrina Lacks. I needed it for the hexes he bought from me."

"You were selling him love spells?" That didn't sound like a gill-man. That sounded more like a vampire to me.

"No. He bought hexes that would make him feel like Corrina was in love with him. It was a challenge to craft initially, but once I got it cold, it was duck soup."

"And this gill-man? I can't imagine your coven would let this go. He sto... er, he kidnapped one of your familiars—your mother and your crone must have been royally cheesed off."

"They are, but their hexes aren't working right either. The coven depends on all three of us fulfilling our roles. All of us need our familiars. If one gets... lost, things are thrown out of balance, and who knows what will happen?"

Not wanting to get her caught in a loop of despair, I did the only thing I could think to do that might help: I grabbed a pad and jotted down everything she had told me thus far. "Could you spell the names for me?"

She did. The gill-man's full rebirth name was Paolo del Mar.

"And what does he do?"

"He's a longshoreman at the Port of Los Angeles."

It was a heck of a drive from Watts to San Pedro, but I guess it was worth it to Paolo to be close to Corrina Lacks. "All right, Hexene. Don't worry about anything. I'm going to find Escuerzo for you."

"Nick, you don't understand." She looked into my eyes, and hers were dim, red, and wrapped in tears. "Everything we cast as a coven is going haywire. Replaying, only wrong."

I swallowed. "Wait, you hexed me a lot, if I recall."

"Sorry about that."

"No, if everything you cast is coming back... "

"That will too. The big ones first, but eventually everything will come back. In the worst way possible."

I remembered something Hexene had told me a few months back. I was on a case, tracking a missing city councilman, and Hexene was a suspect. She had broken into my house in a misguided bid for my trust—that had completely worked, now that I thought about it, though she had no idea I would be such a sap—and had talked about what the Candlemas Coven did.

"Big ones... you mean the weather spell," I said.

She nodded. They were going to cast a spell to even out the weather in the southland. Apparently they had cast it and now it was falling prey to the kidnapping of a toad. I thought of the deluge yesterday at the ballgame.

"The rain?"

She nodded.

"Where did you cast it?"

"Do you know the Sunken City?"

A section of San Pedro not far from Royal Palms, taken by an earthquake and landslide and dumped into the sea. The ruins were still there, poking from the earth, scattered down the rocky cliffs and into the surf. I nodded.

"How much worse is it going to get?"

"A lot worse before it gets any better."

And right on cue, someone in reception let out an ear-splitting shriek.

Four

I hopped up again, toppling another tower of files. Roused from her funk, Hexene craned her head around. I opened the office door and immediately hit the back of Hexene's chair. Instead of asking her to move, I just snaked my way out the door and into reception. I moment later, I heard Hexene getting up anyway.

What I found was Serendipity with her gills in total extension, her webbed hands up, and streams of saltwater running down her face and dripping onto her navy dress from where her goggles had slipped. "It's okay! I'm not going to hurt anyone!" she said, blinking myopically. She couldn't see a thing unless it was through a layer of seawater.

She was ineffectually trying to comfort the couple at the door. Humans, looking as haggard as Hexene did. The husband was standing protectively in front of his wife. The woman's shock had faded and she was already talking, already apologizing. "I'm sorry! I wasn't expecting... I didn't know... I thought... "

And I realized I knew both of them. Henry and Alice

Brooks. Met them at the tail end of the Night War, just after the unpleasantness at Gilmore Field, and hadn't seen them in almost two years. We had gotten together once after the Treaty, when we had all started our new lives. It was kind of a celebration, though it never got a catchy name like V-Day. I think that's because the monsters technically won and were nice enough not to rub it in our faces. We all pledged to stay in touch. We hadn't. And instead I had settled into my routine and not done much of anything.

Aggie wasn't with them. Aggie. Their daughter. She would have been about eleven. Was school in session? I hoped school was in session. I knew it didn't matter. They were here because she was gone, and I didn't want to admit it.

"Henry? Alice?" I said. "What can I do for you?"

Alice pushed past Henry, who never took his eyes off Serendipity for more than a few seconds at a time. "Nick, we need to hire you. You're a private eye, that's what I heard. You find people."

The doughnut I had eaten abruptly turned to stone in my belly. I wanted to sit down. *Not Aggie. Come on, world, show a little mercy here.* "Uh... yeah, yeah, that's right."

"Looks like you already have a client," Henry said, nodding over my head. He did that easily, since I'm on the short side, and Henry's ancestors probably burned half of Europe from longships.

Hexene was lurking in the doorway, shielding herself behind part of it. That was not Hexene at all. She should have been pugnaciously stepping up, ready to find offense in everything Henry said. "It's all right," she nearly whispered.

"Hexene, I'm sorry. I'm taking your case, don't worry. I'll find your, um... I'll find Escuerzo. If I need to talk to you again, I'll come down to your shop." Hexene had an herbalist place on Gower.

"All right. Thanks, Nick."

She slipped out of the office, not even a shadow of her old self.

"Come in, come in." I shook Henry's hand. His grip was firm but clammy, and he would not stop looking at Serendipity. I clasped Alice's hands and she looked ready to fall apart. Not like Hexene had been; while it felt like a part of Hexene was missing and she was less for it, it felt like some of Alice Brooks had been wrenched from her and she was collapsing around an agonizing wound. I pointed out their seats and moved back around my desk to straighten up some of the mess I'd made. Of course, in the cramped and stuffy office, it was difficult to separate the clutter from the functional parts.

I almost asked after Aggie, but a superstitious part of me kept her name out of my mouth. It promised that if I spoke it, it would be to Aggie. I told myself not to speak it then, say something else. Anything else. Maybe it was a social call. One look at either of them said it wasn't.

Henry was sitting sternly on the left, Alice clutching one of his hands.

"What brings you here?" I asked. Sounded neutral enough.

"Aggie."

I collapsed into my seat. I knew it was coming, but the confirmation was worse. "What happened?" was all I could manage.

"She's missing," Henry snapped. "The hell do you think happened?"

"Right, no, I know, I'm just... uh, how?"

Alice was already crying, deep, wracking sobs. She and Henry had already experienced this once. Their son, JJ, had disappeared only a few weeks after I met them. Izzy and I had gone out to look for him. In some ways, that had been my first case. And my first failure, since I never found a single trace of the boy. And now, three years later, their daughter goes missing.

"We put her to bed last night. And when we woke up, she was gone."

"What do you mean, 'gone'?"

"Is there another definition I don't know about?" Henry shouted.

The bellow even stunned Alice from crying.

"Um... no, but... uh, what I'm asking is, were the wards in place? Was the window open? What did her room look like?"

"We keep her wards perfectly updated to keep the snatchers at bay."

"It rained yesterday."

"I know. We went indoors early."

"No, I mean at my house, some of the wards, salt and the like, got washed away."

"I was aware of that. I retouched everything."

"And her closet? Under the bed?"

"We have teddy bears there. Or did you think the rain washed them away, too?"

"Henry, please!" Alice said.

"It's all right," I said. "I know... well, I don't know, but I, uh... I understand? And I want to help."

"You *can* help?" Alice asked me, the hope in her voice heartbreaking.

I had a speech I sometimes gave, when the clients were a little less fragile, and the missing person wasn't someone who had helped keep me sane in the worst year of my life. See, in this business, nine times out of ten, I wasn't looking for a person anymore. I was looking for a monster. And the happy ending, in my well-rehearsed patter, was that their daughter was happy being a fish girl now. There was no way I could give that speech. Not about Aggie Brooks, and not when her mother was looking at me like a dog who thought maybe this one time, the person wouldn't kick him.

"I can help," I lied.

FIVE

That lie haunted me all the way to their home. They were over on 115th Street, not far from where I lived, though the neighborhood was a little more rundown than mine. The open lots were brownish yellow with dead grass and even the trees looked about ready to give up. Wards were hung more openly, from telephone wires, tree branches, road signs; collections of runes, feathers, and beads that probably served only to make a few different kinds of monsters feel vaguely uncomfortable. The entire neighborhood was dominated by a faded billboard for Coca-Cola standing in the lot on the corner, showing just how much advertisers cared about reaching this particular market.

Before leaving, I told Serendipity where I was headed, and the mood was too somber for her to even request the day off. She nodded and settled back behind her desk, trying not to look hurt and sad.

Along the drive, following Henry's faded Oldsmobile, all I could think about was bad luck. I met Henry and Alice after a long night going across the city. It was '52 by then and the war had already hit the turning point. If I hadn't known that before, I sure as hell did then. A small group of us, led by me and Izzy and Mickey, were heading for the rumors of another human holdout in the railyards, hiding from all the different monsters that screamed and gibbered and laughed in the night. There were a couple fights along the way, and Mickey, crazy bastard that he was, thought it was fun. No man ever took more joy in coming up with creative ways to torment monsters than old Mick.

We made it, and only lost one person. We hadn't even noticed she was gone. We just looked around at one point, and it was, "Hey, where's Norma?" Only no one ever saw Norma again. Chances are, she was still alive, she just had some new dietary restrictions and a phobia or three.

The community in the railyard was set between a couple of abandoned cars, with ways in from the north and east. These were guarded and warded; the whole place was hung with enough bizarre things that they were repelling kinds of monsters that didn't even exist yet. It was a minor miracle we found them at all, since most humans hunkered down at night and just tried to see the sun again with the same number of eyes. We were granted entrance into the community and I settled in for what remained of the night. I didn't sleep a wink, not with what I saw at Gilmore, and when the sun came up, we got to look forward to another day.

And who was the first person I saw? Well, okay, it was Izzy, snoring like he had something caught in the back of his throat, because Izzy could sleep anywhere. The second person I saw was little Aggie Brooks. She had that look that kids in war zones get, and I wish it wasn't one I knew so well. She could have been French, Belgian, or German, but she wasn't, she was American. Her dress was a filthy rag by then, and she had an adult's coat thrown over her shoulders even though it was going to be much too hot for something like that. Her cheeks should have been full, but they were hollowed out. I met her eyes, expecting a thousand-yard stare, but didn't get it. She broke into a smile, and though her teeth were smudged, I'd swear it glittered.

She walked over and shyly handed me a steel pot lid, and in it was the smallest fried egg I'd ever seen.

"Thanks," I managed. I almost shoved it into my mouth, but willpower is important. "You want some?"

She shook her head and watched me eat the egg. Just to see the look on my face. It took about half a bite. It was cold, runny, a little spoiled, and the best egg I have had before or since. I handed her the empty pot lid back and she scampered off.

That's when Izzy opened his eyes with a snort. "What? What happened?"

"You missed the breakfast fairy."

His eyes opened up all the way. "Monsters? In here?"

I was laughing too hard to calm him down.

I got to know the Brooks family after that. Henry, Alice, JJ, and Aggie. The perfect little nuclear family. JJ was twelve, Aggie nine—I guess that made her twelve now—and pretty wife and tough husband. I found out later Henry wasn't their natural father. JJ stood for John, Jr., and their father had been a medic killed at Omaha Beach. Henry and Alice had gotten married in '47, before the Night War got really bad, and Henry had stuck with them. He loved those kids, too. You could tell, the way he doted on them. At the time, the Brooks family turned into a symbol of what I was fighting for. There was nothing else, not by '52 anyway.

Aggie had been a tagalong, and I swear, she saved my bacon more times than a lot of my unit back in France. She was nearly silent, for one thing, and her senses were sharp as a mouse's.

I'd get a tug on my shirt tail, and then Aggie—that's Agatha, but we never called her that—would make herself scarce, and I knew the monsters were closing in. If I didn't know better, I'd say she could smell them.

And then, a couple weeks after that breakfast, JJ vanished into thin air.

I pulled up in front of the Brooks house, shaking the past off. It was reasonably big, one story, and looked to have an extra bedroom or two. A squat and craggy California oak shaded half the house from the front yard. The wards were visible even from where I was standing, and that was including wind chimes and feathers hanging motionless in the tree branches.

I got out of the car. The air was completely still, but big white clouds were piling up behind the San Gabriels, just waiting to sweep in and drown us again. The air was unbearable. I had already sweated through my shirt and was in danger of doing the same to my jacket. Just once, I'd like to make it through a hot day and not look like I'd just strolled through a carwash.

The house looked secure, at least from where I was standing. The Brookses had parked on a cracked driveway and I joined them on the walk up to the house. A few crosses were tacked to the house, next to windows. "What do you need to see?" Henry asked.

"Her room. That's where... uh... you saw her last?"

Alice sniffled. "Nick? Do you want to stay for lunch? I'll make you some sandwiches."

"That's... thanks, Alice."

Henry opened up the door, and the house felt empty. It's difficult to put into words, but it was a sensation I'd felt before many times, though not quite as heavy as I felt it at that moment. Probably because I knew whose absence was making it feel that way.

The living room had only a few pictures on the walls, and

like most homes now, nothing before 1953. Alice went into the kitchen at the back while Henry led me into a short hall and opened a door to what had been Aggie's room.

"This is it," he said.

"Yeah." I hadn't seen Aggie in the last couple years, but it fit. This felt right, felt like the girl I knew back during the war. It was all done up in blue. She liked blue, I remembered that, and she always chattered on and on about the last time they had been to the beach when she was little. She was looking forward to going back once the monsters were taken care of. To her, the Night War was a temporary interruption in normal life, even though if she remembered a time without monsters, it was only barely. She took it on faith that we would be able to clean things up. She was wrong.

I made a slow circuit of the room, trying and failing to edit out its contents. She had books upon books about dinosaurs and a few plastic toys standing on her shelves. I picked one up.

"She loves dinosaurs," Henry said. "Wants to be a paleontologist, she says."

"She's a smart girl."

"As a whip. Didn't have nothing to do with me, either. I guess her father was smart. Sometimes she'd get to talking and I would have no idea what she was going on about. Some fossil this, or dig site that... " His expression darkened. "I don't have the heart to tell her UCLA doesn't take humans anymore."

"Things could change by the time she's ready to go."

"They won't. Goddamn snatchers are in charge now."

I shrugged, not wanting to engage. It was the second time he'd used the term. At least this time Serendipity wouldn't have to hear it.

He was having none of it. "Speaking of which, I never figured you would have a snatcher for a secretary."

"She, uh... she likes 'siren.' She's pretty specific."

"A snatcher's a snatcher. You, of all people. Back in the war, you were a killer."

"War's over."

"Yeah. We lost."

I opened up her closet and turned on the lights. Beyond her clothes and a couple of games on the shelf, there was a teddy bear tacked to the wall. I didn't think Henry would lie about that, but it was worth checking on. I shut the lights off and closed the door.

"You have... uh... regular visitors?" I asked, thinking of Mira Mirra, who came to my place a few times a week.

"Visitors?"

"Night visitors."

He scowled. "Oh, yes. There's a headless horseman who wants Alice. We had to buy a real gold coin, and you know how expensive that is, especially supporting a child. But it's still cheaper than digging a moat around the property. Sometimes I think they make these weaknesses up just to bleed us dry."

"I meant for Aggie. Are there monsters who are after her specifically?"

"There's a bogeyman, of course. And a clown."

Typical. I peeked under the bed and found another teddy bear there. The room seemed well-warded. A window looked out onto the walkway between houses. A weatherbeaten fence separated the properties.

"Did you get names from either of them?"

"The bogeyman, no. The clown is—get this—a minister."

"Oh?"

"Yeah. Reverend Bobo Gigglesworth. So not only is he trying to change my daughter, he's trying to make her lose her soul."

"Mmm." Another road I didn't want to go down. Henry Brooks

had never been my closest friend, but he had been fairly reasonable in the war. Had Aggie's abduction pushed him off some kind of cliff? Or maybe my definition of reasonable had changed.

I turned back to the window. This was the way in. "Was the window closed?"

"Of course," Henry said.

I unlocked it and slid it open. It went with nary a sound and held open without trouble. I checked the sill, finding remnants of various powders. Leaning outside, I saw the larger wards. The sounds of the neighborhood—a few birds, the tinkling of chimes and the click of charms—filtered in.

"I warded the sills before we went to bed," Henry said. "The snatchers were already gathering by the time we got home. Guess not even the law means anything to them."

He was not wrong, but it made my skin crawl whenever he said "snatcher." I kept thinking of Hexene and Serendipity, who were not snatchers—they were my friends. And then it made my skin crawl that it made my skin crawl. A monster had snatched Aggie, after all.

I almost shut the window. Something caught my eye, wedged in the corner, caught by an errant splinter of wood. A few strands of hair. I knelt, carefully unhooking it off the splinter and holding it up. Mostly straight, orange, and coarse. I turned it over in my hand. Clowns sometimes had orange hair, but it tended to be curly. This was more fur than hair. Bogeymen might be furry; I'd never gotten a clean look at one, not even when one broke into my house that one Christmas. Neither seemed quite right to me, but this hair belonged to whatever had taken Aggie Brooks. I was holding a physical remnant of the bastard, left behind when he made the biggest mistake of his life.

I stood up, and turned around, fishing an empty vial from my coat. The fur went into that.

"What's that? A clue?" Henry asked.

I nodded. "Don't worry, Henry. No matter what you think, what you saw, I'm still the Nick you knew from the war. I'll find this guy for you."

"And then?" he asked.

I tucked the vial away. I didn't know quite what to say. I wasn't an avenger, and I wasn't even sure if I *was* the Nick he knew. I knew Aggie, though. I knew I'd get her back. "And then we decide what to do with the bastard."

Henry smiled, but it was the most wolfish thing I'd ever seen. And I knew actual werewolves.

Six

Henry and I sat on the cracked concrete of the porch steps, eating ham and cheese on hard rye bread, and looked out across the street to where a sagging house still had a few old burn marks from the war that no one had bothered painting over. We didn't talk about it after I'd promised to help him get revenge. Seemed that was what he had wanted, and I had provided. I had to separate the two groups in my head. Serendipity and Hexene might be monsters. But this guy, whoever he was, was a snatcher.

Henry and I talked instead about our lives now. He wanted to know about the PI game. He only had the movies to think of, or the cartoons where Marty Meatstick was always on the run from Wally Wolfman. The humans were the bad guys in all of those, sneering hunters who thought nothing of hammering on the one weakness of whatever helpless monster they happened to be tormenting. The happy ending was when Wally finally got one over on Marty and locked him in the slammer, usually stealing Marty's girl while he was at it. It was implied that he turned her, but it was only implied. These things were for kids, after all.

I told him it wasn't like that. I had to hide the realities from him, since the last thing a worried father needed was to be told that I probably wasn't going to find his daughter in the same state he left her in. And that's how I was thinking of her: "his daughter," because as soon as she was Aggie Brooks, she was almost as important to me. That was a good way to lose perspective.

He didn't want to talk about his job either. Before the Night War, he had been a factory foreman. Now he swept the floors of the same factory while some monster half his age had his old job.

So we did what men do in those situations. We talked baseball. Human League, specifically. The Los Angeles Angels. Even that was touched a little by the realities of life, as every now and then Henry would bitterly speculate on which of our guys were going to get turned and recruited into the Monster League. I finished my sandwich quickly.

"You can set that down," Henry said. "I'll get to it later."

I put the plate on the concrete. "I'm going to get to work. You can call the office if you want any updates."

"That's all right, Nick. You call when you find something."

I nodded, the food turning over in my stomach at the sound of his confidence.

I wanted to talk to that clown Henry had mentioned, but the trail of Hexene's case was a little closer. That's how I'd have to do this: work the closer case. Hope to solve both, and probably solve neither. I needed to talk to Paolo del Mar. He might not have kidnapped Hexene's toad, but chances are, he knew who did. I drove, leaving Henry behind to brood on his porch while his wife wandered the house like a ghost. I pulled over at the first phone booth I found and paged through the directory. With people getting turned every day, it was a crapshoot on how much was accurate.

But there it was, Paolo del Mar, and his address was listed. He lived in Watts, something I still didn't quite believe even after seeing it. Gill-men weren't the ritziest of monsters, but he could afford better than a human neighborhood. He must really like that girl of his.

I dialed the number and someone picked up. "Hello?" The voice was gummy. Sounded like most gill-men I had talked to. I hung up the phone.

I drove over to del Mar's place, a nice one-story ranch home on one of the better streets in the neighborhood. His paint was new, and his house was the only one on the block not festooned with charms and wards. *Come on in to the gill-man's lair, we have hors d'oeuvres right next to the black lagoon.*

I pulled over and got out of my car. The street was so quiet, I could hear the television in del Mar's house, tuned to the incessant droning of the HUMAC hearings. Monsters had been glued to their sets over that one, and it was nice to see them picking on each other for a change.

I was going up the strip of sidewalk leading up del Mar's healthy lawn and to his door when, from inside the house, there was a crash and a burbling shout. I accelerated, pulling open the screen door and shouting, "Paolo! Paolo, are you there?"

Another crash. Louder this time, but the accompanying cry was softer. I stepped back and kicked the door as hard as I could. The lock tore through the jamb and the door slammed against the wall, almost rebounding shut. The air inside smelled like the ocean, or more accurately, the reception room at Moss Investigations. Stronger, though, the gill-man really marinating in his scent, whereas Serendipity fought against it. The door opened into a tiny foyer and I was just getting my bearings when the wall next to me shook with an impact. I cringed, instantly reverting to my old combat hunch.

I stepped into the living room. I thought there would be carpet, but the tile that started in the foyer seemed to go through the house. Made sense when the owner came home dripping with seawater more often than not. The television was on, but it was also on its side. Congressman Akhenaten I, his eyes glowing with righteous anger, was interrogating some poor vampire from the top of a dais, gesturing emphatically with one impeccably bandaged finger. The vampire cowered. From what I could tell, his crime had been that he was an agent and still represented several human performers.

The rest of the room was destroyed. Shelves had crashed down and there were dents in the plaster walls, with fallen pictures scattered on the floor. I was pretty sure that if I were to put del Mar up to one of those dents, he would fit neatly.

Another thump sounded, through a doorway to my right, though deeper into the house than before. I almost reached for my pistol, now snug as a bug under my left armpit. That was the wrong move. In the old days, everything died from bullets, didn't matter if he was Johnny, Fritz, or Tojo. Now, a gun could do as much harm as good, taking up space in your hand when a pinch of salt was what the situation called for.

I went to the open doorway and peeked through just in time to see a green shape hurtle by at the end of the hall. In the far room, someone was using Paolo del Mar as a poorly balanced football.

"Stop! Police!" It was the first thing I could think to shout. My voice wasn't authoritative. It's high, something that got me teased in school and the service, but I could manage some impressive volume when I was worked up.

Whatever was in there seemed to agree. I heard a hideous groan, then a shriek, both of which sounded mechanical, and then a crash and shatter the likes of which dwarfed the racket that had been coming from the house before. I stepped into the kitchen cautiously and saw what had caused it. The icebox had been torn out of the wall and hurled through the door, where it was now lying, broken and dented, on the back patio. Whatever had done it was gone—I caught a flash of movement and a shadow vaulting over the back fence. If it could do that, I wasn't about to chase it down.

I turned to the other side of the kitchen, where a horribly battered gill-man lay sprawled over a breakfast table and chairs. It was tough to separate the natural scales and bumps from the injuries, though there were some open wounds leaking the fishy ichor they used for blood. His work clothes, simple slacks and a checkered shirt, were torn and stained. The gills were entirely still, and the big black eyes were empty. Well, emptier than usual. He'd been beaten to death.

I was in a bad situation. Put a human in the room with a dead monster and it didn't matter the cause of death. That human was going down for the crime, no questions asked. But this was my one lead in Hexene's case. I could chalk everything up to coincidence, but a big part of being a detective was a firm belief that coincidence is the word for a connection you can't prove yet.

I knelt beside the dead gill-man. Beating one to death took something special. Gill-men were tough sons of bitches. Their scales were nearly bulletproof and they were twice as strong as most men. Whatever had done this had thrown this fella around like a toy.

I stood up and glanced outside. Most of del Mar's backyard was taken up by a kidney-shaped swimming pool. The water didn't look treated, judging by the leafy ropes of seaweed growing up from the bottom. I took a step away from the fallen gill-man, and that's when I noticed the smell.

His blood was overpowering close up, but farther away, I caught another scent. Musky, like an animal. Like an ape. My nose found the memory before I could tell it that, no, I'd rather skip the shell shock today, thanks. Hiding in the tunnels of Gilmore Field, too few of us still left. The roar. And the walls cracking and tumbling down, and the huge, black fist, the fingers curling around Betsy Miller, and that's the last I ever saw of her. The rubble had parted then, and Izzy, Mickey, and I were already running, but we could still hear *him*, roaring and pounding his chest along with the screams of the people he was plucking up like popcorn.

I shook it off. It wasn't *that* ape scent. Similar, certainly, but not as overpowering. And there was something else, almost like an exposed wire. Could be the ozone in the air, the scent of another rainstorm. A glance out the window, at the clouds that were beginning to roll in from both sides, said that was probably the case.

I knew I didn't have much time before someone would call the wolves, if they hadn't already. I went through the house and saw the evidence of whatever the unknown monster had done to del Mar. Every room showed signs of the fight. In his bedroom, the chest of drawers had been turned on its side, spilling out over the floor.

A cigar box was upside down. I righted it and found a series of photos, all of which were shots of the same girl. Very pretty, big eyes, dark skin, looked maybe in her early twenties. In several of the shots, she was carrying an armload of books and I thought I recognized some of the palm trees on the Santa Monica Junior College campus. She dressed like any carefree girl, in white blouses and monster skirts. It wasn't too surprising that the stylized man on the corner of the skirt wasn't a gill-man. The lady seemed to prefer pumpkinheads.

I could always introduce her to one. The back of each photo had a pencil description and a date, written in a wobbly hand. "Corrina after school." "Corrina on the way to the movies." Creepy, sure, but not as bad as it could have been.

I wiped what I'd touched and put it all back on the floor. It was time to get out of this place. At least the street had been quiet. If my luck held, it still would be, and I could go, no one ever being the wiser.

I went out the door and my eyes immediately met those of a woman standing in her yard across the street, wrapped in a housecoat with rollers stuck through her gray hair. So much for anonymity. I pulled my fedora down, got in my car, and drove.

SEVEN

Corrina Lacks was in the neighborhood, and she might know something about what happened to her unwanted paramour. I didn't suspect her for obvious reasons, though it was possible a jealous rival suitor had decided to eliminate the competition. No, the incurable cynic in me was pretty certain that whoever made del Mar call Hexene was the one who offed him. Still, there was a chance Corrina knew something.

I found her in the same book that led me to del Mar and learned she was only a few blocks away. Far enough I felt a little safer after being spotted, but close enough that it made sense as my next stop. I figured I could talk to Mrs. Lacks about her daughter's whereabouts, then possibly make the drive out to Santa Monica to speak with Corrina. I had no idea if she'd be upset about Paolo getting his ticket punched. I tried to think how I would feel if Mira Mirra or Sam Haine bought it in the same way. They were edging into snatcher territory, those two, charming only in their abject failure.

The Lacks home was located on a dirt road between two

paved ones. The city would probably get around to laying down some blacktop eventually, though they would move a little faster if there were any monsters on the street. The house itself was in good repair, on a small lot with dying grass, festooned with an old pickup rusting gently on blocks and the usual array of anti-monster equipment. A quick glance said they were protected and, from the looks of things, particularly protected against several kinds of monsters, with more holy symbols than might normally be needed for home security: several bright lights useful against gill-men and gremlins among others, and clumps of sage burned along the edges to frighten off ghosts.

The yard was about the size of a postage stamp and the house looked as small as mine. Hardly the place you'd want to raise a family. I knocked on the door, and a moment later, it opened. The woman on the other side was in her forties, blinking at me with red eyes. My stomach dropped through the floor as I realized what must have happened.

"Can I help you?" she asked.

"Uh, yeah. Mrs. Lacks?"

"Yes."

"My name is Nick Moss. I'm a private investigator. I was hoping I could ask you a few questions?"

"Is this about Corrina?"

"Sort of. Uh... I'm very sorry. Corrina is missing, isn't she..." It wasn't a question.

Mrs. Lacks sniffed and nodded. I swore inwardly. Every stop and this thing got worse and worse, to say nothing about Aggie Brooks still out there in the wind.

"Can I come in?"

"Who hired you to find my daughter?" Mrs. Lacks asked. She didn't move an inch and even if she hadn't been a formidable-looking woman, there's nothing that could have made me try to force my way in.

"Well, um, no one actually. I was on an unrelated matter and your daughter's name came up. So here I am."

She looked me over and must have decided she either liked or was indifferent to what she saw because she said, "Come in," and stepped aside.

I took off my hat and edged into her tiny living room. Pictures were all over the walls showing a smiling family, but the house felt hollow. Like the Brooks place. She gestured to a chair and I obediently took a seat. "Would you like some lemonade?"

"No thanks, ma'am."

She nodded, seemingly with relief, and settled onto the sofa. "Ask your questions, Mr. Moss."

"Uh... of course, yes." I took out my notebook and the stub of a pencil and poised ready to write. "When did Corrina go missing?"

"Saturday night or Sunday morning. You want to know who did it, you should talk to that del Mar fishhead. Lives a couple blocks over. I'll give you his address."

"No, ma'am. That's, uh, that's all right. I'm familiar with Mr. del Mar."

"He do something?" Mrs. Lacks narrowed her brown eyes and the red looked like it was bleeding into the iris for a moment. I tried to picture Mrs. Lacks, all five feet three inches and a hundred forty pounds of her, throwing Paolo del Mar around with the strength of ten men. The image carried some weight for all of two seconds, and in those two seconds, I was sure I'd solved the case.

"Uh, yes and no, ma'am. Can you tell me about what happened to Corrina?"

She shot me a suspicious look, but acquiesced. "She was out

with that no-good boyfriend of hers most of Saturday and he didn't get her home till barely before dark. Steven, that's my husband, and Brian, my son, had checked all the wards and so on, and we were secure. She should have been home with us. Guarding a home is a family matter."

I nodded at that, because I think that's what she was trying to get me to do, and I was a little frightened of Mrs. Lacks.

"You have a family, Mr. Moss?"

"No. Uh, no, ma'am."

Her face soured.

"Mrs. Lacks, can you take me through what happened Saturday night?"

"No."

"I'm sorry about what happened, but I need to know what happened to Corrina."

"Why? No one's hired you, and we sure as hell can't afford to pay no detective."

I regretted the words as soon as they came out, because they marked me as a sap, but what the hell. Be what you are. "If I come across Corrina in my investigations, who's to say I can't bring her home, too?"

To her credit, Mrs. Lacks didn't laugh in my face. It was the biggest whopper I'd told in a while, even worse than the one I sold to Henry earlier that day. Even if Corrina's disappearance was connected to what I was doing—and that was still one hell of an "if"—odds were I'd be bringing home a monster.

Mrs. Lacks watched me and for a second, it felt like she could look right through me. She would have made quite a cop, assuming a wolfman ever turned her. "All right, Mr. Moss. All right." She took a deep breath, taking away the searchlight to redirect it at the mantel. I followed her gaze and saw a picture of the four of them, a handsome family to be sure. Corrina was right there in the middle in her pumpkinhead skirt, her long curly hair pulled back with a ribbon to explode in a giant pom-pom at the back. I saw what Paolo del Mar had seen in her and instantly felt dirty.

"Corrina went to her room around eight, said she had schoolwork. She's studying history, says she wants to teach. That's the last we saw of her."

"Did you check the wards?"

I regretted that as soon as her head whipped around. "Do you think we're stupid?"

"No, no, not at all. I, uh, have to ask. You know, eliminate everything, make sure there's no assumptions."

"We checked the wards. My son and husband check the wards every night before bed."

"And they were all in place."

She nodded.

"Then how did anything get in?" I was asking myself, but she didn't take it that way.

"I thought you were the detective."

"Uh, right. Can I see her room please?"

She stood up with a sigh and I followed her. The entire house looked too small for all that was packed inside. I had to gingerly edge around the sofa and navigate around a bookcase leaning against one of the few bare walls. She led me into a tiny hall with four doors coming off it, opening one in the center. The room looked sized about right for an infant. Corrina's bed took up most of it, with her dresser and a vanity mirror eating up the rest. There was a swatch of floor that maybe one person could fit on at a time. A window looked out into the backyard, which was scarcely more than a dog run ending in a wooden fence. Textbooks were stacked on the bed, one open to a section on the Salem Witch Hunts. I moved over the window and got an eerie sense of déjà vu.

Second time today, a disappearance out of a bedroom without a sound. I shook it off; now was not the time to get superstitious.

"What is it?" Mrs. Lacks asked from behind me. "You look like someone just walked over your grave."

The woman had a lie-detecting radar. She would have made an incredible cop.

"Not sure yet. Do you mind if I open the window?"

"So long as you close it once you're done."

I had to get onto Corrina's bed to do so, since the bed was right up against the wall. I unlocked the window, and just like Aggie's, it went up clean and silent.

"You said she had a boyfriend?" I asked.

"And just what are you implying?"

"Uh, nothing. Nothing at all. Someone I should probably talk to." Yeah, I wasn't implying that a girl with a boyfriend would have a good reason to make sure her window was nice and quiet.

"Mmm-hmm. His name's Jaime Alvarez, and he's a no-account hoodlum. You can find him with his friends most days at a park on Normandie."

"Does that park have a name?"

"Not any given by the city. It's a bluff no one has decided to build on, and now it's filled up with a bunch of greasers who'd pass out if you ever suggested they get a job."

"Uh... I see."

"They call it El Castillo." Her Spanish was clumsy, and she tumbled over each syllable. *El-cast-EE-oh.*

I knew it. Got the name back in the war when a handful of humans kept it all night against every monster in the city. Or so the story went. I nodded to her, and hunted along the side of the sill. I was hoping I'd find more of that orange hair.

Something to tie the abductions of Aggie Brooks and Corrina Lacks together, even though they were separate cases. There was a tendency to want to do that, since the alternative was accepting that two girls going missing a night apart wasn't unusual. It was almost expected.

Except for a light coating of various powders and dusts, Corrina's sill was bare. The rain had washed away whatever had been here, but I was inclined to take the word of Mrs. Lacks. I peered outside as I had at Aggie's and, once again, I saw a good amount of security. One thing troubled me, though not the bright light mounted in the eave at the corner of the roof, probably left on in the wee hours. To cope, she had thick drapes, not the white lacy kinds you'd expect for a young lady's boudoir. No, what was bugging me was the cross right above the window, with a star of David to the right. She had another kind of cross on the left, one with some extra adornment. Lot of religious paraphernalia, and gill-men never had much concern for the Almighty as I understood it. They just didn't like bright lights shined in their faces.

"Mrs. Lacks? Have you had any trouble with vampires, jaguar people, batb—"

"Vampires. There was one sniffing around earlier this year."

"What happened to him?"

"He stopped coming around. Maybe six months ago?"

"And when did del Mar start bothering your daughter?"

"Maybe April?"

I nodded.

"You think there's a connection?" she asked.

"I don't know yet."

I shut Corrina's window and got off her bed. I never touched her books. The silly part of me wanted them waiting for her when she got back, even if she was going to read them with extra eyes and turn the page with tentacles.

"What *do* you know, Mr. Moss?"

"Not much, ma'am."

EIGHT

I knew if I wanted to canvass the monsters who might have seen who took Corrina, I'd need to be there at night, so I made arrangements with Mrs. Lacks to return and spend the night on her sofa. She was not thrilled by this development, but since it was in the service of finding her little girl and I still hadn't brought up money, she agreed. Not that this altered her jaundiced attitude toward me. She probably thought I had the same chance of finding her daughter as I did of escorting Audrey Hepburn to the fall cotillion and surviving the experience.

There was the temptation to add Corrina to the list that already included Escuerzo the toad and Aggie Brooks, but Mrs. Lacks was right: no one hired me. I'd look for Corrina, but she could not become my primary goal. I had two other jobs, though Corrina's disappearance felt like it fit somewhere in there if only I could see the entire puzzle. I ran through the series of events in Hexene's case on the drive down to the docks.

Problem was, I wasn't certain about the laws surrounding

witches. That wasn't too unusual, since the laws relating to specific monsters were always in flux. The new monsters fought for recognition as the older kinds demanded protection. I made a mental note to ask Hexene about it, and I imagined her bitter response about witches being second-class monsters. I smiled and hoped she would. That would mean the old Hexene was back, at least a little.

It was possible that kidnapping Escuerzo was simple theft, the same as if I suddenly lost my mind and took Mrs. O'Herlihy's blind and incontinent poodle. Only I knew witches' familiars were more than pets, though I was unclear on exactly how much more.

The point being that Hexene was clearly set up so that someone could take her toad, and this person was willing to kill to keep from being discovered. I wasn't positive that del Mar's killer had been the same person who took Escuerzo, but like I said, I don't believe in coincidence. This person was also willing to possibly kidnap Corrina Lacks, but based on what her mother said, there wasn't even a crime there. It had been done after dark, as per the law. A monster came in her window and dragged her into the night, and that was jim dandy.

The Port of Los Angeles was next to San Pedro. I drove to the gates where the ogre security guard waited, dozing. I had spent a little bit of time dealing with ogre security guards on a previous case and I'd learned that honesty was the best policy, so I pulled the car to a stop in front of the colossal savage.

Like most of his kind, he was twelve feet of muscle. His uniform was a little rougher than the ones I'd seen on studio guards, but the billy club he carried, complete with railroad spikes poking from the business end, looked scarier for all the wear and tear. He had an impressive gut and was snoring loudly, bubbles of spit the size of bowling balls forming next to his yellow tusks. I waited patiently, but he didn't rouse.

I shrugged and drove inside, parking in a lot filled with cars only a little nicer than mine. The place was teeming with gill-men, with the occasional swamp monster, siren, and troll thrown in for variety. Martian tripods unloaded great cargo ships. They should get themselves a giant. I only knew of one in Los Angeles, and she was more of a tourist attraction than a stevedore. Maybe they could import. I asked around for del Mar's foreman and was directed to an office.

As it turned out, gill-men have different definitions of "office" than I might. It was a moon pool cut into the docks near the shore. The big rocks that made up the breakwater formed the back wall. The rest of what one might expect from an office was down in the pool. The desk was steel, with sections rusting, and the bottom looked like it might have become home to a colony of crabs. The paper was all sheathed in plastic, and it looked like he had done most of his notes with a grease pencil. I wasn't entirely sure how the paper didn't just float back to the surface. The picture on his desk of him and a siren I can only assume was his wife was the icing on the cake. He had a mirror set up on the far side of the pool, allowing him to see his visitors from his desk, where he was reviewing something in a binder.

I waved.

He looked up, the black eyes blinking a translucent membrane vertically. He held up a webbed finger in the universally accepted "just a second" gesture, turned the page in his binder, nodded to himself, and set it on the desk, where it settled gently. A fish flitted by as he swam to the surface and hauled himself out of the water.

He was dressed in slacks and a shirt, both soaking wet and sticking to his scaly body. "Can I help you?"

"Uh, yeah. Hi. I'm looking for Paolo del Mar's foreman, and I was directed to you."

"Brock Ness," he said, holding out a clawed and webbed hand. I took it and knew my hand would smell like fish for the rest of the day. "What did you want to ask me? Paolo called in sick this morning."

"Can you tell me about Paolo, please?"

"What's this about?"

"I'm a detective, sir. I was hired to find a missing girl, and Mr. del Mar's name came up."

"Came up? What does that mean?"

"Means... that, I guess. No one's ever asked... "

"Paolo had nothing to do with anything like that."

"Sir, with all due... "

"I know what everyone thinks about gill-men. They believe we're dangerous. We fixate on monsters and take them. Well, I'll tell you something, Mr. Detective! We're not barbarians!"

I noticed he said "monsters" and not "humans." I let it go. "Don't worry, Mr. Ness. I'm not here to get Mr. del Mar in any trouble. His name came up, like I said. So you would vouch for him?"

"Without hesitation. I wish I had ten more just like him. Never late, does his job. It was unusual he called in sick. I always figured Paolo would have to be on his deathbed before he missed work."

"What about his personal life?"

"Never let it affect his work, and beyond that, I mind my business."

"Thank you for your time, Mr. Ness."

I turned to go.

"Detective?"

"Yes?"

"You never showed me a badge."

"No, sir. I, uh, I don't have one. I'm a PI. We have licenses."

"What's this all about?"

"A missing girl, Mr. Ness."

When I left, the ogre was still snoring like a lumberyard at the gate.

NINE

The bluff rose out of the ground on the left side of Normandie Avenue: El Castillo. It was yellowish rock, with trees, grass, and clumps of cattails along the top like a bad toupee. Broken stumps pointed to the time it had played host to armed men and women. A low part of the sidewalk led up a grassy slope. Twin yellow tracks went up that slope, saying that cars were a common sight up there.

I could see how the human defenders held out. From the looks of it, that slope was the only way up, and it was narrow, only big enough for one car. Along the left side for the entire way, and on the right for about half, there were forested ledges overlooking the path, where defenders could rain down whatever they wanted. I took the turn and drove up, even though my car sputtered about three-quarters of the way and I had to resort to sweet talk to get it to crest the hill.

I understood what Mrs. Lacks meant and put together what I had just wandered into at the same moment.

The top of El Castillo was a clearing surrounded by nice

big rocks and trees. Cars, primer-gray Fords and Chevys, were parked in a ring and humans were scattered around, on top of rocks or leaning against their cars. Many of them were drinking from bottles hidden in paper bags. One was sharpening wooden stakes. Another was going through combat drills with what looked like a medieval broadsword. There were young men and women here, all tough as knuckles. They were dressed like greasers, but their clothes were old, worn down and worn in. Almost all of them, even the women, were wearing big, steel-toed stompers.

I got out of the car. The people stopped what they were doing and suddenly every hand seemed to be filled with something. Some of it made sense—the broadsword, of course, and the revolver in the hands of a heavily made-up girl with a ratty beehive. Others were artifacts of our time, like the wooden stakes, the flicking lighters, or the bucket of water. Every single one of them wore charms to keep monsters away, and in some cases, even had them tattooed on.

These were the Normandie Knights, and good God, there were a lot of them. Everyone knew about the Knights. They were a menace, a bogeyman for bogeymen. There was supposedly a special unit downtown entirely devoted to putting them behind bars.

"Looks like you took a wrong turn, Fido," said the closest fella, who looked like he was carrying my entire body weight in the form of great, lumpy muscles. His knuckles each had a different symbol inked on them. I could tell because his fists were ready to do a dance on my face.

"Fi—what? No, I'm not a wolf! I'm human!" I held my hands out like this would somehow prove it to the urban predators who were hemming me in on all sides.

"Prove it, boy." The bruiser grabbed me around the neck while the beehived girl jammed her fingers into my mouth. She tasted bitter, and that's when I realized she was shoving wolfsbane down my throat. I struggled and pushed away, spitting and gagging.

"Yeah, Fido? Seems you don't like wolfsbane too much."

"Wolfsbane is poisonous, you dumb mug," I hacked. "I'd do the same thing if you tried to force-feed me arsenic." I straightened up, wiping my mouth with the back of my sleeve. "Hope you haven't been testing everybody like that."

"Just cops."

"I'm not a cop!" Something poked me. "Ow!"

The bruiser grabbed me again, and I got a look at what had jabbed me. A kid, maybe twelve, was holding a silver fork and my arm was throbbing a bit. They pulled up the sleeve. "Wound's not smoking," the beehive girl said.

"Not a pup, huh?" the bruiser asked.

And then I was looking into my face, mashed up by the bruiser's big hand. I blinked. A hand mirror.

"Not a doppelganger either."

"And I'm out in the sunlight, so not a vampire."

"Or a gremlin," the bruiser said.

"You were worried I was a... " I shook my head, slightly insulted. "Can you let me go?"

The bruiser dropped me and I straightened out my suit. The group had relaxed a little, watching me curiously. "Okay, you're not a cop. What the hell are you?"

"I'm a private eye."

"No human dicks in this town," the beehive sneered.

"That's... uh... maybe think your sentences through a little better. I'm a PI, and I have a license if you want to see it." No one did. Or maybe they were too surprised to hear anyone try so brazen a lie. "I want to talk to Jaime Alvarez."

"We don't know a Jaime Alvarez," the bruiser said, but it sounded reflexive.

"Yeah, you do. I was told I could find him here. I'm not asking about anything any of you might or might not have done. I don't care about that at all. I want to ask him about Corrina Lacks."

A leanly muscled man, barely out of his teens, pushed through the gathered people. He was in an undershirt, tattoos crawling up his arms. Some were the same symbols that adorned the others, but more disturbing were the hashmarks on his right forearm. I was pretty sure what those were counting off. His hair was swept up in a pompadour, glistening like an oil slick. His mustache was neatly trimmed, but a little sparse. He was carrying a baseball bat, the end of which was sharpened into a brutal stake, and there were crusts around the point, as though it had been poisoned with something. Jicama, if he was hunting gill-man. Some chemical in the stuff killed them dead.

"What do you want to know about Corrina?"

"Jaime? Uh, right. Of course. Who else would you be? My name's Moss."

They all peered at me a little closer, as though to make certain I wasn't a swamp monster. The silence stretched out and I realized they were content to leave it at that until I left in awkward confusion.

"Right. Okay, can we maybe talk over there?" I hooked a thumb at a fallen tree and some rocks.

"What's over there?"

"Not this," I said, gesturing to the press of people. They did not seem self-conscious about that at all.

Jaime looked from me to the fallen tree, then beckoned me over with his head, like the whole thing had been his idea.

"Excuse me," I muttered. "Coming through."

I followed Jaime over to the tree and the crowd by my car broke up. They went back to what they were doing, but I still felt the weight of their attention on me. I might not be a monster, but I was an outsider. They weren't even subtle about it; a couple were openly staring at me like a gremlin eyeing a Zagnut bar.

"So what do you want, Moss?"

"Right, uh, I was wondering about Corrina."

"You said that already."

"I did. I was wondering when you saw her last."

"Did her mom hire you? Corrina's been missing since Saturday night, or at least that's what the old bag says."

I felt a momentary pang of sympathy for Mrs. Lacks. When she called Jaime Alvarez a no-account hood, I hadn't realized that meant he was a Knight. These kids seemed to think the Night War was still going on, and their vendettas caused more trouble for the human community than they solved.

"No, I was there on an, uh, unrelated matter."

"He take someone else?"

"He? He who?"

"You been looking into Corrina and you don't know?"

"Paolo del Mar. Right, yes. Uh, no, he didn't take Corrina."

"That what he laid on you? Maybe after my *hermanos* and I have a little talk with him, he'll sing a different tune."

"I, uh, I doubt that." I glanced at the baseball bat, and wondered if whoever had murdered del Mar had just made a huge mistake. Could have let the Knights do the dirty work and my trail would have stopped right here.

"Worked last time."

"Last time?"

"Yeah. We pounded the fishy. Told him to stay away."

I wasn't sure if I should point out that if del Mar was still bothering Corrina, their little chat hadn't worked. Then I remembered I was surrounded by armed hoodlums, all of whom were looking for an excuse to pretend I was a wolfman.

"So del Mar is the only monster bothering Corrina?"

"She's a dolly, you know. She gets attention."

She had gotten mine with nothing more than a couple candid shots. She was probably monsterbait. "Anyone specifically? Looked like her room was warded against vampires."

"And kitty cats," Jaime said. I'll give the boy this: he knew his monsters. "She had both in spades."

"Her mom mentioned a vampire."

"Yeah, she means Thirst. He was sniffing around awhile back, and we gave him the same treatment we gave the fish." He paused. "Not the *same* treatment."

"Crosses instead of light. Yeah, I know the drill."

Jaime looked me over as if for the first time. "You fight in the war, Moss?"

"Both of 'em."

"You ever croak a snatcher?"

"I, uh... well, yeah, of course."

"How many?"

"I lost count. It was a war. What? Why are you looking at me like that?"

He looked like a kid asking about Santa. Only it was a muscled, tattoo-covered kid armed with a giant poison spike. He gestured at his gang. "Lot of them never have. Not even one."

"That's, um... unfortunate?"

"Maybe you come by sometime. Maybe you show us how you did it. Teach the anklebiters where the leech keeps his crypt, you know?"

"Thanks, but my monster-killing days are behind me. Well, mostly behind me. I mean, that other time, it was a grem... you know what, that isn't important. Thirst, you said?"

"Yeah, Bud Thirst. He's a lawyer or something. Has an

office on Broadway downtown."

"Great. Thanks, kid. See you in the funny papers." I got into my car and got out of there before they decided to initiate me. I didn't need to explain an evil eye tattoo to my secretary.

TEN

I had to go see a vampire and a clown. It was going to be a stretch to get to both before the sun went down. I had bitten off more than I could chew, taking on two cases and now almost a third. Feast or famine, the curse of the PI game. I was the only one looking for them, so it was all up to me, whether we were talking about Aggie or Corrina or Escuerzo. I decided to hit the more distant address first, which was the Church of Jesus Christ, Remaker in Lincoln Heights, with the intent of catching up with the law firm of Tepes, Tepes, Tepes, and The Impaler on the way back.

I drove through Downtown and into the rolling dun hills of East LA. The puffy clouds continued to build over the purple San Gabriel Mountains, looking impossibly large, like they would collapse at any moment and cover the entire basin in shaving cream. At their base, they were a dark gray and flashes came from within, like there was something evil in there, something waiting to get out.

The church was in the middle of a working-class monster

neighborhood, proudly taking up half a block. It almost looked like a normal Protestant church, the kind from before the war, except someone had painted multicolored polka dots all over it, seemingly without any concern for the lines of the building, the existence of windows or doors, or the thought that someone might want to look at the building without getting an ice cream headache.

The sign on the door said, "LET CHRIST INTO YOUR HEART, BUT THEN LET HIM OUT OR HE'LL SUFFOCATE."

Clowns.

I pulled over and stared at the church. I knew I had to go in. I knew I was on a clock. But there was a clown in there, and he was going to try to drive me insane. I concentrated on his connection to the case. He was interested in turning Aggie Brooks. He might be the owner of the orange hair. Failing that, he might have seen something. I kept those three things in my head, repeated over and over in a litany. I checked my kit and found some makeup remover. It's a shame I couldn't bring in a whole opera. Only thing that scared a clown was opera. Little unwieldy, though. The makeup remover should do if he got too frisky.

I sighed. He was already too frisky and he hadn't even slapped eyes on me.

I crossed the street, flinching as a step pyramid floated overhead. I almost put a hand on the big door handle, but paused. I didn't have much dealing with clowns day-to-day, but I remembered when they first appeared during the Night War. We thought we'd seen everything, then out came the nightmares. There wasn't a monster more sadistically inventive than a clown. Not gremlins, not mad scientists, not brainiacs, not bug-eyed monsters. I peered into the gap between the doors. Yep. There were the exposed wires, electrifying the handle. I pulled the handkerchief from my jacket pocket and used that to open the door.

The guffaw that greeted me was nothing short of bone-chilling. I considered leaving it there. *Sorry, Aggie, but I couldn't handle the clown.* No. Aggie was worth clowns.

"A visitor! Come to find faith and solace in our lord and savior? Hyuck, hyuck!"

Aggie. Think of Aggie.

I stepped inside. The church was big and the air was cool, which should have been a relief after the heat of the day. The sweat patches at my armpits and back turned to ice. The interior was more elaborate than the exterior. The pews were candy-striped. The altar was a giant jack-in-the-box. The Jesus on the cross had vampire fangs and furry arms like a wolfman, with tentacles coming from his back, also nailed to new flanges of the cross. The stained glass windows showed some of the Christian saints and apostles, though filtered through the new weird theology, so Paul was a ghostly banshee, Peter was a troll, Mark was a jaguar person, and so on. In every alcove, a darkened carnival game waited, the faces of the clowns howling in the shadows.

"Reverend Gigglesworth? I need to ask you a few questions."

The handle of the jack-in-the-box started to turn slowly. The plunked notes of "Pop Goes the Weasel" echoed through the church.

He was in there. He was going to pop out and scare me. Even though I knew what was going to happen, it didn't stop the dull childlike terror welling in my guts.

The handle turned quicker. The song got some cohesion, gaining steam as it pounded toward the inevitable end.

I took a step back, reaching into my coat for the makeup remover, hoping I remembered where it was.

The handle turned quicker. And the voice, the mocking

voice, started to sing along, echoing through the church, coming from everywhere and nowhere. "Jimmy's got the whooping cough and Timmy's got the measles."

My hand closed around a vial. Maybe the makeup remover. Maybe not. I was past caring. Why the hell was I in here? Corrina? Wasn't there a toad?

"That's the way the story goes."

There had to be other leads.

"Pop! Goes the weasel!"

And the top of the altar exploded, a man-sized jack-in-the-box popping out on his spring, his sharp-toothed clown face grinning like a maniac, bloody knives in either hand. I yelped, but not as loud as I could have.

And then, from right behind me, "What can I do for you, my son? Hyuck, hyuck!"

I screamed then and whirled, pulling out a vial of salt. Didn't matter, my hands were shaking too badly to open it.

"Don't mind if I do!" said the clown, reaching behind him and producing a plate of french fries, the kind you'd get at a carnival. He carefully popped the cork on the vial and sprinkled some on the plate, then looked at me for approval, his mouth stretching into an impossible grin.

His teeth were razors, and there were more than anything really needed. I thought Serendipity had a scary smile, but at least the rest of her was pleasant to look at. Not the Reverend. He wore vestments, though they were distinctly clownish, in clashing colors and patterns. His skin was stark white, his lips blood red, triangles above and below his eyes making it hard to meet them. He had a bright red puffy nose and a huge mass of curly blue hair.

"Not even a smile, my son? What's got you down? Christ's love, like the inevitable specter of death, is always with you!

Hyuck, hyuck!"

"I... uh... I... "

"Have a french fry!" When I didn't take one, he threw the plate over his shoulder—I never did hear a crash or see a mess later—and pulled a bunch of balloons from nowhere. "Balloon?"

"No, no, I... "

One of the balloons exploded, and with a terrified *buck-CAW!* a featherless chicken burst out and tried to fly.

"Please, please stop."

Reverend Gigglesworth paused and his priestly collar spun around. "Well, if you're not here for your eternal soul, what can I do for you?"

"You're the Reverend Bobo Gigglesworth, correct?"

He reached into his pants and pulled out the end of his underpants, which were brighter than the noonday sun. His name was scrawled there, misspelled and with a few letters backward. "I sure hope so! Hyuck, hyuck!"

"You know Agatha Brooks."

Gigglesworth paused in his schtick. It was the barest moment, but I caught it, and he saw me catch it. It was, in a way, worse than the constant jokes. Laid bare, the clown's boundless rage was uncovered. I was fairly certain he was going to kill me.

He broke into a horrifying grin. "Say, officer, I haven't seen you 'round these parts before! Hyuck, hyuck!"

"I'm not a policeman."

"Not a... " he trailed off, his jaw going slack in mock surprise. Both hands, in giant gloves, smacked the sides of his face in amazement. "Then that means you're a... "

"Private eye. I'm a private eye."

He pulled a giant magnifying glass from wherever he kept his props and leaned in close. His bloodshot eyeball was huge, and I swear it was vertically slitted for a second. His breath stank of raw meat and cotton candy. "Private *eye*, huh?"

I regretted putting it that way, but that was better than at least one of the alternatives.

"Yeah," I said, leaning back.

"Whaddya wanna know about her for? She's probably already changed!"

"Changed? What do you mean?"

Gigglesworth swept away, turned, and when he turned back, he was a clown-wolf thing. I yelped, and he chortled, the false fangs, ears, and fur falling off him. The teeth chattered on the floor. I nudged them away with my foot and wasn't too surprised when they tried to bite. "Changed! Into a mooooooonster!"

"You saw her taken?"

"Sure did! So close, too. She would have made such a good clown! And she would have grown a foot in a single night!"

"You saw what got her?"

"A sasquatch. It was dark. Like this!" He swept over to the candles lit in prayer and blew them out like it was a birthday cake. For a moment, the entire church was plunged into blackness, even though there had been plenty of light streaming in through the windows. Then the flames reappeared, just like trick birthday candles. Gigglesworth was less than an inch away from me, leering. I groped for the makeup remover.

"If it was dark... "

"Then how did I see?" Gigglesworth was suddenly several feet away, reclining on a pew. "That's an excellent question, detective." His voice had dropped a register, and was now an educated baritone. He was gesturing with a pipe. "I suppose the incongruity of my tale would lead one to suspect deception, but I can assure you that I am certain of what I witnessed." He puffed on the pipe. Soap bubbles billowed out of the top. "You see, he was behind a screen of foliage—you know their kind can be somewhat shy, but I clearly saw an arm and a leg. Orange fur, simian, by jove, it was a perfect match." He broke into a grin and bounded up, the manic energy back, whipping a large doll made up to look like a vampiress out from nowhere. "Why, I'd stake my *wife* on it!" And he slammed a wooden stake through its chest.

"Right. Uh. A sasquatch. Thank you for your time, Reverend." I backed away. Slowly.

"Where ya going, detective?" Gigglesworth asked, now lying on the pew with his head in his hands like a besotted teenager. "We're not done playing! Hyuck, hyuck!"

"Oh, no. Thank you. I'm not really, you know, tennis elbow and all that."

He did that thing where suddenly he was in my face, and his voice came out in a feral growl. "I wasn't asking. Meatstick."

I popped the vial open and let him get a whiff of the acrid scent of makeup remover.

That's the thing about clowns. They're just makeup. Get me? *Just makeup.*

"Eeek!" Gigglesworth screamed like every vaudeville housewife and cowered away from the liquid.

"You have a good day, Reverend," I said, and was out the door.

I never thought I'd be so happy to see the sun, but I didn't feel remotely safe until I was in my car and driving away.

Clowns.

Rev. Bobo Gigglesworth

Eleven

The offices of Tepes, Tepes, Tepes, and The Impaler were on the way back to Watts. The sun was getting lower than I'd like, but time was very much a factor for both Aggie and Corrina. In the old days, monsters turned people right away. It was more of an impulsive thing. Catch a human unawares and turn him, and now there's one less enemy and one more ally. Nowadays, monsters were more selective. They tried to pick people who would fit into the lifestyle of the monster in question: meat golems loved medical students, mad scientists turned doctors of any kind, and bogeymen practically demanded that you like kids. Hell, wolfmen put notices in the paper, down to the physical requirements of the recruits they wanted. This kind of thing helped with leads, but far more important was that monsters liked to take their time.

Turning was supposed to be pretty traumatic. The actual act didn't take long, and I'd seen it happen more than anyone ever should. I didn't bother suppressing the shudder working through me. There was fear and sometimes revulsion on the part of the turnee, too. It wasn't pretty.

So these days, monsters preferred to "break in" their prospects, like a pair of shoes. In practical terms, this meant they kept them cooped up for a period of time, sometimes a day, sometimes a week, and gave them a crash course in what it meant to be whatever it was they were becoming. It gave me a window. If the clown was to be believed, a sasquatch snatched Aggie Brooks. He would be holding her in one of the wilder parts of the city—Griffith Park was the likeliest place, though far from the only one—and he would be the world's hairiest scoutmaster. She'd be learning wilderness survival, local plants and animals, and hiding. Sasquatches, for being seven feet of stinking hair, were incredible hiders.

Stinking hair.

Hexene had mentioned her attacker stank. Like a skunk, but less, she had said. That described a sasquatch fairly well.

The same monster took Aggie Brooks and Escuerzo? It was easy to conflate the cases, since I was working them both and things could get wrapped up in each other. The idea that the same creature was behind both was a coincidence the size of one of those tripods from the docks. Then again, if I learned it was a sasquatch who took Corrina, too, well, then there was a connection I wasn't seeing.

A sasquatch. In my time as a shamus, I'd tracked only a few of them. Think I fought all of two during the Night War. As monsters went, sasquatch were peaceniks. Mostly wanted to be alone out in the woods. Take nature hikes. Shit outdoors. That kind of thing. One actually attacking a witch made no sense. And what the hell would one of them want with her familiar?

I pushed it from my mind as I parked in front of the law firm, right in front of a gleaming hearse. Two spaces away, a spectral charger pawed the ground and huffed blasts of brimstone from his nose. The law firm was a Spanish-style building with ornate ironwork for a fence. If there was one thing vampires hated, it was a picket fence.

I walked in the front door and the receptionist looked up. She was a ghoul, her skin gray and drawn, the dark circles around her eyes making her look like she'd been awake for years. Her irises and pupils shone like pennies when the light hit them and she smiled pleasantly, showing off teeth best suited for eating rotting flesh right off the bone. "Good afternoon, sir. How may I help you?"

"Hi. I'm hoping to talk to Mr. Thirst?"

"Do you have an appointment?"

"I'm afraid not."

"I'm happy to make you one as soon as *humanly* possible."

I blanched at the extra mustard she threw on "humanly." She smiled a little wider. "Would you tell him that it's about Corrina Lacks? I believe he'll see me."

The ghoul sighed and stood up, lurching back into the office. I looked around. Other than the cheery Spanish architecture, the vampires had made it their own. Tattered drapes, partly hiding the requisite blackout curtains, hung by the windows. Dead flowers—no roses, out of deference to their ghoul secretary—leaned stiffly in vases. The magazines were the normal assortment for a law firm: *Look, Unlife, Modern Crypt.*

I fidgeted on the deep red carpet until the ghoul shambled back into the room. I suspect she took a little longer than she might have needed to. She knew I was human; she had smelled it on me. For monsters who spent most of their time underground eating carrion, ghouls had incredible noses. "Mr. Thirst will see you. Third door on your left," she said. As I walked up the hall, she said to my back, "Don't be too long."

I glanced at the window, where the late afternoon sun was

getting far too low, and cursed inwardly. She wanted to see my reaction, and I had given her a good one. I went down the hall and knocked on the third door on my left.

"Enter," said a voice inside, rolling the *r* like he was chasing it down a hill.

The room was shrouded in darkness tempered by several standing candelabras, all with guttering black candles. The bookcases were stuffed with law books, though I didn't know why so many of them had pentagrams on the spine. Maybe turning into monsters had forced lawyers to become more honest. The desk looked like a coffin, and I imagined it probably was, just in case the occupant needed to grab a nap or something.

The vampire across the desk stood up and held out his hand. His skin was stark white, a shade unnatural even in vampires. He probably used that makeup I kept seeing billboards for around town: "Get the pallor of the grave without the dirt!" His hair was very black and shiny, swept back from a blade-sharp widow's peak. He wore an old-style tuxedo, complete with a medal. And then there was the cape.

"It is my pleasure to meet you. I am Bud Thirst." The accent was so thick I tripped over it.

"Uh, hi." I took the hand, which was ice cold. He probably kept an icebox under his desk for the desired effect. "Nick Moss."

"You told my secretary you vere here about Miss Lacks?"

"Uh, yes. That's right. I wanted to... "

"First!" He fixed me with his eyes, his right hand undulating at me. "You vill tell me... who... you... are."

"Nick Moss," I repeated louder.

He sighed. "No, what do..." the accent dropped and he sounded southern, then the accent was back, the poor guy stumbling over consonants and his teeth. "Sorry. I mean, vhat do you do?"

"Oh! I'm a detective. Private, that is."

"Our law firm employs many private detectives. I have never heard of you."

"I don't have much of an advertisement budget."

The vampire nodded, and by the way he was focused on my neck, he had probably worked out I was human. To his credit, the next thing he said was, "How is Miss Lacks?"

"Uh, missing, actually. That's what I'm here about. I wanted to speak to you."

Thirst jumped in his seat, making that ridiculous cape billow outward. "Missing? Oh, gawd!" The southern twang was back and it had brought friends. "I know where she is."

I perked up. I could use a break right about now. "You do?"

"Not exactly where. She has this boyfriend, he's a thug. Assaulted me for no reason."

Assaulted you for trying to turn his girlfriend into a vampire, more like. Not that pointing it out would do much more than sour the tone of the interview. Instead, I spoke to the point: "It's not Alvarez."

"How can you be sure? He has a whole gang. Meats... erm. Sorry, humans."

"I just came from there."

"He could have been lying! If he'll beat a man for loitering, no telling what he'll say!"

"Trust me, sir. He doesn't have her. First off, he's got no motive. From what I saw, even if the mother doesn't like him much, he can get into that room when... uh, not to impugn her character, I'm sure she's lovely, but, um. Where was I?"

"The boyfriend."

"Alvarez is clean for this."

Thirst settled back in his seat, staring into the middle distance until he broke into a smile. "Her mother doesn't approve, hmm?"

"Called him a no-account hood."

"That he is." Thirst paused, considering something. "Who hired you... sorry." He cleared his throat and the bad Transylvanian accent was back. "Who hired you to find Corrina?"

"What's with the... no one, actually. She came up in another investigation. I was following the lead to its end, which is you."

"But I don't know anything!"

"Well, yes, but I didn't know that before I got here."

"So you're not looking for her actively?"

"Not, uh, I mean, my cases have priority."

"Let me hire you," he said, leaning forward, the accent forgotten once more. "Find Corrina, detective."

"Why not get someone else? I mean, there are werewolves... Baskerville is good. Gevaudan."

"They'd be in your dust. You're on this thing, and I can see it on you. You want to find her. You want an excuse. I'm giving it to you. Find her and I'll pay you. Take your rate and double it."

I blanched. "Double... " And that was the rate I charged monsters, which was already more than what I charged humans.

"Doubled. And who knows? You find her, maybe there's other work for you."

"You'd work with a human?"

He waved one ivory hand. His fingernails were much longer than a person's really should be. "There are places humans can go that monsters can't. Versatility, Mr. Moss."

"Um, listen, Mr... uh, Mr. Thirst. I don't want to get your hopes up." He was in better shape than the Brookses, so he needed to hear the speech. "Someone hires me to find Susie or Timmy, nine times out of ten, the happy ending is Susie likes being a fish girl now. I look for humans, but I don't bring many of them back."

Thirst nodded, digesting the words. I appreciated that he

took the time to do that. "Whatever Corrina is, it doesn't matter. I will still love her."

"I won't bring her to you."

"Bring her home, Mr. Moss. That's all. Do we have a deal?"

I reached across the table and he took my hand. "I normally charge fifteen dollars a day, plus expenses."

"Thirty it is," Thirst said, giving my hand a hard final shake to seal the deal.

We both stood up.

"Thank you... sorry," and the Transylvanian flooded back into his voice. "Thank you for your service, Mr. Moss."

"Mr. Thirst, can I ask you something?"

"You may."

"What's with the accent and the getup? Doesn't quite seem to fit you."

He sighed, his shoulders slumping. In his southern twang, he said, "I know. It's all the rage with vampires. It's exhausting."

TWELVE

On the way home, I stopped in at a diner with a human-only food counter. The night shift was coming in, mostly zombies, though they did have a blob in the back working the grill. I was one of only three humans in the place. Everyone else was headed home to bunker down for the night. The sky was growing darker, and the flashes coming from the pillars of clouds over the mountains were getting brighter, and much more purple than I liked. The other two humans at the counter were in shabby coveralls, tired from a long day, and wolfing their food down.

A zombie waitress approached me. She was almost pretty, though she was rotting a tad more than I'd normally like. In particular, she had a missing patch of flesh disappearing up into her skirt that almost put me off food entirely. "Brains?" she asked.

"Can't complain," I said.

"Brains."

"Well, you know, the weather and all."

"Brains?"

"Yeah, I'm ready. The meatloaf any good?"

"Brains."

"All right, I'll have that."

"Brains?"

"Vegetables, please."

"Brains."

"Oh... iced tea?"

"Brains."

She wrote it down with a stubby pencil and hung it on the order carousel. She spun it once. In the kitchen, the blob, all flailing pink pseudopods, seemed to peer at the order with one of them while continuing its spastic work. I glanced at the monsters around me out of the corner of my eyes and was horrified, though not surprised, to see that nearly all of them were paying close attention to the three humans in the place. The diner was quiet, the conversation amongst the monsters unfocused. There was a good variety around us, so no telling how we'd turn if the sun went down.

One of the humans must have heard my thoughts, because he dropped a bill on the table and was out the door. In the old days, doors had bells. Now, anything jangling randomly like that was a way to keep phantoms out, and there were a couple enjoying the blue plate special.

A plate clattered in front of me. The meatloaf was smothered in ketchup and bolstered with mashed potatoes and steamed vegetables. The food wasn't tasty, but there was a good amount of it and I'd had worse during both wars. The other fella got up halfway through my meal and scurried out, leaving me alone in a diner full of monsters. The weight of their combined gaze made me hunch over. I had the absurd urge to hide what I could of my body, as though the problem was that they were seeing too much of it and not that they were predators by nature.

"Brains?" said the waitress.

"Huh?" I looked up, and she was nodding to the sky. It was turning pink. I didn't have much time.

"Brains," she said more clearly.

"Yeah." I put some money down. "Thanks."

"Brains," she said. For a second, I saw the woman she had been before a zombie had made a meal of the only word she could say anymore. She was sad and beaten down and now she was the lowest monster there was. Forever. She could have been any one of the people I never found. Hell, maybe I'd told her husband she was happy being a fish girl.

So I did the only thing I could. I left her a good tip.

I drove into Watts much closer to sundown than I ever wanted. The monsters on Corrina's street were waiting by their cars and brooms and flying machines and carts, buzzing with excitement. In some cases literally, as a moth flew into the hissing arc of electricity between a robot's antennae and promptly exploded into dust. The monsters eyed me hungrily, then glanced at the sky, willing the sun to go down so they could pounce. I knocked on the Lacks' door, resisting the urge to pull vials from my jacket and sprinkle the nearest monster with everything I had. It didn't help that a scarecrow was standing just off the porch, staring at me, the straw in his body rustling with minute movements.

I knocked again, wondering if I had somehow gotten the wrong house. If the people who should have been inside were on vacation somewhere, enjoying themselves while I got turned into a sack of dried hay on their porch.

The door opened. The man on the other side of it was in his shirtsleeves, rolled up over his big forearms. His gut strained against his buttons.

"Mister, you picked a strange time to come calling."

"Mr. Lacks? My name is Moss. Your wife invited me over."

"Pull the other one, vampire. I ain't pulling down the crosses."

"Please, Mr. Lacks. Call your wife. Tell her Nick Moss is here like we discussed."

He looked me over, rubbing the stubble on his pockmarked chin. "Lorraine! There's a man at the door said you invited him!"

Behind me, the sun inched lower in the sky. The monsters were getting subliminally louder with each passing moment that I was defenseless. I wasn't, though there was no way I could fight off every last monster on that street. Not being helpless does not equal being safe.

A moment later, Mrs. Lacks bustled into view. She peered around her husband, and though her expression didn't soften, her eyes showed recognition. "That's the detective I told you about. He's looking for Corrina."

"What's he doing here, then?"

"Sir, if we could just continue this conversation in your living room... "

"Oh, come in before you drop dead of a heart attack," Mrs. Lacks grumbled. She opened up the screen door and I scampered inside. Then they shut the door and threw several locks.

I took off my hat and addressed Mr. Lacks. "I'm sorry about this, sir. I'm, uh, I'm looking for your daughter... "

"No, he ain't," Mrs. Lacks said.

"Actually, things have changed. I've been hired."

Her eyes narrowed. "By who?"

"That's not, uh, that's not important. And there's a confidenti... doesn't matter. The point is, I'm hired to bring your daughter here. To you."

Mrs. Lacks watched me. Mr. Lacks was just confused. "Why are you here?"

"I wanted to talk to the monsters who visit you, and the

best way to do that is to spend the night."

"Visit us," Mr. Lacks huffed.

"That's why I put the blankets out," Mrs. Lacks said, indicating the pile of linen on the couch.

"I thought you were mad at me."

She smiled at him with real affection, the kind that hadn't been directed my way since just after I got home from France. "Silly man."

"Mama?" A boy, maybe seventeen years old, had come into the room. Corrina was in his face, and it was an odd feeling, seeing the girl I was tracking right there. He was a little taller than his father and much leaner. He looked like a tough kid, but not a hood like Alvarez.

"Don't worry, Brian. Mr. Moss here is a detective looking for your sister." She managed to say that without the editorializing tone.

"Hi," I said.

"Uh, hi."

"Well, Mr. Moss, we were going to have supper if you'd care to join us."

"Oh, no thanks. I don't want to impose. Uh, more than I already am. I'd like to stay by the window here so I can talk to them as soon as they get going."

Mrs. Lacks nodded, not looking too disappointed at my refusal. "We'll leave you to it. Change your mind, you come on in."

"Thank you, ma'am," I said, settling into the chair by the window. The Lacks family left me in the front and soon the sounds and smells of family wafted from the back. I wanted to bring Corrina back to them. Even if she wasn't my original goal, she had joined Aggie and Escuerzo on the roster.

I parted the curtains just enough to see out without making myself too visible. The sun was gone, the sky falling past purple and on to full dark. The monsters had started their nightly ritual, probing the defenses of every house on the block. Some seemed to ignore humans altogether to cavort in the street like it was a block party in Hell.

I watched the monsters gravitate to the houses of their favorite people. An invisible man, appearing only as a suit floating in midair, poked around a house down the street, trying futilely to scale a copse of banana trees. Across the street, a phantom had begun singing scales and for a moment, I had to pause to appreciate the haunting beauty. A ghost appeared on the Lacks lawn and I remembered the burned sage at the eaves.

I checked my kit and set the vials of sage and holy water on the table in front of me. I slid the curtains aside and several monsters turned. Eyes of all different colors, and one the size of a beach ball, narrowed. I pointed at the ghost and beckoned.

The ghost pointed at himself, or more accurately, at the gaping hole through his chest. I nodded. He shrugged and moved closer. His legs faded into transparent mist at mid-calf. I had no idea what pumping his legs actually did to move him over the lawn, but he got there. He stopped at the edge of the flowerbed right beneath the window and shot a look of pure hatred up at the corner of the house where a clump of sage shed fragrant smoke.

"You want to be a ghost?" he moaned at me. Beneath him, insects and worms billowed out of the earth.

"No thanks." Our voices were muffled by the closed window. "Were you here Saturday night?"

"No," he said.

"Where were you?"

"Why should I tell you, meatstick?"

"Because I'm holding a vial of holy water."

"All right, all right. Saturday night I was out with my wife. We went dancing."

"How do you... you know what? Never mind."

"Are you going to put out the sage?"

"Not a chance."

"Can't protect the house every night, meatstick. Lorraine Lacks will be mine."

I shook the holy water at him and he took the hint.

I scanned the street again. The phantom was directly across the street, singing loudly, trying to drown out the wind chimes that tinkled and sent her scurrying away, hands clapped over her ears, only to return when the wind died and she could sing again. I tried to get her attention several times, and during one retreat, when I was jumping up and down and waving through the front window, she caught sight of me. She was, like most phantoms, pale as cheesecloth, her lips drawn back over too-big teeth, her eyes buggy in their deep black pits. She came over cautiously, probably expecting some sort of trap. Phantoms. Always think everyone is just like they are.

"Hi," she said hesitantly.

"How do you do, ma'am. I was wondering if I could ask you some questions?"

She looked around, probably expecting a piano or something to fall on her. "I think so?"

"All right."

"We could talk inside," she said hopefully.

"This is... does that work?"

"I can barely hear you through the window."

"You can hear me perfectly. And you could probably identify the key I'm speaking in."

"It's higher than I normally hear from a man."

"That's not... that's not really... um. All right. Were you

here last night, Miss... ?"

"Fontaine," she said with a truly horrifying smile. "Belle Fontaine. And yes. There's a girl who lives across the way, and she plays the viola like an angel. Oh, if only she would let me in. I could teach her so much, bring her art to such new heights." She shook her head wistfully.

"Right, uh... Miss Fontaine? I don't really... were you here on Saturday night?"

"No."

"Oh," I said, already looking for another monster who might have had a clear view. There didn't appear to be one.

"I was over there," she said, pointing to where she had been standing when I called her over.

"That's what I... all right. You were there on Saturday night. Someone in this house was taken out of her room. Did you see what happened?"

"The girl, wasn't it? She's popular. Has a gill-man beau."

Not how I'd heard it. "Uh... a beau? You've seen them being, um, romantic?"

"Oh, no. It's only a matter of time, though. She lets her guard down and he takes her to live by the sea. Probably would get a sea hag to turn her. They're like family," she confided.

"They, uh, they like the term 'siren.'"

"That's ridiculous. They're part of a long and proud family of hags. There's forest hags, and mountain hags, swamp hags... "

"There are swamp hags?"

"Oh yes. Ugly as sin, but much more reliable than the forest variety. Less distractions, I think."

"We're getting off track."

She blinked. "Are we? Human, I don't mind speaking to you. You're remarkably polite. No screaming, no threats, but my purpose here is to turn young Miss Pearlman and you're distracting me. If you played any instruments, I might have an excuse."

"Sorry. I tried to learn the harmonica in the service, but everything came out like duck calls."

"I said 'instruments.' Harmonicas give voice to the transient murderer inside us."

"Oh. I see."

She glanced at the Pearlman house. "If you would get on with it?"

"Right. Well, I was wondering if you saw the monster who grabbed the girl who lives here."

"I believe so. I only saw one approach the house, but I wasn't really watching."

"Could you see what kind of monster?"

She nodded, and I saw it. She was going to say it was a sasquatch, and I could connect Corrina to Aggie. Both cases would get a break as I uncovered the inevitable connection between the two of them. I broke into a smile.

"It was a robot," Belle said, her eyeballs rolling skyward as she conjured the memory.

My stomach sank. "You're certain?"

"Well, as I said, I didn't get a good look. I saw something go around the side of the house. A big shape. It stepped into the light briefly, and I caught a glimpse of shiny metal or plastic where its head was. And then there were the antennae."

"You certain? About the antennae?"

"Oh, yes. I saw them hit a hanging feather."

"Thank you for your time," I said to the phantom.

"Think nothing of it." Belle Fontaine flitted off across the dirt road to haunt the viola player and I settled back, the cases seemingly even farther out of my reach.

THIRTEEN

None of the other monsters in the neighborhood knew a thing either, and I talked to every last one I could coax over. They made their threats, tried to get inside, and finally answered my questions. I got to sleep later than I would've liked. The Lacks couch was soft enough, thankfully. I had a dreamless few hours and woke up just before dawn, as the Lacks family was beginning to move around. I thanked them for their hospitality and assured them that finding Corrina was a priority. Mrs. Lacks offered me breakfast, but I didn't want to impose. I accepted the offer of coffee, though, because I'm not crazy. As I sipped, standing in their kitchen with the Lacks men at the kitchen table and Mrs. Lacks at the stove, I asked, "Have you had any trouble with robots in the past?"

"No," Mr. Lacks said promptly.

"Not a one," Mrs. Lacks confirmed. "Why, that one who bothers the Wong boys come over here last night?"

"No, nothing like that. But your robot wards are in place, correct?"

Mr. Lacks nodded. “Got an optical illusion tacked up by every window, every door. It’s this horseshoe thing where it looks like two prongs, only there’s three at the end.”

“I’ve seen that one.” It was a pretty common option at any apothecary. I used an M.C. Escher postcard myself, the one with all the staircases. I didn’t trust anything too simple. I always imagined the robots would figure it out somehow.

I went over Corrina’s movements from the week before. She had classes at Santa Monica College on Monday through Thursdays, and she worked at an industrial bakery on her other days. She spent most of her free time with Jaime Alvarez, something no one, not even her brother, seemed to approve of. I noted everything down, just in case.

I thanked them again for the hospitality and drove home for a shower, shave, and a change of clothes. The clouds had begun to spread again, as though they couldn’t stack any higher and were spilling out over the city. From the looks of it, everything east of Pasadena was covered in a second night. At least the lightning had stopped.

By the time I pulled up in my driveway, the monsters had emptied out of the neighborhood. Evidence of them was everywhere, from simple things like tipped-over trashcans and torn up flowerbeds to odder sights like pink residue glistening in the early morning light and discarded batteries half-sunk in the turf. As I opened up my front door, a note fluttered to the porch. I picked it up and went inside. A clue? A confession? You never could tell. Sometimes cases turned on the oddest of things.

Nope.

The lipstick kiss gave it away immediately.

Dearest Nick,

You never came home last night. I know you were not making time with another girl. Serendipity says you’re not the type, and the only time you did anything indecent was in the service of your job. I missed you and wanted you to know I am thinking of you.

Yours Always,

Mira

I sighed and dropped the note in the garbage. My cat trotted out of the bedroom and yowled at me. I opened a can of food and set it down. The cat hissed, swatted me, and only after securing my retreat did it deign to eat. I swear, if jaguar people weren't such a hazard, I would have given him to the Pearlman girl for new viola strings.

The shower was quick and the shave even quicker. I nicked myself once and reflected that it was a good thing I'd visited the vampire yesterday. I put on an old gray suit with a blue bowtie, checked my equipment, and drove into the office. I dropped yesterday's suit off with Mr. Rodriguez at the laundry and picked up the clean one, then headed up to the office. I opened up the door and failed to register the panicked look on Serendipity's face over the pained howling of my empty belly. I turned to find the pink pastry box by the door.

"You got doughnuts! Bless you, Ser."

"Nick?"

"One second." I opened the box up. It was empty.

"Ser, that's just a mean trick." I turned around, and her eyes were even bigger, nearly bugging out of the goggles. Her gills were fluttering nervously. "What?"

"Hey there, Moss. Your secretary said you'd come in eventually. You meatsticks love to sleep in." I didn't have to look to know who had spoken, but I did anyway, since I like to see danger coming. And there he was, leaning against the doorjamb and devouring the doughnut my secretary had bought for me. The navy blue suit was as cheap as always, the ugly tie had to be a clip-on. The hat matched the suit, worn low so his glittering eyes were always in shadow. He already had five o'clock shadow and it was barely eight in the morning. His name was Lou Garou, homicide detective for the Los Angeles Police Department. And, like nearly everyone on the LAPD, he was a wolfman. He said he wanted to turn me, but I could never be sure. Garou was a bully—I'd seen enough of them over my life to recognize the type. He liked making humans squirm and had figured out my buttons pretty quick.

"Hi, detective. Just to warn you, I'm very busy, so if you're looking to hire me, now's not the best time."

A raspy chuckle filtered from my office. That would be Garou's partner, Phil Moon, the elder and more reasonable of the pair.

"Good to see your sense of humor is intact, Moss. Can't even find your own ass and you want to help find mine." Garou took a single step, grabbed me by the back of my jacket, and shoved me into my office, all while munching on my doughnut.

Moon had his feet kicked up on my desk. Unlike Garou, who was mostly muscle, Moon had a bit of a gut and was working hard on that second chin. He had a raspy voice, like every cigarette and every glass of whiskey in the city had found a home in his windpipe. He wore a checkered jacket that didn't match his pants or hat, but I don't think it matched much of anything. They say dogs are colorblind, and Moon was out to prove it.

I caught myself on the desk. "Siddown, Moss," Garou said from behind me, his hand coming down on my shoulder and pushing me into the chair. I didn't fight. Getting shaken down by the cops wasn't exactly a new experience for any human. At least I knew these particular wolves.

"So what can I do for you fellas? See you already helped yourself to breakfast."

"Thanks, Moss," Moon said, waving the tiny corner of his doughnut. It had sprinkles on it. I love sprinkles.

"Tell your secretary to go to a better place. These taste like yesterday's," Garou said.

"They probably are. I don't really pay her enough for fresh doughnuts every day."

"Pretty girl like that? You should pay her more," Moon said.

"And since she's the only thing keeping you human," Garou said. He was talking about the Verity case, when I'd met the two of them. Like I said, they had been keen to turn me, but I had successfully leaned on Serendipity's status as a good, trustworthy monster to keep them from doing it illegally.

"Did you come here to discuss how I pay my secretary?"

"Don't get smart," Garou snarled into my ear. I froze. Didn't matter that he looked human at the moment. There was enough wolf in him to talk directly to the terrified caveman inside me. I knew I could spar with them to a point, but they had all the weapons.

"We left you alone," Moon said philosophically, "not because of the dame in the other room. We did it because we thought maybe you were one of the good ones. The rare meatstick who actually contributes to society. Does his job, pays taxes, doesn't bother anybody."

"That's, um, nice of you to say," I said, still acutely aware of Garou right behind me.

"So why did somebody matching your description come out of a murdered gill-man's house yesterday?"

"I can think of a couple different possibilities." I was doing my best to remain calm, but the sweat sprang up in my armpits.

"Those possibilities explain why that same guy was seen later at the gill-man's work asking about him?"

"What were you doing with the dead fish, Moss?" Garou said. His breath smelled like sugar and dog.

"All right, all right. Look, we both know I didn't do anything, and if you try to pin anything on me, I'll clam up."

"And we send you down for it," Garou said.

"Then you're trusting the leeches to get it right." I figured if they were throwing around racist terms, I might as well join in.

The eyeroll from Moon said I picked right. "Talk, Moss. You have something."

"Yeah, uh, there's confide—"

"There's nothing unless I say there's something," Garou snarled.

"Moon, can you put a leas... uh, I mean, can you call your partner off? It's tough concentrating when I'm worried about him ripping my face off."

"Why d'you have to concentrate, meatstick? Coming up with a story?"

"Lou, let him be."

Garou stood back up. There was nowhere really for him to go, but at least I wasn't smelling his breath.

"Talk, Moss. And if I don't like it, I'll let Lou ask."

I took a breath, hoping to see some kind of comfort in Moon's florid face. I got nothing. The fella might be the nicer of the pair, but he was still a wolf. "Okay, like I said, I've been hired for a job. A couple jobs, but this only concerns the one of them."

"Missing person? Some co-ed get turned and you need to find 'em?"

"Uh... not exactly."

Garou shoved my shoulder. "Cough it up, Moss."

"A toad."

"A what?" Moon asked.

"You know, like a frog, only dry?"

"I know what a goddamn toad is, Moss. What are you doing looking for one?"

"A friend of mine misplaced one."

"Who has a toad to misplace?"

"A witch."

"You making time with witches? Dangerous game," Garou said. Moon shushed him with a wave of his hand.

I went on, "Yeah. A witch had her toad kidnapped. Toadnapped? She hired me."

"Why didn't she call the police?"

"Your sterling record?"

"Careful, meatstick," Garou said.

Despite the rebuke, I was on firmer ground. "Mind if I smoke?" I didn't wait for the yes, knowing they'd give it even if wolves hated the smell, just to avoid looking weak. I removed the battered pack of Luckies, shook a cigarette into my hand, and promptly lost it. I scooped it off the ground, and after a couple tries, got the thing lit. I was never any good at smoking, but it came in handy sometimes, so I still tried. "The point is, she hired me. A client of hers arranged a meeting and at that meeting, she got jumped, sapped, and when she woke up, the toad was gone."

"Meeting?" Garou snorted. "Your friend's a working girl, huh?"

The urge to flick wolfsbane in Garou's face was almost overwhelming. It also defined the phrase, "useless, empty gesture" pretty well. Defending Hexene's honor to the dog wasn't going to win me or her any points.

"Careful," Moon said. "I think Moss is a little sweet on her."

Garou laughed. "So's anyone with a buck."

I stood up so quick I wasn't even sure I was doing it. The cigarette fell out of my mouth to burn on the floor. Moon was so shocked he didn't do much more than gape. Garou was ready. I never got turned around before I heard the snarl and felt his hand, now furry, clamp down on my shoulder. The claws bored new holes into the fabric, and he pushed. Hard. "Siddown, meatstick," he snarled. I didn't have a lot of choice in the matter.

"Everybody settle down," Moon rasped. He looked more annoyed at having been caught with his pants down. Had I pulled silver on him, and had his partner not been there, he'd be on the way to the big sleep. Didn't really matter that it had been his partner who had provoked me, either. From now on, he knew that if I ever wanted to take him, I could. He wouldn't be the first wolfman, either, and I think he knew that, too. The balance of power had tipped between us, and we were both on much shakier ground. "And you," he said to me, "You're exhausting our goodwill here."

Of course, it had been Garou I wanted, and he couldn't care less. Pack politics were worse than any fraternal organization had ever been in the old days.

"This is goodwill?" I picked up the smoke and set it in an ashtray to let it spiral gray threads into the dead air.

"We haven't hauled you in yet," Garou said.

"Tell us about what happened to your witch," Moon said. There was no editorializing this time.

"The client she was arranging the meeting with was a gill-man by the name of Paolo del Mar."

"The dead guy," Moon said.

"So, Moss, you plug the fishy to make time with the witch?" Garou said, his voice having lost the animal snarl.

"Far from it."

"But you were seen at the house where the gill-man was beaten to death and you were poking around his work."

"Um, well... okay, I'm not saying I was there, but you fellas have to know for a fact I can't beat a gill-man to death on my best day." They were silent, and I could tell they were waiting for me to get to the point for them. "You want a description of the monster who did it."

"Who says it was a monster?" Garou asked.

"The scene. No human alive throws a gill-man around and you know it."

"He's got you there," Moon said.

"Let's take him downtown and stick him in a lineup. We'll know for sure he was there, then make a case," Garou said.

"You two have nothing."

"And not reporting a crime is a crime," Moon said.

"You're not going to arrest me for that."

"And why not?"

"Because right now, I'm doing your job. I'm investigating something else entirely, and you can play dumb if I step out of line. It crosses with the del Mar murder. You got more shoe leather on the case."

"Earn it, Moss. We want a lead."

"Okay, again, let's say I showed up at del Mar's place right when he was being killed. It sounded like he was getting thrown around by a gorilla. I never got a good look at what did it, but my friend the witch said she was grabbed by something furry right before she got knocked out. Sounds like a sasquatch to me."

"Doesn't sound like something one of them would do," Moon said.

I shrugged. "Search me. Uh, and if you take that literally, I have licenses for everything."

Moon ignored it. He was like a dog with a bone, and I regretted thinking that, only because I was sure he would somehow hear me. "So you're saying whoever forced del Mar to set up the meeting with the witch is the one who later offed him?"

"Yeah, that's what I think happened."

"And whoever set it up did it all to get his hands on a toad?"

"Uh... yeah. I mean, it doesn't sound as good when you say it out loud like that."

"What does a sasquatch want with a toad?"

"I'll ask him once I find him."

"What does the witch know?"

"Not much. She would have told me if she had anything. She got set up."

"Give us a name," Garou snarled.

I sighed. She was going to hate me for this, but hopefully she had enough connections to stay out of the big house. "Hexene Candlemas."

Moon chuckled. "All right, Moss. You find anything else out, you call us." He stood up, his knees popping when he was vertical.

"Don't make us come back," Garou said. They filed out, and I heard Garou say, "Miss," when he passed Serendipity's desk.

The front door closed and a moment later Serendipity came in, still looking as distressed as she had before. "Are you all right, Nick?"

"I should probably go see Hexene. I need to talk to her about her day, but now I should warn her about the two homicide dicks who are going to stop by."

Serendipity nodded, wringing her webbed hands together.

I stubbed the smoke out and stood. "Take the day, Ser. Go get discovered."

She brightened. "You sure? I could stay here. Just in case."

"I have three cases. I need another one like I need a pair of wolfmen in my office. Besides, if they come back, I'd rather they find a closed-for-business sign."

She grinned, turning from a pretty blue-and-yellow girl into a terrifying avatar of needle-toothed death.

"Good luck at the drugstore."

"Actually, I have a new spot. They found a girl at the library.

Can you beat that?"

"I sure can't."

FOURTEEN

I drove into Hollywood, rehearsing my apology to Hexene for spilling my guts to the wolfmen. She'd understand. She would have to. At least, that's what I told myself. With some luck, Moon and Garou wouldn't be heading directly to her. Following up other leads, rounding up other suspects. Be nice if our relationship went both ways, but the fact that they'd shaken me down said they didn't have anything. Asking a meatstick for information was really scraping the bottom of the barrel.

Hexene's shop was on Gower, south of Melrose. The thoroughfare held shops and the odd restaurant, while the side streets were cluttered with houses. Small lots, mostly, populated by studio employees.

The shop itself was a two-story Spanish building, the stucco doing its best to pass as adobe. The windows were small and the display was haphazard. It looked like the space in front of the windows was used as storage, and I smiled because that was probably exactly what Hexene had been doing. The sign in black letters said only, "CANDLEMAS" and had a sigil on either side that I didn't recognize.

Inside, the lights were dim, but since the sign in the door said "OPEN," I did.

The air inside the shop was heavy with scents. A couple I knew intimately: wolfsbane and others I used to fend off the various creatures of the night. Moon and Garou were going to have a hell of a time getting anything from Hexene while they were inhaling that. The other scents were the turgid mix of an exploded spice rack. A few candles burning away in lanterns threw some fitful illumination over the shelves, and I wasn't sure whether or not to be grateful. The dolls, skulls, fetishes, and devices I didn't have names for might become more horrifying in the light, or else my imagination was running away with me.

The counter had an old cash register, but no one was minding it except for what looked like a large otter made entirely from snot. It peered at me with antediluvian suspicion.

"Uh. Hi. I'm looking for Hexene. Um, Candlemas."

The creature, whatever it was, shifted, stubby legs slapping over the surface of the counter. A moment later, a curtain opened and a woman came into the room. She was very short, maybe half my height, which put her squarely into dwarf territory. She was heavy-set, too, with wide hips and breasts like the prow of a very tiny battleship. She looked squarely in her forties, and her shiny black hair held more than a few streaks of gray. Her eyes were nearly black, sizing me up with formidable intelligence and power. Her skin was a reddish brown, something I'd associate with the few Indians I'd met, or the Mexicans from deep in the country. She wore a patchwork dress that looked made by the same hand as Hexene's.

"Hola," she said, lifting the massive amphibian into her

arms and cradling it like a baby. It was almost as big as she was. "¿Còmo le puedo ayudar?"

"Uh, hi. I'm Nick Moss. I'm here to see Hexene."

"Oh, eres el novio de Hexene. Te ves más como una comadreja de lo que ella dijo."

"Um, yes. That's right." I had no idea if that was right or not, but I thought it best to play along.

She nodded like I had spoken a great truth. "Soy Hechalé. Soy la madre de Hexene. Sígueme." She turned around and waddled to the door, paused, turned back, and jerked her head in that direction.

"Oh!" I followed her. She parted the curtains, and for the first time since I could remember, I had to move them too, so the parts higher up wouldn't hit me in the face. I found myself in a hallway leading to a back room. New smells billowed from the back, and I was reminded that I hadn't eaten breakfast. Someone was cooking back there and it smelled incredible.

She parted another curtain, revealing a kitchen with a circular table in the middle. Hexene and another witch were sitting at it, Hexene still looking drawn and listless. The other witch was hunchbacked and green-skinned, her nose long and warty, her hair iron gray under a tall, pointed hat. Her dress was similarly patchwork, though the colors were much darker than the other two. This had to be the crone of the Candlemas Coven, and possibly the most powerful witch in Los Angeles. She was squinting at me like she wondered what I tasted like in stew.

A television was on in the corner, showing the HUMAC hearings. That's the House Un-Monster Activities Committee to you and me. Congressman Akhenaten I was grilling some blob about harboring human fugitives during the Night War. This was the most unpatriotic thing a monster could think of: another monster treating human life with respect, and if this blob were convicted, he could say goodbye to his career, social life, and romantic prospects. Depending on how much of those a blob had, anyway.

The Imbolc Investigators, Akhenaten I's personal witch coven and attack dogs, were arrayed behind the mummy, grinning like Cheshire Cats. They were severe-looking women, with about ten years difference between maiden and mother, mother and crone. Their hair colors couldn't be seen on the black-and-white television, but with how unforgiving their hairstyles were, it was possible the color had been pulled clean out. They wore conservative suits, and in a stunning display of historical irony, their pointed hats managed to look Puritan. Maybe it's me, but even though HUMAC and the Imbolc witches had no care for a human amnestied by the Treaty of St. Louis, I still reflexively loathed them. I don't like witch hunts.

"Mija, tu novio está aquí," the mother said. The short woman had to be the mother of the Candlemas Coven.

"Ya te lo dije, no es me novio," Hexene snapped, color momentarily returning to her cheeks. I was no expert, but her accent sounded flawless. "Hi, Nick," she said to me. "Did you find anything?"

"Todavía no deberías estar saliendo, pero cuando lo hagas, se podría hacer mejor que él. Eres muy bonita," the mother said.

"¡Madre de dios!" Hexene cursed.

The crone grunted in vague disapproval.

"Cuida tu lenguaje. La Virgen fue uno de nosotros," the mother said, and her lecturing tone, at least, translated.

Hexene looked chastened.

"Ahora, invitas al hombre comadreja para sentarse y preguntarle si le gustaría algo de comer. La forma en que sigue mirando la cocina me hace pensar que no lo ha tenido una buena comida en muchos años."

Hexene sighed. "Nick, Hechalé, our mother, would like me to invite you to sit down and have some breakfast." .

"Really? Thank you!" I turned to the tiny woman, who had put her giant salamander on the counter and was feeding him strips of bacon. "Thank you, ma'am."

On the television, the blob broke down under the relentless questioning and was just quivering like last week's Jell-O. The Imbolc Investigators must have gotten something good on him.

"De nada. Siéntate, por favor." She nodded to the empty seat.

"Right." I plopped into the chair and was eye level with the crone. She stared me down.

"This is Hermosa, our crone."

"Pleased to meet you. And you, ma'am," I called over to the mother. She turned her head and smiled, and I felt nice and warm.

Hermosa grunted and continued to stare. A scrape came from under the table. I peeked and found a snapping turtle the size of a couch cushion staring at me with the same look.

"Don't pet him," Hexene said.

"Wasn't planning on it."

"Pretend he's not there."

"What if he bites me?"

"He won't. Probably."

Hechalé slid a plate in front of me. It was covered edge to edge in eggs, beans, tortillas, and red sauce. One taste and it was all I could do not to upend the whole thing directly into my mouth.

"Por lo menos puede comer," the mother remarked.

Hexene got another plate, which she absently picked at. Hermosa's breakfast looked mostly liquid, which was good since she only had a couple good teeth left, and those looked ready to abandon ship.

"Had no idea you spoke Spanish," I said to Hexene between bites.

"I'm from Mexico, so yes."

I blinked and looked up at her. She was the perfect Irish lass, with her wavy red hair, green eyes, and freckles. "Oh, so the... you changed, then."

"Not all Irish people went to the US," she said, apparently reading my mind. "Some went to Mexico, including my family. One of the reasons Hermosa and Hechalé picked me was the hair and eyes. The closer you are to the supposed ideal, the more power you and the coven get. And those that don't look the part change physically. Sometimes."

I glanced at the television, where the shot of the Imbolc Investigators revealed none of that. They looked closer to sisters than the three phases of womanhood. Then again, they hardly looked female. Like Congressman Akhenaten I, their commitment to the cause had rendered them sexless.

"Huh. Always wondered about that."

"Now you know."

"You don't have an accent."

"I worked hard to lose it."

"¿Quieres otro plato?" Hechalé asked. I looked down and realized I'd cleaned my plate completely. There wasn't a scrap of anything.

"She's asking if you want seconds," Hexene explained.

"Oh." I thought about it. I was pretty full, but there was room in there, and if she was offering... "Uh, yeah. But not as much."

"Él dice que sí, por favor," Hexene translated.

Hechalé beamed at me, took my plate, filled it back up to the brim, and put it back in front of me.

"Wow," I said. "A lot of food." I dove in.

"What brings you here, Nick?"

"Uh, a couple things. I wanted to talk to you about your day, so I can retrace your steps. But first, you should know that a couple cops visited me this morning, and chances are they'll be making an appearance here."

Hexene dropped her fork, and I was happy to see a little of her former fire. I wasn't thrilled it was directed at me, but better me than nowhere. "And why is that?"

"They braced me. Your friend Paolo del Mar got himself killed, and I was spotted coming out of his house."

"You killed him?"

"Why does everyone think I killed him? No, I think whatever grabbed you on the beach killed him. Cleaning up loose ends. I explained that to the wolves, so they might want to talk to you while they try to sniff out a lead."

Hexene sighed. "All right."

I finished the second plate of food. Hechalé took it instantly with a questioning look. I held my belly and said, "I couldn't possibly. It was delicious."

"Él dice que no, gracias."

Hechalé beamed again, filled my plate halfway, and put it in front of me. "Uh, I said... it's not important." I ate, but it was getting progressively more difficult.

"Hexene," I said to buy some time, "Can you tell me what happened that day?"

"Nothing. I would have told you if something happened. I spent all day in the shop. No one came in. Paolo called around four, I think. I rode my broom out to Royal Palms and... you know the rest."

"What about the week? I need a list of the people you met, especially any new clients."

"You want a list of my clients after you told me you spilled your guts to the cops?"

"I wouldn't, um, I wouldn't tell the police."

"And I can trust you why?"

"You're trusting me with this."

"And wondering if I should be doing that."

That hurt. I think she saw it in my face, because she looked away just after she said it. I forced out what I was going to say. "I just need some leads, is all. The more I look at this thing, the weirder it gets, but yeah. You can trust me."

"This is the worst thing that can happen to a witch," she said.

"Don't worry. I'll find something." The truth was, I was beginning to worry that my best clue was already at the morgue Downtown, ready to be filleted by the coroner. I smiled at Hexene, faking some confidence I didn't feel. "Hey, how about those Imbolc Investigators. You said they never let witches do anything?"

"Those fairy godmothers?" Hexene sneered. "No thanks."

FIFTEEN

Hexene gave me a list after complaining about hex-slinger/client confidentiality, which she still seemed to believe was a concept that existed outside of her head. She made me promise to burn it after I'd memorized it, and if it fell into the hands of the police, I could kiss pretty much everything goodbye. I checked over the list of people, and saw that she met one, a Percy Katz, at the Isla Calavera Casino on Catalina Island. Name like that, he had to be a jaguar person. Well, I wouldn't be seeing him, for more reasons than one. I shuddered, feeling guilty and glad that the island was off-limits to humans.

I don't know why I drove to the kidnapping site. I guess I thought I should have a look, even if the odds of finding something were basically nil. Royal Palms was a beach very close to the southern tip of Los Angeles. Even the housing developments didn't extend this far, as the local topography had already proved it didn't want people when, at the turn of the century, it dropped an entire street in the drink.

The road to the beach was a wide yellow track leading to a

dirt parking lot that was nearly empty. A few cars with wood-paneled doors were lined up at one end, and the owners, a large group of gill-men and sirens, were heading up from the beach. The gill-men were in the big trunks favored by the body-surfers and some of the sirens were in rather daring two-piece bathing suits. The most adventurous matched their skin tone and even sported thick stripes in similar colors to those looping over their bodies. Some of them nestled in the scaly crooks of the gill-men's arms, and there was a good deal of laughing all around. Every last gill-man wore thick, dark glasses, blocking out the morning sun as best they could.

"Excuse me," I said to the group.

They paused, checking me out with faint curiosity. "Yeah?" one of the gill-men asked.

"Were any of you here on Sunday afternoon?"

The entire group laughed, the sirens' gills frilling outward in big red collars.

"What's funny?"

"Surf in the afternoon? Talk about squaresville," the biggest gill-man of the bunch responded. A siren was doing her best to drape herself over him.

"Oh. Thanks."

The fish people dismissed me and continued their walk up to their cars. Must be nice, to be young and a monster.

The beach was empty by the time I got to the sand. The waves pounded the shore, and back at the lot, the cars made dusty semicircles before heading up the slope and onto the street above. I was left alone on the site where, on Sunday, Hexene had been mugged for her toad.

The sandy beach was bordered on either side by jagged rock, and with no one around, the whole place was surprisingly peaceful. What I couldn't understand was how anyone could have snuck up on Hexene. Even if she was the oblivious sort, and she wasn't, the only way onto the beach was the path I'd just traversed. She would have at least been aware of anything coming from that direction. Other than that, it was down fifty feet of cliff or over the rocks. Either way, there was no place to sneak up on her.

Another mystery piling up. Had her attacker actually been Paolo del Mar or some other gill-man, he could have come from the ocean, but she described fur and didn't mention it being wet.

I looked out into the churning surf. Off the coast, Catalina Island rose in a dark hump against the endless blue of the Pacific. There was a casino out there now, one of the larger tourist traps in LA. At night, the southern end of the island would be lit up like a New Orleans Christmas, but in the day, it was a dark, uniform lump. The lights were for monsters, and I was still human.

As I looked at the island, I shuddered. I knew what was out there. At least he was staying there.

SIXTEEN

With Hexene's case giving up nothing, I turned to Aggie. I drove back to the Brooks household and knocked on the door. Alice answered, looking almost as bad as she had yesterday. She brightened a little when she saw me, and the light died as quickly when she saw I didn't have her little girl.

"Hi, Nick. What are you doing here?"

"I was going to retrace Aggie's steps. Could you take me through her day?"

Alice nodded and invited me in. I sat down at their dining room table and saw with a sick feeling there were four chairs. Two for Henry and Alice, and one for each of their missing children, one of whom never had a chance to see there was a place waiting for him at home. I wondered whose seat I was in.

"Where's Henry?" I asked as she went into the kitchen.

"He's at work. Can't take any more time off."

Alice returned, carrying a tray with two cups of coffee, a ceramic bowl of sugar shaped like a cartoon pig, and a tiny pitcher of milk. I put my coffee together in silence.

"I'm sorry about this, Alice."

"I thought I was done losing people." A sniffle turned into a bitter chuckle. "I thought it was the worst thing that could have happened when I got the letter about John."

"John. Their father."

She nodded. "It was such a long time ago, I don't think I remember what he looked like. Lost all the pictures of him in the Night War."

"I'm sorry to hear that."

"He died in the invasion. He was a medic. Didn't even have a gun." She wiped her nose. "Where were you on D-Day, Nick?"

"Scared out of my mind in the French countryside behind enemy lines." She frowned at me, and I saw I was distracting from her pain. So I went on. "I was a paratrooper. You know why? When I enlisted, I saw they paid paratroopers fifty bucks more a month than normal soldiers—Jump Pay, but it's more like Falling Out of a Plane Pay—and I figured, how hard is falling? I can do that without any training. So I signed up for that. The night before the invasion, they piled us into planes and spilled us out over France. My plane got hit, and at the time, I figured that's why I completely missed my target and ended up alone. Turned out we were all scattered to hell and gone, whether or not our planes stayed in one piece. I had a bunch of my equipment in a leg bag, and when my chute opened, the shock pulled that off, so I lost most everything. Found out later there were fellas who lost their rifles, which made me lucky. Missed the beach, too, which made me extra lucky."

"John died on the beach." I knew the story. Maybe not this specific one, but enough like it. I didn't interrupt; she needed to say it. "I got the letter, that he died a hero, and I thought that at least it was the worst thing that could happen to us. I was wrong. Telling JJ was the worst thing. Aggie was only a year old, so she didn't understand. She had only met her father once, and she was too young to know what was happening. JJ was four, and he understood. At least, he understood his father was never coming home."

She was quiet, so I said something just to say something. "I'm sorry, Alice."

"And then the Night War began. You remember what it was like at first. A lot of disappearances, some news articles that sounded like the press had lost their marbles. Then it happened to someone you knew. Then you saw something. And then the world went crazy. I had met Henry before things got really bad, and he loved JJ and Aggie. I thought I was the luckiest girl in the world, you know? Aggie never knew another father, and Henry never treated the kids as anything other than his. We had their names changed, too, from D'Agostino to Brooks, and I swear, it was the happiest day in our lives."

"Alice, I'm going to do everything I can for you."

She met my eyes, and hers had gone red and wobbly. "I know, Nick."

"I need you to tell me what Aggie did on Sunday."

"We went to church first."

"Which church?"

"The Church of Christ. It's a few blocks away, human congregation."

"And after that?"

"We had a picnic in the park. Aggie liked to push the smaller children on the swings. She's a sweet girl."

"She is," I told her. I talked Alice through the rest of Aggie's week, which was mostly spent at school and at home. I knew that the monster I was looking for had either lurked outside the Church of Christ, or in the park, or was a regular nighttime visitor. Not now, though. Now, he was gone with Aggie somewhere.

When Alice was finished and I had a page of notes scratched into my notebook, I gulped the rest of my coffee. “One thing: if there was a monster you remember seeing around that’s suddenly not around anymore, you call me. I’m going to get back out there. No reason to waste any time.” Though the statement was factual, it wasn’t the truth. I just couldn’t be around poor, grieving Alice Brooks for a second longer.

SEVENTEEN

This had been the second time I'd been to church in as many days, shattering my previous record of once every couple of weeks when I was a kid. Aggie's church wasn't in the same shape as the Church of Christ, Remaker, either. It was rundown, still scarred in places from the Night War. Churches had been a popular place to gather in those days, since the holy symbols kept several of the more common monsters at bay. Problem was, the other kinds of monsters realized this, and churches turned into all-night buffets.

I went inside and was relieved that as uncomfortable as this might get, I wasn't going to have to deal with a clown. I found the minister talking to a family who seemed to be listening to what the man had to say. I waited by the door and attempted to smoke just to have something to do with my hands. When their conversation finally let up, the minister sized me up and headed right over, a beatific smile on his face.

"You look like you have a lot on your mind, Mr... ."

"Moss. Yeah, I do. I wanted to discuss Aggie Brooks with you."

"Oh, yes. I heard. Horrible. Are you with the police?"

I smirked at that. "Come on."

He chuckled. "Yes, I suppose that was naïve of me, wasn't it?"

"I'm a private eye."

"Moss. Moss, yes, that sounds familiar. Some of my congregation must have mentioned you."

"Probably."

"And yet you're not here on Sundays."

"If Jesus played baseball, that might be a different story. Look, I'm not interested in talking about my immortal soul. Aggie Brooks. You know her. Have there been any monsters hanging around the church? Maybe taking an interest in her? Maybe a sasquatch?"

"No, nothing like that," he said. "With the Fair Game Law being what it is, we don't have many monsters troubling us." He was referring to the fact that holy ground was considered "home" for the purposes of turning humans. It was why hotel rooms had Bibles in the drawers.

"I see. Can you think of anything that might help me?"

"I'm afraid not, Mr. Moss."

"Well, if you think of something, call my office. My secretary might even be there."

I turned to go.

"I'm sorry, Mr. Moss, but before you go, can you indulge me for a moment?"

I stopped. "Sure."

"Just because the Night War altered what we know to be true, it does not mean God is not a part of us."

"It wasn't the war that ended my churchgoing days, Reverend. Thanks for your time."

I drove to the park Alice had mentioned, only a few blocks from the church. It was one of the sadder places I'd seen. The bluff the Normandie Knights occupied boasted more greenery. The grass was dying and the play equipment looked like it was made from the rusted remains of reclaimed military hardware. It was a Tuesday afternoon, and likely not as busy as it had been on Sunday, but there were still a few people there: mothers with small children in carriages and a few tykes playing in a sandpit my cat would have loved. Two clowns stood at the border of the park, holding bunches of balloons, silently staring at the people within. Their ice cream trucks played competing versions of "Pop Goes the Weasel." What was it with clowns and that song?

I approached a knot of mothers sharing an afternoon gossip, apparently unaware of the clowns watching them.

"Hello, ladies," I said, and the conversation stopped immediately to regard the intruder. "My name's Nick Moss, and I was wondering if I could ask you a few questions."

"Are you a policeman?" one asked me, a pretty and plump brunette whose baby was fast asleep in his carriage.

"No, ma'am. I'm a private eye. Human."

They relaxed instantly. "You should have said that first," said a blonde, keeping one eye on a little boy who was busy cramming fistfuls of dirt into his mouth.

"Yeah, probably. Can I ask you... do you want me to do something about them?" I asked, jerking a thumb at the clowns.

The women looked like they were considering it. Finally, the blonde said, "No thanks. As long as they stay over there, they can watch."

"Were any of you here on Sunday?"

"I was," the brunette said.

"Were the clowns here then, Mrs... ."

"Lowery. They weren't."

"What about other monsters? A sasquatch maybe?"

She shook her head in the same rhythm that she moved

the carriage. "No sasquatches. I mean, I've never seen one, but then, I didn't see a monster here that I'd never seen before."

"Oh, all right." I was getting desperate, and the day was moving on. "What about fur? Any furry monsters around here?"

She frowned. "Do bogeymen have fur?"

"Maybe?"

She pointed to a hollowed-out log. I followed the finger and glimpsed some movement inside. "There are always bogeymen in there. We tell the kids not to play anywhere close."

There had been a bogeyman sniffing around Aggie Brooks, and who was to say they didn't look like sasquatches when pulled out. They hated light, even more than vampires and gremlins. Even a nightlight could burn them, and the sun would kill one in seconds. They were also horrible cowards. That fact gave me some confidence.

I walked over to the log, passing the sandpit where the children played and slipping into the dappled shade. I tapped the log with a foot. "Anybody in there?"

After a long moment, a forlorn voice inside said, "No."

"That's good," I said, settling down next to a large hole in the top. There were holes in the side as well, and the bogeyman would be peering through them at the kids. I put my legs directly in front of two of them. That left one peephole: directly beneath the opening next to me. And then I waited. Just like fishing.

I heard the bogeyman shifting below me. The unexperienced man might have lunged, but I gave him a little time. I wanted him to feel safe. Little by little, he inched toward the peephole, the only sound his claws scrabbling on the wood every few minutes. I stared off in the direction of the street. The clouds had come in and the sky was darkening. Pretty soon we'd have the same false night we'd had on Sunday. I was going to have to cut the day short.

I plunged my hand into the log and grabbed something

furry and a little elastic. The bogeyman howled in dismay and struggled, but they're best suited for grabbing kids. Even little fellas like me can hold one without too much trouble, especially in the daytime. At night, in the dark, they got a hell of a lot bigger and stronger. The way he was thrashing and carrying on, you'd have thought I was killing him.

I glanced around. The clowns were heading for their ice cream trucks, studiously pretending nothing had happened. They would probably call the cops about the crazy meatstick assaulting a monster in the park. I'd have to make this quick. The women were openly smiling. The kids just looked confused.

"All right, bogey. You got a name?"

"M-m-murphy. Murphy Bedd."

"Tell you what, Murph. If you don't stop wailing, I'm going to pull you out of that log and let you take your chances in the daylight."

He howled again. His skin felt a bit like flesh, but there were soft scales under my fingers, and some coarse hair. Felt like the stuff in Aggie's window, but I couldn't be sure. I shook him. "Knock it off."

He fell silent, except for some sniffling.

"All right, I'm going to ask you a few questions. Understand?"

"PLEASE DON'T SHOW ME DAYLIGHT, MISTER! PLEASE!"

"That's not a yes." I yanked him into the top of the log and he wailed.

"YES! YES! JUST LET ME GO!"

Letting Bedd go was a good way to never see or hear from him again. Bogeymen had some weird way of traveling between closets and beneath beds and other hiding places. Soon as I let him go, Bedd would vanish and probably find another park to haunt.

"I'll let you go, Murph, but like I said, I have a few questions.

I'm looking for a little girl named Aggie Brooks, and she was playing in this park on Sunday. Something furry took her out of her house that night. I could be mistaken, but it sure feels like I'm holding something furry."

"OH GOD! NO! IT WASN'T ME! I SWEAR, MISTER, PLEASE!"

"You sure about that?"

"YES! TOTALLY CERTAIN! ONE HUNDRED PERCENT!"

"What about other bogeymen? Is she hiding in there?"

"OH GOD! I'D KNOW! I SWEAR I'D KNOW! SHE'S NOT IN HERE, PLEASE, MISTER, LET ME GO!"

"And what will you do if you find a little girl named Aggie Brooks?"

Bedd was silent, and then, cautiously: "Turn her?"

"Nope," I said, yanking him toward the hole.

"TURN HER IN TO THE POLICE! THAT'S WHAT I WAS SAYING! YOU DIDN'T LET ME FINISH, MISTER! I'M SO SORRY!"

"Okay. Now when I let you go, you find a new park, got that? Something across town, where monsters live. Because if I see you again, you're sunbathing."

"YES! YES! I'LL DO THAT! THANKS, MISTER!"

I dropped Bedd, and heard the scrabbling of his claws under my butt, and then nothing. I knew if I looked into the log, it would be empty. I got up, dusted myself off, and walked back to my car. The women threw admiring looks my way. I puffed up my chest and walked a little taller, at least until I was back in the car.

EIGHTEEN

The spot where JJ disappeared wasn't on the way home, but I stopped there anyway. Actually, it was several miles out of my way, in a monster neighborhood, and this was with the premature night of the storm closing in. But something drew me up there, out past Watts into the working-class neighborhood of Vernon. JJ had been scavenging pretty far from home that day. Nearly everything close by had been picked over. He had mentioned some apartment blocks that hadn't been looted, trying to get an *attaboy* from Izzy and me. JJ's face had lit up, the combination of his ruddy complexion and red hair making him look like a smiling sunrise.

Thing was, when he told us, we were exhausted. We'd finally beaten back a siege of headless horsemen and pumpkinheads, and we needed some shut-eye before we all made tracks to find a new place to hunker down.

To this day, I don't remember exactly what I said to JJ. Sometimes it's, "Be my guest, kid." Sometimes it's a little crueler. Didn't matter. JJ vanished, and we all guessed he went out to loot that find of his and found it wasn't as deserted as he thought.

As I pulled up outside that apartment building, those thoughts were simmering right at the top of my head.

The buildings were different now, of course. Mostly restored, even though the monsters in there were zombies, blobs, ghosts: the kinds of working-class monsters who had been changed but not necessarily much improved by it. The apartment building lacked the kind of marks you'd see on a human tenement. There were no bullet holes, no acid burns, no piles of rubble the city hadn't yet got around to clearing. But it was far from the gleaming mansions in Hollywood where the uptown monsters, the crawling eyes and vampires, the mummies and brainiacs made their homes.

I last stood in the courtyard of that place three years ago, right at the tail end of the Night War. We knew it was the end. Hell, I knew it was the end as soon as that monster tore the ballpark in half. I saw the same looks on the faces of my friends that I saw on the Krauts when we rolled into Germany. It wasn't despair so much as exhaustion and resignation. And under the circumstances, the treaty was better than we could have hoped for.

None of that helped JJ. He was still missing. Maybe dead. Wouldn't that be the cruelest. Turned and then killed by a human right as the Night War was ending.

I felt like the biggest sap who ever lived, but I promised JJ something. He wasn't around to hear it, but I could pretend. I'd find Aggie. It was probably already too late, but at least they could have contact with one of the kids. Assuming they accepted her new form, whatever that was.

The sky was almost pitch black and it sounded like a giant was pounding on huge kettledrums over the mountains, so I drove home.

I was finally hungry after the relentless breakfast the Candlemas Coven had served me and I was looking forward to a night of playing the cases out in my mind, trying to find the thing I'd missed. The thing that would unravel and lead me right to all the missing.

The monsters were gathering on Juniper Street. The usual suspects had already assembled, including Mira Mirra, sitting on my lawn with a starlight picnic, and my old admirer Sam Haine brooding several houses away. I was hungry enough that I considered at least grabbing a sandwich from Mira.

And there was a car I didn't recognize, parked right in front of my place. A Rolls-Royce, buffed and shined until it was the sparkliest thing on the street, and there was a newly polished robot waddling on the Mendozas' lawn. A Rolls meant money, and if there was one thing I knew beyond a shadow of a doubt, money meant trouble.

NINETEEN

A blob oozed out of the Rolls, and some prankster had crammed the top half of a chauffeur's outfit and cap on his quivering pink form. I got the vague impression of a face, due to the strategic placement of some objects in the part of his body between the neck of the uniform and the jaunty hat. Blobs looked like runny pink Jell-O, so why not treat them that way?

"Nick!" called Mira. She stood up, smoothing a rather attractive sundress. Across the street, Sam Haine glowered at us in impotent jilted fury.

"Mr. Nicholas Moss?" the blob burbled at me.

"Depends on who's asking."

"Mr. Nicholas Moss! You are getting into my car! I have hooch and plush seats and you have no choice in the matter!"

"Just wait one se—"

Mira had crossed the lawn and was right up next to me. Her hair was a cornsilk blond , her eyes bright blue, and she smelled like summer. As I watched, her hair, eyes, and complexion darkened, like she was trying to find the combination that would work best on me. "Nick, who's the blob?"

"I don't... what are you doing?"

She had blue skin with yellow stripes now, and long greenish-black hair. She looked like my secretary. "I thought you liked sirens."

"Not like... uh... oh, darn." I said this last part because a pink pseudopod had wrapped around my body and was already starting to dissolve my suit. The blob had slithered halfway up the driveway and was reaching the rest of the way.

"Mr. Nicholas Moss! You're getting in the car! This is going to be so much fun! A quick drive and the knowledge that we are everywhere!"

"Wait, what?" And then I was sailing fifteen feet over the earth, still wrapped in the pseudopod.

"Nick!" Mira shouted.

I reached into my coat for the vial of potassium. That would take the stuffing out of a blob pretty quickly. The blob must have seen that coming. Of course he did. Just because he had a couple chunks of coal where a head should be didn't mean those were his eyes. His entire body was eyes. I was in the middle of shuddering about that fact when he plowed me into my lawn. He didn't come close to turning out the lights, but he did ring my bells pretty good. Another pseudopod opened the back of the Rolls and he chucked me inside, making a lump of Nick Moss in the back.

"Nick!" screamed Mira.

"Call Ser!" I shouted at her, and maybe she heard it before the door clunked shut. The blob got into the front and the Rolls drove away.

"Mr. Nicholas Moss! Feel free to help yourself to the bar, and be comforted that soon we will all be one single mass!" The blob had maybe the most cheerful voice I'd ever heard, even if it sounded like he was addressing me from the bottom of a bowl of pudding. Unlike the clown, he seemed genuinely friendly, which somehow made the threat or whatever it was at the end of the sentence even more frightening.

"Uh... thanks?"

I sat up and considered going for the potassium. The blob was looking at me. He was looking at everything while he drove, really. I could see the beads of his false eyes and nose and the chain of his mouth through the translucent lump at the top of his body. So it felt like he was looking directly at me.

"Mr. Nicholas Moss! Don't go for a weapon! We are friends, and the outer layer of your shirt is delicious!"

"What?" I looked down and saw that the pseudopod had eaten partly through my shirt.

"Mr. Nicholas Moss! My boss would like to speak with you on a matter of employment which will soon become unnecessary in the coming age of flesh!"

"Oh. Uh. If your boss wants to talk to me, why not come to my office? Why send his goon?"

"Mr. Nicholas Moss! When you see my boss, it will all make sense! Now make yourself a drink and properly season your flesh! You are a whiskey man, are you not?"

"Uh, yeah. How did you know that?"

"My boss wanted you to be as comfortable as possible! 'Keyes,' she said to me, 'You are to treat Nick Moss with the utmost respect!'"

"Keyes? That's you?"

"Gelatin Keyes!" the blob said, extending a pseudopod from the back of the part I'd been calling its head. I shook it, and when I got my hand back, all the hair was gone. The skin underneath was positively glowing.

"Nice to meet you."

"The pleasure is all mine! And now, with the taste of your skin, I can always find you!"

"Uh. That's... great?"

The car was aiming for the coast, and at first I thought I was returning to San Pedro, but then it turned north. We were heading for Palos Verdes, where the wealthier monsters made their homes. It fit with the Rolls. With no escape in sight, I opened up the liquor cabinet and poked around. The glass bottles were filled with a variety of liquids in bright colors, the bulk of which were smoking. I sniffed a couple and probably gave myself brain damage. Every one of them smelled like industrial cleaner. No idea what the blob thought "whiskey" meant, but he had a generous idea of what that might be.

With things calmed down, I had a horrifying realization. I tried to keep the panic out of my voice when I addressed the chauffeur. "Listen, Keyes, I can't really be out after dark. For, you know, obvious reasons."

"My employer is rarely on the mainland! And she said, 'Keyes, fetch Nick Moss at once!' I waited at your office all day! Good thing I tried your home!"

"Yeah, that's a relief. Look, I don't want to tell you how to do your job, but I'm human. And this is kidnapping."

"Nonsense! It's after dark!"

"Night! The law says night!"

"It's always night somewhere!"

We were going up the coast at over thirty miles an hour. Jumping out of the car wasn't an option. Because of the clouds, it was full dark. The Pacific was an endless expanse of black velvet. With a sick feeling, I realized I could see the lights twinkling on Catalina Island. That would be the Isla Calavera Casino. I didn't want to think about what was in that place, but my mind had already made the connection, so I saw it anyway. And then, inevitably, the side of the ballpark cracking open and that huge hand reaching in.

The car pulled off the road down a winding street that led up to a huge house. I mean that in every possible way. It was maybe not quite a mansion based on its number of rooms, but it would have been two or three based on its square footage. It looked like a charming Spanish beach cottage, sized for someone who was fifty feet tall. It was then I knew exactly who Keyes's employer was. Didn't know who she'd misplaced, but I really wanted to throw up.

The house took up the entirety of the cliff, stretching from a private beach at the base to the top. The road led to a garage on the second floor, where a small addition to the house was sized for humans and the vast majority of monsters. Keyes pulled the car inside and turned off the ignition.

"Mr. Nicholas Moss! We have arrived!"

The blob slithered out of his door and landed on the concrete floor of the garage with a wet plop. He opened up the back door.

"Say, what do you call a fly with no wings?" he asked me.

"I don't know. What?"

"A trombone!" He chortled, which sounded exactly like someone blowing bubbles in mud. "Come with me, Mr. Nicholas Moss! I'm to make your stay as pleasant as possible! I can taste smells!"

Keyes led me into an elevator. He shut the grating and hit the lever, and we were going down. The door opened much later than I thought it should have and he pulled aside the rattling cage. We were in a living room, once again sized for a woman fifty feet tall. She had impeccable taste, even if the furniture looked to my eyes like vast mountains.

Yeah, I knew where I was, all right. There was only one giant—well, giantess—in Los Angeles. Most places only had one or two, just because of the strain it took to feed them. She was something of a tourist attraction down here, too, on her daily swim out to the Isla Calavera Casino and back. Wasn't everywhere you could watch a gorgeous giant blonde in a bikini climb out of the water. They sold postcards with her in her signature leopard-print bathing suit at every gift shop in the city. I was at the home of Pilar O'Heaven, LA's famous giantess.

And she was the kept woman of that goddamn ape. I shuddered, the queasy feeling getting worse and worse.

"Is it cold? Would you like a fire? I no longer feel the chill because it is all places!"

"Uh, no. I'm fine."

Keyes led me to an end table by the sofa. A spiral staircase, sized for me, led to the top. "Can I get you another whiskey?"

"Uh, do you mean actual whiskey, or what was... you know what? Never mind."

"Please wait up there! My boss will return soon! I will talk to other parts of my body!"

I climbed the staircase. It looked fragile, like an errant kick from the mistress of the house would break it off entirely. The steps were white and immaculate. One of the benefits of having a blob for a manservant. Still, it was an odd choice. Blobs tended to be a little dim, and from the looks of things, Keyes was no exception. Probably took the same kind of eccentricity that made her kidnap a human right before dark.

I made it to the top and found a comfortable chair with a human-sized end table. A microphone sat on the table with a speaker underneath. I settled down to await Miss O'Heaven. One thing kept me from running out of there, kept the panic at bay: Pilar O'Heaven had a bad reputation amongst monsters.

She was one of the first monsters Akhenaten I dragged in front of HUMAC to grill about their actions during the Night War. She was also the first high-profile monster. Even though she wasn't really anyone important, the fact that she was beautiful and a giantess meant she would be famous no matter what.

She was from back east, and they'd probably turned her for the same reason any of the giant monsters got made, to scare the living crap out of the humans. And it worked. Pilar, though, supposedly retreated into the Catskill Mountains and waited out the war. That in itself didn't mean much. Sure, Akhenaten I had gone after people for less, and once they invoked the Fifth, he could slam them for contempt of Congress and let public sentiment do the rest. But the persistent rumor with Pilar was that she was actively harboring humans. She did the predictable thing, got a short sentence, and then no monster would hire her.

Almost no monster. She came out to the City of Devils and transformed herself. Kept woman of whatever you wanted to call that ape—crime lord, businessman, public menace—and now she was a tourist attraction. Sure, she wasn't trustworthy enough for an important job, but as cheesecake, why not?

I didn't know how much of this was true. I hoped all of it. I never followed the HUMAC hearings closely. Didn't concern me. I remembered a few positive things folks around the neighborhood had said about Pilar O'Heaven, usually tempered by a frank assessment of her assets. I was essentially hoping that the biggest pinup girl in Los Angeles—no pun intended—was as unsavory as her reputation suggested.

A slurping sound came up the stairs. Keyes shortly emerged, carrying a tumbler filled with a green smoking liquid. "Made you a Manhattan! Who doesn't love a Manhattan? Manhattan would make me much larger!"

"Uh, thanks."

"Say, what did the ocean say to the other ocean?"

"I don't know. What?"

"I didn't do it on porpoise!" Keyes burbled on his way down the steps.

I glanced at the "Manhattan," which smelled like something I'd use to strip the grease off an engine.

Outside, the thunder crashed again, and the rain started to fall. I hoped that wasn't an indictment of my present situation, though it was difficult not to find significance in the weather patterns.

The door opened, and the rain grew even louder. Lightning flashed, silhouetting someone who didn't need that kind of theatricality to get her point across. It was Pilar O'Heaven, all fifty feet of her. She was dripping from the swim from Catalina Island to the mainland, her blonde hair hanging loose around her shoulders. She was in her famous leopard-print bikini, and I am a little ashamed to admit looking at her more closely than I might have otherwise. She was a well-built woman, with a body sculpted by her daily swim. As she pulled a giant towel from a hook in the foyer, she looked strangely vulnerable, not something I would have expected to see in a giantess.

I had to remind myself of a very simple fact: she was fifty feet tall. She came into the living room, wrapping her towel around herself to end the show, and looked down at me with a pair of brown eyes so warm I no longer needed that fire.

Yeah, I was in trouble all right.

Pilar O'Heaven

TWENTY

I've heard of women having legs that go all the way up; well, hers extended twenty feet past all the way up, finding a new place amongst the clouds.

"Well, hello there, Mr. Moss. You're taller than I thought," Pilar O'Heaven said with the kind of smile that could turn an average man into a quivering blob. Maybe that's where Keyes came from.

"Feeling's mutual," I said, and instantly regretted it.

She smiled. "I need you to speak into the microphone. Otherwise you sound like mice squeaking."

I picked up the microphone. "I said 'feeling's mutual.'" And then I wondered why I hadn't used my second chance to come up with anything better. My voice boomed out from under the table, sounding high-pitched and tinny.

A girlish laugh escaped her and she put one giant hand up to stifle it. "Would you be so good as to wait here? I need to wash up before I can be presentable."

"Uh, yeah."

"Microphone, Mr. Moss."

"Yes. Please, make yourself comfortable."

"That's my line, detective. I'll have Keyes bring you a drink."

"Uh, no, that's not necessary... "

"Keyes?" She took a step and looked down. "Oh, dear." She brought up her foot and Keyes was smashed onto the sole. He dribbled off. I guess that explained her choice of help.

"Yes, Miss O'Heaven!" he burbled, the voice coming simultaneously from the bits of goo still stuck to her foot and the growing blob on the floor.

"Bring Mr. Moss a drink while I freshen up. And we'll be having dinner in the dining room tonight." She disappeared and I heard her thundering footsteps going upstairs, and then the sound of a shower. Or maybe that was just the storm.

"Did you want another Manhattan, Mr. Moss?" Keyes gurgled from the floor.

"Uh, no. No, still nursing this one. Thanks."

"Let me know when you want another! In the space between stars we wait and hunger!"

"Wait, what did you... ?" But Keyes had already slithered off. I was not looking forward to dinner after what he thought a Manhattan was. To confirm my fear, the glass next to me popped and sent a spiral of smoke on a long and lonely journey to the ceiling.

The only window I could see was the one in the front door. Outside was the deep blue-black of a fresh bruise, with occasional bright stabs of white. It was definitely night now, and according to the law, I was fair game. Any monster that caught me was in his rights to turn me into one of them. I had a giantess and a blob within shouting distance.

Well, I supposed I could hope the giantess won out. Being fifty feet tall—and all giants were precisely fifty feet, and no one knew why—would make PI life impossible. I'd probably have to get a job down at the docks unloading ships. Wouldn't that be funny, end up working for del Mar's old boss. It would still be better than ending up a gelatinous pink thing everyone was worried would eventually devour the world.

While the nervous part of me, which was the largest but fortunately not the only part, ran through that scenario, the rational part had some work to do. If Pilar O'Heaven wanted to turn me, chances are she would have done it already. I had the normal anti-giant wards—I wasn't growing a beanstalk in my backyard for my health—but she was a giantess. She could have plucked me up off the ground whenever. Which led me to the assumption that she actually wanted to hire me like the blob had said.

Pilar came back in and I realized her footsteps had been obscured by thunder. It was booming pretty frequently, rattling glass and angrying up the "Manhattan." She had changed into a dress of a muted yellow color utterly at odds with the pandemonium outside. Her hair was still wet, but she had corralled it with some conservative pin work. Her makeup was so light as to be almost nonexistent. I had the sense I was seeing the real Pilar O'Heaven, rather than the sexpot who surfaced every morning, gleaming, from the surf in front of the biggest casino outside of Las Vegas.

"Mr. Moss, if you would step into my palm, I'll carry you into the dining room." She put a hand out to me that was about the size of the dining room table at the Brooks house. I glanced at it, then up at my host. "Don't be afraid, Mr. Moss. I've never dropped anyone yet."

I gingerly stepped onto her palm. It was like a very squishy floor, and the strangest part was that I was seeing all the detail of a hand, but rendered around nine times larger than I was used to. She stood up straight, and vertigo planted me solidly on my ass. She held me close to her bosom, and I had the momentary uncomfortable image of being crushed by breasts whose scale could only be described as geographic.

She carried me through several open doors, winding up at a lovely, if giant, dining room at the front of the house. She placed her hand carefully on the doilied tablecloth. A one-person table of my size had been set up there, complete with microphone and speaker. I got up, dismounted her palm, and waited by my chair.

Pilar took her seat and broke into a smile when I only then sat down. "Such a gentleman," she boomed overhead.

I shrugged.

"It's all right, Mr. Moss. Use the microphone. I brought you here to talk."

"Uh, thank you, Miss O'Heaven, but it's after dark... "

She waved a hand. "You won't be harmed in any way, Mr. Moss. And that includes being turned. You have my word on that."

I knew it was bad form to question her word, but it was the word of a monster.

She might have read the look on my face, because she smiled and said, "HUMAC might have left me alone if I had any such designs."

The flippant way she said it was surprising. I laughed, but it was a bit brittle. Fortunately, it wasn't into the microphone, so she probably never heard a thing. "I suppose so."

"You have nothing to fear. I have a small safe room for my human guests. And it locks from the inside."

"Do you often entertain, uh, human guests?"

"What a thing to ask a girl!" She giggled, but it was an act. An act that probably worked on most men, despite the fact that she was fifty feet tall and whatever her shape made men think about, any action would result in crushing death.

As I was contemplating this, an electric whine started below me and got steadily louder. A platform rose into view on the far side of the table. Keyes was on it, carrying a plate sized for Pilar, and thus bigger than my car. A smaller pseudopod carried another, normal-sized plate. He deposited the big one in front of Pilar with an undulating wave through his entire pink body. I was a little disappointed when he merely set mine in front of me. The dinners were echoes of each other. On mine, a pair of small cooked birds—probably squab—along with vegetables and mashed potatoes. On hers, the vegetables were the swollen mutant kind the mad scientists spliced and the killer vegetables called a war crime. Instead of birds, she had a pair of whole cooked cows, which she ate with a daintiness her mammoth frame belied.

The food smelled fine, and tasted even finer. Whatever mental block Keyes had when mixing drinks was gone when it came to cooking.

After I'd taken the edge off my hunger, I leaned over to the microphone. "Miss O'Heaven? I was wondering why you had me brought here."

"I do hope that wasn't unpleasant. I told Keyes to bring you, but sometimes he can be rather oblivious to the needs of those of us with bones."

"Uh... I've had worse."

She didn't ask for elaboration, instead dabbing unnecessarily at her face with a napkin. She shifted in her seat and wouldn't look right at me. I waited this out. Finally, she said, "It started in June." That was two months ago. "I noticed I was feeling a little weaker than usual. I would get light-headed if I stood up quickly and was more winded than usual after my daily commute. Eventually, I found the source." She tilted her head to the side, showing off a neck that was far more climbable than kissable.

"I can't see anything," I said into the microphone.

She leaned closer. I squinted.

"They look like two pinpricks," she prompted.

"Wait, are you saying you have a vampire, uh... caller?"

She straightened up and blushed. I briefly considered the amount of blood that would have required, then realized if I kept thinking about it, I would have to stop eating. "Yes, I believe so. I've never seen him, though."

Her skin had to be several inches thick. Any vampire feeding on her would have to be packing some serious chompers. I kept that to myself, as it seemed a little gauche to bring up.

"I see. When does he, um, visit?"

"At night."

"Right, no, obviously, but when? What days of the week?"

"It varies. Sometimes he's not here for several weeks, then he's here three nights in a row."

"And you want me to... "

"Find him, Mr. Moss."

That was the spear of ice I'd been waiting for. I wondered if that's how that poor hapless vampire was going to feel if I actually took the job. "What, uh, what for?"

"Is that a question you ask all your clients?" she asked, leaning back and accentuating her attributes. Frankly, it looked like more of a threat.

"Well, no, but most of my clients are human. And missing a loved one. 'Find my daughter' is a pretty normal thing to ask of a private eye, and the reason why is very rarely 'she owes me money.'"

She smiled. "This vampire does not owe me money."

"Then what does he owe you?"

"An explanation, perhaps?"

"How about he gets thirsty and you're the biggest source of blood on the mainland?"

"Don't be crude, Mr. Moss." Though it sounded like a rebuke, she was still playing me, pretending it was the most titillating thing she could have said.

"Fine, fine. There's a whole city of humans out there—okay, not a whole city, but a couple neighborhoods' worth. And we ward against vampires every day. We hang crosses, or stars of David, or in the case of my neighbors, the Yamamotos, this arch thing that looks very elegant... anyway, the point is, I have lived in my house since the end of the war, and I've never had a vampire in it. If you need a place to pick up some wards, I know a great herbalist shop on Gower. But that's not what you want, is it? You want me to find this twilight visitor and arrange an introduction."

She paused, the blush growing sunnier even as outside it sounded like the biblical Flood. Finally she nodded. "Yes, that is what I want to hire you to do, and I will pay you quite well for it and for your discretion."

I shook my head. How was I going to tell a fifty-foot woman no? "Uh, okay, we need to go through this point by point. First off, why me?"

"You're a private investigator who finds missing persons."

"He's not technically 'missing.'"

"I don't know where he is, and would like to. That defines 'missing.'"

This was getting me nowhere, so I switched tactics. "There are other detectives in town, there's B—"

"I can't trust them. I need to keep this secret."

"How did you find me?"

"Imogen Verity," she said, naming not only my most famous

client but several of the most famous faces on the planet. She was a doppelganger, the star of nearly every one of Visionary Pictures' releases. She was a sex symbol and an Oscar winner, and I had helped her out of a jam a few months ago.

"Oh?"

"She came to the casino as a special guest," and here she made a face. "My... beau... invites a lot of women out to the island. Imogen came, but was more interested in speaking with me than him. I had a little time in private with her, explained my problem, and she recommended you."

"Well, that's always nice to hear, but it does beg the question. You mentioned your beau," and I shuddered because even though I could dance around his name, I couldn't dance around the memories, "and if you want me to find this vampire for, um, romantic purposes? What's your boyfriend going to think?"

"He's a brute!" she burst out. I nearly fell out of my chair. "Those women he invites to the island? You think it's plain admiration? You think he's calling up Imogen Verity because he likes her movies?"

"Well, there's the matter of, uh, of logistics. I mean, your... um, beau is your size, and Imogen—"

"Mr. Moss!"

"It's relevant! In this case. Which also, of course, I mean, a vampire is pretty small, and you're, well, you're not... "

She cut me off. "What I want to do is my business. You find him and arrange the meeting. I take the meeting and pay you a good deal of money. As for the reaction of others concerned, there need not be one. If you're discreet, then no one need find out."

"Um... I'm in the middle of cases. Three, actually. And they're really taking all... "

She leaned over the table showing off cleavage that was more aptly described as a canyon. I was fairly certain she still thought she was seducing me. “Come now, Mr. Moss. This can’t be much of a challenge for a man like you.”

“Well, I don’t exactly, um... ”

“Money, Mr. Moss. For very little work.”

I thought about my three other cases. Then I thought of the name on Hexene’s list: Percy Katz, who she met on Catalina Island. If this gave me the chance to interview someone I might otherwise miss, I owed it to Hexene. Much as I didn’t want to admit it, I was at a dead end with the others. Maybe this could clear my palate, and I’d come back and see what I’d been missing.

“Well,” I said, drawing out the word as I thought, “if someone developed a crush on you, he probably likes to watch you swim to the casino. My guess is that he catches the ferry in the morning, watches you come in, and catches a later ferry to watch you on the other side. If you wanted me to get started immediately, I’d need a ride on that ferry.”

“Easily done. I have complimentary tickets from the casino.”

“Not so easily. No humans allowed on the island.”

“Stay away from the monsters who can tell. Most of the employees at the casino are zombies and jaguar people. You should be fine.”

“Uh, do you know the name ‘Percy Katz’?”

“Sure, he’s the head of security.”

“Oh.”

“Why do you want to know about Percy?”

“Not important. I’ll do it, but you have to understand I’m working a couple other cases right now.”

“You have all the time in the world, Mr. Moss. Find my vampire for me.”

“And I charge by the day?”

She waved a hand. “Find him, bill me what you think is

fair." She gazed down at me, and I knew she was not used to being swindled for a very good reason: she could crush me with nary a thought.

We were finished with dinner and I once again boarded the hand. She transported me to an alcove sized for a human, with a short staircase leading to a heavy steel door, where I dismounted her hand.

"You can spend the night in there. It's sealed, so you don't even have to worry about Keyes. I told him you're not to be touched, but he'll likely forget before long. So I apologize for that. If you need anything, there is an intercom, and I can convey requests to Keyes for you. Good night, Mr. Moss. I'm sorry about the way I brought you here, and I'm glad you can look past it."

I nodded to her and opened the door. It gave a little puff, attesting to the seal she had promised was on the inside. I pulled it closed and saw it did, in fact, lock from the inside. Felt strange to have a monster tell me something totally true. Maybe the reasons HUMAC had gone after her were genuine. Saving humans was the most Un-Monster Activity she could have been doing. All she wanted me to do was find this vampire. Should be easy enough. A quick trip out to the island, an interview with Mr. Katz, and I could return and follow the trails of the two humans and one toad who needed me, and hopefully with fresh perspective.

The room was much nicer than I expected, and spotless like everything else in the house. Maybe hiring blobs was the right way to go. Most of the richer monsters used ghosts, out of a combination of ease, stability, and ambience. Both ghosts and blobs were blue-collar, but ghosts were at least elegant about it.

There was a bed big enough for two, made up with military corners. A closet was empty save for a few pairs of clean pajamas and some nightgowns. I hung up my jacket and hat inside. Another door led into a tidy bathroom, where I washed up for bed.

Isla Calavera Casino. That was a hell of a way to get a man to face his fears. With any luck, I could continue my streak of avoiding that particular monster. He wasn't someone I needed to talk to, and in fact, I had good reason to leave him alone.

I stripped down to shorts and undershirt and lay back on the bed, playing the cases through my head, looking for the stone I'd left unturned. If it degenerated to me retracing their steps over the previous weeks, I was increasingly unlikely to find anything. The feeling I was missing something big kept nagging at me, but the more threads I pulled, the more it unraveled into the present mess I was in.

"Mr. Nicholas Moss? Open the door and we can become one!"

"Go away, Keyes. Ask your boss. I'm not supposed to be turned."

He didn't respond. I just heard a sucking sound, and that was the lullaby that put me out.

Gelatin Keyes

TWENTY-ONE

My eyes opened as a bolt of terror shot through me. The room I was in was completely unfamiliar and my groggy mind tried to string together whatever odd events had led to my kidnapping. The guy who took Escuerzo had taken me too and now Hexene was going to have to hire a wolf to track me down. Baskerville was supposed to be good.

I realized then I was in Pilar O'Heaven's guest vault. There was probably a nicer word for it, but the heavy steel door, like the door of a bank vault complete with a wheel lock in the center, demanded a name like that. I showered and dressed, leaving my rapidly growing beard. Might help convince people I was a werewolf if it came to that.

I checked the clock and guessed Serendipity was in. I called the office.

"Moss Investigations," she said.

"Ser, it's Nick."

"What happened? Mira said you were kidnapped!"

"Uh, yeah, I was, kind of."

"Do you need me to call the police?"

"No, it was a... well, a client. We have another job."

Serendipity sighed. "Someone kidnaps you and you take a job? What's the name? I'll start the invoice."

"Pilar O'Heaven."

"Why do I... wait, the giantess? The one in the leopard... Nick, you can't mean her."

"I can and do. I need to go out to Catalina Island today."

"That's illegal!" she squeaked, and I had a mental image of her gills extending in scandalized delight.

"Right, well, I still need to do it. Unless the operator is listening in, in which case I wouldn't dream of it."

"Watch yourself, boss."

"Believe me, I will."

"Say, if you're not coming in today... "

"You took yesterday off!"

"Only half. And I think I'm really close. There were some well-heeled sorts I'm pretty certain were from the studios. If I look my best, they might look my way."

"Watch yourself, Ser. Get the office in order, get my laundry from Mr. Rodriguez, and then yes."

"Thanks, Nick!" She hung up before I could change my mind, which was the smartest thing she could have done.

Dressed in yesterday's rumpled suit, I opened up the door and let out a yelp at seeing Keyes lying protoplasmically in the way. He surged upward into his normal shape—something like a half-melted bowling pin—and gurgled, "Mr. Nicholas Moss! I hope you like ham and eggs, for that is what awaits you in the kitchen! I hope you like the symphony of every cell in your body speaking with its own voice, for that is what awaits you in the future!"

"Is there coffee?"

"You bet! Say, what do you get when you cross a wendigo and a vampire?"

"I don't know. What?"

"A walk!" Keyes giggled as he slithered up the stairs, which had the weird look of jelly being poured backwards.

The legs of the dining room table looked like trees designed by an obsessive god. The chairs were more of an abstract idea, size rendering what should have been soft and comforting into a geologic formation on the verge of collapsing. Pilar was already at the table, body wrapped in a silk dressing gown. I briefly wondered how they'd found enough silkworms to spin that before remembering that mad scientists had made great strides in the field of giant insects.

I rode the elevator up, and at the top, she smiled down at me and boomed, "Good morning, Mr. Moss. I hope you slept well?"

I waved to her as I walked across the white tablecloth to the table where I would eat. Her blonde hair was in rollers and her face was scrubbed clean. She looked less like the pinup face of Los Angeles and more like your standard gorgeous fifty-foot woman. She was eating an omelet the size of a small whale and was drinking from a glass of orange juice I would drown in.

I took my seat and leaned over to the microphone. "Like a baby."

"Oh, good." She looked up at the clock. "You have time for breakfast before catching the first ferry to Catalina. Is there anything you need beforehand?"

"Just the ticket."

"Keyes has them. I'll be sending him with you. That will smooth your way, since he's known around the island as my employee. They're unlikely to question your identity if you're with him."

Keyes came up on the elevator with an omelet, coffee, and

orange juice for me. Sometime during the night, his makeshift face had gotten scrambled and he had not corrected it. His expression had turned into that of a man trying to pass a very large kidney stone.

"And he can be, uh... subtle?"

"Don't worry about him. Remember, the last ferry of the day is at seven."

"I'll be done before that."

"Good," she said, rising from the table. Her plate was clean. "I need to put my face on and get ready for my swim. If you leave now, you should beat me to the island. Thank you for your help, Mr. Moss."

I wolfed my breakfast and joined Keyes on the table elevator where he had been waiting, jiggling with what I hoped was just ambient wind and not some kind of alien joy at the prospect of us taking a trip to Catalina Island.

"Come with me, Mr. Nicholas Moss! The car awaits, as does the end of your singularity!"

"Right, listen, Keyes, could you not call me by my name?"

"Of course! Distinguishing you from me is a waste!"

"That's not what... you know what? I'll take it."

Keyes led me past the mountainous furniture of the O'Heaven home and back out to the garage. I got into the car and settled in as Keyes pulled out and drove down the hill. He was moving at a much greater clip than yesterday, which was saying something. The sun was coming up over the mountains on my left, but you'd barely know it with the woolly clouds. The ground was still wet from the previous night and would get even wetter when the heavens inevitably opened up.

Catalina Island was perversely clear. The normal haze was gone, absorbed into the clouds or blown away, letting me pick out individual details on an island twenty-two miles off the coast of Los Angeles. That included the Isla Calavera Casino at the southern tip. The place was huge, formed of five distinct sections. The first, and only one touching the ground, was the central casino, where the games and theaters and restaurants were. The others were step pyramids, like the kind in the Mexican jungle, that the jaguar people somehow figured out how to make float like balloons. These were tethered to the earthbound structure with chains and gondola lines. As I understood it, these were where the bulk of the actual hotel rooms were. Great views and classic architecture. Sometimes the monsters got it right.

The car wound down to the harbor in Long Beach and parked alongside other cars, brainiac carts, gremlin contraptions, and some even more exotic conveyances. It was a Wednesday morning, so the press of monsters that would be there on a weekend was thankfully absent. The bulk of the monsters would either be house players or the career gamblers who made their living playing against the proposition guys. Work commuters.

The boats in the harbor ranged from the pleasure yachts of the very rich to some smaller vessels for charter fisherman. The Night War had changed air travel, but for the most part, water travel remained the same. Gremlins stayed away from water—they found it intensely embarrassing for whatever reason—and so their contraptions were rarely even remotely seaworthy. Martians relied on their tripods and never bothered with anything else. Brainiacs and mad scientists made seagoing vessels, but for the time being, they were very similar to normal boats, at least until the engine fired up and the thing streaked over the water at a hundred miles an hour.

There were, of course, exceptions, and one of these was the ferry I was boarding with Gelatin Keyes. It was a ghost ship.

It floated in the water, a little higher than a totally solid boat of its size, and gave off a fitful green glow. It looked like it had once been a pirate ship, complete with rope rigging and tattered sails. The wood was worm-eaten and the figurehead was a screaming, skull-headed banshee.

I wondered when she got time off, or if they always had her tied there.

The ship had been modified, perhaps some kind of concession to the changing times, or else it had somehow combined with other wrecks when they summoned it from the deep or however it was they got ghost ships. Sections were covered with bolted-on plating already curdling with rust. A propeller covered in strands of sargasso dripped on the rear. A skeleton lashed to one of its blades grinned at me. The name, emblazoned across the back, was *Merry Celestial.*

We moved onto the docks, and a waterlogged zombie dripping with seaweed said, "Brains."

Keyes handed over the tickets. "Glad to, sport!"

The zombie punched holes in the tickets and handed them back. "Brains."

I followed Keyes up the gangway. The crew of the ghost ship went about their business, ignoring the milling tourists taking up the center of the deck. I looked down at the rickety wood and rusting steel that made up the deck and found that if I tried, I could see partially through it. Since that was a recipe for vertigo, I looked up at the horizon.

I separated from the crowd of monsters and went to the railing. It had been a long while since I'd been on a ship. Not since they stuck me in one and I sailed back to the States. Wound up in New York and took a train back to Los Angeles. There was a whole group of us on the way home. Every stop, we hemorrhaged more and more guys, and we always made the same promises to stay in touch. We might have even kept them if not for the Night War. I hadn't seen the old crew in ten years. I wondered how many of them were alive. How many were still human.

"Ladies and gentlemen, monsters of all stripes!" announced a voice sporting a Spanish accent so pronounced it had to be put on. The speaker was a ghost, dressed as a Spanish conquistador. Maybe he *was* a Spanish conquistador, or maybe he just liked the style. If memory served, there was a boutique in Hollywood that sold to ghosts. Something about ectoplasmic stitching or something. In any case, this partially transparent man had a neat van dyke, metal breastplate and helmet, and some garish pantaloons. His cause of death looked to be the dozen or so arrows piercing every part of his body, though they didn't seem to bother him. "I am your captain, El Acerico. Please enjoy the short trip to Catalina Island."

With that cue, the ship's propeller started up, chopping into the gray water. The sails filled with spectral wind and the *Merry Celestial* churned out into the channel between Los Angeles and Santa Catalina Island. The island grew steadily larger off the bow. I looked out over the ocean, trying to pretend I wasn't marching into the lair of the one monster I still had nightmares about. The sky seemed to agree with me, echoing my unease. It was low and gray, and out beyond the island, lightning clawed at the water.

The crew went about the business of the ship, but most of it seemed to be functioning on its own. A drunken pirate ghost hobbled by on his peg leg, perpetually moments from tipping over onto the drink. A serviceman who looked like any of the scrubbed Navy boys from '43 was working with the rigging. He was missing most of his head, but seemed reasonably cheerful for it. Not so the woman in the flowing white gown standing on the crow's nest and peering out over the choppy sea. Unless, of course, she was intentionally crying spiders as some kind of ambience. Lastly, a massive man in an old-timey diving suit waddled from bow to stern and back again, whistling a bizarre atonal song as he went. Keyes followed him, transparent pink tissues humming.

"Not one for ocean travel?"

I turned. It was the swabbie, the Navy kid. I met his remaining eye, since the rest of his skull was just plain missing. "It's been awhile."

"Day War, huh?"

I nodded. "Army. Spent my time under Ike."

"Navy. The *Nevada.*"

I knew the ship. She was in both theaters, if I was thinking of the right one.

"As you can see, didn't turn out quite as well for me," he said.

"What happened?"

"Jap plane rammed the deck. Deck rammed me."

"Sorry to hear it."

He shrugged. "Could have been worse, I guess. I died instantly."

"Small favors, right? Nick Moss," I said, holding out a hand. I winced, not knowing if I should have lied. Would have felt wrong lying to a vet.

"Ensign Pulverized."

"Pleased to meet you."

"Moss, huh? Strange name for a... wolfman?"

Common misconception when seeing me. I was hairy enough to pass, and you could mistake the fearful hunch in my posture for ferality. "Yeah, I'm not that creative."

He shrugged. "Not like we knew we were going to have to do that when we turned."

"Say that again." I watched the lightning walk over the ocean. "Listen, Pulverized, are there a lot of vampires on the island?"

"Some. We normally keep them belowdecks on the trip over. We have a section of the hold for coffins. You can avoid them pretty easy." I opened my mouth to protest, but Pulverized held up a hand. "It's all right. Pumpkinheads give me the heebie jeebies. Being a monster ain't all it's cracked up to be."

"You said it." I shook a cigarette out of the pack just for something to do.

"You think I could have one of those?"

I handed it over and got one for myself. I lit his, which had the odd look of being the one solid thing held up by the greenish gray ghost. "Those things'll kill you."

Pulverized grinned and sucked the smoke into the space where his lungs should have been. I could see it moving around in his body. I had a little more difficulty lighting mine and coughed through it.

"Careful, Moss. Don't cough up a lung."

"Doing my best."

The diving suit man passed by and Keyes was following along, singing counterpoint to him, but whatever words he was using weren't in English.

"You get a lot of regulars on the ferry?" I asked him.

"Most of them are regulars. After a little while, they usually figure out that the passage costs too much and they might as well move to Avalon," he said, naming the town on the southern end of the island. "Other ones are movie stars or studio bosses, and they have to live on the mainland."

"So someone coming out on the first ferry of the day every day wouldn't be unusual."

"Not at all. Besides, most of them do that anyway to catch the show. You know." He did a reasonable impression of a woman emerging from the surf and shaking her long hair. I was impressed that none of his brains fell out.

"Looking forward to that myself."

"You won't be disappointed. Hell of a thing." Pulverized flicked the finished cigarette into the surf. "Good to know you, Moss. I have to get this scow ready to land."

The ship was getting closer to the island, and while talking to my fellow vet, I had completely forgotten about it. Fear twisted up in my guts at the thought of the place. I managed a nod. Pulverized went about his business. The casino was in sight now, like a volcano rising up from the island, a skull carved into the face of the stone. Palm trees waved in the wind. A winding path, bordered by jungle greenery, led to the skull's mouth, which was also the front door of the casino.

I saw with a lurch of my stomach that the door was built to accommodate someone very large, but who didn't walk entirely upright. Someone, oh, about fifty feet tall.

TWENTY-TWO

The Isla Calavera Casino seemed to stare down at us with fires burning in its eye sockets and its skeletal mouth open wide in undead hunger. I didn't understand what it was about monsters that possessed them to be so ghoulish. Maybe the pressures of existing like that.

The chains connecting the floating pyramids to the volcanic skull of the island were huge, the kinds that should be on battleships for their colossal anchors. The gondola lines, like delicate filaments next to the bulky chains, ran up parallel. The cars ferried guests from the rooms to the entertainment. The jungle plants had greens so vibrant they seemed phony, with flowers larger and more exotic than anything I could have imagined. The whole place looked like some fantastic version of a South Pacific island, which was exactly what the boss had likely wanted.

As the *Merry Celestial* pulled into the harbor, the only other vessel waiting there was a giant pleasure barge. It was a great, wallowing tub built like a cargo ship, but the deck was an ostentatious announcement of wealth. A large portion of the center was curtained off like a palanquin. It looked like comfort was the primary purpose, and speed a distant second or even seventh, depending. I knew it hadn't been used in some time, since its arrival in Long Beach was something of an event every time. An event that kept me indoors for a few days until it was safely docked back here.

A figure was standing on the pier, and even from a distance I could tell it was an impressive one. Her posture was relaxed, but it was a languid, feline pose that implied she would be ready to move at a second's notice. This was doubly impressive considering the height of her heels and the black dress that looked like it had to be sewn on. Her black hair was immaculately styled, and her green eyes seemed to glow brighter than the ghosts on the ship. Wasn't hard to know this was one of Catalina Island's many jaguar people. I also knew to stay far away from her.

The excited murmurs of the passengers grew, turning into a full-blown hubbub by the time the gangway was lowered.

"Good morning, everyone!" called the jaguar woman on the pier. "I'm Leona Pryde, the head concierge here at Isla Calavera. If you need anything, please do not hesitate to ask. In the meantime, I would like to direct you to our private beach, where Miss Pilar O'Heaven will shortly be arriving! Welcome to Isla Calavera and have a wonderful stay."

The mention of Pilar got the crowd going, with the men almost exploding into full Tex Avery wolfishness. As we all disembarked, following the pier up to the beach and then along the path, Leona Pryde stared at each of us. It was a predatory look that seemed to undress each one of us, dress us in something else, undress us again, and have her way with us six or seven times before, exhausted, we were fit only for consumption, at which point she would season, cook, and devour us. She radiated sex that was threatening in ways I previously thought only clowns trying to batter down my door at two a.m. could be. I stayed very close to Keyes, knowing that no woman had ever found a blob attractive a day in her life.

Based on the look she gave him, I was wrong.

Keyes was oblivious. "Mr. Ni—" he got out before I clapped a hand over where I thought his mouth was. My hand sank into pink gel, but at least he stopped from giving me away. "—ght Ranger! Let's go see Pilar O'Heaven surface from the cursed brine!"

"Yeah, let's do that." I pulled my hand out. It was slick, and all the hair on the back was gone.

"Say, what did zero say to the number eight?"

"I don't know. What?"

"Nothing! It just waved!" He gorped happily. Glad someone was.

We followed a decent-sized portion of the ferry's other passengers through a section of fake jungle and down onto a secluded beach, shielded from view from the main building by a cliff. Deck chairs were lined up near the back, with overhanging trees for shade. Vampires, nosferatu, and even a gremlin claimed places back there, umbrellas and parasols blocking out what little sun peeked through leaves and cloud. The other monsters were gathered out on the sand, the ones you'd normally expect to want to ogle a fifty-foot bathing beauty: gill-men, bug-eyed monsters, and even a mad scientist, half his skull replaced with a clear dome, electricity flashing from within. Zombie waiters, dressed in island garb and skull makeup, circulated through the crowd with trays of drinks. One stopped in front of me and offered a Bloody Mary that smelled like actual blood, a pungent smoking thing that stung my nostrils, a glass of live newts in water, and a mimosa. I took the last one, and Keyes selected the thing that smelled like one of his "Manhattans."

We saw her when she was still a mile off. She started out as something massive flopping through the water, the splashes from her kicks going twenty-five feet into the air in some cases. The conversation hushed as she got closer to shore. The dunk and slush of her moving through the water was louder than the waves. Long expanses of tanned flesh and leopard print peeked through the stormy gray surf. And then she stood. The water flowed off her in streams that looked thick enough to knock me unconscious. She seemed to take ages to get fully upright, as though she kept standing, and standing, and standing, and would still be in the process of standing if I left for a quick game of cards in the casino and came back. At some point, she was finished, and she struck a pose, hand on one ample hip, bust pushed out, her expression somewhere between "C'mere, big boy," and "Touch me and die."

She was also shivering. She was fighting it, and maybe the monsters didn't notice, but I did. I bet if her lipstick wasn't so cherry red, her lips would be a deep blue by now. She picked up a huge towel from a wooden deck and made her way up a cleared path to the casino, patting the water off her form, but not wrapping it around herself as she probably would have liked. The assembled monsters applauded.

I kept my eye on the vampires. They had formed a knot, like crows, crowding together under the pooled shade of their umbrellas. They all wore large sunglasses like Audrey Hepburn, a sidhe that Serendipity seemed to both love and despise. The nosferatu, despite being cousins in good standing (and, some claimed, one of the genesis monsters for vampires) were excluded. They hadn't gathered together themselves, each choosing to lurk by his lonesome. The gremlin shoveled candy into his mouth and loudly smacked his lips.

I counted up the vampires: nine of them. Add in the three nosferatu and that was twelve suspects. As Pilar passed us, water raining off her body, the sun broke through the angry clouds. The vampires hissed and made for the foliage.

Pilar moved up the beach toward the hotel, her footsteps thudding like miniature earthquakes. She stooped slightly to get through the front door as the tourists gaped in amazement. Then she was gone, and I was left with a jury of bloodsuckers to track.

TWENTY-THREE

The vampires were first back to the hotel, scurrying under the shade of banana trees or their parasols, trading excited babble in their bad Transylvanian accents. The nosferatu followed at a discreet distance, apparently wanting to be part of the group, yet not accepted. It seemed a shame, since to the layman, there wasn't much difference between vampire and nosferatu—but to them, those differences were all-important. It was much like the beef between werewolf and wolfman, though at least some of that could be chalked up to jurisdiction.

Vampires generally looked like extremely pale humans with sharp canines and blood-red lips. They liked to cultivate a certain Slavic mystique, which meant dressing in evening wear, inventing fake titles, talking in ridiculous accents, growing unseemly fingernails, and shaving their hairlines into the perfect razor-sharp widow's peak. They either practiced law or became agents for actors, musicians, and writers, which turned every court case and contract negotiation into a bizarre battle of one-upsmanship in which each vampire tried to prove he was the most mysteriously Slavic. Legal practices, at least in the States, had gotten decidedly weird over the past several years.

Nosferatu were treated like the vampires' inbred hillbilly cousins. They were more German than Slavic, and the Krauts still weren't the most popular of people on the world stage. Can't imagine why. Anyway, the nosferatu were generally taller and thinner. Their skin was gray, their heads bald, their ears pointed. Instead of elegantly pointed canines, their incisors were long and sharp, like carnivorous bunny rabbits. Some nosferatu tried to follow their brethren into law, but a nosferatu defense attorney was a good sign you were getting convicted. Most went into fields like pest control. Made good use of their odd powers.

Outsiders saw very little difference, and holy symbols and daylight were just as effective against either one. But then, wolfsbane and silver worked just as well against both werewolves and wolfmen, and any suggestion that this might indicate a relationship would be rewarded with a night in the clink and a Disturbing the Peace rap.

Keyes churned along beside me, sounding like an upset stomach. "Mr. Night Ranger! I am so—"

"Keyes! Keep your voices down."

"Oh. Sorry, Mr. Night Ranger. Sometimes I forget that I speak with the voices of every cell." He lowered his voice to a hissing whisper that sprayed little gobbets of caustic pink jelly. I made a mental note to charge Pilar for a new suit. "I am so thrilled to be part of a private investigation, Mr. Night Ranger. I enjoy reading the works of Cleave Hunter and Chaz Standard."

Serendipity had gotten me one of Hunter's books for my last birthday as a joke. It wasn't bad, but I knew instantly the killer was the only human in the cast. "You know it's not really like that, right?"

"*Dial M for Meatstick* is my favorite," Keyes went on, apparently oblivious to the idea of conversation as a two-sided affair.

"I, uh, haven't read that one."

"It's very good. The human was the killer."

"Yeah, I gathered that."

"*The Seventh Demon* is my favorite."

"I thought you said—"

"It's very good. The human was the killer."

"Well, yeah... "

"*Hydrophobia* is my favorite."

"Keyes, I might be detecting a pattern—"

"It's very good. The human was the killer."

"*Kiss Kiss Bl*—"

"Let me stop you right there. It's your favorite and the human is the killer."

Keyes wobbled happily. "I knew you would understand."

"All right, so you like private eye books... "

"I like Visionus, the crawling private eye, best."

I rolled mine. "Yeah, all right, I understand. You like to read. I like to read too."

"You like *Dial M for*—"

"I like westerns, okay?"

"You should read private eye books."

"Do you read blob chauffeur books?"

Keyes wobbled more quickly, and a space opened up near the top of him. I thought he was going to rise up and crash over me like a wave. "There are blob chauffeur books? Do they capture the delightful contradiction of being an ever-hungry amalgam of a hundred minds? Do they get the uniforms right?"

I sighed. This wasn't working. "What you read in the books isn't what it's like. For one thing, we're not even looking for a killer."

"We might be!"

"Keyes, I never look for killers. That's what police are for."

"Oh. In all your cases, you have never encountered a killer?"

"Well, no, actually. I mean, the other day there was a thing, and I mean, I'm not looking for him, except maybe I am?"

"See? You're looking for a killer! Soon you will be drawn into a world of moral compromise and sexy dames. And then you will find the human and you point him out, and you have your killer."

"Wasn't a human," I said, back on terra firma.

"I know," Keyes said. "This will end with a human killer and you can be ready for your next adventure."

We were at the top of the winding path, terminating at the entryway into the Isla Calavera Hotel and Casino. A smaller automatic door was set into the frame of the larger door used by Pilar and the master of the house. I walked through it, beneath the sharp, jutting teeth of the casino's skull face, feeling like I was heading into my own funeral that everyone inside was very pleased to finally be attending.

The lights in the central room came from torches burning in sconces that appeared to be made of wood and bones. The walls were fake lava rock, dotted with planters spilling over with emerald green ferns. Ornate South Pacific masks decorated everything. The room was filled with tables for blackjack, roulette, craps, and the like. Gambling was still mostly illegal in California, though I knew a loose confederation of casino operators was fighting to change that. In the meantime, they skirted the laws with house players: monsters who played using the casino's money and won enough to keep everything profitable. A wide path led from the front door and turned right into a vaulted room. That's where Pilar had gone, and that's where the one monster I had to avoid was waiting.

The dealers, croupiers, pit bosses, and floor bosses were all of a type: the same as Leona Pryde, the gorgeous dame who'd greeted us on the pier. They were black-haired and green-eyed. Depending on their ethnic background, they either got *very* white, a kind of ivory that was much healthier than the washed-out pallor of vampire. or their complexion darkened to a smooth, pure ebony, or burnished into even more stunning hues of bronze and gold. These were balam, the jaguar people, and though they might be among the most beautiful monsters there were, it was a mistake to comment on it or even give them a second look.

Zombies circulated amongst the gamblers, serving complementary drinks. These zombies were like the ones outside, done up in bones and makeup, trying their best to play the savage. They asked for drink orders with a simple, "Brains?" and confirmed them the same way, staggering off to the bar to get the order filled. The bartender, a tiki-masked martian, made good use of his many tentacles.

A stage was erected against one wall and a good number of monsters were ignoring the games to watch the big band. The leader was clearly a jaguar man, his skin clean bronze and eyes glowing green, wrapped in a gaudy white suit in contrast to the black-suited band. He was crooning a love song, and he swept the audience up with a combination of leers, acrobatic eyebrows, and a buttery voice, bringing everyone along in a skillfully alluded-to festival of carnal delights. And he managed it while singing about an old rocking horse. His backing band was split up between zombies, jaguar people, and gill-men, though he had somehow landed a phantom on cornet and a bug-eyed monster on drums. The marquee, done up in flashing letters, called them JUNGLE JIM and the HEPCATS.

I might have enjoyed the place if I were a monster. There was a certain glamour to it, the kind of shine you get when money and risk have an illicit rendezvous in broad daylight.

For a moment, I was lost in the snap of cards and the clack of the wheel.

"He's right this way. He is *so* happy you accepted his invitation." I knew that voice. Leona Pryde. She'd made quite an impression in her short stint in my life. She breezed past me, escorting a well-developed blonde to the vaulted room. It took me a moment, but I recognized the blonde too, since she was wearing her most famous face, the face that had been staring at me on Sunday from the third base line at Gilmore Field. It was Jayne Doe, the doppelganger who'd found an easier way to make a living than starring in films. She was the in-house model at *Twilight Visitor* magazine.

I wasn't the only one who recognized Jayne Doe. Her status as Miss Hollywood Star made her something of a local celebrity, and the tawdry nature of her specific claim to fame ensured that only a certain kind of monster would dare approach her.

"Miss Jayne Doe! Oh, look, Mr. Night Ranger, it's Miss Jayne Doe! You remember, Misses March 1954 to August 1955!" Keyes slithered after her, extending a pseudopod that immediately made me wish I hadn't drawn an inevitable comparison.

Both women turned to Keyes, their expressions curious but predatory. They looked like they were wondering if they could eat him. "Yes?" Jayne Doe said.

"Miss Jayne Doe! I am Gelatin Keyes, an employee of Miss Pilar O'Heaven! I am a big fan! I long to add your mass to my own!"

"That's lovely," Jayne said with a demure smile. "Thank you for reading."

"Mr. Keyes," Leona said, "if you would excuse us, Miss Doe has an appointment to keep."

"You said to contact you if I needed anything! I would like to do so now for an autograph! From Miss Doe, not you! You are not famous enough to write on anything!"

"Of course, Mr. Keyes," Jayne said. "I would be happy to, but not right now."

"Oh, thank you, Miss Doe! I love how frightened and yet happy you look when you are home alone and the monsters are outside!"

They both smiled, but it was getting pretty strained. I grabbed Keyes and had to immediately yank my hands out of him. "Come on, Keyes. You can get your autograph later."

"Oh, Mr. Night Ranger! You should get one too!"

"Big fan," I muttered to Jayne, but she was finished with us, turning to head into the other room. Leona followed, giving the both of us a final once-over.

"Can you believe that? What luck!"

"You need to keep a lower profile, Keyes."

"But that was Miss Jayne Doe! Oh, if only real humans were like her, so beautiful and inviting and careless with locks and wards!"

"Uh... right."

I glanced around. I knew tracking down vampire-specific rooms would be possible, but I'd need the supply rooms first. They wouldn't be accessible from the main floor, since a big part of any glamour industry is rendering the people who do the work as invisible as possible. I watched the paths of the waiters as they wove between the tables. They seemed to be coming out of a hallway in the northeast corner artfully concealed by the folds of false lava rock. "Come on."

Keyes followed me to the hallway. "Where are we going?"

"We? You're staying here with this fern."

Keyes extended a pseudopod to absorb one of the hanging fronds.

"Don't do that," I told him. "You stay here and, uh, keep

watch or something. I'm going in there." I didn't wait for another conversation with the blob. He didn't seem very good at those, or at understanding what was being said, even when he was the one who said it. The hall turned a few times. A zombie passed me holding a tray of drinks and I stumbled and lurched, hoping he wouldn't give me a second glance. He didn't. At the end of the hall was a pair of swinging doors with windows in them, looking like the kind of thing that might lead into a kitchen. I slipped inside.

The room was filled with zombies, all of them scrabbling around and moaning *brains* at each other while they loaded up trays and carried them out onto the casino floor. Other than the bar, where the overworked waiters would stop and build their drinks, there were several metal shelves stuffed with glasses and trays. Another swinging door opened and a zombie in the white uniform of a dishwasher came in carrying a tray of freshly cleaned glassware. There was a fresh chorus of "Brains!" as the dishwasher put things away.

I went through another swinging door, emerging in a maze of trays, glassware, carts, tablecloths, plates, and all kinds of things the zombies would need to keep the guests happy. I crept down the aisles of supplies, searching for the hub, which should be around here someplace. Zombies shuffled through the back room, the echoes putting them all around me. I reflexively checked for my salt and took comfort in the fact that I was surrounded by things that could cause blunt-force trauma. At first, the only voices were the low mutters of "brains," the zombies talking to themselves as they hunted for whatever it was they needed for the outside. I hoped it wasn't brains.

There was another sound, and as I made my way deeper into the huge storage space, it grew louder. The crackling of an old radio, the voice coming from it feminine but deepened by scotch and cigarettes into a throaty purr that sounded like industrial equipment trying to flirt. I couldn't make out words, and wasn't sure I wanted to. After all, was I going to get a break in a case just by wandering around and magically overhearing the crucial bit of information from someone I'd never heard of? Hadn't happened yet.

At the corner of the shelves, the room opened up, and I saw my likely quarry: a clipboard hanging from a pillar by a nail, a pencil tied to it with a fraying string. I broke cover and could make out the voice now.

"... business matter between us. Zombies stick with zombies."

I couldn't help it. I glanced. Two zombies were off on the other side of the central space, right next to the wall, partly hidden by more overstuffed shelves. One was one of the Isla Calavera zombies that I had gotten used to. The other was a big zombie nattily dressed in a blue pinstriped suit and matching fedora. He looked stiffer than most zombies, but that was because his neck was encased in a collar of old gray steel, all the way from clavicle to jaw. Right at the throat was a battered speaker, and that's where the voice was coming from. The zombie's face was rotting right off the bone, his eyelids and lips seemingly gone.

The voice coming from the speaker got quiet as the zombie saw me. I turned away and walked quicker to the clipboard, which fortunately put the pillar between me and him. The voice started up soon after, but this time quieter. I could only hear the sharp fricatives and the hissing sibilants.

I flipped through the clipboard. It was a blank form, with the room numbers printed on the page. Next to it were notes scrawled in the unsteady hands of zombies for the special requests of each. Room 213 asked for eyedroppers. Room 310 needed several large batteries. Room 818 needed extra germ killers. I shifted through it until I found the rooms that wanted grave dirt. There were fourteen of them, meaning there were two vampire or nosferatu guests who had no interest in watching Pilar rise from the surf. Probably excused them from suspicion, but I was going to toss their rooms anyway since there was no way to tell from the list who was who. I noted the rooms down and slunk out, hoping not to attract more attention from the well-heeled zombie with the U-boat radio on his neck.

I came through the two doors and back out into the hallway on the heels of a zombie carrying a tray of drinks with flopping tentacles coming from the top, trying to wind around one another. I did my best to ignore it and emerged into the echoing main room of the casino. Keyes was right where I left him, industriously devouring the fern I'd asked him not to. I couldn't testify to it, but he seemed a little bigger, too. As soon as I came into view, the pseudopod engulfing the fern retracted into his gelatinous body.

"Mr. Night Ranger! Say, why don't skeletons fight?"

"I don't know. Why?"

"Roberto!"

I shook my head and walked briskly toward the rooms. Maybe he would lose interest and wander off. He didn't.

The first room on my list was only one floor up, on the mezzanine. We took the elevator, emerging at a balcony overlooking the gaming floor. I wondered if any cheaters had ever used the vantage point to feed information to cohorts below. If anyone had been stupid enough to rob the Isla Calavera, they were probably mashed perfectly flat by now.

I found room 142 without much trouble and went to work on the lock. Thank you, Night War, for turning an honest man into a housebreaker. With a few twitches of my picks, the lock clicked and the door opened.

"Say, Mr. Night Ranger? Is that legal?"

"No. Very illegal. That's why I need you to stay in the hallway and keep watch. Got it?"

He extended a pseudopod that extended another smaller pseudopod. I stared at him for a long moment before I realized it was an attempted thumbs-up. "Okay, thanks."

I went into the room where one of the vampires was staying. The bed had been removed, and in its place was a coffin. Just to make sure, I opened it up. The vampire was in there, sleeping away the day. The show on the beach was probably his bedtime entertainment. I had hunted vampires during the war; I mean, who hadn't? They were easier to take out than some other monsters, because unlike gremlins or phantoms, vampires weren't big on traps. The worst you had to deal with were ghouls, hunchbacks, or zombie manservants, or the occasional hellhound. And other than that, vampires slept like the dead, no pun intended.

We had grown up with the legends of vampires, which, in my quieter moments, had given me chicken-and-egg thoughts about the legends and the realities. So we knew enough to drive a stake through the heart, behead them, and stuff the mouth with garlic. I had a buddy during the war, Janina Rakoczy from Poland. She had a thing about nailing them—with literal nails—and burying them at crossroads, which is why if you were to tear up the blacktop on Hollywood and Vine, you might find a few sharp-toothed corpses. Anyway, what I learned was that while sunlight will fry a vampire to a crisp, killing them was still possible without it. A stake through the heart will kill just about anything (not brainiacs, robots, or martians, but I digress). Same for tenpenny nails hammered through the temple. And beheading is just about the most reliable method of death there is, so much so that headless horsemen wouldn't even exist without it. Turns out once you have a vampire helpless, you can kill it like you would anything else. The legends only existed because our distant ancestors got very sadistic when they had a bloodsucking corpse at their mercy.

This particular vampire was a good-looking man with sharp Eastern European features, a kind of ideal for the race. His hands were folded over his heart and he was sleeping in his full eveningwear. He had the most disturbing vampire habit in that he wasn't bothering to breathe, but at least that meant he was solidly in dreamland. I replaced the top of the coffin and searched the rest of the hotel room.

I found nothing incriminating in his belongings. Just some extra tuxedoes, a change of medals, and some grave-flower-scented pomade with the holding power of plaster. I moved on, collecting Keyes from outside.

The next several rooms were the same. All but one had its occupant slumbering peacefully in his coffin, oblivious to me rummaging around. So long as I didn't start kicking the coffin, screaming the National Anthem, or firing my pistol in the air, they would stay sleeping. None of them had anything that implied they were anything other than wealthy visitors from the mainland.

Room 232 was different. After telling Keyes to stay outside and watch, I picked my way in. The occupant was inside, a nosferatu sleeping soundly in his coffin. He was fairly typical for the race, with grayish skin, sharp buckteeth, and a bald head. I hadn't been expecting any nosferatu until I got to the middle rooms. Those were usually the cheapest of the bunch, lacking the quick access to the casino floor of the lower levels and the commanding view reserved for the upper echelons. This was a reasonably big room, unaffordable to someone without a good income, which meant one of the vampire lawyers and agents LA was infamous for.

I shrugged that aside and opened up the closet. When I moved aside his hanging cloaks, I knew I'd found my man. Or batboy, as the case may be.

Tacked to the wall was a picture of Pilar O'Heaven. The famous one she'd done when she was just out from New York. I don't know who originally took the photo, but it was bought and run by *Twilight Visitor* magazine, in the only issue any normal human ever bought. She wasn't nude, though the bikini she was wearing in it made the one she wore every morning look like a nun's habit. It was clinging to her curves precariously, like a man holding onto a mountain peak with his fingertips. Any second, it would fall to an ignominious death.

As gorgeous as Pilar was, a mere picture of her wouldn't have become famous. Even given her notoriety from the HUMAC hearings, and the delight the establishment would have taken in seeing her debase herself. No, this was a brilliant way for her to advertise who she was and where she was. She leaned against the H in the Hollywoodland sign, her head back, eyes half-lidded, lips parted. Those letters were forty-five feet high, and she was only shorter than the H because of that seductive, promising lean. That picture was on the inside of more lockers than stink.

Sometimes the cases were easy. I snorted at that. Yeah, easy once you get on a monsters-only island and break into the rooms of half a dozen vampires. Maybe this was a new line of business for me. "At Nick Moss Investigations, I find that certain special someone who doesn't want to be found." No way *that* backfires on me horribly.

I opened up the guy's suitcase, which was shaped like a coffin—all the rage amongst the undead—and found even more pictures of Pilar. Magazine clippings, a newspaper story, all of it in a photo album, carefully protected behind plastic. Nothing specific about her blood, but then, he had only harvested what was out there. Perhaps not wanting to court this kind of attention, she had never given any interviews about what she had in her veins.

I set everything aside and looked over at the coffin. From where I was, kneeling at the closet, I could only see the very tip of the nosferatu's gray hooked nose. He wasn't a looker. Not even by the standards of his kind. As my secretary would say, he was no Rock Hudson. Pilar was probably going to be disappointed.

That wasn't really my problem. She hired me to do a job, and I'd done it. Now all I had to do was interview Percy Katz on the off chance he knew something about Escuerzo's kidnapping and I could call it a day.

I duckwalked over to the coffin and gently reached in. This was the kind of thing that could wake him up. Nosferatu might not be respected, but if you ask me, they're tougher customers than vampires. Stronger—and vampires are already plenty strong—and able to call in every rat in a five-block radius to do his dirty work? *Trust in the Lord*, I reminded myself, *or at least his signature.* I touched the pocket where I kept the cross.

I patted the batboy down as gently as I was able, keeping an eye on his stonelike face. He wasn't breathing, so I couldn't wait for a hitch to know I'd gone too far. I found what I was looking for in the breast pocket of his tight-fitting suit. I lifted up the side of his jacket and paused, glancing at the motionless face. His teeth were long and flat, coming to a wedge-shaped point at the end. They were faintly yellow.

I reached in with the other hand, trying not to touch his chest. What was it with nosferatu and fitted suits? It's like they weren't happy unless everything was skin-tight. And it wasn't like with the jaguar people, who had something to show off. No, these looked like sad gargoyles made out of matchsticks.

With my thumb and forefinger, I hooked the wallet and gently extracted it from the batboy's pocket. I kept waiting for his eyelids to snap open, his mouth to open up nice and big, give me one of those hisses, and lunge for my throat. We could see how fast I was then.

The wallet came out and I froze, watching him a little longer to make sure this wasn't some kind of trick to catch me off guard. He kept lying there, his eyes shut and his teeth poking over his lower lip, so I figured either he was still asleep or he was waiting to see where I was going with the whole thing. I opened up his wallet, which was shaped like a bat, and fished out his ID.

Count Morlock of Santa Monica. I noted down his information so Pilar could visit or, more likely, send Keyes out there to abduct the fella and bring him back to the house. I replaced his ID and tucked the wallet back where I found it, just as carefully. As before, Morlock slept through the whole thing, or else had decided nothing was happening that he really needed to be involved in. His wallet safely tucked away by his heart, I closed the coffin so he could sleep the rest of the day in peace.

That was one case in the books and I could go back to the important things. Having the others out of the forefront of my mind, at least for a little while, should do some good. I could approach with a fresh perspective and maybe make some headway. Things were finally turning my way, and considering all the grief I'd been absorbing, I could use it.

I made for the doorway when it was suddenly eclipsed.

She'd rolled around the corner languidly, and now she was leaning against the doorjamb, a knowing smirk on her perfect lips. Her lambent green eyes regarded me from toe to head and back again, and I felt that I'd been ravaged, comforted, married, cheated on, divorced, remarried, trapped in a loveless relationship, and returned to her in an illicit affair that destroyed both our lives. It was Leona Pryde, as though it could be anyone else.

"Well, hello there," she purred.

What had happened to Keyes? Had she sapped him? No, I would have heard the hissing if she had sprinkled him with anything.

"Uh, hi?"

"This isn't your room," she said, pushing herself fully upright and beginning to make her way to me. If she threw those hips around with any more vigor, I might get knocked unconscious.

"I, um, was just about to talk to the concierge. I didn't order a coffin."

"I don't imagine you would, Mr. Ranger."

"Oh, so you remember me."

She was still advancing, and I was retreating. This was because I knew about jaguar people, or balam, as they liked to be called. They turned into jaguars whenever they got turned on. Only problem was, once they transformed into killing machines perfected by millions of years of evolution, they forgot about the sex part and decided they needed to tear everything in the area into meaty ribbons. Sort of like thinking you're going to be hanged and finding that the iron maiden is back in style. And because they never got a chance to satisfy themselves, jaguar people walked around in a constant, humming state of arousal. Nothing, and I do mean *nothing*, could sniff out a double entendre like a balam.

"Oh, I'd remember you anywhere... detective."

I was rapidly losing real estate to back up into. A few more steps and I'd be pressed against the blackout drapes they'd so thoughtfully provided Mr. Morlock. "How'd you know I was a detective?"

"Just look at you," she said. And did. I got an even more rapid feeling of a doomed romance, though this one ended with me in flowing white, casting myself into the sea.

"Well, good eye," I said, chuckling nervously. There was a light thump and I had no more room to back up.

"There's a lot of me that's good."

"That's nice to hear."

"There's even more that's bad."

"Uh-oh."

"So tell me, detective. What are you doing snooping in one of our guest rooms? That's mighty naughty."

"Nope! No, it's not. It's not good. Or bad. It's, uh, it's entirely devoid of morality."

"Answer." She took a step forward. "The." She took another step forward, and I was officially crowded. "Question," she finished, and one more step brought her well within my comfort zone. Whatever perfume she was wearing smelled like jungle flowers. I had to lean back to look anywhere other than the smooth expanse of her neck, and doing so I managed to hit my head on the wall.

"Police business," I squeaked.

"You're out of your jurisdiction." I don't think I have to mention which syllable she threw the emphasis on. "Catalina Island is the purview of the local sheriff."

"And how do you know I'm not with the sheriff?"

She chuckled, one crimson fingernail running from my gut up to my neck. "I know every deputy on the island."

"I bet you do."

She slapped me, but it was light and playful, which somehow made it more terrifying. "Fresh," she said, like she liked the idea of it.

"No, I just mean, what with the overhead, and the, uh,

nature of the establishment... ”

“What are you doing in this room?”

“Investigation!” I thought quickly, which was very hard to do, what with Aphrodite in a tight black dress attempting to make an honest man out of me with nothing more than simple eye contact. “Murders. On the mainland. Vampires. Ferry ticket!”

“I see,” she said. “You’re on the trail of a killer. How very brave of you.”

“It’s all in the job.”

Her ivory skin had flushed, and I swear there was more heat coming off her than a car engine. Her hand fell to the hem of her dress. “As it turns out, we have a reward for that sort of thing.”

“But I haven’t caught him yet.”

“Call it a down payment.”

“I’d really rather not.”

“Oh, come now, detective. I can tell what you want.”

“What if he wakes up?”

She glanced at the coffin, and when she turned back, I could tell I had said the wrong thing. Her eyes had always been faintly glowing, but now they burned with terrifying green fire. The color had bloomed in her cheeks so emphatically, she was almost beet red. Her breath was coming in sweet, short bursts. Her left hand snaked over my shoulder to grab a handful of drape. “Oh, what if he *does* wake up? And we’re right here, doing God knows what?”

“Oh no.”

“Oh yes!”

I have no idea how she got that dress off. It must have been tearaway or something, because suddenly she was in her unmentionables, and of course they were black, showing off everything and hiding nothing. The garter belt seemed entirely unfair. She leaned in for a kiss, and that's when she began to change.

Her face lengthened, sprouting black fur. Her teeth elongated and sharpened. Her body, already sleek, grew muscles. I slipped around her and backed off.

She was half-jaguar, half-woman, turning around to track my movement. Her back had twisted, and she was on all fours. Her fingers and toes had disappeared into padded feet, and I knew she now had claws like switchblades waiting in those paws. She was still wearing the garter belt, too, which didn't look quite right, and her back claws were going to shred her stockings.

And then she was a jaguar. Perfectly black, six feet from nose to tail of ferocious jungle beast, and looking at me like I was the dinner special at Musso and Frank. Her lips peeled back from her teeth and she hissed. For an absurd moment, she reminded me of my cat. Was my cat female? I'd never thought to find out, since it only lived with me to keep the jaguar people away, and it was never around when I needed it anyway. That expression was the same one my cat used at the slightest provocation, down to the bared teeth, the hateful eyes, and the angry hiss. Only Leona was much, much bigger, and the result of her anger wouldn't leave enough of me to bury.

Her green eyes flashed—those at least were recognizable, if much larger. I briefly wondered if they had been vertically slitted before, or if I had provided that with my overheated mind. Fortunately, I was saved from pondering that for long, as she pounced.

Leona Pryde

TWENTY-FOUR

While I would like to describe the sound I made as a manly war cry of the kind that would have made any Kraut within a hundred yards tremble in his boots, it's probably more accurate to say it was a scream more at home in the lungs of a young girl at her surprise party. What can I say? I'm really more of a dog person.

Leona Pryde came at me trailing lingerie. Her powerful muscles shifted and bunched like wind-up toys dancing under a mink coat. Then she was springing through the air, teeth and claws unsheathed like she thought she'd need all of them to take down such dangerous prey.

I uttered the aforementioned yelp and fell backward. I had the presence of mind to regret both the verbal ejaculation and the trip that sent me sprawling. Not only was I going to die, I was going to do it on my back and sounding like a schoolgirl.

Fortunately, while my conscious mind was busy spinning in useless circles, my reflexes knew what to do. They were reflexes trained first in that Army camp in Georgia, then in the chaos of warring France, Belgium, and Germany, and perfected in my hometown when the lights went out for a good eight years. The monsters hadn't gotten me back when there was no law forcing them to pretend to play fair. They sure as hell weren't going to get me now. My hand snaked into the same pocket I'd checked before. Later I could wonder if it was pure luck, because if I had been breaking into the room of a ghost or a pumpkinhead or an ogre and my muscles had focused on *that* deterrent...

Luck maybe, that jaguar people hate crosses as much as vampires and Jesus do. She let out an agonized yowl, and midway through the air, twisted and flopped her body like a cat seeing a full bathtub for the first time. I rolled aside as she thumped into the carpet where I had been, howling and spitting and hissing. I scrambled to my feet, using the dresser behind me for leverage, the cross held out at her. She focused on it with such hate, I expected some kind of green fire to lance out and burn it up. Fortunately, she wasn't a robot.

I backed off. "Look, Miss Pryde, you're very pretty and all, but I'm a nice guy, and this isn't how I like to do things. I'll be out of your hotel soon. I promise."

She sounded like a cat facing off with an intruder into her yard, as long as the cat was two hundred pounds and had canines the size of .30-06 shells. She stayed low, glaring balefully up at me while I backed out of the room and slammed the door.

Gelatin Keyes was waiting for me in the hall. "Keyes?"

"Mr. Night Ranger! Did you see that jaguar lady? I sure did!"

I stared at the blob. "This is because I didn't tell you to warn me."

"I kept watch! I watched her come up the hall! I watched her go into the room! I watched you come out!"

"You never thought to mention it?"

"Mr. Night Ranger! Is she the human we're looking for?"

"We're not looking for a human!"

"Not yet!"

"Goddamn it, Keyes! I found the guy bleeding your boss! I need to go tell her before the jaguar lady you didn't see fit to warn me about calls security. You stay here, and grab him if he tries to go anywhere, got it?"

"Got it!" He extended the pseudopod and the subpseudopod in his thumbs-up gesture and I ran. I had no idea how long it was going to take Leona to get unhot and unbothered, but based on the time it took to wind her up, I had a feeling the answer was "not long." She'd be on the horn for security soon, and I'd be a dead duck. I thought briefly of heading for the ferry, but I couldn't remember the schedule, so I might be running for an empty slip. The other option would be hijacking the pleasure barge, which would add piracy to my potential crimes, and that was not something I wanted to explain to the court-appointed attorney.

My only option was Pilar. I had to get to my client and hide with her until she could sneak me back to the mainland. She owed me that much for wrapping her case up as quickly as I did. I should charge her for hazard pay anyway. This was worse than jumping out of a perfectly good airplane, and the Army had seen fit to compensate me for that. There was one likely spot for Pilar, considering her most distinctive feature. It was that vaulted open area to the right of the main casino floor. The halls looked to be giant loops rather than spokes in a wheel, so I was able to follow the hall I was in back to the center, using the smooth big-band sounds of Jungle Jim and his Hepcats to guide me.

The jazzy swing pulled me to the central room, and soon the rest of the casino sounds joined it. A little farther and I was going to see the entryway. Considering who else was down that hall... no, just think of Pilar for now. Get to her, this gets solved. I was a step away.

The jaguar people rolled into the hall, like they'd been waiting just around the corner. All three were big fellas, the one in the lead an ebony-skinned giant. They were dressed in the black suits of security, impeccably tailored and probably extremely expensive. The man in the lead held out a hand.

"Stop right there, Mr. Ranger."

Well, my cover was intact. Small blessings. My eye went to the gold pin on his lapel. KATZ.

"Wait. Are you Percy Katz?"

His handsome face twitched, like I had done something very rude and smelly, but he was too polite to mention it. "Give the man a cigar. Percy Katz, head of security at the Isla Calavera Casino."

"Do you know Hexene Candlemas? Of course you do, I know you d—"

The rest of the sentence came out of me in something like an *oof*, because Percy, all two hundred and fifty pounds of chiseled Percy, slammed me into a wall. His forearm pressed into my windpipe and I noticed that my feet weren't touching the ground. Good way to bridge the twelve inches of distance between our heights. Percy smelled subtly like expensive cologne. His eyes seemed even greener than Leona's had, his teeth much larger and whiter. He didn't even have to turn into a jaguar to ruin my day. I suddenly had the intense hope I wasn't turning him on. "I don't know what you're talking about," he growled.

I tried to say something, but given the sounds I was able to force out, only ducks would have understood.

He reached into my jacket, hissed, and recoiled. He opened it up gingerly. "Quite an arsenal you have in here."

Normally, I would have politely explained I'd had licenses for everything. As it was, I was busy concentrating on the stars exploding across my vision.

More carefully this time, Percy reached into my jacket and found my wallet. He opened it up, and the licenses fluttered to the floor. "Get those," he said over his shoulder, and one of his men picked them up. Percy looked at my identification. "Moss? Never heard of you. Don't look like a swamp monster."

"Blerg," I managed.

He let me go and I collapsed in a heap. "You a meatstick, Moss? No meatsticks on Catalina. There's a law."

I coughed.

Percy hauled me to my feet and ripped the jacket off. "I'll take this." A moment later, the shoulder holsters with my gun and knife joined it. "Won't need your weapons here, meatstick." He threw me to his men. "Carry him."

The two security goons, who were as ivory as Leona, each hooked an arm under my armpit and pulled me along the casino floor. My toes dragged over the carpet. With Percy shielding me from the front and the two men on either side, I was fairly well concealed. I saw a few looks, through the small gap between my escorts, but most monsters seemed content to let security deal with the drunk. They were heading for the front door and my mind started racing. I had to figure out a way back in, some way to get around Leona Pryde and Percy Katz.

Until we turned to the left, heading for the wide vaulted area I had been trying to get through. I must have croaked something, either audible enough to jaguar ears or far enough out of the direct path of Jungle Jim's version of "Cherry Pink and Apple Blossom White."

"Oh, you thought we were going to throw you out on the docks? No, the boss likes to deal with this kind of thing personally."

I've seen a lot of boys freeze in combat. It was practically a rite of passage. It's impossible to know how you're going to react when the bullets start flying. It's the worst experience of your life, and so outside the reference of anyone who's never been there that it's only possible to describe in terms usually used for hyperbole. In that first moment, with the screaming, and the death, and the ground exploding all around, fellas you thought were tough as nails can break down into little sobbing lumps. Doesn't mean they're cowards, it means they've looked into the mouth of hell, and it had an effect. In the Civil War, they called it "seeing the elephant," I guess because they didn't know what elephants looked like back then.

I had been somewhat lucky. In the night before D-Day, when they dumped me out over France and I ended up lost, I got to sort of ease into combat. Didn't stop the shots of ice I got in my veins whenever the first shot cracked, but I started the night in a skirmish and got to move up from there. It was hell, but at least it was hell I got to acclimate to, and as any devil will tell you, it's not the heat, it's the humidity.

Well, I knew what it was to freeze right then, when Percy referred to "the boss." My body seemed to turn to ice, because there wasn't a damn thing I could do to move any of my limbs. I wanted to run, hide, probably cry. I had the insane feeling that if only my mother were here, everything would be all right. I wouldn't be dragged in to see the one creature on earth I feared most.

They hauled me around the corner and my body tensed even further. I felt like a good tap and I'd shatter. At least then I wouldn't have to face him. Though I was seeing the walls of the Isla Calavera, the sculpted false lava rock, the potted ferns, and the "tribal" decorations turning it into a sensory riot, my brain was showing me the wall at Gilmore Field. I heard the thump, saw the cracks webbing outward, the dust shedding. We were huddled in there, not sure what to expect, but knowing we couldn't leave without being set upon by every monster in Hollywood. Then the wall breaking in half. And the hand, bigger than anything...

I could feel him, beyond the wall. He was going to break it in half at any second. He was going to smash it, and that was the end of me. The one monster I couldn't fight, couldn't repel. Oh, I had something I thought might work. Something Serendipity had said, and I clipped it out of *Look* magazine, and she had yelled at me until I explained, and the look on her face said she didn't really understand but she was being nice to her human boss. There was that, but it was a last-ditch thing. And it was in Percy's arms with everything else I could use to defend myself.

The double doors were huge. My panicked mind desperately, crazily registered that Pilar would have to stoop to get through, but he wouldn't. Not because he wasn't as big. Because he wasn't as upright.

The doors had smaller ones in the base, and those were what Percy opened to give me and my escorts a clean path into the next room. I had barely enough presence of mind to clamp down on the scream I felt building in the back of my throat.

The room was done in the same style as the rest of the casino, only this was where power sat. The walls, ceiling, and floor were all fake stone, the floor flattened and smoothed into something almost like flagstones. Two rivers of glowing red-orange liquid went by on either side. Thank a mad scientist or brainiac for that, I guess. More light came from waterfalls of this same turgid liquid flowing over the walls to join the main rivers. Skulls decorated the walls, the largest at the other end of the room. I noted that they appeared to be from dinosaurs;

Aggie Brooks would have loved to see that. They were displayed like trophies, as though the lord of this room—and there was a lord, as this kind of room had to have one—had personally killed each one. While I knew there was no such thing as living dinosaurs, or else the mad scientists would have thrown them at us during the war, a little superstitious voice in the back of my mind kept whispering, *What if?*

And then I saw him.

Kublai Kong.

A gorilla the size of an office building. Not bad, right? Not until you've seen him pull houses apart with his bare hands, throw cars around like they're toys, or cram people into his mouth like popcorn. There were rumors about how to deal with the so-called monkey khans. They were scared of airplanes, everyone said. No idea how I'd fit one of those in my jacket. Right next to the cold iron dagger, I guess. No, instead I had that picture of Ser's favorite actress, Audrey Hepburn, because someone told me they brought a monkey khan down in New York and beauty killed the beast.

Well, Percy had it anyway. Maybe he'd let me borrow it to kill his boss?

First Kong. He'd changed a little. His belly was bigger than last time, and what I could see of his back when he turned or shifted was more silver. He sat on a massive throne, made in the same style as the rest of the casino, out of what I hoped were fake skulls and bamboo. Kong wore gold bracers on his wrists, with skull designs picked out in jewels, and a gold necklace with a grinning skull pendant. He topped it all off with a crown of golden bones.

His throne was up on a dais, with steps sized for him leading up to his massive and tacky chair. Pilar was nearby, in a similar but far less ornate chair, wrapped in a green floral-print island dress, her hair down around her shoulders. A slit showed more leg than I had previously thought existed in the entire Los Angeles area. Her eyes were wide when she saw me, and she fought to put on her bored poker face.

On the other side, resting on the arm of Kong's chair, was another, human-sized chair. Jayne Doe was there, gazing at us in bewilderment.

Kong hooted and grunted, gesturing at me. I flinched with each one.

"His imperial magnificence, the Mighty Kublai Kong, would like to know what this creature is doing in his potent presence." The voice was high and reedy, and after a moment of confusion, I located the source as the shadowy space under Kong's throne. Something moved around under there. A bogeyman.

Would Kong remember me? No way he could. I was barely an insect to him and did I remember every grasshopper I pulled out of my rose bushes? Of course not. He couldn't remember the face of one of the humans at Gilmore Field, back when Kong arrived in Los Angeles and showed us that the Night War was not only futile, it had already been lost.

"Miss Pryde called security on this one," Percy said. His voice echoed loudly through the room, the acoustics making it audible to the giant and the ape. "He was breaking into room 232. The guest is Mr. Morlock, a nosferatu."

Kong hooted.

"Was anything stolen?" the bogeyman translated.

"I don't believe so, sir," Percy said.

Kong grunted.

"Then why is he here?"

"Miss Pryde is on her way, and she can—"

Percy's explanation was cut off as the door opened behind us and I heard Leona's heels clicking on the fake stone floor.

"Great Kong," Leona said, "I'm very sorry to have to use security here. This man caught me off-guard with a... " and she hesitated to get the proper disgust dripping from her honeysuckle voice, "*cross*. I was momentarily incapacitated, and he escaped." She hadn't mentioned the exact circumstances of me pulling the cross on her, but I wasn't expecting monsters to suddenly discover honesty. I was hoping they still thought I was a monster, or better yet, a cop, so maybe I could work some leverage.

She walked ahead of me, showing her back. Now that I was beaten, her contempt was complete. Her outfit wasn't quite on straight and she was no longer wearing stockings. I had a feeling this was fairly common for all the jaguar people, and no one mentioned it.

Kong beat his chest and ululated.

"The Invincible Kong would like to know who he is."

"He says he's a police detective. From the mainland. His name is Night Ranger." I'd said no such thing.

"He was lying about that," Percy said smugly. Leona shot him a horrified glare and he pressed on. "His identification says Moss. He's a meatstick."

Kong grunted and growled.

"Meatstick? On Catalina?"

Kublai Kong's attention was straight on me, and it was heavy, coming as it was from eyeballs about the size of Percy if he decided to curl up. The whites were bloodshot, the irises a golden brown. A pinkish scar ran down the side of one, and I had to wonder what had done that. We were fresh out of tanks and artillery by the time Kong showed up in Los Angeles. Maybe it had come from one of the other cities where the rumors whispered he had smashed the last bits of resistance before coming here to mop up. As he stared at me, his black lips rippled, showing off teeth that had no business being in the mouth of a gorilla; they were built for killing.

"Answer the Potent Kong," the bogeyman snapped. "Are you a meatstick?"

"Uh... yeah. I'm a... " I couldn't bring myself to say the word. Didn't matter. They heard it.

Kong growled.

"The Mighty Kong would like to know what a meatstick is doing on Catalina Island."

My gaze slipped to Pilar. Tell the truth to Kong, and she was going to catch a beating. No way I could sic Kong on anyone. So I had one option. Lie. To the monster who had lived exclusively in my nightmares. And hope he bought it.

"I'm a detect... er, I'm a private investigator. I've been hired to, uh, there's some hanky panky. An affair! I'm here to prove whether or not someone's having an affair." I got those jobs from time to time. The truth was, the Night War was the best thing to happen to marriage, at least amongst humans. It was too dangerous to go out at night to cheat. These days, it was usually some human seeing a monster, trying to get turned behind the spouse's back.

Kong nodded, his crown slipping slightly on his massive, sloping forehead. He corrected it, leaning back and hooting with a flinging gesture thrown in. I flinched, as the last time I had seen him do that with his hand, a '46 Chrysler had come tumbling out.

"The Great Kong would like to know what you were doing breaking into the room of a guest."

"I was looking for the, uh, the guy."

"You told me it was a murder," Leona said, raising one of her perfectly arched eyebrows.

In my panic, I had completely forgotten the lie I'd tried on her. "I was lying to you, because of the whole... human... thing."

Kong's enormous eyes narrowed. He grunted.

"The Puissant Kong wants to know how he can be sure you're not lying now," the bogeyman said.

"Well, uh, Great Kong, if I were to lie now, that'd be, well, that'd be the dumbest thing I could ever do. So I'm not. I'm telling the truth. Sir." I felt like I might be making some headway. Maybe Kong was buying this after all.

Kong hooted.

"The Divine Kong does not trust you," said the bogeyman. Or there was that. That could be a problem.

"Well, uh, if I could just... "

Kong leapt from his throne and charged up the stone at me, snarling and gnashing teeth better suited to pulping cars. I cowered, positive that he was going to finish what he had started that day at Gilmore Field. The worst part was that he didn't remember. To me, he was the personification of fear. To him, I wasn't even a memory. I felt the falls of his feet and fists as thunder in the ground as he charged. His cries pummeled me from all sides. I curled up, too terrified to do anything than to gibber mindlessly.

He stopped twenty feet away and pounded his chest, snarling and wailing. His crown had slipped to a cocked angle. Even Leona and Percy had backed off a few steps.

And just like that, he stopped. He stood there on knuckles and feet and hooted softly. Softly for *him*, which was still a boom, made worse by the room's incredible acoustics.

"The Immortal Kong would like the meatstick arrested and put in the pit until he decides what to do with him."

Percy's men hooked their arms under my armpits and dragged my boneless body from the room. All I could think on the way was, *The pit?*

Kublai Kong

TWENTY-FIVE

I'll say this for the designers of the Isla Calavera Hotel and Casino: when they said "pit," they meant it. Percy's men dragged me off to another annex of the throne room, somewhere near the back of the hotel. The pit felt like it was in a far corner of the building, in a single room where a normal casino might have had a makeshift jail. I suppose that's what this was, though I didn't have much time to think about it when the two goons chucked me in like last week's trash.

I fell the twelve feet to the sandy floor and winced when I landed. At least I didn't have to worry about landing on any vials and breaking them, as Percy had already taken my jacket, all of my weapons, and—just to be a jerk, I guess—my hat. So I hit the ground on my side and lay there, sucking air.

"Wait here awhile, meatstick," Percy said.

I tried to talk to him, mention Hexene again now that he was out of pummeling range, but all that came out was a croak. He was gone a moment later, the door closing out of my sight with a depressingly firm click.

I couldn't see much. The pit was fifteen feet across, sand on the floor, or maybe as the floor. The walls were ringed with bamboo, which, after trying to work my fingers between the poles, turned out to be fake. At the top, they terminated in an irregular railing, the tops sharpened. If I squinted, I could see that some of them were decorated in more of the fake skulls, teeth, beads, and feathers. Good to know their commitment to the island gimmick extended to their pokey.

There was a light overhead, which they kept on. It didn't do much. The bulb was either tired or they had never once replaced it, and it was in the midst of a death spiral. It illuminated the paneled ceiling, where water stains crept outward like a lost blob.

I tried to climb the bamboo a few times without any luck. After a bit, I slumped down and waited. Pilar knew where I was. She'd get me out. Not her specifically. She'd send someone, probably Keyes, once they found each other.

So it was time to hurry up and wait.

And wait.

It was slow going in the pit. My watch hadn't told time in years. I only wore it out of misguided sentiment. So I was left measure time by the steadily growing rumbling in my stomach. I hadn't eaten since sunrise at Pilar's, and it had to be at least noon by now. It was probably too much to hope that they'd throw something down here.

As it happened, they did throw something down a couple hours later. After a fashion. I heard the door open and I scrambled to my feet, sending sand spraying out in every direction. Percy peered over the side, his green eyes blazing. He broke into a humorless smile. "Enjoying your time at Isla Calavera, meatstick?"

"I'd love it if you'd send a zombie by to take my drink order."

"I'll do that. In the meantime, we brought you a little company."

Percy's goons threw a man over the bamboo picket, but of course it wasn't a man at all. I was the only man on the island, and it didn't hurt to remember that from time to time.

"Gimmicked the roulette wheel," Percy said. "Lucky Kong has a soft spot for you, Doc. If it was me, you'd already be in the bay."

I recognized the man, though it took a moment to place him. I had seen him on the shore when Pilar surfaced. He had been part of the larger crowd down on the beach. He was a mad scientist, as obvious a one of those as ever there was. Half of his skull was missing, replaced with a transparent bubble. His brain pulsed within it, burning with St. Elmo's fire. His left eye was huge and bloodshot, his pupil likely permanently dilated. His other eye was covered with a red lens. His hair was reddish, shot through with streaks of snow white, but thick and shooting out in every direction. Other than the two-toned hair and the skinny frame, he didn't seem old exactly. More prematurely aged, the whole getup adding thirty years to him without throwing in the wrinkles and liver spots. He wore a long lab coat, spotted with the requisite mystery stains.

"The bay? *The bay?!*" The mad scientist threw back his head and cackled. "The bay is mine!"

"Sure thing, Doc. Mind your Ps and Qs. Your new roommate is a meatstick. Real hard case, too, probably bumped off more mad scientists than lab-created abominations."

"Hey, Katz," I called up.

"What do you want, meatstick?"

"Hexene Candlemas. You know her."

He fixed me with a finger. "Mouth off that, meatstick. Or you and I are going round for round, and you ain't got a corner or a towel."

The jaguar people left. The mad scientist was staring at me across the pit. His brain was giving off more light than the bulb in the ceiling, giving everything a ghostly pallor. "Meatstick," he said.

"Um, human."

"Don't worry, Marty Meatstick. They will suffer for what they've done today. All of them! Percy Katz, Lurkimer Closett, Pilar O'Heaven, and Kublai Kong. *He will suffer most egregiously of all!*" And cue the maniacal laughter. Mad scientists were always swearing vengeance on a world that wronged them. It could get pretty violent at times, but fortunately, most monsters seemed to get how dangerous mad scientists were. They were probably only still around because of the persistent rumor that the first monster ever had been that mad scientist Oppenheimer.

I knew all the names he mentioned except one, and judging by it, Lurkimer Closett was the bogeyman under Kong's throne. Just another monster out to get me.

"Actually, my name's Moss."

"And I am Dr. Uriah Bluddengutz, the future master of all I survey!"

I glanced around the fifteen-foot pit. "Impressive."

He didn't seem to notice, instead rifling through the pockets of his lab coat and finding them empty. Percy had to have given him a pat-down and taken anything that looked even remotely mechanical. Give a mad scientist a pencil sharpener and he'd turn it into a flamethrower.

I watched him, wondering where I'd heard the name before. Mad scientists all had names like that, so it's possible I was thinking of something else. "Say, Doc, do I know you?"

Bluddengutz looked up at me, his enormous eye twitching. "Did you fight in the Night War?"

"Uh... yes."

"Then you knew me! I was supreme commander of all forces south of San Francisco, where that fool of a martian

PX-60 ruled with a vampiric tentacle! *Called me mad, did he?! He and all his ilk will suffer!*" There was the laugh again, echoing all around like we had a choir of madmen instead of just the one.

"So you were, um, you were down here."

"Oh yes! Perhaps you remember my *atomic pigeons!*"

In point of fact, I did. They showed up sometime in '51, these glowing man-sized pigeons. The weird thing was, they didn't really do much. They would land, eat whatever was on the ground, and fly away if you got too close. Other than the size and the glowing, they were your basic pigeons. We even killed and ate them from time to time. Sure, the meat made your tongue glow, but that went away after a day, day and a half tops. "Right, the pigeons."

"The human resistance was down to eating crumbs! *So I would make something to eat all the crumbs in the world!*" He threw back his head and got maybe one *ha* out before I interrupted.

"Wait, you designed giant pigeons to eat crumbs?"

"Of course! It was a brilliant plan, though none of the others could see it. *Kong called me mad, called me—*"

"But they were big."

Bluddengutz blinked. Or, he tried to, but the big eye didn't do much more than twitch and the other one could barely be seen behind the red lens. "Well, yes. Kong is very big, but it is the mind that—"

"No, the pigeons. They were big."

The shock might have injected some sanity into him. "Well, yes. You see, to eat more crumbs, I had to expand the stomach, and of course, if they were still to fly, I had to expand the wings, and by that time, it just became easier to make the whole bird larger."

"Right."

"And then, I would—"

"Why not just make them...I know I'm not an expert or anything, but why not have them crave human flesh?"

"For what?"

"To eat?"

Bluddengutz chuckled. It was an avuncular chuckle. He should have had a podium and a blackboard upon which to make his point. "Pigeons eat crumbs," he said clearly.

"Well, yes, but pigeons are also yea big." I demonstrated.

"It was a simple matter of replacing their blood with a uranium-rich slurry—"

"You couldn't have made them eat meat?"

"Mr. Moss, I could make them dance. *Dance to my every whim!* Had I wanted them to eat meat, they would have eaten every human in Los Angeles! *And then the world!*"

"Right. Wouldn't that have been better?"

His laugh ended with an awkward cough. "Um. No. Because of... the... well, there was... crumbs, I think."

"Oh, I understand. Good job, Doc." At least now I understood why mad scientists hadn't been wiped out for everyone's safety.

Placated, Bluddengutz stared up at the lip of the pit. It felt strange to say, especially because I could see his brain thinking, but he was probably pondering the same problem I had been prior to his arrival as my pitmate. "Moss. Let me stand on your shoulders."

"Uh. And you'll lower a ladder or something?"

"Doubt my word? *Call me mad?*"

"You never gave your word."

"Oh. You have my word." He gestured with both hands like a magician.

"All right then."

I knelt, and Bluddengutz put his feet on my shoulders. He was in wingtips, though they were worn and battered, the leather caked with some kind of white crust. Salt, I found out later, when I was wiping it off my shoulders. The zombies must have loved the footprints he was leaving around. I held onto his skinny ankles. His sock garters bit into my fingers. He carefully rose to his full height. If he strained, he wouldn't even make it to one of the phony bamboo stalks poking up from the mass, and even if he could, he would probably just impale himself at the top. It was pointless, but at least it gave us something to pass the time.

He got fully upright, promptly lost his balance, and we both tumbled into the sand.

"You did that on purpose!" he shouted at me.

"You were swaying up there like a drunk scarecrow!"

"Call me mad?"

"I did no such thing! Come on, we'll try again."

We did. And again. And again. We tried so many times, I was developing bruises on my shoulders, though at least they'd be footprint-shaped to prove to Ser how I had gotten bruises there in the first place. I could already see her patiently explaining how that explained nothing. The falls hadn't hurt at first, but after a couple they started to. After a few more, they started to hurt worse.

"You have to be doing this on purpose!" Bluddengutz screamed at me.

"Why would I? You can't even reach one of those stalks, let alone haul yourself up with those chicken arms!"

"Chickens don't have arms!"

"Do you want to try to hold me up? See how hard it is?" I shouted back.

"I am the doctor! I am the head! You are fit only as feet!"

"Then maybe you learn to fly, huh? Jump on one of your pigeons? *Oh, that's right, the jaguar people ate all your stupid pigeons!"*

Bluddengutz looked about ready to jump on me, clawing me with his emaciated old-young hands. I would have welcomed it. I was tired of Uriah Bluddengutz, and pummeling him might make me feel a little better. Truth be told, I was still smarting from that shameful display in Kong's throne room. Pilar and Leona had seen it, and though I had no romantic interest in either of them, there was still a part of me that couldn't handle it. If Hexene had been there, I'd probably have to live out the rest of my life as a hermit.

I really was a sap, if I thought a witch would have anything to do with me in that way.

I balled up my fist and was about to show him the boxing I'd learned in the war when a rope ladder clattered down the side of the pit.

We stopped, looking at each other, then the ladder. No one called down.

Bluddengutz ran for it, scampering up, and I followed, hoping that whatever was up there was better than being in a pit with him.

TWENTY-SIX

I knew the zombie waiting at the top of the pit. He was in his blue pinstriped suit with his fedora tipped rakishly at an angle. He had no eyelids or lips, and a steel collar poked up from his shirt, covering his neck entirely. “Dr. Bluddengutz. Mr. Moss.” The voice came out of a battered speaker at the zombie’s throat.

“Brains,” whispered the zombie. If death had a voice, it would sound exactly like that. With his lack of lips, it came out more as “Hrains,” but I knew what he meant and he was terrifying, so I gave him the benefit of the doubt.

“You, my good zombie, will have a place in the world I shall leave behind! *When I perfect my race of atomic supermen—*”

“Yes, Doctor, I appreciate your... ambitions,” said the voice. It was a deep rattling purr, like a mile of rough road finished off with a jazz singer. “You two are probably wondering why I chose to rescue you from that ape’s jail.”

“Why wouldn’t you save your future master?” Bluddengutz asked.

I decided to play along, even if I thought I knew how this game ended. "Yeah. Can't help but wonder."

"I am a local businessbeing," the voice crackled. "My name is Sarah Bellum."

I swallowed with an audible click and hoped she took that to be one of the many soft clicks and pops coming out of the speaker at her zombie's neck. I knew the name. Who didn't? She was the Al Capone of the West Coast, the single biggest crime lord, and the only one the LAPD had thus far been completely unable to take down. Worst of all, she paid her taxes.

The Bellum Mob was infamous for dumping rivals, rats, and monsters they just plain didn't like off a specific turn on Mulholland. The canyon was littered with bones, slime, and all manner of effluvia that was once a monster, to the point that a copse of trees had turned purplish gray. I had no doubt in my mind that the pinstriped zombie who was lacking in the lips department was responsible for more than one tumble off Mulhollhand Falls.

"I regret that I could not greet you in person," she went on. "This is my associate, Mr. de Kay."

"I'm, um, I'm pleased to meet you," I said, sticking out a hand and hoping it wasn't as clammy as I knew it was.

"Brains," de Kay whispered, accepting the hand with a mitt that felt like a vise wrapped in parchment. When I got it back, I wiped off dry scraps of his flesh.

Bluddengutz accepted the hand as well, but he was distracted. I couldn't imagine what was more important than being in the presence of a Bellum enforcer. Ever since he got out of the pit, the guy had sounded a bit brittle, like if I tapped him, he'd shatter. Didn't ease my mind that the lunatic with the giant pigeons seemed even more nervous than me.

"Not that I don't appreciate the save," I said, "but it does beg the question."

"Of course, Mr. Moss. If you both would accompany my associate from the building, you should be able to avoid security."

"Brains," de Kay whispered, going to the door like he knew we would follow. Bluddengutz did, almost hypnotized by what was happening. I glanced back at the pit and something caught my eye.

A swatch of orange.

De Kay was at the door now, Bluddengutz right behind. I rushed over to the stakes. A few threads of orange fur clung to the sharpened ends. Identical to the fur I saw on the windowsill of Aggie's room. I picked it up, cursing inwardly when I realized Percy Katz had my jacket and array of vials. I couldn't compare, but I didn't have to. This was the same stuff. I knew it. I stuck it in the breast pocket of my shirt and followed de Kay and Bluddengutz.

My mind was spinning. Aggie's kidnapper had no connection to the island at all, except for the vague possibility of being the same monster who grabbed Hexene, and she was connected to Percy Katz.

There was one thing I knew: it was no coincidence. Orange fur in two places, possible fur in a third. Could the solution to both cases be on Catalina Island? Had I stumbled onto both girl and toad?

De Kay led the way confidently. There was no concession to stealth, just the squared-shouldered, stiff-legged gait of a zombie with somewhere to go. Bluddengutz's head kept whipping around, hunting for the source of his fear. Couldn't blame him. The last thing I wanted to do was get on Kublai Kong's bad side again. Even if escaping his pit was a surefire way to do just that.

De Kay took us down back hallways. The casino hotel was a maze back here. Probably riddled with secret passages letting servants and security get where they needed to without disturbing the guests too much. We passed the occasional zombie as we went, but they played dumb. Not even an acknowledging mutter of "Brains."

De Kay only paused once. The bones of his hand, which he held back to halt Bluddengutz and me, were yellowed like old cigarettes, peeking through the ragged holes in his papery flesh. I obeyed, flattening myself against the featureless white wall. Bluddengutz merely froze, arms out, like he planned to pounce at whatever was coming down the hall.

A group of the black-clad jaguar people marched purposefully past, the men in their stylish suits, the women in short dresses. Security. Never once gave us a glance. I had the vague sense they were on a direct route to the pit, while de Kay had taken us the long way around.

De Kay beckoned us forward, and we went in the direction the jaguar people came from. After few more twists and turns, we found ourselves at a swinging door. De Kay opened it slowly, and the three of us were outside. The sun was rapidly going down, but the only way to tell was that the glowering sky was just the tiniest bit darker. The air was damp and chilly and I shivered without my jacket, mentally cursing Percy for the umpteenth time.

We had emerged by the outdoor swimming pools, a large area taking up the entirety of the back of the casino, terminating only at the slope of the scrubby hill. Like everything else, the pools were fake sculpted lava rock designed to appear as natural formations, and lit from below with orange and red so the water looked like lava from a distance. Though it was too cold to be swimming, there were a few monsters in the pools, mostly gill-men and sirens who seemed not to care about the temperature.

De Kay led us to a copse of meticulously cared-for banana trees that shielded us from the bulk of the monsters enjoying the water. We gathered into a little circle and I tried to put my companions and the greenery between me and the cold wind spinning down from the storm. It didn't help, and I was left to fold my arms and hope for the best.

"I can only imagine how your hearts are full of gratitude at this moment," Sarah Bellum said through the speaker at de Kay's neck. "And you are wondering how you can possibly repay such a selfless benefactor."

I knew the next part of the pitch. That was going to be when we found out how they already had a price in mind and wasn't that convenient?

"Mr. Moss."

It took me a second. "Huh? Sorry, it's... uh, it's cold."

"Then I'll make it quick. Tomorrow you will bring a cat to my associate."

"A cat?"

"Yes."

"Any specific kind of cat?"

"I'll leave that to you. Fetch a cat and bring it here."

"Here? To the pool?"

"Mr. de Kay will be waiting for you by the harbor."

There was only one reason they would want a cat on the island. They wanted some balam dead. I hadn't paid close attention, but it wouldn't shock me if Kong had made cats illegal on the island. Not the best way to be welcoming to witches, but then I hadn't seen a single one since getting here. The feline population suddenly became very valuable when we learned they could kill a jaguar person with a single swat of the claws, and the little bastards seemed only too happy to do it.

Bellum was arranging a hit, and they were using me.

"Why me?"

De Kay remained stiff, the voice at his throat far more animated. "You're a meatstick and you made it onto the island. That speaks to a certain amount of resourcefulness. If you can smuggle yourself, you can smuggle yourself *and* a cat."

"How?"

"That would be your problem, Mr. Moss. Because the alternative is Mr. de Kay alerting security to your escape."

I swallowed. "All right then."

"Then we have a deal."

"We have a deal."

"Remember those words, Mr. Moss. We will hold you to them."

"Uh, right. I should get going. Try to catch the ferry back." The sky was nearly black. No guarantee there was a ferry running.

"Yes."

I turned to go, and Bellum lowered her voice to say something to Bluddengutz. All she got out was, "Doctor... " before I turned back and she stopped talking instantly. She had some way to watch, probably built into de Kay's collar. Brainiacs were to be feared: almost as smart as a mad scientist, but with none of the crazy.

"One thing. You wouldn't happen to know of any monster on Catalina Island with orange fur?"

"Uh. Um," Bluddengutz said.

"Brains."

"Foote," Bellum said after a moment. "The park ranger. Harry Foote."

"Sasquatch?"

"Of course. His cabin is up that hill, a few miles hike along the path. You can't miss it."

"Thanks."

Of course, I wasn't going to see Foote today. No time. I

would have to find a way to see him later, and not have de Kay take me on a personal tour of Mulholland just because I didn't bring him a murder weapon. This past Sunday, I had nothing to do but take in a ballgame. Here it was Wednesday and I was rapidly losing track of just how many monsters wanted something from me, and how many would like to turn me into a thin paste if I didn't deliver.

At least they weren't trying to turn me.

Oh yeah, this was *so* much better.

I made my way around the hotel with one final glance at de Kay and Bluddengutz. The mad scientist was still oddly subdued. Maybe it had finally sunk into his pulsing electrified brain who he was talking to. The wind picked up further, biting through my shirt and undershirt. The jacket probably wouldn't have helped much, but it would have given me some wool to huddle in. I felt half dressed, wandering around hatless and in shirtsleeves, and it probably made me the most conspicuous person on the island.

Well, the most conspicuous person under fifty feet tall.

The wind and clouds had driven most of the monsters inside. I rounded the hotel, coming down the forested paths where the wind rattled through the dense undergrowth. I skipped the path leading to Pilar's beach, instead taking the one that hugged the hotel itself. I emerged from the greenery and had a clear view of the harbor.

The only boat, now rocking on the increasingly choppy water, was Kong's barge. Of the ghost ship, there was no sign. I swore and turned to Pilar's beach. A huge white streak moved at the corner of my eye and there was a colossal splash. Flecks of white seawater shot skyward. I ran down the path to the beach. The wind tried to push me back into the foliage, but I fought it.

The beach was empty save for a few vampires on the lawn

chairs, basking under the clouds, their skin so white as to be blue.

Pilar O'Heaven was there too, offshore and paddling for the mainland. I called after her, but the wind ate my voice. She was already gone. And I was stuck on Catalina Island. At night. As a fugitive.

Thanks, Pilar.

TWENTY-SEVEN

The first step in any decent plan is to stop screaming inwardly and making deals with any number of supernatural entities who have never shown the slightest desire to save my ass. It can be a very difficult step when you're in so much trouble that the fact that you're surrounded by vampires at night qualifies as the least of your worries.

The vampires had only just noticed me, peering over their dark glasses at this bedraggled interloper on their beach. I knew they could smell blood pretty well, but couldn't tell the difference between many monsters and humans without tasting it. For all they knew, I was Pilar's biggest fan. I shot them an embarrassed smile and retreated onto the path I'd come from.

The fact that I was human was probably known only to casino staff. They wouldn't want it getting out that a human had broken their quarantine. What would the neighbors think?

I was blocked on all sides from clean sight lines and had only to worry about running into a monster taking an evening walk. The storm stayed my ally there, but it was an abusive one, doing its level best to knock me over and freeze me.

I needed a telephone. The casino was lousy with them, but I couldn't go back in there. They had to know I was gone by now, and even if not, every balam in the joint probably had a picture of my mug. Foote's cabin. It was possible he had a telephone. He was also the prime suspect for the kidnappings of Aggie Brooks and Escuerzo Toad. Two incredibly dangerous birds with one stone.

The pathways around the hotel all looped back into one another, built as they were to keep the guests on the property and funnel them back to the gaming floor where they could buy Kong more of those snazzy crowns. I had to cut across some of the fake jungle. Inside, it was easier to see how it wasn't completely authentic. The ferns were planted at constant distances, the trees arranged in dignified groups. The wind laid everything bare, displaying the perpetually wet substrate that looked more like wood pulp than anything else. The palms cracked as the other trees fluttered and shook. The air hadn't turned to rain yet, but by the taste of it, that wasn't terribly far off. Salt stung my eyes and I wondered how zombies handled being outside when the wind was up. Since I hadn't seen a single zombie since leaving de Kay, the answer was probably that they didn't like it at all.

The landscaping ended at an irrigation ditch separating the property line of Isla Calavera from Catalina Island proper. A dirt path led up the hill and away to someplace above the lights of Avalon. The little town was also in walking distance, as long as I used the old definition of that term I'd learned in Basic: *Have you heard of it? Then you can walk it.* I not only had heard of Avalon, a sleepy little community of gill-men and the like, I could see the lights twinkling invitingly in the dark.

They would get me no closer to the end of the case. Harry

Foote, park ranger, just might.

Only a few steps up the path, a crash reverberated from the hotel. I turned. Kublai Kong had emerged from the casino floor. He paused at the dock and peered off to sea. The wind hammered him, but couldn't do much more than ruffle his fur. It was fairly obvious who he was looking for, and even more obvious when I saw the blonde hair whipping around on top of the woman gripped tightly in his fist. Kong had Jayne Doe in hand, and wanted to make certain his kept woman was long gone. It paled in comparison to the other things I'd seen Kong do, yet for some reason, this petty sin took my atavistic fear and burned it into solid hatred. This new thing diminished Kong. He wasn't the unstoppable engine of destruction that still woke me up in the middle of the night covered in sweat.

He was just a cad, like any other.

A cad that could throw cars around. But it was a start. I was unarmed and freezing, but I swore I'd bring him down somehow. Probably the most useless and unrealistic vow I'd made in a week full of them.

The great ape climbed the wall of the Isla Calavera Casino, the doppelganger in his fist. He transferred his weight to the chain leading to one of the floating pyramids up and off to the side and swung upward with a mighty leap to land on its stone steps. He opened a door that had been concealed in the stonework and disappeared into it with his lady friend.

I trudged up the path, my arms tightly folded over my body while the wind attempted to explain, in no uncertain terms, that I should not climb this hill. I was as stubborn as ever, though, and I leaned into it. Back in Basic, I had run Currahee Mountain every night, and with full gear. But that was thirteen years ago by now, and we'd never had a storm like this one, brought on by a witch coven's spell gone wrong.

The path was heading roughly east, and the wind blowing north to south, so I was leaned over like a drunk with vertigo. I kept on the dusty path while the dark, scrubby terrain loomed on all sides of me. The only light I got was from Avalon, and that didn't do much more than give me a rough idea of where I was, along with the occasional flash of lightning, promising rain. So far, it was just flash and thunder. Wouldn't last. I'd get drenched and then we could see how well I could climb a hill—hill? make that mountain—while soaked to the skin.

I kept my feet on the path by virtue of staying where the largest bushes weren't. Those were mostly shadows, but occasionally the lightning would flash and I'd get everything picked out in blinding detail.

I have no idea how long it took. Too long. It was freezing, but I'd spent the winter of '44 in a snowdrift outside of Bastogne. I was miserable on Catalina, but it was still a vast improvement over Belgium. At least there was no Kraut artillery pounding me. No jacket? I could handle that. I kept repeating that in my head, occasionally conjuring memories of the Ardennes in an attempt to trick my body into ignoring the present cold.

I'm not sure if it worked or not. I do know the palpable relief that flooded into me when I saw the cabin was no dream. Felt like the temperature raised a full five degrees. It was a little house, shielded on three sides by stubby oaks and rough bushes. Golden light spilled from the windows, and by the way it was flickering, I knew there was a fire crackling in there. I could already feel it in my bones.

Stiffly, I picked up speed, cutting off the path and heading for the cabin. It wasn't until I was on the porch that I realized I could be knocking on the door of a multiple kidnapper at night. A sasquatch had several times the strength of a man, and I was going to walk into the house of one without a camera to scare him off. Goddamn Percy Katz right to hell.

I raised my hand to knock on the door, but it whipped open before my knuckles made contact. The heat billowed out and enfolded me. The being standing in the doorway, which was sized neatly for his eight-foot frame, was very obviously a sasquatch. Even if I hadn't known who lived there, I'd have realized as soon as the smell hit me, like someone ran over a skunk in the rain and then cooked it in rosemary. Furry legs poked out of some tight khaki shorts, beefy arms from a similarly tight khaki park ranger's shirt. He wasn't wearing his wide-brimmed hat, because it was hanging by the door, with ample room in the crown for his pointy head. He wasn't wearing shoes, because with feet like those—like snowshoes with toes—he could have walked barefoot through fire and not even noticed he'd done it. His honest face split into a flat-toothed grin at the sight of me, some concern softening his already soft brown eyes.

"Goodness! What are you doing out in that without a coat or fur? Come in, come in!" Harry Foote, because it had to be him, ushered me inside with his massive arms.

The shivers hit me when I made it inside the door, the fire crackling in his hearth unraveling all the cold my body had sucked up while it was outside. The cabin wasn't large, at least for a monster Foote's size. The ceiling was vaulted, the walls plain wood. We were in a combination living room and kitchen, with a couch and a few chairs around the fire. A sink and stove were in one corner, with a pot over one of the burners. A single door led into a bedroom, and I hoped a bathroom, but I wasn't going to inquire. The place smelled mostly of him, and in another situation, might have sent me for the hills. Here and now, there was nowhere else to go.

"Please, make yourself comfortable. What were you doing

out in shirtsleeves? Did you get lost on a hike?"

"Uh, yeah... "

"Sit down by the fire. Get warmed up."

I sat in one of the chairs. The fire snapped and leapt in front of me. "Thank you, Mr... ."

"Foote. Harry Foote. I'm the local park ranger. Who was your tour guide? Harchok the Hammer? I've told him to stay on the path, but he wants to show the tourists... " he finished the thought with a frustrated wave. "I'll be sending him a strongly worded letter tomorrow, don't you worry."

"You live up here?"

"Oh, yes. Doesn't pay to get too close to Avalon, or to that big new hotel on the coast." Sasquatches were notoriously shy. One on one, they were like anyone else, though it sounded like Foote wasn't keen on confrontation.

"Do you have a telephone, Mr. Foote?"

"It's Harry. Yes, yes, you probably want to call your motel. There's one in the other room."

"Thanks, Harry."

I was starting to feel comfortable, and even though the wind was howling outside, the fire had put the warmth back in my bones. I got up and went into the other room where Foote had pointed, and found his bedroom. The smell of pine was strong in here, and after groping around for the light switch, I found out why. He was sleeping on a pile of pine needles and branches. I had seen stranger. That very day, even.

I glanced in his closet, where a bunch of identical khaki shirts, scarves, and shorts hung in neat rows. No Aggie Brooks and no Escuerzo. I checked the back wall and floor and was reasonably certain there was no secret passage there. The only other door in the room led to a small bathroom. Other than some matted orange hair in the tub, there was nothing of note.

I suppressed the gagging and fished some out to compare to what I'd found on the pit spikes. It looked like the same fur, but I couldn't be certain. Foote remained a suspect, but if he was holding them, it probably wasn't here.

I picked up the handset of the phone on the wall, dialed the operator, and asked her to connect me to Ser's place.

"Hello?" said a voice. I knew that voice. It was Serendipity's roommate, Mira Mirra.

"Can I speak with Serendipity please?"

"Of course, I think... Wait, Nick, is that you?"

"Uh, yes, but if you could... "

"Nick, you stinker. Where are you?"

"Um, that's not, I mean... "

"I stopped by your house, but it was dark. Two nights in a row now. Do you have a girlfriend?" Hard to miss the edge in her voice with that last. If I leaned too close to the phone, she could have shaved me with it.

"No, no, nothing like that. I'm on a case, Mira. It's not important."

"Nick, you know you can tell me about that stuff. I'm very... discreet." I pictured her winding the cord around one slender finger.

"Uh, right, I know. You're of a high moral character and all."

"Are you in danger right now?"

"A little."

"Oh my god, Nick! Tell me where you are. I'll be right there. What face should I wear? What do you like? Oh, that doesn't matter. Where are you?"

"Mira, I need to talk to Serendipity."

Mira's voice was a little farther away, and I realized she had moved her mouth away from the phone to talk to someone else. "Oh, it's nobody." A voice responded, but I couldn't make out the details. I recognized it, though.

"Ser! It's Nick! Pick up the phone!"

"It's no one," Mira said emphatically.

From the other end came the clicks, rushes, and muted cursing that came with a fight over the phone. A moment later, I heard Serendipity's voice. "Nick?"

Mira's voice was still clear, probably standing no more than an arm's length from her roommate. "I don't know how you can butt into a private conversation!"

"He called me and you know it."

"You're all wet."

Serendipity was quiet. I knew enough to know that wasn't something you said to a siren, and probably not to a gill-man either. When she spoke again, it was low and cold, and I had only ever heard that tone from a mother scolding some seriously wayward offspring. "Go back to your room and we'll talk later."

There was pure silence. The phone didn't even pick up Mira's chastised footsteps.

"Nick?" Ser's voice was mostly back to normal. After that, I was little concerned about the favor I was going to ask.

"Hey, Ser. You all right?"

"I'm fine. She's just... what did you do to her?"

"This is my fault? She's the one who won't take no for an answer."

"Have you tried, I don't know, yelling it at her?"

"Sometimes with a mirror!"

Serendipity sighed. "Why are you calling so late?"

"I'm, um... I'm stranded on Catalina Island. I need you to come get me."

"You're what?"

"Stranded? The last ferry already left."

"How are you stranded?"

"I got thrown in a... you know what? That's not the point. If you want the whole story, I'll tell it to you... at the marina on the south end of the island."

She sighed again. "All right, where exactly?"

"Head for the lights of Avalon. There will be a marina." I said this pretty certain I'd be right, but not positive. Such was my present situation.

"Find a beach," she said. "I'll be there in... I don't know. A few hours?"

"Thanks, Ser."

"See you soon."

I hung up the phone and glanced again at the pile of pine branches. What was wrong with a bed? He could put pine in that. Monsters. There's no explaining them.

I came out into the living room. Harry was at the table in front of the stove, ladling soup into a bowl. The one across the table was already full, and there was a loaf of dark bread between the two. My stomach, awakened from its hibernation, growled in renewed hunger.

"Have some soup?" Harry said. "It's just Campbell's."

"No, that's fine." It was better than fine. I sat down and ate a few spoonfuls before I realized he might be trying to poison me. I laughed a little at that. If Foote wanted me dead, he was eight feet of muscle and located at the top of a steep hill. He could find an easier way that would prompt no questions. I glanced up at him and he smiled, apparently pleased I was enjoying myself. He picked up the bread in one massive mitt and tore off a hunk. I thought of Hexene's description of the furry arms grabbing her, and his long, beefy limbs certainly fit the bill. I knew if I was going to get the information out of him, I couldn't brace him, especially since I was unarmed. I had to be smart.

Damn.

"I never got your name," Foote said pleasantly.

"Uh... Ranger. Night Ranger."

Foote laughed. "Ranger! I guess it's fate that we'd meet."

"Or serendipity."

"Or that," he agreed. "What brings you to Catalina?"

"Uh... charter fishing."

"Very good for that," he said amiably. "I'm not much of an angler myself. I prefer the dry land. Hope your adventure hasn't put you off it entirely."

"Do you get off the island much?"

"Oh no. Haven't been since I moved here in... '51, it was. Wanted to get away from all of... well, you know." The distaste in his voice when referring to the Night War sounded real, and though his apelike face had different tells than a human, I was pretty confident I was reading it right. Even if he wilted as soon as he noticed me staring.

"Never took the ferry?"

His eyes widened. "Oh, goodness no! There are... " his voice dropped to a horrified whisper. "*Tourists.*"

Right. Tourists have cameras, and he'd never get anywhere near those.

"Find you like it here?"

"Oh, very much. It's beautiful. Even in this weather we're having, though it's a different kind of beauty."

"Don't get lonely up here?"

"Oh no." He chuckled. "Maybe it's who we were before, or what we are now, but we sasquatches like the solitude. There are exceptions to every rule, I suppose, but I'm not one of them."

It was hardly damning proof, but I liked Foote. I was getting absolutely no caginess from him. He seemed like a normal, nice monster doing what he could to help out a fellow monster in need.

"Any other sasquatches on the island?"

"Just me, so far as I know."

"And how far do you know?"

"Oh, I know the whole island. I suppose it would be possible there's another one of us at the other end—there's a lot of park there—but it's unlikely. We're solitary, not antisocial."

"How about orange fur? Is there something else out there with orange fur or hair?"

"What is this about?"

I couldn't tell him the truth. Saying I was a human looking for another human was a good way to get laughed at and turned, in that order. So I lied like I'd done to Leona. "My name is Detective Night Ranger, from Harbor Division."

"You're a police officer." He said it with awe. No fear whatsoever, which might stay out of his voice for something as mundane as a human kidnapping, but had to be there if he was stealing from witches.

"I'm investigating a crime on the mainland."

"Where's your badge?"

"I, uh... I had a run-in..."

"...with the people running that hotel," he finished, smearing a little disgust over "that hotel" while he was at it.

"Yes."

"The element that place brings! I'm no prude, I love a good time as much as anyone. There's nothing better than some suds around a warm campfire, roasting weenies, and a couple good songs." He sounded like a fun guy. "But *that* place. Gambling. Low character. And not one arrest, did you know that?"

"I had an inkling."

He shook his head. "Sheriff Thorpe should be ashamed."

"I think he's too busy counting his money."

Foote nodded sadly. "You're investigating them?"

"Not exactly, but there have been a few troubling connections."

"Troubling connections?"

"Yeah, you know, connections that imply wrongdoing but aren't actually..."

"No, I meant, like what?"

"Oh. The orange hair for one."

"Witches have orange hair," he said, and then brightened. "I've seen a witch! She flies in from time to time. She really stands out, since we don't get much air traffic. Gargoyles have trouble with the distance, gremlins don't like sun or water, and the balam are already here."

"A witch, huh?" I had a feeling about who he was describing, but I wanted to see him get there naturally.

He nodded. "Young. Orangish hair, like I said. Long and wavy. She wears these dresses that look like old quilts." He paused. "And she has a toad. I've seen the toad."

I watched him as he rattled off a perfect description of Hexene Candlemas. Still no sense of deception. More and more, Foote was looking like an innocent in all of this. I cursed silently. He'd been my best suspect.

And besides, Hexene's hair was more coppery than orange. Just, you know, for the sake of accuracy.

"When was the last time you saw the witch?"

He wracked his brain. "A few weeks ago. She was meeting with one of the local balam. He's dark-skinned, very big for them. Green eyes, though that doesn't help." He was describing Percy Katz, which was good enough for me. "I was out walking, and sometimes I like to cut through the foliage on the edge of their property. It's more densely planted than anything else on the island. And the witch landed and had a conversation with the balam. He gave her money, she gave him some paper, and then she flew off on her broom."

A hex deal. Nothing there, since I wasn't a vice cop. Not

even in my hasty cover identity.

"And you haven't seen her since?"

"Not once. Does she have something to do with all this?"

"You could say that. Is there anything else on this island with orange hair?"

He thought again. "I haven't seen anything. That hardly means it's not there, though. I spend most of my time up in the hills, and most of the time, I'm the only thing I see."

I nodded. "Anything else out of the ordinary or weird?"

"The lights, you mean?" Foote asked.

"What lights? The casino?"

"No, off the coast. About a mile off the southern tip of the island."

"Lights in the air?"

"No, from under the water."

I paused to consider. "Um... what kind of lights?"

"Blue and red ones."

"When did you first see them?"

"Last year. I was out walking at night and I saw them shining. I waited to see if anything surfaced, but nothing ever did."

I tried to map that to what I knew, some sort of aquatic robot—unlikely, considering water shorted them out—or an orange-furred merman. It didn't come together, and considering all of the strange and unexpected changes the sudden influx of monsters into the population had caused, there were a hundred similar stories that never panned out.

"Thanks, Harry. I appreciate the time."

I finished my bread and soup and cursed the luck that made Harry Foote into a nice guy. Still, something with orange hair had been at the edge of that pit, and it wasn't Foote and it sure as hell wasn't Hexene. I was willing to bet it was Aggie's kidnapper, and he was shadowing me.

Twenty-Eight

Foote refused to let me out of his house without a jacket. He deflected any attempts to pay him, telling me the jacket was something someone had left behind and he didn't need anyway. That it was sized perfectly for an eight-foot, broad-shouldered frame and smelled like wet dog said he was lying to me. That and the fact that, as it turned out, he was an awful liar and could barely stutter through a story that had more holes than a zombie's burial suit.

So I wrapped myself up in a foul-smelling jacket that fit me like a cloak and went back out into the cold. I regretted it fairly quickly. I thought about turning around and asking Foote if I could sleep on his couch, but I'd already called Ser, and if she sailed into the harbor and I wasn't there, there would be hell to pay, and for good reason. I trudged down the dusty path with the orange, green, and blue lights of Isla Calavera to my left and the soft glow of Avalon to my right.

The swaying step pyramids floated in the dark, casting shadows only in the irregular flashes of lightning. I kept an eye on the one I saw Kong disappear into. Though I didn't think he would emerge again until morning, it never paid to lose track of a fifty-foot gorilla.

He didn't come out, though his casino looked to still be hopping. The exterior lights were on, and though no one appeared to be outside from what I could see, I could imagine the inside, hazy with cigarette and cocktail smoke, Jungle Jim schmoozing through another set while making goo-goo eyes at some dowager bug-eyed monster in the front row, the games rattling along and everyone a winner. It was a party in Isla Calavera, and no humans were invited. I had seen worse when monsters chose to get together, so a few games of chance and the occasional thrown adrenal sac hardly seemed out of line.

But there was always something underneath. The Bellum mob moving in on Kublai Kong, which was the clearest case of bad meeting evil since Hitler stabbed Stalin in the back. While I hated Kong, at least he had stayed on his side of the channel. The worst thing that would happen with him in charge was maybe California would legalize gambling. Wasn't like folks didn't already have regular dice games and numbers rackets. Just make things nice and legal so every monster would get a slice.

The Bellum mob, on the other hand, was a pack of killers. Sure, maybe they only killed other monsters, but how long would that last? I knew Sarah Bellum would personally chuck every man, woman, and child off Mulholland Falls if she thought for a second it would make her a buck. Giving her access to Isla Calavera's coffers meant more money to expand. More money she didn't need and I didn't really want her to have.

I sighed. I was going to have to warn Kong. Well, maybe not Kong. Pilar. If he didn't listen to her, well, that would be his problem.

No, that would be everybody's problem.

I was wrestling with this dilemma as I cut down a side path, illuminated by some white lightning. It was a little ridge, passing between what were probably gentle gullies filled with the friendly island fauna. In the dark, it looked like two bottomless pits. The ocean crashed, wind giving the waves intimidating height. When the path finally spit me out onto a weather-beaten boardwalk paralleling the shore, I saw that the waves had nearly swallowed the beach entirely.

The storm building over Los Angeles was going to make the one that had rained out the baseball game look like a nice summer drizzle. The clouds spat lightning onto the ocean and the ocean rose in great humps, trying to strike back.

I followed the line of the beach until I came to the first bit of sand that wasn't covered by the oncoming waves and sat down on a berm. I huddled in Foote's musky jacket and waited for Serendipity to arrive. A boat could probably get in pretty close; a combination of darkness and high waves would serve to hide it well. When the lightning lit up the world, I tried to quickly scan the horizon to see where she'd be approaching. I hoped she was able to borrow a big boat. I knew her "family," that adopted group of sirens and gill-men, had some fishermen in it, and I could handle the twenty-two miles back home in a boat that smelled like fish. I wondered what she'd tell the gill-men about me, if anything. I didn't have a flashlight to defend myself, to say nothing of jicama, not that I would have pulled jicama on a Sargasso.

I was still hunting the horizon when a shape stood up from the surf and trudged inward. A flash of lightning revealed it to be Serendipity, her gills only just beginning to settle back into her neck. She was wearing a black bathing suit, and I learned that the thick lines of yellow on her skin apparently extended to her legs. And her toes were indeed webbed.

"Nick! Nick?" she called out, pushing her green-black hair away from her face. She was squinting into the dark. "Nick!"

"Right here!" I called back and waved, hopping up from the berm and into the sand.

"Nick?" she asked, squinting in my general direction. "Is that you?"

"Who else would it be?" As I got closer, I realized the problem. She wasn't wearing her goggles. She couldn't see a thing without them, at least not on land. "Hey, silly question, but where's the boat?"

"What boat?" she asked.

"The boat. That you brought here to bring me back."

"I didn't bring a boat."

"You didn't bring a boat? Why didn't you bring a boat?"

"Because I'm not stealing one! If you wanted someone to steal boats, you should have hired a pirate ghost!"

"Pirate gho... Ser, you have family! They have boats! You've told me this!"

"Boats that are all being used at the moment. And if you think you'd be safe around my family, you're crazier than I thought."

I blinked. "You think I'm crazy?"

"Who's the human on Catalina Island in the middle of the night, asking a siren to swim him back to the mainland with a storm brewing?"

"In my defense, I assumed there would be a boat involved."

We faced each other in the sand. Lightning turned the world white. Ser's big yellow eyes were blinking frantically, first the vertical inner eyelid, then the horizontal outer one. Her face was screwed up in great concentration, trying to turn what was probably a Nick-shaped blob into her boss.

"So what are we doing?" she asked.

"I don't know. What's involved here?"

"Oh, Judas priest," she muttered. "Hold onto my shoulders. Not my neck. I'll need to breathe. Wrap your legs around me, and you know, don't let go."

"Um... Ser... this seems... "

"Dangerous?"

"I was going to say inappropriate."

"You're freezing to death on a monsters-only island and you're worried about decorum?"

"I'm afraid of the other thing too."

"Come on, Nick." She reached out, and I think she was trying to hold my hand, but she slapped me across the face. "Sorry."

"It's all right. I needed that."

I followed her out into the surf and instantly regretted it. The water somehow managed to be colder than ice, but retained its liquid form entirely through spite. The waves staggered me, even when the foam was only pooling around my freezing ankles. Serendipity moved through it effortlessly. She should have been colder than I was. She was soaking wet, and though her one-piece bathing suit was hardly scandalous, she was showing a good deal more skin than me.

And more than I'd ever seen from her. As pleasant as it was, she was my employee, and I was not going to think of her that way. She got down in the water and beckoned to Avalon, by which I think she was probably trying to mean me. I knelt down and awkwardly got on. My hands found her slick shoulders, and I sat on her rear end, my legs under her. A wave slapped me in the chest, finishing the job the others had started, soaking me to the bone.

Serendipity started swimming, and if I thought she could walk through the water effortlessly, there was no comparison to the way she could swim. She seemed to use a modified breaststroke to zip through the water, though there was no need for her to surface. Her head was a few inches under the water, her gills moving in and out of her neck, the red filaments drifting like seaweed.

We surged out into the channel between Catalina and the mainland. All around us, the wind howled and the clouds bellowed. Lightning snapped with increased frequency, but then, maybe I was just more conscious of it as I was speeding through the drink. The lights of the island shrank behind us, but we were still too far from the mainland for those to grow appreciably.

My left hand slipped off her shoulder. I grabbed back on, but then my right gave. Then the left again. I swore and pulled my hand from the water. A sheet of clear mucous sluggishly dripped from it. I shook my hand in disgust and noticed Serendipity had stopped moving. She shrugged out from under me and surfaced.

"Ser, what the hell is this?"

Her gills were still out, and out of the water. "That's... that's, um, that's my slime coating."

"Your what?"

"My slime coating," she mumbled, not able to look at me, both out of embarrassment and from the way her eyes worked. Despite all of this, she had a webbed hand clamped on my upper arm, somehow keeping us both afloat.

"You have a slime coating? How have I never... I mean, I would think... " The choppy water cut me off by giving me a salty mouthful of the Pacific.

"It only kicks in when I submerge in salt water. It helps, you know, move me."

"It makes it hard to hold on."

"Sorry," she mumbled.

"No, I mean, it's great for... hydro... uh, water locom... er, swimming. Just caught me off guard is all."

"Can you hang on?"

"Oh, yeah, now that I know, you know..." Now that I knew holding onto Serendipity underwater was like grabbing a giant ball of snot. Not that I'd ever say that to her.

She let go, leaving me to tread water, and showing me just how much energy that took in rough seas. She dove, and I felt her, or else a friendly dolphin, swim up and under me. I put my hands back on her shoulders and the slime coating kicked back in. I spent the rest of the ride losing and regaining my grip on her shoulders, a task that got harder and harder as the freezing water numbed my hands. I blinked out salt spray and just about everything was simultaneously soaking wet and being chewed on by wind that was almost as cold. She hadn't brought a boat. She thought she'd just swim us both back.

It's not every secretary that would do that for her boss.

On the ride back, I had time to think. The cold occupied some of my thoughts, if only to reassure myself that the winter of '44 was still worse. Then my thoughts turned to what was below the surface. Harry's lights last year, whatever those had been. More importantly, there were a few leviathans tooling around the ocean. I had been lucky enough never to have seen one, but we all heard about the Battle of the Chesapeake, when the first of the leviathans pretty effectively ate a good chunk of the American fleet. At the time, I had chalked it up to hysteria, but that was before I'd seen my own giant and grasped how much the world had changed.

The odds of a leviathan being in the channel were next to none—supposedly there was only one per ocean and they ruled their territory like kings—but fear is seldom rational. Soon as the thought entered my chattering brain, there it was. I could feel the colossal eyes on me from below and imagined the monster surfacing to swallow Serendipity and me in a single bite.

The far shore had finally begun to grow. The lights glittered, the air clear underneath the angry sky. A tripod worked on loading a ship at the harbor, but other than that, very little was out. As though to prove why, a lightning bolt ripped from the sky and wreathed the silvery martian vehicle in a crackling blue glow. I thought of the mad scientist's brain, sizzling under its clear dome. The tripod never stopped moving—martians build to last—and the light faded from the clean gray surface.

Serendipity wasn't headed for the harbor. I squinted at the shore and figured out where we were going: Royal Palms, where Hexene had been attacked. I hadn't told Ser to go there, and I wasn't even certain she knew its connection to the case. I made a mental note to ask her why she picked that particular landing spot.

Or I would have, if I hadn't chosen that moment to pass out.

TWENTY-NINE

Everything was bright and beautiful. I heard the surf, but instead of the cruel tides of the last few days, it was the gentle caress of the water on the perfect summer day. The radio was playing one of the Andrews Sisters tunes, "Rum and Coca-Cola," that had been big right when I was coming home from France. That song told me that the worst was over, and I could settle into the kind of life I was supposed to have. Get married, have kids, go into business. The notes, a heavenly close harmony, were tinny over the radio, but grew in power until the tides merged with them, washing the song in salt and summer. I was on the shore, leaning back on a bench with a bottle of Coke—and just a snap of rum in there—sipping my drink and watching the pretty girls in the water. One of them was my girl, the tough redhead with all the freckles. No, it was the sweet brunette who was blind without her glasses. Don't be silly, it was the tall blonde with the figure that would make a priest forget his vows.

Something sloshed in my lap. I blinked. It was night, and

I squinted at every oncoming car's headlights. I was also in a car, an unfamiliar one, slumped back in the passenger's seat while someone else drove. I looked down into my lap and found a clear plastic container filled with water. In the corner, a tiny sea anemone waved its minute tentacles. A bright purple-and-yellow fish darted back and forth. I blinked again and looked at the driver's seat. Serendipity, now wearing her goggles, turning opaque as the headlights from oncoming cars hit us. She was sitting on a towel, and I noticed that I was as well.

"What happened?" I asked. My brain was still half-frozen, and I had worked out what happened, but my mouth still made the noise.

"Sorry. I was singing," she said. She *was* a siren, after all, and had shown me once before what her singing voice could do. Namely, hypnotize everything within hearing. She occasionally did so without thinking about it. "You were sleeping, so I thought... I don't know."

I wasn't as cold anymore. I looked for a place to set the box aside, which I had figured out was the case she kept her goggles in, complete with the water she would need to see. I could put it on the seat, but I imagined if she had wanted that, she would have put it there herself. "Where are we going?"

"I was going to take you to my place. We have a couch."

That was enough to wake me up. "Are you crazy?! Mira lives with you!"

"Oh, I don't think she'd try anything."

"Ser, I don't want to sound, you know, arrogant, but that girl has a serious jones for me. Take us to Pilar O'Heaven's place. It's... " I found the ocean out of my window, "in the other direction."

"Pilar O'Heaven?"

"The giantess? Remember, I told you, she's our client."

"I remember. Isn't it a little late?"

"Probably. But her place is safer than mine right now, and a lot safer than yours."

Serendipity *hmph*ed, but pulled over onto the gravel at the side of the road and swung the car around. Between the headlights and the low black clouds, it was completely dark. I had Serendipity's pleasant salt smell to keep me company, and everything was bright again, and soft and gentle and...

"Ser, could you please not hum?"

"Huh? Oh, sorry about that. It's just when I'm driving... "

"No, I know, but you're... "

"Beguiling you."

"Is that what you call it?"

"That's what it's called."

"Just a little. I mean, it's not as bad... well, as good... as when you're really singing. I'd just like to stay, you know, aware and all."

She nodded.

"Where did you get a car?"

"I borrowed it from my neighbor. He's a phantom, and I think he likes Llorona." That was her other roommate, a ghost who worked as a maid in a hotel downtown.

"A phantom's car." I shook my head.

"You're going to have to get over your thing about phantoms at some point."

"Give it a case or three."

We were quiet. After a moment, she said, "I'm not old, am I?"

"What?"

"Old. I'm not old. Do I look old?"

"I don't know. How do sirens look old?"

"Nick!"

"I'm sorry! You're blue! And yellow! You're a very pretty

girl, with, you know, gills and so on. You don't look old."

"I'm *not* old."

"Well, all right then," I said, and looked out the window.

"*He* said I was old."

"He? He who?"

"The man at the library. The producer."

"You talked to a producer?"

"Who said I was old!"

"What does he know?"

"He still said it."

"You're not old, Ser. You're in the flower of youth."

Her gills popped out, but she retained a poker face. "Thank you, Nick."

"Just out of, you know, curiosity, what happens to older sirens?"

"Our hair turns green. Really green. Like your lawn."

"My lawn is more yellow. There's these werewolves having a territorial dispute... "

"All right, not your lawn. *A* lawn. An imaginary lawn that's very green."

"I'm picturing it."

"Our color darkens a little. We get scalier."

"Then by that standard, you're a perfect and unassailable model of, um, maritime youth."

She was silent, then, "Maybe I'm old."

"What?"

"For getting discovered. I'm nearly twenty-five. People get discovered before then."

"Not everyone."

She thought it over. "Thanks, Nick."

"You can thank me by making sure I stay human tonight."

"I'll do my best."

THIRTY

Serendipity looked at the giant beach house, and I knew she was having the same reaction I had when I'd first seen it. Maybe more, since Ser had probably been fascinated with Pilar's place when it was profiled in one of her magazines.

"Bigger than I thought it would be."

"Pilar is, too."

"Well, yes, that's one thing to hear, but another to actually see it."

I directed her to the driveway at the side of the house where Keyes had parked. A narrow stone staircase led down to the beach and up to Pilar's front porch. The wind buffeted us, but I was mostly dry at that point. My backside was still damp, though, having never aired out, and I shivered anew. At least it wasn't that all-consuming cold my body absorbed on the trip across the channel. It was an uncomfortable, unpleasant, human cold.

The staircase ended at a walkway that went to Pilar's porch, where everything ballooned to giant portions. She was nice enough to have built a staircase for smaller visitors into her larger one, with nine normal steps for every one large one. A doorbell was set close to the ground, the front door looming above us. Her house was otherwise dark. I had a moment of fear, wondering if Kong had made the crossing. No, he was making time with Jayne Doe. Pilar would be alone.

I rang the bell. A few minutes later, I rang it again.

The light came on, and giant footsteps thudded through the ground, making my teeth chatter. The door opened on Pilar, wrapped in a dressing gown, hair in rollers, blinking sleepily down at Serendipity and me. I don't know if it was relief or shame I saw on her face, or maybe some combination of both. "Mr. Moss?" she boomed. "What are you... oh, of course." It had dawned on her that she wouldn't hear us anyway. She knelt and put her hand flat on the porch.

I got on and Serendipity followed. Pilar stood up, and Ser immediately fell onto her rear. I made it a little more gracefully, simply because it wasn't my first trip on the Pilar-o-coaster. The giantess shut the door and carried us into the front room, carefully depositing us on the dais. She glanced around, found another chair on her dining room table, and put it out. We both gratefully took our seats. She settled back on the sofa, carefully re-wrapping her gown.

"Now, Mr. Moss, what are you doing here?"

"I found your admirer."

"That could have waited until morning. I wouldn't want you to endanger yourself."

"I was already out," I said.

"I... I'm sorry about that. I couldn't get to you. Those halls are too small. I needed Keyes."

"I know."

"Where *is* Keyes?"

"He's not with... of course he's not. The last I saw him, he was at Isla Calavera."

"Oh dear. He can get lost quite easily."

"Not the best trait in a chauffeur."

"I had to choose, that or squashable, and unfortunately I was forced to pick the former."

"Understandable."

"And you've brought a guest?"

"Oh, sorry, Miss O'Heaven, this is my secretary, Serendipity Sargasso."

Ser leaned over to the microphone I was using. "It's very nice to meet you."

"Likewise, Miss Sargasso. So, Mr. Moss, you said you've located my admirer?"

"Um, yes, I believe so."

"You believe so?"

"Well, I wasn't able to speak to him. Leona Pryde cornered me, then called Katz and his goons."

"Yes. I'm sorry about that, too."

"Even if he's not the one who's been your, um, regular, it's fair to say he's just as interested."

"Who is he?"

"A nosferatu named Count Morlock. He's staying in Room 232." I watched her face fall when I said "nosferatu." She had been hoping for someone dashing and delightfully old world, or at least able to fake it. What she got was a baldheaded freak with buckteeth whose closest friends were best known for carrying plague. I felt a little bad for Morlock, even though if any attempt were made to consummate the relationship, he'd be smashed flatter than a hammered pancake on the interstate.

"Count Morlock? You're certain?"

"Well, like I said, I'm not a hundred percent certain... "

"I hired you to be a hundred percent certain."

"That means going back to the island."

"I know."

"And tangling with security again."

"If you get pinched, I'll get you out."

"I did get pinched."

She winced. "I'm sorry—"

I cut her off, not needing to hear the same apology again. "So if it happens again, you can and will get me out?

She hesitated, then nodded. I knew I should do my best to avoid it if I could, since a nod was far from a definite yes. She probably wanted to be able to help me, but the world had beaten that level of defiance out of her. She was left with her fantasies about a vampire sweeping her off her feet. Oldest story in the book.

"I could use my stuff back," I said to her. "They took my jacket, a lot of wards and whatnot, my gun, my wallet, my licenses, my identification."

She held up a massive hand. "I've got the idea. I can get those for you."

"Don't send Keyes. He'll just eat them."

A ghost of a smile touched her lips. "Anything else?"

"Don't leave without me."

"If you miss the final ferry, I swim out at seven. I can't stay much later than that without Kublai knowing."

"I'll be there."

"You'll do it, then?"

"I'll do it." Not even a question. Whatever had taken Aggie was on that island. The hair on the lip of the pit proved it. Couldn't be a coincidence, not even in a city as big as this one.

She nodded. "May I carry you into the bedroom you used last night?" She looked between Ser and me. "I'm very sorry, but it's the only guest room I have. I'm not used to entertaining so many smaller guests at one time."

"It's fine," Serendipity said, for which I was grateful, because no matter what I said, it would feel presumptuous.

Pilar put her hand on the table and Ser and I climbed aboard. She took us back to the vault, set us down, wished us goodnight, and returned to her bed. Her footsteps shook the whole place.

I walked into the bedroom with Serendipity right behind me. "Thanks for everything, Ser. You can go home if you want."

"I'm not leaving you here," she said, closing the door. "I have to drive you back."

"I can call a cab."

"You're not calling a cab, Nick. You're getting some sleep, and I'm driving you home in the morning."

She was still by the door, standing demurely in her bathing suit, staring back at me with her eyes massive behind the goggles. I must have stared just a bit too long, because she looked away, her gills coming out, and chewed on one of her claws. I turned to the bed, partly to hide my own rising blush.

"Well, I, uh, I can sleep on the floor."

"Why would you do that?"

"So you can have the bed. So there's no, you know."

"Why would I want the bed?"

"I don't know. You're supposed to give women the bed. That's how this works."

"Oh! I don't sleep in a bed," she said. She moved past, still not looking directly at me, into the bathroom and I heard the tub start to fill. She poked her head out. "The bathtub's big enough."

"You sleep in a tub?"

"Of course. My skin would dry out otherwise. I wish she

had some salt, but fresh water is better than no water."

I stared at her, trying to process this new information about my secretary.

She smiled awkwardly, keeping her deep-sea murder-teeth hidden. "Goodnight, Nick."

"Goodnight, Ser... Ser?" She turned around. "Thanks again."

She paused, hand on the doorknob. "You're welcome, Nick." When she shut the door, her gills were still out, trying to strain water that wasn't there.

THIRTY-ONE

We were a sight, me in a rumpled two-days-dirty suit and a jacket that would fit maybe three of me, her in her bathing suit and a towel, her hair in frizzy tangles. When she saw me looking, she scowled and muttered, "Fresh water," and refused to elaborate. Pilar fed both of us breakfast and left a couple of ferry tickets, in case Serendipity wanted to go with me. Our massive host was out the door shortly thereafter, trusting us to see our own way out.

Serendipity's eyes lit up as she held the ticket.

"I'm on a case, Ser."

"Oh, not today. A night of real glamour, though? That could be fun."

"Sure. Head into that bastard's den for a good time."

She put the ticket down. "Are you all right?"

I sighed. "This is a rough one. All of them."

"Then we should get moving."

"You can say that again."

We left Pilar's place as the sun was rising and Ser drove

me home. Not that the rising sun made much of an impression with the weather we'd been having. It could almost have been night, and any light was mostly from lightning strikes that barely had a second in between them.

After the night I'd had, returning to the mundanity of my neighborhood felt strange. Isla Calavera couldn't exist in the same world as my little house. They would never touch each other, never even be aware of one another. One couldn't be more mundane. The other would have sounded insane ten years ago.

Serendipity pulled up in front of my place. "Here we are." I opened the door and stepped out. "You need me in the office?"

"You worked last night, the way I see it."

She smiled then, her teeth making her face go from pretty to horrifying. "You'll find them."

"Yeah. Tell me another one." I shut the door behind me and Serendipity drove away.

I looked at my house and sighed. Just like always. Faded bluish stucco walls, wards hung at every eave and window. Sconces with burned-out torches. Holy symbols that could use a buffing. The line of dust that normally encircled it, more important than any lock, had washed away in the rain. My little fortress. Just a house.

I trudged up the lawn. A shower and a change of clothes, then I could attack the case fresh. Go back to that island, find what they didn't want me to find. It was all there, at least two of these cases I'd found myself in. Wrap them up and turn to the others, and try to ignore the fact that it was almost definitely too late for any of them.

I reached under the mat for the spare key, unlocked the door, and my cat came bolting out of the house. I tripped over its streaking form and fell face-first into the carpet.

That was probably what saved my life.

The television smashed into the wall where my head had been, shattering into pieces and raining down around me as I covered up. I didn't even have time to yell or curse. Whatever had thrown it now stepped over me, and I smelled something almost like a sasquatch, but not nearly as bad. I tried to see it, but got only a vague shadow.

Hands grabbed me by the coat, impossibly strong hands that lifted me up like nothing. My feet were closer to the ceiling than the floor. It, whatever *it* was, hairy, big, and strong, was behind me. It threw me as easily as someone tossing a baseball. I flew across my living room and slammed into the wall, knocking free a photograph of Echo Park Lake.

My head was trying to swim away, but I knew if I let it, that was it. Lights out. Strength like that, it could beat me to death, and I got the impression that was exactly what this thing's purpose was. I fought unsteadily to my feet, but those gave, and I caught myself on the back of the sofa.

From behind me, a thump-thump-pause-THUMP, like something had taken a running leap and landed directly behind me. I tried to turn, at least to get an idea of where the next attack was coming from. Instead, those iron hands clamped onto my left shoulder and the seat of my pants and I was hurled unceremoniously through the doorway into the hall.

I slammed into the wall, more pictures falling onto me. I managed to take the impact on the back this time, cold comfort that was. This was how Paolo del Mar had bought it. Exactly. It would take a lot less to bump me off in the same way. I didn't have that protective coating of scales, and I was only as strong as one small man.

I blinked at the silhouette in my living room. It was big, the size of Harry Foote, but if it was him, he was wearing some kind of helmet, like a spaceman. It started to advance.

The footlocker.

Maybe it was the smooth, metallic lines of the monster's head. Maybe it was the lightning outside, hitting me obliquely with a bolt of inspiration. Maybe it was just that I didn't want to die that morning. My footlocker, in my closet. All of my monster-fighting equipment was stashed in there, the big guns from the bad old days. I hadn't gotten a good look at this thing, but something in there *had* to be perfect for it.

It was moving. I could see it out of the corner of my eye. It hunched over and ran, almost like a man, but with the weight distributed all wrong.

I scrambled to all fours, launching myself at my bedroom. I slammed into the door, partially upright, and fell inside. My body felt boneless and livid like a giant bruise. I ripped open my closet and hauled out the footlocker, scrabbling at the latch.

The hands grabbed me again and flung me backward. I hit the other wall and lost whatever breath was left in my lungs. I lay there, trying to get enough air into my body to make it possible to move again. What I'd do with that, I had no idea, because I couldn't beat this monster. Especially not with it standing between me and my only salvation.

I had enough strength to look up, and I finally saw the thing that was beating me like it thought I was full of candy.

It was about seven feet tall, give or take. Its body was apelike, covered in orange hair. Its head was not. It looked almost like the helmet of a space suit, round and bubble-like, with antennae scraping the ceiling. A thread of electricity climbed the antennae to pop and spark at the top.

A sasquatch. A robot. Two monsters, one body. No wonder the thing got in. There was no way to keep the damn thing out because it was new. No way to know what frightened it. What killed it.

It was also the key. The connection to three of my cases. He took Aggie Brooks, Corrina Lacks, and Escuerzo. The cases had been the same thing all along, and I wasn't even going to get to know why.

The ape-robot stared down at me, the screen in his bubble face nothing but a blank line. When he spoke, the voice registered as humps and dips in the line, but what he said in his deep, artificial voice surprised me.

"Mr. Moss?"

I blinked. "Yes?" Was this where we found out that he had the wrong house? He really wanted Mr. Motts, who lived across town. He would apologize, offer to help straighten up, I'd politely refuse, and we would go our separate ways.

The ape-robot reached for me with his powerful mitts and I flinched, bracing for another throw. He hesitated. Unfortunately, it was just that, a hesitation. He nodded to himself and grabbed my lapel. It was a weaker grip than before, but still so powerful I wasn't going to be able to get away. He hurled me into the wall, though not as hard as the other times, maybe still wrestling with whatever had stunned him. I bounced off it—even his half-strength toss was enough to ring my bells—and fell onto the bed.

He grabbed the front of my shirt again and threw me almost carelessly back into the hall. I hit the wall and slid to the floor. I wondered what Paolo del Mar had thought in this same situation. Had he known why this monster had paid him a visit? Had my attacker set up the whole thing?

"What do you want with them?" I said.

The ape-robot was through the door. He looked down at me, his blank television face more than unnerving.

"You have all of them, don't you? Corrina Lacks. Escuerzo. Aggie Brooks."

He hesitated again, though not for long before grabbing

me, slamming me into a wall, and then hurling me into my bedroom. It was getting repetitive. I thumped off the wall and back onto the bed. The throw was weak, and I rolled off the bed relatively unharmed. The footlocker was right next to me. I blinked, forgetting for a moment what I had wanted it for. Oh, yes, to deal with the monster trying to kill me. That's right. He wasn't going to talk. Maybe he'd change his mind if I found what scared him. I fumbled with the lock, my fingers big and clumsy.

The ape-robot came through the door.

I opened the footlocker.

The ape-robot took a step toward me.

I held up a camera and snapped a shot. He batted it out of my hand and it shattered against the wall. "All right," I muttered, and reached into the case again. "Aha!" That came with the postcard of an M.C. Escher painting called *Relativity*. The monster kept coming. "Okay, not that." I pulled out a shot of Audrey Hepburn. Nope, that didn't work either.

"Oh no," I said as the hands closed over my lapels. He hefted me this time, and it seemed like the kid gloves were not only off, they had been hopelessly lost. He wound up and threw, and I sailed out of the bedroom to hit the doorjamb into the main room. I fell heavily to the floor. Something opened up in my forehead, which I only noticed when my shirt started turning red. I put my hand to my head and it came away wet. I couldn't take much more of this, and the monster coming through the door was as fresh as a daisy.

I rolled over and the world swam around me. I almost lost my breakfast. That would probably have been the end of me, hunched over and upchucking while the big thing bounced me off a couple more walls. I bit the bile back and crawled. If I could just make the front door, still partially open, maybe one of my neighbors would call the police. The one time I'd be happy to see those wolf bastards. The one time they wouldn't be hassling me for being a meatstick in the wrong part of town, which seemed like everywhere.

Otherwise, it would be Moon and Garou standing over my broken body, writing up a report. They wouldn't even have bothered to show if I hadn't had the connection to a monster killed the same way.

The ape-robot's heavy tread came over the floorboards behind me and I kept crawling, knowing that there was no way I could get there in time.

The door swung open. A flash of lightning silhouetted a shape in the doorway. A distressingly slender silhouette.

Thirty-Two

"Nick?" I knew that voice. Hexene. "Nick!"

I kept crawling. I could tell Hexene had switched her attention to the ape-robot, and although I wasn't listening too much, I didn't feel the footsteps anymore. She had stopped him in his tracks.

"You," Hexene said. "You stay where you are."

Thump-thump. Not for long, apparently. Getting closer. The floor dimpled under my hands and knees. I put on a burst of speed and nearly retched.

Hexene spoke again, this time in some bizarre language. I saw motion, and I heard her rummage in her satchel. The ape-robot paused again, and actually recoiled when Hexene threw something at him. I felt her arms under my armpits as she hauled me up, putting my feet under me. "Nick! We have to go!"

The world kept swimming, and I wasn't fully aware of where we were until we were down the street. I was leaning on Hexene, my arm over her shoulder. She was still paler than usual, her skin grayish rather than ruddy. Her freckles were washed out and her green eyes faded. Her hair wasn't as vibrant as it had been, looking more frazzled than usual. But I saw the old Hexene in the set of her jaw, and the fact that she'd just faced down a monster twice her size to save my life.

"Are your powers back?" I slurred at her.

She shook her head. "No."

"But you... "

"He didn't know that."

I had to shut my mouth, otherwise I'd just start gushing at her, and that wasn't impressive. The shock of the beating was beginning to fade, and my body was learning that it no longer had to adapt to short, abrupt flights. My feet were under me again and I could walk without the whole world swaying like the deck of the *Merry Celestial.* I touched my forehead and found that I had stopped bleeding.

"You look terrible," Hexene said.

"So what else is new?"

We kept moving down the block, my house receding quickly behind us. Every foot we got away, the more my balance returned, the more the world decided to be the nice solid place I had become used to over the course of my life. The ringing in my head had retreated a bit and I could concentrate on the lush panoply of aches and pains blooming over my body from my recent savage beating.

Hexene noticed I was walking more on my own now and let me bear more of my weight. She let out a small, relieved groan. "That bastard moves fast," she said.

"What bastard? That thing in my house?"

She nodded. "I caught him in the shop this morning. He was in the back, standing over Hermosa and Hechalé. They were beaten pretty bad. I scared him off with more flimflam, but he made it out with Erasmo and Ernesto."

Fortunately, none of my brains had been beaten out of my head and I was able to put that together on my own. "Those are the other two familiars?"

"Yes." She rummaged through her satchel and removed a photograph of the Candlemas Coven, the three of them up by the Griffith Observatory, a three-domed art deco stargazing facility on Mount Hollywood. Hermosa was in the middle, scowling, her snapping turtle making the same face she was. Hexene was on the left, holding Escuerzo, smiling and looking away, clearly embarrassed by the whole operation. Only Hechalé, the portly, diminutive mother, looked at all pleased, and it was a happy beam that would have put a smile on my face in another situation. She held her giant salamander, and the thing looked like it was grinning along with her. "Ernesto," Hexene said, pointing to the snapping turtle. "Erasmo," pointing to the snot otter.

"So all three are gone now," I muttered mostly to myself.

"I called the police and an ambulance, and then I took a red car over here." The venom she smeared over "red car" was the kind of thing normal people might reserve for "door-to-door salesman" or "fugitive Nazi."

"And you'd never seen that monster before he broke into your shop?"

"No."

"Seems like he matches fairly well with whatever grabbed you on the beach."

She thought about it. "I would need for him to grab me to be sure."

"Trust me, that's the last thing you want."

She looked me over. "How are you feeling?"

"Been better."

"Sit down," she said, and it wasn't a conversation. We were at the corner of the street, next to a low billboard for police recruitment with the motto of the LAPD in big letters: TO PROTECT AND SERVE MAN. Despite the thunder and lightning, it hadn't started raining yet. We were both grateful for that; neither of us wanted her melting in the streets. She looked me over, first the wound on my forehead, and then at the rest of me. She leaned in to feel at my ribs and though I winced, I never cried out. At this point, I was going to call that a victory. As close as she was, her hair brushing my face, I expected a whiff of her normal scent, this sort of earthy herbal smell, a lot like the hills of Los Angeles on a nice spring day. That was gone, along with her familiar. "I don't think anything is broken," she said.

"Other than my house."

"You should think about another line of work."

"You know anyplace that hires humans?"

She reached into her satchel, rummaged around, and removed a wooden box and a gourd. From these, she extracted some dried leaves and powder. "It's not perfect, but swallow this, and chew these." She dumped a pinch of the powder down my throat and handed over some of the leaves. The leaves tasted like burnt cleaning solvents, but I chewed anyway.

We sat there by the billboard, watching ball lightning bounce around the skies. Thunder rattled the windows and the billboard, and wind buffeted us. At least I was dry, even if my clothes were a little stiff and probably tasted like salt. Whatever was in the leaves helped, and the pain receded further into the background.

Experimentally, I stood. The only thing swaying me was the wind. I could live with that. Hexene got up, her dress and hair whipping around her, looking like the portrait of one of those Irish girls watching her brother get carted off to Australia. The difference was, that girl would have been mournful. Hexene looked angry, and more so because she couldn't punch the cause of her present misery.

"What now?" she asked, raising her voice over the persistent booms in the sky.

"I have the outline of it all now, and I know where he was. You were attacked on the beach, and I found signs of him on Catalina. Means I'm taking the ferry back there and I'm going to find him. He's at the center of the disappearances of two girls and three amphibians."

Hexene nodded. "And what are you going to do when you find him?"

"Hadn't thought about that yet."

"He's a new kind of monster. No telling what he's afraid of."

"Yeah, I know."

"Then I guess it's lucky you have an ex-witch willing to help you."

"Hexene..." Saying that it was too dangerous seemed wrong, since she'd just saved my life. Her flimflam had worked twice, but I didn't think there was going to be a third time. I needed a witch, and she was an ex. But then there was the way Hexene was staring at me, her jaw out, head held high, even if she looked sick enough that she should be in bed. No way I could say anything about that and then, of course, that silly feeling that I just wanted her around. I opened my mouth, confident I could craft a response by the time the words hit the air.

"Can it, Moss," she said, cutting me off. "Whether you like it or not, you've got a partner."

THIRTY-THREE

The monsters on the red car gave Hexene and me a wide berth, probably assuming by our dress and general state that we were one of a new breed of hobo who only needed to ride the rails as far as Hollywood. It was no small wonder the crawling eye who slithered on at Melrose watched us the whole way to his seat.

Hexene wanted to go straight to the island. She had money for the tickets, she said. She resented the idea of having to ride the ferry, as she was used to zipping over to the island on her broom, but she would deal with it, if it meant getting Escuerzo back. I had a stop to make first, one that might upset Hexene for more reasons than one.

I was turning things over in my mind. As much as this monster broke the other cases open, I was still wondering. I had no motive for any of it. Stealing those familiars only made sense for something trying to either weaken the Candlemas Coven or steal their mojo for itself. Hexene had bluffed the ape-robot, so that wasn't it. Even the eating motive didn't make much sense. The monster had no mouth to speak of, and there had to be an easier way to get a toad than taking one from the most powerful maiden in Los Angeles.

Hexene had one connection I still hadn't probed, and we had the duration of the ride, all the way from Watts to Hollywood. It would take some time. "Percy Katz," I said.

"Huh?" Hexene blinked. When we hadn't spoken for a while, she had the tendency to slip back into that disturbing fugue state she had been in when Escuerzo first went missing.

"One of your customers," I said, not wanting to actually blurt out what it was Hexene did to the entire red car.

"Yes. Um, once every few weeks or thereabouts."

"For what?"

She glanced around the red car. A phantom dozed in the back, clutching a saxophone to his chest like a brass baby. He was the monster on the red car with the best hearing, and nothing else seemed to be paying much attention to the gypsy and the hobo. Still, Hexene dropped her voice to a near whisper. "A kind of hex that... um... well, balam have this... er... desire..."

"I've seen it."

Hexene raised her eyebrows.

"It was not pleasant."

The eyebrows went down. "Well, he's trying to control it. With hexes."

"How so?"

"When he's thinking about certain things, the hex makes him think about other things. Get it?"

"So he doesn't change at the drop of a hat."

"He can still change, but he has to *really* concentrate on the things that, you know, get him... going?" I had never seen Hexene this uncomfortable before, and I had the sense that if her complexion weren't so sickly, I would have been seeing some Celtic red cheeks.

"Right. How expensive are we talking?"

"Not very."

"That's all he's into?"

"As far as I know."

I nodded. Katz, as much as I hated to think it, was probably not my problem. Just one of the many monsters standing between me and the end of the case. I turned it over and over for the rest of the ride, and eventually came to the conclusion that I wouldn't know much more until I could talk to him. The challenge being that I would have to do that without getting thrown into the pit or torn apart. Percy might have more control than most jaguar people, but that didn't make him a monk. And he had my cross.

We got out on Hollywood Boulevard and took the short walk over to Bronson. My destination was a converted theater that was now a nightclub called The Gloom Room. The doors were closed, but I knew the girls were in there rehearsing. They always were.

"What are we doing here?" Hexene asked.

"You've never seen that monster. I've never seen that monster. Doesn't mean no one's ever seen that monster."

I opened the door onto the carpeted and curtained lobby. The Gloom Room was in the seedier part of Hollywood, but no one had told the decorator that. If anything, the location added a sense of danger, which for monsters was in short supply. A short trip east and the city belonged to the Howlers, the biggest motorcycle gang around and not my biggest fans. I had no intention of adding them into the mix, not after I'd hospitalized four of their more famous members.

"What is this place?" Hexene asked.

"Um... you might want to follow my lead."

I headed through the empty lobby and opened up the doors to the club proper. Tables and chairs were arrayed around a central hardwood dance floor. The stage was against the opposite wall, though the lights were down, giving the front area a pleasant, lived-in illumination. The band reclined in their chairs taking five, some smoking, others just chatting. They were mostly phantoms, with two zombies and a gill-man thrown in for color, I guessed. They were dressed in street clothes; at night they probably had matching tuxes, something subtle so as not to distract from the main attraction.

I was there to see the main attraction: the Salem Sisters, a close-harmony group with the voices of angels and bodies to make devils. All three of them were gorgeous and they knew it. Dresses that tight—and they were always dressed to the nines, even at rehearsal—were the strict purview of the confident. They didn't look like a witch coven, as they appeared roughly the same age, but it had been explained to me that a year separated the maiden from the mother and the mother from the crone. They even had the same hairstyle, victory rolls at the tops of their heads with the rest trailing glossily down their necks. The three of them lounged around a table just in front of the stage.

The crone, not that you'd call her that without already knowing, was Hyacinth Salem, or Hy to her friends. Platinum blonde hair was her stand-in for gray. She wore white, and a white sparrow was perched on the lip of her gin and tonic, bobbing in and taking a gulp from time to time. Relaxed, she wasn't nearly as frightening as she could be when her attention was focused on something she didn't like.

The mother was Verbena, or Verb, which I would never call her, since she hated me. A little misunderstanding when we first met, you know. Her black hair was just as shiny as Hy's, and her matching dress made her look like the queen on the other side of the chessboard. Her bluejay was perched on top of one victory roll, periodically whistling snatches of "In the Mood."

The maiden was Lily, and something of a friend. She was one of those I'd failed to find, but at least she had a happy ending. She liked being a fish girl, as it were. Some of that might have been due to the fact that she had been this little mousy thing, but once she had been turned, she became a bombshell. Her hair was much redder than Hexene's, a thick, unnatural red she assured me wasn't dyed. Her dress was green, and I did my best to keep my eyes on her face. It wasn't easy. Her robin was on her shoulder, and it was what saw me first. It warbled, and all three witches turned in my direction.

"Nick?" said Lily, getting up and smoothing her dress. That wasn't helping.

"Oh, great," said Verbena, sipping her drink. Even her bluejay looked disappointed in me.

"Hi, Lil. I'm not, uh, interrupting anything am I?"

"We were just about to get back to rehearsing," Verb said.

Lily shot the mother a look. "We can take a little more time. What's buzzing? And who's your friend?"

"He has a type," Verb muttered.

"Uh... this is Hexene. Hexene, um, Hexene Candlemas." We moved closer to the coven in the dimmed lights of the stage.

Recognition flickered over Hy's features. "*Her*," she said.

"We didn't mean it, Miss Candlemas," Lily said, dropping the vamp act and looking more like the scared girl who had been kidnapped on her way home from school.

"Didn't mean what?" Hexene asked. We arrived at the edge of the table, and now all three of the Salem Sisters were staring at Hexene with open fear.

"The scrying," Hyacinth said.

"About two months ago," Lily added.

"It was his fault," Verbena finished.

Hexene pursed her lips. I could tell she was trying to decide how much to reveal to the three of them, and how mad to be. There was always a secret culture with every monster, a code that only those with the same fur, scales, or slime knew about. Witches were no exception, and from what little I had access to, probably had a richer one than most. Since they were among the more powerful and less respected monsters out there, you had a recipe for some tense interactions. I gathered that most covens weren't too fond of one another as a rule, and the ladies of the Candlemas Coven were the top dogs in the city. When I mentioned the Salem Sisters to Hexene after the scrying incident in question, she had dismissed them as so-so witches. I wasn't going to bring that up.

Hexene said, "It's forgotten."

All three Salem Sisters heaved sighs of relief, which, combined with their low-cut dresses, managed to be both very pleasant and potentially embarrassing to me. The band, which had grown quiet at the intrusion, relaxed and went back to their conversations, though at a much lower volume than before. A few were openly eavesdropping.

"Nick, what's wrong with you?" Lily asked, coming to my side. She still looked a little nervous about Hexene, but Lily wasn't going to let that stop her.

"Probably reduced to riding the rails," Verb said.

"This case. I tangled with a monster. A new kind of monster, at least to me. I was hoping one of you might have heard of it."

"Ask," said Hy, sitting back down and sipping from her drink. The sparrow never got up, merely waiting its turn and taking another gulp. Had to be the first sparrow lush I'd ever seen.

"All right. He's about..." I tried a "yea high" maneuver and realized I wasn't tall enough, and stretching just aggravated the bruises all across my back. "Seven feet high. Looks like an ape, an orange one, except for some kind of robot head. Domed, television for a face, antennae."

"Never heard of it," Hy said with authority.

Lily winced when she saw me stretching painfully, then shook her head to confirm what Hy had said.

"This new monster, you saw it in your dreams?" Verb said.

"Try my living room."

"Your house is warded?" Hy asked.

"Against the stuff I've heard of."

"Witches included," Verb said, taking her bluejay from her head to let it perch on her wrist. Every time she fixed me with her clear gray eyes, I felt that I'd let her down, and this was a terrible thing.

"Sorry," I mumbled.

"Knock it off, Verb," Hy said. "He hasn't pulled anything on you except the one time you tried to hex him."

"Still rude," she sniffed.

"A new monster could conceivably go anywhere it liked. Granted, most inherit weaknesses from their parent species. Sea hags, for example, got our aversion to evil eye charms, and the jicama weakness from the gill-men."

"They, um, they like 'siren' actually," I said.

Hy waved that away. "The point stands."

"The new monsters don't always get their weaknesses from the parents?"

"Not necessarily. Though it would be unusual if they got nothing." Hy paused, looking at Hexene, who had retreated to that gray place she went now. "Are you all right, sweetheart?"

The question was odd, since Hy couldn't have been much older than Hexene, if at all. Still, some crone magic or whatever it was leaked through, and Hexene blinked and came back to reality. She nodded, taking a deep breath.

Hyacinth's icy blue eyes narrowed, then widened in shock. "You've lost your familiar."

The other two witches put their hands over their mouths in horror. The three birds huddled closer to their mistresses. Hexene nodded, wiping at a stubborn tear, and refused to break. I wanted to comfort her, but I knew that was the last thing she would want.

The Salem Sisters didn't know Hexene as well as I did, so went with their instincts. Verb's standoffishness melted, and she was up and holding Hexene so quickly I didn't even see her move. She was already in the middle of "there, there" as Hexene continued to valiantly refrain from crying. Lily had taken Hexene's hand and was patting it impotently. Hyacinth turned to me, and I quailed when I saw the rage in her face. "Why didn't you mention this immediately?"

"It's not, uh, I have certain policies... client privilege and so on..."

"You should have told us at once," she scolded. Her eyes softened when she looked at Hexene. "Tell us what happened, dear."

Hexene spilled, the story coming between bouts of doing her best not to cry. I listened, trying to comb through her story for something that I had missed earlier, but came up empty. Same as before: called by del Mar, went to Royal Palms, got jumped, and when she came to, no toad. I put the orange-furred ape-robot in the story now, and it tracked, at least in terms of what I had to work with. He must have come in from the water. A submarine? Apparently he lacked the robot vulnerability to water. What did he need with two humans and three familiars?

"And you're tracking this poor maiden's familiar," Hy said, the implication being that if I wasn't before, I sure was now.

"Among other... yes, I am."

"And?"

"And I'm going to Catalina. That monster was there yesterday, at least briefly, and I'm willing to bet he lives somewhere around there."

Hy nodded. Verb was too concerned with Hexene to pay attention to me, which was a relief. "Find the toad, detective. The alternative..." Hy trailed off, shaking her head.

"It's happened before?"

A frown creased her face, and those were the first wrinkles I'd ever seen on the Salem Sisters' crone. "When I was first turned, I heard about a witch who had her familiar taken."

"Is she still alive?"

Hy shook her head, glanced at Hexene, and lowered her voice. "She drank." The nod supplied the rest: she drank herself to death.

"When was this?"

Hy frowned again. "I was still a maiden then, so... '52? I can't pin it down more than that, I'm afraid."

I shuddered. She didn't even mention Kong, but referencing the year he showed up was enough. "Did you know who took it?"

"Sadly, no. If it had been the monster you described, I believe that would have been a bigger part of the story."

"Thanks, ladies," I said, standing. "I need to get back to Catalina."

"You should stay here, sweetheart," Verb said to Hexene.

"Nick will find your toad for you," Lily said. "He found me." She didn't say "too late," and for that I was grateful.

"No," Hexene said, rising, and wiping her nose on her sleeve. "I'm going too. Escuerzo needs me."

"All right then," Hy said. "Good luck, dear."

Hexene nodded to them and we walked out. I glanced back, and all three witches were staring at Hexene, faces a mix of horror and sympathy. I knew it would do Hexene no good to see that. She didn't have much hope. I was all that was left.

Thirty-Four

The *Merry Celestial* plowed through the stormy seas on a course for Isla Calavera with the ghost in the old-fashioned diving suit walking next to it along the surface of the water, peering down through the choppy gray whitecaps. I was in my makeshift suit, shivering in the stiff wind. The clouds looked close enough to touch, but that would be like sticking your finger into a wall socket, judging by the skeletal hands of lighting ripping over the surface. The ghost ship was admirably stable, as it rode higher in the water than a real physical vessel would have, but even it could not totally resist the fury of the brewing storm. The tattered sails snapped and ropes strained against the wind. One of the ropes had been torn in half, and that was what the diving-suited man was hunting for, using the green glow from whatever was in his helmet to illuminate the depths. The noises he made, somewhere between the creaking of an old battleship and the groans of a whale, had a distinctly subconscious feel to them. Maybe that was his version of humming under his breath.

Hexene and I stood together on the deck of the ship, close but not too close, both of us with arms folded across our chests in a vain attempt to stay warm. We were both in borrowed coats, me in Foote's and her in one from the Gloom Room's Lost and Found that Verbena had insisted she take. The ferry was nearly empty, with only the truly diehard gamblers braving the waters to try their luck. Once again I'd be the only human on the island, though Hexene might as well have been one, what with her powers gone. Or maybe it was worse for her. She knew what it was like to have power, and it had been taken away.

By a new kind of monster, probably created just for that purpose. In all likelihood, one of his parent monsters was a robot. The other... Foote? Kong? Both made sense. Kong needed an influx of muscle, especially now that the Bellum mob was closing in. And zombies probably weren't sexy enough to prompt his balam to change. A jaguar person who was more person than jaguar was significantly less powerful and therefore less use in a fight. Then what was this new monster doing collecting familiars? If he took Corrina and Aggie, that made sense: more new monsters like him. But the familiars? Was he making yet another monster?

"Nick Moss?" I turned, and found a navyman glowing greenish gray.

"Pulverized," I said, smiling in spite of myself and holding out a hand. He took it and I shivered, not from cold but from feeling like someone was tap-dancing on my grave. One of the hazards of touching ghosts.

"What are you doing back?" he asked, looking me over. I knew about how bad I looked, and I got depressing confirmation from the expression of a man who was missing more than half his head.

"I have some business on the island."

"Yeah," he said, scanning the horizon, or what there was of it. In the distance, funnels of wind touched the ocean. "You doing okay?" he asked.

"I am."

"All right. Don't lose your shirt in there."

"I won't." I wanted to tell the guy what I was doing in there, just so he didn't think I was some kind of degenerate. He'd earned it. We were in the same war, though only one of us made it back intact. But it was pure sentiment; I didn't know the ghost from Adam. So instead I let him pity me while Hexene and I made the crossing.

The *Merry Celestial* pulled into the little harbor next to Kong's pleasure barge. Even a hundred yards out, I could see the deathlike silhouette of Mr. de Kay waiting in front of the hotel. I knew he had seen me as well, even though that was a silly thing to think. I hadn't made it out on the first ferry of the day, and this was the second, so of course he was waiting. But I knew, I just *knew*, that de Kay's lidless eyes tracked me across the channel, fixed square on me.

I swore under my breath.

"What?" Hexene said, turning to me. She pulled the hair out of her face where the wind kept flipping it.

"That zombie up there."

"There are a lot of zombies."

"The most dapper one."

"Oh. Him."

"He's an enforcer for the Bellum mob. He asked me to find a cat for him."

"I thought you didn't find animals as a rule."

"Not a specific cat. Any cat."

"You have a cat."

"Not my cat."

"You said any cat."

"Hexene, he wants a cat because he's trying to off one of the jaguar people. My guess is either Leona Pryde or Percy Katz."

"So you didn't bring him the cat."

"Of course I didn't bring him the cat!"

"He's probably going to be angry with you."

"That's the whole reason I'm bringing this up, Hexene."

"What do you want me to do?"

"Do you have any salt in there?"

"I don't think so. I have some eye of newt."

"I'm not trying to scare newts!"

"It's more for focusing love spells and other curses."

"Love spells are a cur... never mind. I don't want to know."

Hexene watched de Kay as the ferry drew closer to him. "So what are you going to do?"

I cast around for something, anything. The captain, the Spanish conquistador, held onto the ship's wheel and guided us in, ignoring his arrow wounds that were bleeding shipworms. The lady in white stood on the bowsprit, ready to cast herself into the waves for whatever love caused her to fall into despair. The man in the diving suit trudged across the water, his reflection smeared over the surface of the ocean like a smudge of gray-green paint, ready to tie the ship to the dock. The pirate wobbled over the deck, sucking down some ectoplasmic rum. Ensign Pulverized was at the other side of the ferry, holding a few ghostly ropes that writhed with spectral life.

Leona Pryde stood at the end of the dock, radiant with the same expectant smile, and posed just so, making certain the second sight visitors took in—after the glowering skull of the casino itself—was the balamshell on the docks. That was it. Leona Pryde. She was my salvation. Or my doom, but those things were tied up so intimately in my present life that it was getting difficult to distinguish them.

The few monsters who were on the ferry got off first, and Leona went through her spiel. “Good morning everyone! I’m Leona Pryde, the head concierge here at Isla Calavera. If you need anything, please do not hesitate to ask. In the meantime, I would like to direct you to our main stage, where Jungle Jim and the Hepcats will be starting their lunchtime show! Welcome to Isla Calavera and have a wonderful stay.”

Hexene and I went down the gangway. Leona made it a point to undress the both of us with her leering eyes, from the bottom up, so that by the time she got to our faces, I was a little surprised we were both still wearing clothing. “You!” she exclaimed.

“Me,” I confirmed.

Her eyes blazed, but her expression instantly softened. “Coming back to the island when you know what’s waiting—you got some balls, meat... stick.” She drew the racial slur out. Maybe she thought that was attractive.

“I’m here to turn myself in.”

“Do you know what kind of punishment is waiting?” She slathered “punishment” with so much syrup, she had to lick her lips afterwards.

“Nope! No concern! Just turning myself in. For no real reason.”

I hooked her under the arm and escorted her up the pier, Hexene following us. “Oh!” Leona squealed. “So forceful!”

“Sorry.”

“Grab harder!”

“Stop that!” I had to swat her other hand away, and she was breathing a bit more heavily than I’d like, her ivory complexion flushed. “I need you to arrest me!”

Leona nodded. “Come with me.” Did she have whiskers? I

thought I saw whiskers. Even though I was the one gripping *her* upper arm, she was the one dragging me toward the side entrance of the main building. De Kay had spotted us and was following. He probably saw that I wasn't carrying a cat.

"Faster," I said, jogging. "We should move faster."

"Yes... faster..." she breathed. Her arm bulged. Her face looked darker.

"So... about war crimes?" I said.

She stopped. "What?"

"No, no, we're still moving," I said, dragging her along now. Her arm didn't seem to be bulging quite as much, and she no longer had the shadow of black fur on her jaw. "Which door? That door?" De Kay was still behind us, his silhouette faintly visible as a sepulchral shadow between the jungle trees.

"That's the door. I have a room I like to stay in. To... entertain." She grinned, and her teeth looked sharper.

"Do you know much about leprosy?"

"What are you talking about?" Her teeth went blunt again, and she was still moving forward while trying to stare at me at the same time.

"You know, leprosy? Limbs just falling off willy-nilly?"

"I know what leprosy is." She yanked her arm out of my grasp. "You are a strange little man."

"So they tell me."

"How strange?" she asked, slowing, her finger playing up the sasquatch's jacket I still had wrapped around me like an army blanket. "How strange do you get?"

"In Malaysia, they eat grasshoppers. Big ones."

"You... eat insects?"

"Oh, sure. Whatever I can get."

She shuddered and smiled. Those teeth were definitely sharper. "That's... interesting."

"That too? Damn. How about..."

"Nick?" Hexene said. "He's getting closer."

"I almost forgot our little tagalong. Hello there, Red," Leona purred.

"Don't call me Red."

"Fiery, too."

"Focus!" I shouted. "On roadkill! And spoiled food! And dead things!"

Leona blinked as she opened the door. "What on earth is wrong with you?" She didn't wait for a response, slipping inside.

Hexene paused at the door. "What *is* wrong with you?"

"Balam change when they get, you know, aroused."

"Oh! Oh. I thought you were just being, you know, Nick." She followed Leona in.

"Do I do that normally?" I asked no one in particular. I checked behind us, and de Kay was still there. Even the best of zombies weren't very fast, moving at a semi-controlled forward fall. With any luck, he hadn't seen us through the foliage and we could get away clean, leaving him to wander aimlessly around the outside. *Enjoy the salt air, dead man.*

I closed the door as silently as I could. Leona and Hexene were waiting in the hallway, starting down it when I got the door shut. The smooth crooning of Jungle Jim filtered down the hall. I almost started tapping my foot. There's nothing I could do; the guy was good.

We arrived at the elevator, which opened quickly to a zombie operator. "Brains?" he asked.

"Usual floor, Shamble."

"Brains."

The zombie moved the lever and the elevator went up. It was surprisingly silent on the way, and spacious too. We stood in awkward silence, waiting for the short ride to be over. The door opened at our floor and the zombie retracted the safety gate. "Brains," he said.

"Thank you, Shamble," Leona said, leading the way to one of the rooms along the hall. She produced a small keyring from somewhere. I didn't have any idea where she'd been hiding it, since all she had was the shiny black dress that fit like a snakeskin, and that clipboard with the casino's schedule. Probably best never to know. She unlocked Room 580 and led the way in.

I probably shouldn't have been too surprised at what I found inside. "Don't the maids come in here?"

"Only I come in here," Leona purred, whirling on me.

The room had been destroyed. Claw marks raked every wall. The curtains were tattered ribbons. The bed had been disemboweled, the mattress spilling springs and stuffing. The sheets weren't really sheets anymore. At least there was no blood that I could see.

Leona sashayed her way over to Hexene and me, both of us recoiling to slam into the door behind us. Leona ran her nails softly over our cheeks. All I could think of were the retractable claws that had carved this place up. "Now, what shall we do?"

"Arrested, remember? I'm surrendering. Not in a sexy way."

"I think it's sexy."

"Rat feces!"

"Why do you keep doing that?" She sighed, turned, and walked into the room.

Hexene was glaring at me so hard I was worried her eyes might pop out of her skull. She probably wanted to hex me and was upset she couldn't. "Who is this maniac?" she whispered.

"Leona Pryde. She's the concierge."

Leona was at a tray of crystal decanters, mixing herself a drink. "Want something while we talk?"

"Sure. Scotch and soda?"

"And what about you, Red?"

"Shirley Temple?"

"Oh, that's adorable," Leona said.

"Shirley Temple?" I whispered at Hexene.

She shrugged.

We advanced into the room side by side, watching Leona intently for any signs of her transformation into a jaguar. So far she had shown none, unless jaguars were nature's bartenders. Leona turned, holding a glass of amber and a glass of red. "Scotch and soda for the man, Shirley Temple for the witch." She winked. "Oh, come now, Red. I know a maiden when I see one."

We accepted the drinks.

"Now try to loosen up," Leona said, "and tell me why you'd sail all the way over here just to surrender."

"Well, that wasn't the original plan," I said. "Things changed when I saw... there was a man, well, not a man. I mean, he *was* a man. He's not now."

"Get to a point, detective."

"Mobster!"

"What?"

"He's some kind of enforcer or button man or something for the Bellum mob. He's a zombie. You've seen him. Natty pinstriped suit, matching fedora? And there's the steel turtleneck."

"I see," said Leona.

"He's moving against your boss somehow. The Bellum mob wants Isla Calavera, and you know them. They're not a bunch of social workers. They tried to get me to bring a... a *cat* to the island."

Leona nodded. "Thank you for bringing this to my attention, Mr. Moss."

The door opened behind us. I turned. De Kay lurched into the room, pistol trained on me and Hexene.

"You're talking about my associate, Mr. de Kay," Leona said.

"I don't see a cat," said Sarah Bellum, her voice crackling from the speaker at de Kay's throat.

"Brains," de Kay whispered.

THIRTY-FIVE

The .45 in de Kay's hand was as blunt and gray as the zombie holding it. I half-expected skin to come off the thing in sooty sheaves. As it turned out, it was difficult to look past the barrel leveled at my heart to notice much more about the situation. "It's loaded with silver bullets," Bellum rasped in her smoky voice. "Isn't that funny? I haven't had to kill a meatstick in so long I don't have any lead bullets lying around."

"Brains," de Kay agreed.

"I can wait if you want to save the cash."

"Very funny, meatstick."

Hexene and I backed up into the room, hands raised. From this range, de Kay didn't have to be much of a shot, and I had a feeling that when applying for a job as mob enforcer, one's aim was something that came up on the interview. Bullets would kill a witch as well. Not as easily as dousing them in water, and not as easily as bullets killed a human, but a witch, especially one without her powers, was far from bulletproof. Hexene knew it too, and was visibly seething.

Sarah Bellum must have noticed as well. "Got a beef, sweetie?" she asked.

"Get that mug's gun out of my face," Hexene growled. "Or I'll turn him into a tadpole."

"I don't think so, Red. You make a move, and my 'mug' will put so much silver in you, they'll be using your corpse as werewolf repellent."

"Brains," de Kay confirmed.

"Drop the satchel, Red," Bellum said.

"Brains," de Kay implied.

Hexene, still seething, unshouldered her satchel and set it on the bed.

"Oh, you two," the purring voice came from between us, soft breath on my neck. Smooth white arms came around our shoulders, holding drinks. Leona leaned in, trying to get as much of her body on the both of us as she could. Just like that, I realized I had some hope, but I'd have to ease into it.

So to speak.

"Look, I see what's happening here. Leona, you want to stab your boss in the back... which is fine. He's a jerk, a goon, you name it. If it's bad, it applies to that palooka. You hooked up with the Bellum mob... er... company. Fraternal organization... they're sort of like the Elks, I guess..." Hexene elbowed me. "The point is, you want this casino. Here's the news: I don't care. This doesn't involve me in the slightest. You're all welcome to it, and when you take out Kong, I'll be the guy jumping for joy."

"And I'm supposed to believe that?" Bellum asked.

"It's the truth."

Bellum laughed, the rasp in her voice and the crackle in the speaker turning it into a horrible scratching, like the sound of a hundred zombies trying to pile into a red car. "Truth is remarkably fluid. What's true during the moments I have Mr.

de Kay's pistol pointed at your heart becomes untrue when you're home and safe. You might honestly believe you're no threat to me, but you already proved what a weasel you are when you didn't bring the cat."

"He mentioned you asked for a *cat*," Leona said in horrified disgust. I felt her recoil, as though the cat were suddenly in the room. "I figured he was lying like a meatstick."

"Relax. It was for our mutual friend."

"I don't like this."

"Stop playing the wide-eyed girl off the bus from Grover's Corners. You want this the same as us."

"Not if it involves *cats*."

"You three seem to have a lot to work out," I said, and started to leave.

"Stay where you are," Bellum said.

"Brains," de Kay agreed. The gun came up again.

"I thought we decided since I don't care, I should just... you know, and if de Kay here needs an alibi, we can say he and I were at a ballgame."

"You and I had a deal. You broke that deal. Now I'm going to pay you what you're owed."

"It's all right. I work gratis a lot of the time."

That didn't work, either. Not that I expected it would. So I was going to have to use the only weapon I had at my disposal. "Hey, Leona. I was just thinking about... you know... sex and so on."

"What?" Leona said.

"What?" Hexene said.

"What?" Bellum said.

"Brains?" de Kay said.

"You know, sex. Um, when men and women are sort of... you know... intimate. Together. In various states of, uh, of undress. In the dark?"

"Oh?" Leona said.

"Nick, what the hell are you doing?" Hexene hissed at me.

"Yeah, so I was thinking all four of us should have sex. In the next five minutes or so. Yeah. I am very ready for sex." I tried to sound convincing. It did not work.

"Oh, you *are* a naughty boy, aren't you?" Leona said. She wasn't asking, no matter what the lilt at the end said. I was a naughty boy in her mind, and that was the best thing in the world. Of course, what I was doing was also extremely stupid. But that's what you're left with, with a gun in front and a not-yet-furry killing machine behind.

"What are you doing? Cut that out!" Bellum snapped.

"Brains!" de Kay insisted.

"Yeah. All four of us. Five if you count the brainiac on the other end of the radio. Ooo. Yeah. Um."

"Mr. de Kay, shoot him, please!"

"Ohhhhhh, yeeeeee..." And the moan turned into a snarl. I knew what was happening behind me, and I knew I was a dead man if I hesitated. I was probably a dead man regardless, but Mama Moss raised an optimist.

I dropped to the floor and yanked Hexene along with me. "Nick! I'm not going to—"

She didn't get the rest out, because she saw what I had done. The jaguar that had been Leona Pryde was sailing over our heads. She would have tackled us both to the ground and had our backs all for her own. Instead, she slammed into de Kay and they both went sprawling to the floor. The gun went off like a clap of thunder in the room. A shatter came from behind, and then a stiff, chill wind. Leona reached for his head, her mouth opened wide as a snake's, her huge canines ready to drill into his skull. He caught her, undead strength barely keeping the big cat from finishing him. The gun was dropped—somewhere, I couldn't see—and forgotten. Now it was time for the two monsters to battle it out.

I got up, untangling myself from Hexene. "Come on!"

"My satchel!"

It was on the bed, right above their wrestling forms. "Leave it!"

"Stay where you are!" Bellum crackled, almost drowned out by the jaguar's growls and hisses. "We're not finished yet!"

Leona tore into de Kay, shredding the natty suit with swipes from her terrible claws. They were effectively blocking the front door. I turned to the window. Well, it wasn't like my business was in the hotel proper anyway. I ran to the window and poked my head out.

We were up on the fifth floor, with several more above. Each floor had a terrace of jungle plants, all lush green with flowers and fruits in all the colors of the rainbow, running around it in irregular loops. All the vegetation was thrashing around in the salty wind tearing off the gray Pacific. Lightning crawled over the black surface of the clouds, sometimes spinning off into a globe of crackling energy. It was angry and unnatural and terrifyingly close.

I stepped out of the window and the wind tried to rip me off the side of the hotel and fling me into the bay. I pressed myself against the stone wall, putting as much of the greenery between the wind and me as I could.

The *Merry Celestial* was just setting off across the channel, a few tourists huddling in groups along the deck. The glowing crew moved about, free of any worry about rough seas or cold wind. There was a freedom in already being dead. There I was, envying ghosts. Not the best sign.

"Nick! What the hell are you doing?" Hexene had poked her head out of the window, the wind tossing her hair around in an angry, fiery mass.

"Getting out of there!" I shouted back.

She glanced back in the room and must have seen something worse than what was out here, because she crawled out next to me. The terrace was a little over a foot wide, bordered in stone, with moist soil and the plants now whipping around and smacking my legs. This planter ended and another one a foot higher started, then another a foot lower. I guess the idea was to show off the kinds of ledges you would see on a volcano. Then again, by shaping the front like a giant skull, they had already made some concessions as to verisimilitude.

"Do you have a plan?" she shouted. When those waterspouts dancing through the ocean got closer, talking was going to be impossible.

I pointed. "There!"

She followed my finger to one of the floating step pyramids tethered to the main hotel with chains and slender gondola lines. The pyramid seemed to move in the wind, the lines bouncing and shifting. The car was at the crown of the hotel.

"What about it?"

"That's where Kong lives. If he's created a new monster, that's where he's hiding it!" That, or information about it. I didn't have to elaborate. Hexene nodded and followed me from the terrace we were on to the next one. Gusts of wind kept coming and the salt bit my eyes. I concentrated on the fact that I had held onto Serendipity through the freezing Pacific. I could hang onto some stone that didn't even have a slime coating.

I climbed to the higher planter and Hexene clambered up after, having some difficulties between her dress, the bulky coat from the Gloom Room, and her hair. I offered a hand and was strangely happy when she slapped it away. Turns out, imminent death was the best thing to bring out the old Hexene. I kept an eye on her just in case and kept moving along the terraces. At the highest in the level, I reached for the lowest on the next. My fingers curled around the stone and I hoisted myself up into the soft, wet dirt. For that maneuver, Hexene accepted a hand, but only after she tried it herself first. I didn't make a big thing of it, just reaching down and feeling her hand curl around my forearm. She barely weighed anything, and between the two of us, we got her hauled in.

Concentrating on the climbing was the key. Ignore the increasing distance to the ground. Ignore the apocalyptic weather. Ignore the fact that as soon as Leona came down from her present mania, she'd be unleashing the entirety of the Isla Calavera security staff on us. Ignore the fact that I'd just tried to kill a Bellum mob enforcer. We climbed up through the plants that smelled like every exotic piece of fruit I could imagine, going higher and higher for a gondola that would take us to a stone structure somehow floating even higher.

The gondola itself was not visible from where I was. The cable disappeared into what looked like a cave in the phony lava rock, and I figured the car would be inside, waiting to be loaded up. I had no idea how we were going to get into it. It was unlikely that someone as important as Kong would leave it unguarded, especially with the Bellum mob sniffing around.

We were several floors away, clambering up another set of terraces, when a grinding sound cut through the howl of the wind. I knew what was happening before I saw it. The gondola was moving. No telling when it would come back down again.

"Hexene! We have to move faster!" I'm not certain she heard me or if she came to the same conclusion. She quickened the pace, even though her breathing was ragged and her skin had gone stark white. I probably didn't look much better. Wouldn't that be funny? A world full of monsters, and it would be weather that killed me. Yeah, that's hilarious, let's all take some time to sit down and laugh.

I hoisted myself up to the next terrace and hauled Hexene in behind me. She staggered, her chest heaving so hard I thought she was going to pass out. I tried to catch her, and she feebly shook me off and mounted the next terrace. I boosted her and this time she gave me a hand, but truth be told, she didn't have much strength behind it. I used the ledge just as a gust buffeted us both into the wall. The storm was turning angry. It had probably started to rain over LA. Out here, it was wind and lightning, as though the thing knew it had a shot at taking out one of the people who had bottled it up for so long, now that she was without her powers.

I got to my feet, staggered again, and the grinding grew louder. The gondola was emerging from its cave. It was about the size of half a bus, and through the windows, I could see the shadows of large maid carts and what I assumed were their attendant maids. The car was only a few terraces away, and there was no way I could miss my window. I jumped up to the next terrace, pulled Hexene up behind me, and repeated, trying not to concentrate on the gondola crawling from its lair.

We scrambled up the side, around the cave. The car was almost all the way out. I fell onto the terrace just above it and my legs tried to give out. *No more standing for you today, we've been pushed to the limit.* One thing ten years of war taught me was that the human body had limits, but the minute you accepted them was the same minute you died. So I got to my feet and staggered forward, out of control, tipping and falling off the edge of the terrace.

I had no way to check to see if the gondola was still there or not. I was either going over at that moment, or I was missing my ride.

I plunged over, and was relieved to see the white metal roof of the gondola rushing up to meet me. Here's where some very specialized training I had came in handy: the U.S. Army had drilled into my brain how to fall from a great height, and while this wasn't more than ten feet, my body responded like the gondola was Normandy anyway. I hit the surface and rolled, coming up in a relatively graceful crouch. It barely made any noise, and over the howl of the wind and the frequent crash of thunder, the zombies in the car probably wouldn't attach much significance to it. I turned to grin at Hexene and saw she was still on the terrace. The gondola was clearing the station. In few moments, it would be out of reach.

"Hexene! It's all right! You can stay there! We'll meet up later and..."

But this was Hexene we're talking about. My attempt at reassurance had the exact opposite effect as intended on her, and she went from a slightly sick expression swaying on the edge of the terrace to a full-blown leap. The wind really did have it out for her. A gust chose that moment to plow off the Pacific, slamming into Hexene while she was in midair. With the wind plastering her dress to her body, it was clear that she was mostly skin and bones under it. Wearing a dress that could almost be a sail.

I had no time to think. I lunged for the edge of the gondola, reaching for her. She reached back, more terror on her face than I'd ever seen, and I knew, just *knew*, the wind was going to be vindictive and send her spinning to the earth. I was on the edge, only inches from falling myself, and another gust could easily nudge me over the side to join Hexene. I didn't care. I reached.

My hand closed over her wrist.

And hers over mine.

She swung over, and I hauled her in. She hit the side of

the gondola with a muffled "oof" and lost her grip. I didn't, though. I pulled her in and we lay on the gondola, me looking up at the gray sky and her face-down, both of us crouched in the partial lee of the steel beams connecting it to the cable.

I tried to listen for the zombies moving around inside, giving some indication they'd heard us land on the roof or glimpsed Hexene out the window. I couldn't hear anything. Whatever the wind wasn't muffling, my pounding heart did an admirable job of drowning out. I huddled in Harry Foote's jacket and waited for a zombie to poke her head out of the hatch near the back to have a look.

A thump nearly popped me out of my own skin. Another followed, then another. Something hit me in the head. I winced, pressing backward into the steel, trying to get something above me, as I reached down to the white roof and chased around what had got me. An irregular cylinder of ice, about the size of my knuckle.

Hail. It was hailing.

I nearly laughed. Hexene, looking as bedraggled and miserable as I'd ever seen her, glared at me. "What?"

"Hail. Of all the luck."

"Not seeing the humor in this, Nick."

"You think zombies are going to check on us when hard things are falling from the sky?"

"They're falling on *us*."

"I know—ow—but they won't kill us."

"Any bigger and they might."

I shrugged. "I take it where I can get it."

The roof of the cable car was freezing, the hail drumming off it in parade cadence. Across the channel, martian tripods and gremlin flying saucers moved through the black fog like the smoke of a burning town. Three waterspouts twirled for the mainland, ready to chew up some of the city. Hell of a thing I was into. For want of a toad, a city was lost.

I kept my back up against another piece of steel, and Hexene did the same across from me. I took the odd hailstone in the leg and shoulder, a small price to pay for the relative safety of the ride.

Safety—there was something really funny. Only I could think of being on top of a giant metal box a hundred feet off the ground and filled with zombies in the middle of a lightning storm as safe. And then there was the ultimate goal: the floating step pyramid that was home to Kublai Kong.

Thirty-Six

It was my first time seeing a floating pyramid up close. Oh, like anyone else, I saw them flying around the city every now and again. They weren't the most common sight, but they were far from rare, and with the size of them, pretty hard to miss. In their pace, they were either stately or plodding, depending on your point of view. I suppose it hinged on how impressed people were that a multi-ton stone building was levitating above them. The jaguar people never revealed how they did it; some kind of trade secret. I wondered if their presence here meant Kong was in on the secret, or if the balam merely gave him a few to keep the big ape happy.

But I wasn't here for industrial espionage. I was here looking for something on that robot-ape at the center of this whole mess.

The pyramids were the kind that came from the jungles of Central and South America. Or so I'd heard somewhere. Supposedly, the balam first appeared somewhere south of the border and had spread fairly rapidly. Easy to understand how an extremely attractive group with flying houses could find ways to acclimatize to new places. There was some anti-balam prejudice, or so I'd gathered from a few dropped comments by other monsters, calling them loose and immoral, with a few pushes to increase the sky patrols at the border. Seemed like a waste of time to me. Just set some cats out. But monsters had a real squeamishness when it came to using one another's weaknesses. If they started with one, where would it stop?

The pyramid had nine terraces, each one several times the size of a human, and staircases on three of its four sides. The remaining side had a door for Kong. It had been mostly concealed from the casino below, but on this side it was plainly visible. A small, square building stood at the top. That was where we were headed, into a structure that looked like a temple on the outside, but was a station for the gondola on the inside. Along every surface, reliefs had been carved into the stone, visible at this range even through the storm. They all had a similar theme: giant ape fights something and wins. He even kept the crown on in most of the depictions.

The cable car ground upward, the hail continuing to drum and the storm continuing to howl. Hexene huddled miserably in her corner, her hair hiding her face except in isolated moments when the wind would expose a slice of stark white skin beneath the fluttering copper-red.

The shadowed station enveloped us. The hail stopped its pervasive drumming. The wind was cut; not absent, because of the open doorways on all four sides, but blunted somewhat. The room was gray stone, with a line of frescoes along the top displaying Kong—there's no real polite way to say this—*cavorting* with a variety of women. These women were, by and large, human-sized, rendering some of the reliefs objectively horrifying. For no logical reason, I was ashamed. As though I was the sculptor, and I had dragged Hexene up to my flying pleasure temple to show her some banned etchings. At least the blushing put some warmth back in my skin.

Hexene started to move, and I put a hand out, mouthing, "Wait." She did.

The doors of the gondola opened. Immediately following were the choruses of "Brains" that told us the zombies were moving. After a second, the first one came into view, pushing a room service cart piled high with bananas. The next one followed with a similarly laden cart. The next cart held several jugs filled with daiquiris, and I was willing to bet they were banana-flavored. Two more carts followed with assorted fruit, and the final one was covered in several roast suckling pigs. The zombies weren't maids as I'd thought, but porters. They were in simple uniforms of slacks, shirts, vests, and bowties. Probably delivering Kong's afternoon feast. They shambled to the end of the room, where an industrial elevator waited. It fit the whole crew, carts and all, and a moment later, Hexene and I were alone in the room.

I hopped off the gondola, stumbling on stiff feet. I reached up and Hexene let me help her down. I kept my hands on her waist, doing my best to ignore how good that felt.

Hexene scowled. "If I could use my broom, we would have been up here in seconds."

"If you could use your broom, we wouldn't be here."

"I know," she said, like it was my fault.

"We're close, Hexene. I can feel it."

She nodded and turned away to look out one of the openings. I saw her angrily wipe her nose, so I let her think she'd fooled me. I poked around for a way down that didn't involve using the same elevator as the zombies. The cable car swayed in the center of the room, fitting snugly into a groove carved for it, with less than half a foot of clearance between it and the floor. The rest of the room was mostly bare. Kong saw no reason to impress his servants, and any real guest would be carried up by the monkey khan himself.

I found a doorway on the other side of the room. The door itself was incongruously normal. I would have expected some carved stone, but it was the same kind of exterior metal door found on the hotel below. It was unlocked, opening to reveal a narrow staircase going down. I smiled at Kong's hubris. Of *course* no one would be breaking into his place. Someone would have to be crazy to do that. That seemed to be the consensus on me, though. Crazy Nick, the only human PI. I called Hexene over and started the descent.

A little more than one story down, we came to the first door. I opened it up and found that we were on a narrow walkway some eighty feet above the floor. The room was huge in a way that I had not previously understood something could *be* huge. I hadn't been around anything so big except for the few times I had been on a naval vessel and got a look at the real behemoths of the fleet. This counted, a vaulted room built for someone fifty feet tall who really liked his headroom and was an excellent climber. The walls and floor were stone, and there were more of the obscene frescoes everywhere. A copse of fake trees sprouted from some fake turf on one side of the room, and a miniature Empire State Building stood on the other. I had to pause at that one. I had heard those stories of the monkey khan taken down in the Big Apple, but I figured those were hokum. Begged the question why Kong would want a reminder. Maybe it was religious. Cultural. Or maybe Los Angeles didn't have high enough buildings to scale.

The walkway ran around the room, just above the frescoes, and what looked like an impossibly delicate spiral staircase led to the ground in one corner. A single exit sized for Kong was open off to our right, next to the staircase. Beyond, a few shapes loomed, but the sheer size of everything made it difficult to understand what anything was.

The doors to the elevators opened. I hadn't noticed them until they moved, as they were done up as fake bricks. The zombies came out, pushing their carts with a strange combination of drunken staggering and military precision. I nudged Hexene and the two of us started creeping toward the staircase.

It was then that I noticed what I had taken to be nothing but a pile of tiger furs around the base of the trees start to move. Jayne Doe, wrapped in a leopard-print bikini that looked more like Pilar's than seemed decent, freed herself from the pile. Her hair and makeup were, of course, perfect. Doppelgangers.

"Good morning," she said to the zombies. Though nothing colored her face, the subdued tone said embarrassment.

The zombies responded with a series of respectful, "Brains."

Jayne Doe flashed a brittle smile, but the zombies didn't pay any attention. They delivered their carts and shambled back to the elevator.

"Excuse me?" Jayne said

One of the zombies turned.

"When will Mr. Kong be back?"

"Brains."

"Oh. Right. Sorry."

The zombie shrugged sadly—or maybe I was projecting my own frustration on him—and continued his shuffle to the elevator. Jayne went to the cart and selected some kind of spined fruit that had to be the product of a bored and fruit-loving mad scientist, or perhaps a cross-breeding killer vegetable. She bit into it with a worried expression that brightened immediately. I waited, crouched on the walkway, silently cursing at Jayne

Doe while she ate that fruit. *Go somewhere else, for God's sake.*

Eventually she did, wandering off to someplace below my feet I couldn't see. I thought I heard the thunk of a door, and she didn't reappear. It was good enough for the time being, and Hexene and I eased down the spiral staircase. It was thin metal, but not delicate. It just looked that way in comparison to the skyscraper that Kong clearly had in the room to do some climbing.

On the ground, I had the same feeling I'd had in Pilar's house. The furniture here was far more customized, but it loomed over me just the same. The door Jayne disappeared into was human-sized. Probably a bathroom for kongquests to clean up after whatever it was they did. I didn't want to think about it too much, but the frescoes had already given me an unwelcome education.

I crept to the corner of the open doorway and peered inside. It was an office, maybe half the size of the living room. It was far more human-looking, in that it actually had a desk, though where there should have been a chair was another fake tree. There was also a fake skull on the front of the desk, leering at whoever was coming through the door, and angled for visitors my size. A little extra intimidation for those for whom a fifty-foot ape wasn't enough. Masks decorated the walls, the same tribal styles as the ones in the casino, but these were sized for someone like Kong. A stuffed dinosaur stood by the wall. At this point, I was just going to assume it was real. That way, when one inevitably jumped out at me, I could die with a smug, know-it-all look on my face. Aggie Brooks would have loved the thing. It had the leathery skin I saw in her books, stood on two powerful clawed legs, and had a head that looked like it could comfortably bite a ship in half.

I gave the door beyond which Jayne Doe was doing whatever it was she was doing a final glance and slunk into the office proper. Getting closer did not do much to mitigate the sheer size and power of Kong's furnishings. The dinosaur in particular only grew meaner. I would not have been at all surprised if the thing started moving at any moment. Whoever had created that beast had done an impressive job.

We jogged over the stone floor to the desk. The main skull was decorated with other, smaller skulls. Kong had apparently missed one of the most well-known of design secrets in the post-Night War world: one skull goes a long way. Then again, what does a five-thousand-ton gorilla decorate his office with? Whatever he wants.

We got to the desk just as the sound of the door faintly reached us. Hexene and I easily hid behind its leg. Jayne Doe, now dressed, passed in front of the open archway. From that distance, it was tough to see what kind of expression was on her face. The only thing left for me was whether to mention it to Pilar. Probably not. She knew what Kong was up to. She had to. And besides, she had already decided to leave the ape. Or at least give as good as she was getting.

Jayne glanced into the office once, but her gaze was too high to be searching for a couple of human interlopers, and after a moment, she made her way to the elevator. As she crossed a room built for someone nine times larger than she, I had a little time to look around. The desk appeared to be constructed like an actual building. Close up, I could see where some of the boards were fitted together, and I bet if I started pulling those away, I'd find sections of concrete and rebar. The space beneath the desk was dark, and dust bunnies as big as I was occasionally rolled over the floor like giant black tumbleweeds.

When Jayne was gone, I went to Kong's chair.

Well, "chair."

It was a gnarled and craggy tree rooted in a circular opening in the stone filled with wet soil. The bark appeared to have been stripped away, leaving some raw white flesh a vampire would have been proud of. It was an illusion, of course; the tree was as fake as everything else, or so I thought until I touched it.

It was real. Kong had gotten some mad scientist to grow him a full tree and shape it like a chair. There were even a back and arms formed from the pale branches. I grabbed a knothole and tested my weight on the tree. I felt like an idiot pretty quickly, since this thing, as brittle as it looked, habitually bore the weight of Kublai Kong. It could hold Hexene and me, and all our friends and relatives, without bowing.

Because it was at least partly natural, the tree had numerous handholds to make the ascent easier. I was doing a lot of climbing on this job, more than usual, even. I guess that's what happens when there's an ape and a robot-ape in the middle of a case. I paused at the seat, which was a densely interwoven mat of branches, hard but probably spongy enough to make Kong comfy. Hexene clambered up after me, sitting down when she saw me do the same, and sucking in great gusts of air. I let her recover, and made sure not to mention that's what I was doing.

"What are we looking for?" she asked when she got most of her wind back.

"I'm not entirely sure. Something."

"Something? Your plan is to look for *something*?"

"I never said there was a plan."

She groaned in frustration.

"I'll know when I see it," I retorted.

She flipped some of her hair from her face only to fix me with a baleful look I'd ever only seen on the face of her missing toad previously.

"I'll keep climbing," I said.

The rest of the ascent took me up the arm of the chair and ended with a leap to the top of Kong's desk. I felt like someone in a fairy tale, breaking into the giant's lair. Pretty soon he'd come home booming about the blood of an Englishman, and though I wasn't sure where my family hailed from, he was unlikely to see much of a distinction. Besides, Kong was worse than any giant. He was regularly knocking one around.

The lamp was a repurposed streetlight, presently shut off. The clock looked to be taken out of a tower and remounted in cement, a pair of life-size lions growling at it. He had a few other knickknacks, including a sculpted stone head from somewhere in the South Pacific, a green 1948 Studebaker, and a stuffed rhinoceros that looked real. I peered over the side, gave myself a shot of vertigo, and leaned back.

"Hexene?" I called. She looked up from her resting place.

"What?" she shouted back.

"I think I need you!"

"For what?"

"It would be easier if you came up here!"

She sighed and started the rest of the climb. She was so awkward between the dress, the fatigue, and the wasting whatever-it-was afflicting her while her toad was out of reach, that I instantly regretted calling her up. Yet telling her to stay would only make her more determined to climb up and probably earn me a punch in the jaw now that she could no longer hex me as she liked. She made it to the arm of the chair, then had to contend with a five-foot leap to make it to the top of the desk. She jumped, and didn't object when I caught and steadied her on the other side.

"Nick?"

"Yeah?"

"You can let go."

"Oh, right. Sorry. I, uh, I wanted to steady myself." I let her go.

"Why am I here?"

"We need to open the drawers. I don't think I can do that."

She peeked over the side. The desk drawers had gold handles about the size of hammocks. "How?"

"Well... um... I'll show you." I hunkered down, grabbed the edge of the desk, and hung over the side. I tried to forget that slipping would lead to a pair of broken legs in the office of the monster that had constituted my nightmares for years, and instead concentrated on putting my feet into the desk. There was a tiny gap between drawer and desk, and if I could wedge enough weight in there, I might be able to get it open wide enough to slip inside.

"You just look like you're hanging there and turning red."

"Right," I gasped. "I'm moving... I'm trying to... just don't let me fall."

Hexene knelt and took my wrists. Someone a little stronger, which could have been almost anyone in her present state, would have been preferable. Or the old, strong, flying Hexene would be even better. At least I could still trust her not to turn me.

I wiggled my feet under the desk, knowing I was tilting my weight dangerously far from Hexene, where I'd be even harder to hold. I tried to take solace in the fact that though I was heavier than in the old days, I was still light and lean. Hexene promptly turned red, her fingers biting into my wrists.

My heels slid into the gap. I wedged my feet in there and levered my body up. My fingers slid on the desk, white and aching from bearing almost my entire weight. I wiggled. I pushed. The drawer was too heavy. All that time and risk to get nothing.

The drawer creaked. I wiggled some more. My fingers felt like they might like to fall off. I bore down, pushing and shoving. The drawer steadily opened. And then my fingers gave out.

Hexene might have screamed, had shock let her do much of anything. I had time to reflect that this wasn't the way I thought I'd go.

And I landed on a not-entirely hard surface only a few feet down. I sat up, and whatever I was sitting on kept sliding around. I reached down and found something to pick up. It was a photograph.

"Nick? Nick, are you okay?"

"Yeah. I think so. Photos broke my fall."

"What?"

I looked up. Hexene was peering over the side into the open drawer. What little light got in showed me a massive pile of photos. To Kong, these would have been about the size of a postage stamp, and that's what this looked like: the stamp collection of a man who had yet to mount them in a book. I stood up carefully, the slick surface shifting underneath me. I held the picture up to the light coming through the gap in the drawer.

Kublai Kong was scaling the fake Empire State Building in his living room, and clutched in his hand was a woman, her blonde hair fluttering outward. I tossed it away and picked up another. Same thing, only he was in the tree, and she was in a leopard-print bikini. I knelt and picked up picture after picture. In most, he was scaling something with the woman in his hand. In others, he was facing off against the stuffed dinosaur in his office, beating his chest while the blonde—she was always a blonde; even in black and white, I could tell—cowered beneath them. I looked at the massive pile I was standing on and shook my head.

"What is it?" Hexene asked.

"Well, I have a heap of evidence he's a cad."

"Nothing on the mystery monster."

"Not unless it's under all of this." I looked around, knowing I didn't have the time, and whatever I needed to find was probably not in here. I boosted myself up onto the lip of the drawer, turned around, and climbed onto the desk.

"Time for the other side."

My fingers were still throbbing and after I wedged the second desk drawer open, they were in full revolt. When I wasn't using them to bear my entire weight, I was cradling them close to my chest. In the other drawer, I found pens sized to Kong's liking and an inkwell I could have bathed in, but nothing that indicated any knowledge of the new monster. Not even any orange hair that I could see. I cursed Percy Katz again for taking my flashlight, then wearily boosted myself out. Hexene and I climbed back down the tree-chair to the floor.

I led the way over to the other doorway. The room beyond, hidden by a small foyer that blocked a clean view inside, was a bedroom. At least, that's what I took it to be. More trees like the one Kong used for a desk chair grew out of a larger hole in the stone floor. These were woven together, and unlike the picked-clean chair, were covered in lush branches and leaves. A pair of slippers, each one the size of a sedan, sat side-by-side next to the bed. I peeked into another archway and found a bathroom. Kong had a bathtub and a toilet, and I could have gone my whole life without thinking about the unholy amount of waste he had to be making.

"Are you all right?" Hexene asked.

"Yep. Nope. Had a... a thought."

She nodded sympathetically.

I went back into the bedroom with the growing realization that I was going to come up empty. If not Kong, then who? Foote? There hadn't been any evidence of another monster at his place. Granted, any discovery of orange hair wouldn't have proven a thing. I went to the other doorway, which led into a darkened closet. By what little light was filtering in, I could see what Kong thought were clothes. There were silk robes that could have provided parachutes for an entire company, bangles and bracers, and a whole selection of crowns. I always figured that one crown was all anyone needed. Turns out I was wrong.

I turned to Hexene to tell her we were out of luck when I heard a voice from behind me say, "What the hell are you doing in here?"

Thirty-Seven

The voice came from a set of eyes glowing softly amongst a mass of shadows that might be limbs. The eyes were almond-shaped with no iris, and only a slit pupil. A bogeyman. More specifically, Lurkimer Closett, the coward hiding under Kong's throne and translating the monkey khan's grunts and ululations for the rest of us. The bogeyman was in the shadows under a rack of giant gold and silver tubes I realized later were greaves for Kong's shins when he wanted to play Caesar.

I was at the end of my rope, and the last thing I needed was Closett running back to his master via whatever shadowy back roads bogeymen used to suddenly appear in dark places. I don't think he was expecting what came next either, and our mutual surprise at what it was let me manage it.

I lunged at him. My left hand grabbed a wad of hair. My right hand wrapped around something that might have been scales. And I hauled him in.

"No! No! What are you doing?!"

"Closett, you are going to tell me everything you know or I

am dragging you out into the sun!"

"Oh, please no!" Closett blubbered.

"Everything you know!" I growled, yanking him farther out.

"Okay, okay! The internal combustion engine works by creating tiny explosions! Roulette has the worst odds of any casino game! Kublai Kong passes gas whenever he has milk and it's awful! The grizzly bear is surprisingly social in the wild! Ghouls cheat at dice by using their teeth!"

"What?" My grip slackened, but Closett never noticed.

"Ghouls. They take out their teeth and rattle them when the dice are rolling, it changes what numbers come up. It's like weighted dice, but not as reliable."

"No, I mean, what are you saying?"

"You told me to tell you everything I know."

"Oh. Okay, well, that was my fault. Sorry. I want to know a few things specifically."

Closett's elastic bogeyman eyes had gone from menacing almond shapes to almost perfectly round, just like his pupils. "Which things?"

"Kong created a new monster, probably with the assistance of a robot. I want to know about it."

The eyes were now upside-down arcs. "The Mighty Kong has never made another kind of monster."

"Don't lie to me!"

"I'm not, I'm not! Oh god, I promise I'm not!"

"The monsters, they look like orange apes with TVs for heads. What do you know about them?"

"Prime-8! You mean Prime-8! I know him!"

"You know him? Who is he? What is he?"

"I don't know! I see him around every now and then. He stays at the casino, I think. He's the only one of those I've ever seen... orangutrons! They're called orangutrons!"

"Who called them that?"

"I don't know!" Closett howled. I was inclined to believe him.

"All right, Closett, I need you to calm down. Can you calm down for me?"

"Oh god, I'll calm down, I swear!"

"Closett. Come on. I need you to think: where did this... orangutron? Orangutron. Where did he come from?"

"I don't know. I swear, I don't know. The Great Kong didn't make him. He would have mentioned something. And he would have put Prime-8 up somewhere special. A room or a suite, and Leona would have handled it. But it didn't matter! He was just another guest! We had to kick him out."

"Kick him out? Why?"

"Because he's like a robot. He calculated the odds on everything and he was winning too much. And when he did lose, he started shrieking and destroying gaming tables. The Imperious Kong slapped him with a lifetime ban. I still see him around the island from time to time, but not in the casino."

Maybe Closett hadn't been around for the creation. I switched tracks. "What about robots? Does Kong have any robot associates?"

"The Invincible Kong had a robot ally..."

"Who? Where?"

"His name was Zzzolt."

"Was?"

"He was killed three years ago. Meatsticks got him with a bucket of water."

1952 again. The witch and her kidnapped familiar, Kong's arrival, JJ's disappearance. That year was dogging me throughout this whole thing, like I was supposed to make up for every mistake, every moment of cowardice, every last failure in the final year I thought humanity had a shot.

What this particular mention of '52 meant was beyond

me, at least for the time being. That Kong knew a robot didn't guarantee he created these orangutrons with him, but it was an indicator of... something. '52 was still the Night War, with the Treaty not getting signed until March of the following year. If a monster was created then, why hadn't I seen it? Why hadn't it hunted me?

Closett must have seen me woolgathering. He lashed out, shoving me with half a dozen arms, and I lost my grip on his scales. He skittered back into the dark, leaving me with a handful of brownish hair. His shadowy mass was abruptly gone from the closet. He would be down in the casino, calling security.

"We have to get out of here," I said to Hexene.

She nodded. We ran for the stairs, not wanting to wait for the elevator. The spiral staircase rattled under our thudding steps. My legs were screaming at me, but I could ignore it. Not tomorrow. I'd be in pain then, but better pain tomorrow than another session before Kong's throne. We raced along the walkway to the stairs, and from there, to the temple on the roof.

The gondola was far across the cable, just emerging from the hotel. Jayne Doe had ridden it down, and now security was on its way. Closett was efficient, I'll give him that. The wind staggered us and the hailstones had become icy fat drops of rain, blown sideways into the temple to sting our eyes. Hexene winced when the drops hit her exposed skin. She wouldn't dissolve in rain, but it would hurt. I wished there were another way—or even one way. I went to the edge of the temple and looked down. The effect was dizzying: the stone staircase led to more than a hundred-foot drop. The tops of trees were distantly visible below. It was an invitation to die.

"Come on," I said, starting down the stairs.

"Where are you going?" Hexene shouted over the wind.

"We can't wait for the cable car!"

"There's nowhere else to go!"

The swimming pools were far away, behind the hotel, but the bay was fairly close, assuming we went around the pyramid. There was definitely the ghost of a chance we could make it. "The ocean!"

"Are you crazy?"

Oh. Right. If Hexene went swimming, she'd melt. In my panic, I had forgotten, even though she was huddling deeper into her borrowed coat, trying to keep the rain off her. She had kept her weaknesses, but lost all of her powers. Great deal for her.

"Right! Sorry!" I staggered down the steps, leaning backward so if the wind ripping at my body knocked me off my feet, I would be thrown into the stone pyramid rather than the earth below. "We'll figure something out! I promise!"

"You can't promise me that," she screamed, but followed me down nonetheless. The wind was crueler to her, just by virtue of there being less of Hexene than there was of me. She was nearly blind, too, what with all that hair hitting her in the face, though at least it was blocking the rain. I reached out and grabbed her hand and she grabbed back. Her hand was warm and her grip was tight. I felt little puffs of warmth when raindrops hit her: smoke coming off her skin. I had no idea what I was doing, yet Hexene was trusting me, and I would get her out of this. What had I done to inspire that, exactly? Or was this the more likely scenario of any port in a literal storm?

The gondola was halfway up the cable when we reached the bottom of the staircase. The stone just ended. Where there should be earth, there was air. No railing. Just better than a hundred feet of drop. The wind wanted to introduce me to that drop, and unlike the last time I had stood staring at an impossible fall, I wasn't wearing a parachute. And instead of armed Germans waiting down there, there were a variety of monsters right out of a nightmare.

I'll say this for Kong, he knew his cue. He burst out of the Isla Calavera casino with a boom, landing on the open roundabout that welcomed guests to his West Coast pleasure palace. Had there been anyone out front, on a day when the sky wasn't falling, I imagined them scattering like tenpins as Kong bounded through the door. The monkey khan's crown was askew and his face was contorted in rage. He looked up at the pyramid I was clinging to and roared.

I froze. The last time I heard that particular roar, the wall of Gilmore Field had come tumbling down, and that monster gorilla's mitt had come through it like the judgment of a hungry god. He hadn't spotted me, but he was here for *me* specifically—whatever had the temerity to break into his home—and was going to take what was due. There wouldn't even be enough of me left to bury. Eclipsing the perfectly rational fear of a giant and hopping-mad ape was the instinctive fear. I was a prey animal, and even though there was no point in freezing, I did it anyway.

"Nick! Nick?" Hexene was screaming. At first, I thought maybe the wind had learned my name. She was pulling at me. "Nick! You have to move! He's coming!"

I might as well have been a statue. I wanted to tell Hexene to save herself, but there were no words.

Tiny figures boiled out of the building, stopping well away from Kong. His security, most likely, those who couldn't cram into the gondola that was partway up the cable. Kong roared again and I shivered helplessly, unable to move.

Until the slap. I blinked and gaped. Hexene cradled her hand, the wind shoving her around, her hair whipping over her face. Puffs of smoke rose into the air whenever a raindrop tapped her ashy face. "Nick! Snap out of it!"

I focused on Hexene. She was here, and not going anywhere without me. She was taking the pain and keeping it together. I nodded. "Sorry. Let's..."

Another boom sounded from the casino. I whirled around in time to see Pilar hot on Kong's heels. The antlike figures around her feet scattered. She was dressed as a jungle queen, her thin gown scarcely concealing her curves. She was already shivering. She reached out for Kong, and without hesitating in the slightest, he backhanded her across the face.

Pilar clutched her cheek with one hand, staggering backwards and catching herself on the hotel. Fear of Kong blackened to hatred. Hate. I could work with hate. I thought about the Bellum mob and wondered what I'd do if they wanted me to help rub out Kong rather than one of his flunkies, whose only crime was being a goon. Then again, that would have meant smuggling an aircraft or something, which was pretty far above my pay grade.

Kong loped for the pyramid. I had seen him leap up the night before and knew how easily he could get to us. I looked down and I saw salvation.

Or maybe just death. One or the other. So close in this line of work.

I took Hexene's hand. "We're jumping."

"You are crazy." Might have been wishful thinking, but I swear I heard a tinge of admiration over the wind.

I don't know if she saw what I had, or if she just trusted me. Regardless, we jumped off the floating pyramid into the wind and I hoped I wasn't doing the dumbest—and most final—thing of my life.

THIRTY-EIGHT

On the upside, Kraut flak wasn't exploding all around me like the world's worst Fourth of July. On the downside, the closest thing I had to a parachute was a skinny girl in a dress like an Amish quilt. I concentrated on the target below, coming at me far too fast. When I jumped out of planes, I usually had between six and eight times the space. Now the ground was right there, and it was looking mean.

I aimed for the target. I hoped the wind wouldn't pull us too far away. I hoped he was as spongy and strong as I assumed.

The nice part was, I didn't have time to check on Kong. He could do what he was going to do. I was in the process of something that very nearly qualified as a suicide attempt. That is, if this entire debacle hadn't qualified already.

I should really charge more.

I plunged into the sticky pinkish mass with a sound like someone throwing a ham hock into pudding. I had to fight the urge to take a deep breath. That wouldn't help anything. The wind was suddenly gone, only a muffled howling and a queasy wobble shaking through my surroundings. It was pleasantly warm, or at least not cold and wet.

I struggled in the mass, my eyes squeezed shut because I might be crazy enough to jump off a flying pyramid, but there's no way I was going to get blob in my eyes.

My hand burst out, the wind chilling it instantly. I fought in that direction, my lungs screaming at me. I yanked my head and shoulders out of the blob and opened my eyes. My skin stung a bit where the blob's residue clung.

I reached back in, grabbed Hexene, and hauled her out. She gasped and opened her eyes, holding onto me while our lungs reinflated. "Keyes," I gasped. "Stop trying to digest us."

"My apologies, Mr. Night Ranger!" Keyes burbled happily. "I saw you falling and I thought I should catch you! And your lady friend!" The slime flowed off of us, even the stuff that seemed like it was little more than residue, joining the central pinkish mass wobbling in the wind. We were in one of the forested plots of the Isla Calavera, and it was only by virtue of the wind moving the tree cover that I saw salvation in the form of a blob.

"I'm not his lady friend," Hexene said, but she huddled close to me. It was only to stay out of the rain, but I wasn't above counting it.

"Thanks for the catch," I said.

"Say, what do you call a man with a rubber toe?"

"I don't know. What?"

"They don't have the guts!"

Kong leapt through the air and landed on the pyramid to disappear inside. I watched the giant ape sail overhead and felt something close to religious fear.

"You said it."

"Who...?" Hexene asked, indicating the chauffeur she had just emerged from.

"Gelatin Keyes, Hexene Candlemas."

"Pleased to meet you, Miss Hexene Candlemas! I'm Gelatin Keyes!"

"Yes, um, Nick mentioned that..."

"The distance between stars is not as far as that in the human mind!"

"...he didn't mention that."

I glanced upward and could swear the pyramid was shuddering with whatever tantrum Kong was throwing inside. "Come on. Let's get somewhere else."

I headed for the back of the hotel, where the pools should have been mostly deserted. After Keyes had digested its outer layer, my skin felt both cleaner and thinner. Along the way, I paused, pulling a pair of sticks and some kind of climbing vine off a nearby tree.

Sure enough, no one was by the pools. It had grown too inhospitable even for the gill-men and the sirens. I couldn't blame them; the rain was pounding us now. Hexene had her borrowed coat up over her head, keeping the worst of it off her. She didn't look like she was dissolving—and I had never heard of a witch buying it due to rain—but the little puffs of smoke didn't look at all pleasant. Keyes didn't seem to mind the weather. He had half-absorbed his chauffeur's outfit. He probably forgot he was supposed to wear it and had mistaken it for food. To a blob, anything that couldn't outrun them was technically food, so it was hard to blame him.

"Not that I'm not glad to see you, Keyes, but what are you doing here?"

"I tasted your scent! So I followed!"

Like most things Keyes said, I tried not to think about it too hard. Otherwise they'd have to break out the butterfly nets and the jackets with the extra-long sleeves.

"Okay. And?"

Keyes just wobbled there for a moment. The decoration he had been using for a face had been entirely digested, so he was a featureless blob of pinkish ooze. "I found the man you wanted, Mr. Night Ranger! He tastes like sadness and sloth!"

"...right. And where is he?"

The blob shuddered and rose up in a gelatinous pillar, then vomited up a dark shape that had been lurking in his depths, along with the tattered remnants of the chauffeur outfit. I almost mentioned that, but figured it was between Keyes and his employer.

The shape that fell out of the blob and slid over the wet concrete, with strands and chunks of pink blob-material still clinging to it, was not Count Morlock. He was about man-sized, with a hunched posture and stone-gray skin. He had claws, a bestial face, horns, and a pair of bat wings. He was, in short, a gargoyle.

"This isn't him," I said. The gargoyle lay there as still as a statue. This might have unnerved me if it hadn't been a gargoyle.

"Are you certain, Mr. Night Ranger?"

"Why is he calling you that?" Hexene asked.

"It's a long... it doesn't... yes, I'm certain that's not him. Is that a nosferatu?"

Keyes extended a pseudopod to inspect the gargoyle.

"Don't taste him," I said.

The pseudopod recoiled. "I think that is a nosferatu!"

"That's a gargoyle!"

"How can you tell?"

"Because of the... and the... I can just tell, all right? That's not the man I told you to collect."

The gargoyle opened his eyes and blinked a few times. He clambered to his feet, fixed a stern gaze on Keyes.

"I'm terribly sorry, sir," I said to him.

He grunted, flapping his wings, and slowly, clumsily, fluttered off into the air, only to land on one of the casino's many terraces and stand there motionlessly with a fierce look on his face.

"How long was he in... you know? I don't want to know."

"What now, Mr. Night Ranger?"

"We're going to get the man I was talking about. The one you somehow managed to mistake despite me leaving you *right outside his door.*"

"Really?" Hexene asked.

I nodded.

"Wow."

"The world is a very large place! Especially with so many individuals polluting it with their confusing presences!"

I shook my head. "All right. We're going back to Room 232." I led the way into the casino via the side door, alert for any signs of jaguar people. We were quite a group, a bedraggled human, a similarly frazzled witch, and of course, the ravenous pink mass slithering along and occasionally making sounds almost like chanting. At least with Keyes, we had a fighting chance against security, though I wasn't certain I wanted to be responsible for a blob growing out of control and eating half a city. We didn't need another Philadelphia.

We entered the elevator, and the zombie operating it didn't give us a second glance. "Second floor?"

"Brains."

"Thanks."

The cage rattled shut and the three of us waited side-by-side, not talking as the elevator rose. We got out on the second floor and the zombie took his elevator elsewhere. If anyone asked him if he'd seen us, he could answer "brains" honestly.

"Say, what kind of bone will a dog never eat?"

"I don't know. What?"

"Frostbite!" Keyes blorped.

"He... he does that," I explained in the face of Hexene's baffled annoyance.

We got to the closed door of Room 232. I patted my pockets and swore.

"What?" Hexene asked.

"My tools. They're in my jacket."

"Where's your jacket?"

"With security."

"Oh. That might be a problem."

"Thank you, Hexene."

"Don't worry, Mr. Night Ranger!" Keyes extended a pseudopod and enveloped the doorknob and lock. Both were cloudy shapes under the pinkish layer of blob, and they seemed to be growing more and more blurry until a thunk came from the door. Keyes retracted. The knob, lock, and a section of wood were now gone, though a few fragmentary remainders had fallen into the room.

"Thanks, Keyes."

"Should I keep watch?"

"I remember what happened last time."

"So, yes?"

"Just come in."

The three of us went into Morlock's room. The coffin was shut. I flicked the lights on, but kept the drapes closed. Not much sunlight, but there was no reason to risk the guy's life. Whatever damage Leona had done had been repaired or hidden by the staff. They were probably used to that sort of thing, what with this place being lousy with jaguar people.

While Hexene and Keyes took up places in the room, I

opened up the coffin. Morlock was dozing peacefully inside. I shook him. He kept dozing. I shook him harder. "Morlock! Wake up!"

His lids fluttered and he smacked his lips sleepily. Then his eyes widened. "What are you doing in my room?"

"Mr. Morlock, I'm a detective..."

"I'm not doing anything illegal!" His gaze darted around the room. "And you brought a blob and a... is this another witch hunt? Are you with HUMAC?"

"Nothing like that, sir, I assure you."

"Officer, I'm just an admirer! Photography isn't illegal!"

"Mr. Morlock, if you'd just calm down for a moment."

He retreated from me only to bang his head on the coffin. He barely noticed, gathering up the rest of his long, skinny limbs into a terrified ball. "Officer! I swear! I'm not dangerous!"

His abject fear got to me. I wanted to wrap one thing up, just one thing, and his whining wasn't helping. "So breaking into her place isn't dangerous, huh? What do you call that?"

Morlock's ugly gray face contorted in confusion. "Breaking... officer, I've never done anything like that!"

"You're telling me you never went into Pilar O'Heaven's house?"

"No!"

"And you never drank any of her blood?"

Morlock swallowed, and the expression washing over his face was pure bliss. "No. N... nothing like that. I mean, I've always wanted to. Who hasn't?"

I looked at Hexene and Keyes.

"Present company excepted," Morlock said.

"You've never been to her place?"

"I never said that. It's not illegal! It's a public road, and her house is on those maps they sell on Hollywood Boulevard."

"Yeah, I guess it is." Serendipity had a collection of those things in her desk, newest on the top, and discrepancies pointed out in pen. I would have complained, but they seemed like one of those things that would inevitably come in handy before long. "So you've been to her place. At night, I expect."

"But I never went in! When I'm on the mainland, sometimes I need a... break. You know, from the stress. So I go to Miss O'Heaven's house. I just look at it! I swear!"

I frowned. "You do this a lot?"

"No."

"Don't lie to me."

"All the time."

"All right. Have you seen anyone break in?"

"It didn't look like a break-in! He went in the side door! He looked like he had a key!"

"Let me guess. It was a new kind of monster, one you hadn't seen before, or maybe only ever saw on Catalina Island. He looked like an orange ape with a television for a head."

"No. He was a mad scientist, I think. He was missing half his head, and he had this red lens over an eye."

Dr. Uriah Bluddengutz, my cellmate from my short incarceration in the pit. A mad scientist. What would... "What was he carrying? He had something with him, didn't he? Something big?"

Morlock nodded eagerly. "He did! It looked like a pair of tanks, like divers wear. He had them on his back. And there was some kind of gun!"

Not a gun. Something to draw blood. The mad scientist, right there in front of me. The hair on the lip of the pit: Prime-8 had been there. That's why Bluddengutz wasn't overly concerned with what would happen in the pit. He had his backup getting ready to spring him. Then Mr. de Kay showed up. Best laid plans of robot-apes and men.

"You're certain about this mad scientist," I said to Morlock, trying to keep my expression as neutral as possible. I didn't want to push him into a false lead, especially since this was the one that broke everything open.

"Positive. Why? Who is he?"

"No one," I said. "Sorry to bother you. You might want to call the front desk in a second. My associate had to eat your lock."

"I see," Morlock said carefully.

I stood up, the cases spinning in my head. They were all the same thing. Aggie, Corrina, Pilar, and the familiars. Worse still, I think I understood what these separate ingredients led to, and it was not good.

"Come on," I said to Hexene and Keyes. We entered the hall right as the elevator opened. Percy, Leona, and several impossibly handsome security men came out and into the hall.

"Stop right there, meatstick," Percy said.

Thirty-Nine

It wasn't a street at high noon and I wasn't Randolph Scott. It was the hallway of an opulent casino hotel with brand-new carpeting and, well, a door that could use some attention since a good chunk had been apparently melted out. I was more than a little damp from the rain, sporting a few days' growth of beard, and still wearing a jacket lent to me by a sasquatch. Hexene was just as damp, her hair hanging in clumps, and looking like a cat that had been dunked in a bath. Keyes was his usual blobby self, though now completely absent of any sort of identifying markers. Morlock wasn't with us, but he was peering out from behind the doorjamb in fear.

As for the jaguar people, well, if anyone were to guess which side was the heroes, they would be picked ten times out of ten. Other than Leona's dress being slightly askew and a few strands of hair escaping their rolls to hang artfully over her flawless face, they could not have been more perfectly put together. I felt like a group of carnies about to get run off by a crew of movie stars.

"Stay where you are," Percy said, pointing at me. I couldn't prove it, but I swear he was posing.

"You still owe me a jacket," I said.

"I owe you a lot more than that."

"But I brought a friend of yours."

Hexene pushed her hair out of her face and Percy hesitated. Leona filled in the gap. "Take her too."

They eyeballed Keyes, and I knew what they were thinking. There was very little more dangerous than a blob. Unless they had some very specific blob-fighting equipment on them—ironically enough, available in the jacket they had confiscated from me—there was little they could actually do against Keyes. Even moving him was nearly impossible. He could just eat whatever they used to push him, or simply devour the hotel itself. Blobs existed in a strange corner of the social contract: we knew they could destroy us all, but they politely agreed not to, so we wouldn't destroy them first. It was probably inevitable that this would change sooner or later.

And this is what the balam were thinking as they looked from the relatively non-threatening figures of me, Hexene, and Morlock to the blubbery pink apocalypse that was whistling atonally through his skin, apparently unaware of anything that was happening.

Leona sighed and started to advance on us. "Don't worry," she said over her shoulder. "The blob won't do anything."

"Hey, Percy, maybe you should ask Leona about some of her business associates."

Because Leona was in front of them, they couldn't see the flash of sheer terror on her face.

"Pull the other one, Moss," Percy said. That had never sounded so threatening before.

"All right," I said, "I guess we're doing this the hard way." I reached into Foote's jacket and pulled out the twigs and vine I'd torn from the jungle plants, now fashioned into a crude cross, and leveled it at the jaguar people. Leona screamed and shielded her face. Percy snarled. One of the goons fainted dead away and the other one dropped to the floor like I had tossed a grenade. Behind me, Morlock let out a shriek and slammed his door, which, lacking anything to keep it shut, promptly bounced open.

"Sorry, Count!" I yelled.

"Just go away, please!" he yelled back, his voice muffled under something.

I grabbed Leona, one arm around her shoulders, pulling her to me like a hostage, keeping the cross bared at security. Leona cowered back from it, right into me. She was wiggling a little more than she had to.

"Okay, see you cats later," I said to Percy, pulling Leona along behind me. Hexene and Keyes made way.

"Zombies! Someone get some zombies up here!" Percy fumed. We turned the corner and I tried to shove Leona away, but she wasn't going anywhere.

"Great, you kidnapped the concierge," Hexene said. "What now?"

"I can think of a few things," Leona said.

"I wasn't asking you!"

The irony of me kidnapping anyone aside, I had the barest hint of a plan. "Keyes. Keyes!"

"Yes, Mr. Night Ranger? Is it time to usher in a new age of the pink tide?"

"Wait... um, no, it's not that. I need you to find Pilar. Tell her it wasn't Count Morlock. It was Uriah Bluddengutz and it wasn't romantic."

"You got it, Mr. Night Ranger!" The floor began to creak and smoke as Keyes dissolved it.

"Repeat it to me, Keyes."

"It. It. It. It."

"Oh, goddamn it."

"Oh, goddamn it."

"Keyes!" I shouted. "Tell Pilar it was not Count Morlock. It was Uriah Bluddengutz."

"It was not Pilar! It was Uriah Bluddengutz!"

I sighed. "Close enough."

The floor gave way and Keyes crashed into the hall below. With any luck, Percy and the others would assume we went that way and distract themselves while we slipped out the back.

"Bluddengutz? What do you want with that has-been?" Leona asked as I hustled her down the hall, looking for the stairs.

"You know him?"

"Every monster knows him. He showed up in '51 and was one of the bigwigs in the war."

Right, '51, when his pigeons made their baffling debut on the war's stage. I swear, as frightening as the Night War could be at times, it was much funnier than its predecessor.

"Someone put him in charge?"

"Mad scientist," she said, slowly, like a teacher trying to reach the slow kid. "They take charge whether you want them or not. And they refer to everyone as a monstrous minion. That's why Kong kicked him to the curb. Now why don't you drop that cross and the three of us can get better acquainted?"

I showed it to her and she cowered into the wall, hissing like a cat. "I don't think so. Bluddengutz had a beef with Kong?"

"Kong took over!" she howled, sliding down the wall and squirming under the cross's attention. I stopped leveling it at her, mostly because the squirming had taken on a decidedly sensual air. "Bluddengutz stepped aside, but you could tell he wasn't happy about it."

"You knew them back during the war?"

"We hunted meatsticks together! All of us. Kong, Bluddengutz, Zzzolt, Closett..."

I almost didn't ask her, but curiosity was always my weakness. Killed the cat, which in itself was pretty ironic, considering.

"If you were pals with Kong from the war, why are you trying to off him?"

"Kong's weak! After the war he came out here and just stayed. I thought we were going to have the whole city, but all he wanted was this island."

"So you sell him out to the woman who does run things on the mainland." Sarah Bellum, the brainiac crime boss.

"Yes," she said, relaxing slightly now that the cross wasn't held up boldly in front of her.

"The cat was for Percy, huh? Thought he was the only thing standing between the Bellum thugs and Kong, 'cause the ape just isn't what he used to be, right?"

"You're pretty smart for a meatstick," she said, sizing me up. "I'd like to see what else you're good at."

I sighed and brought the cross up. She hissed and spat like a soaked cat. Strange how the cross thing worked, and it did more or less the same for any monster who didn't like the sight of holy symbols. They worked pretty well as wards, but there was no substitute for squaring your shoulders and holding it in front of you, sure that the Lord was your shepherd or whatever. The fact that it worked for me at all said the symbol itself was a more important part of the equation than any devout feelings.

"I'm good at not getting involved, Leona. You monsters want to kill each other tugging on the same money, that's fine by me. Just leave me out of it."

"You're already in deep," she said, writhing.

This wasn't going to work. Time to get back on track. "What

happened to Zzzolt?"

"He was an electrolic, fried his circuits on the juice."

"When?"

"After the Treaty."

"Why?"

"How should I know? He was a robot." She smiled up at me from her place on the floor. "Robots are no fun. Not like we could..." and she drifted off into an agonized and titillated moan as I brought up the cross again.

"Cut that out. What about another monster? Prime-8? Orangutron?"

"Yeah, I remember him. Bluddengutz introduced him right around the time Kong took over. Didn't talk much... he was just Bluddengutz's little errand boy."

Little errand boy. Kong arrived in '52. I would remember that until the day I died. I ran over the timeline in my head. It fit. It couldn't be. And yet... I dragged Leona to her feet. I thought I had it. All of it. I wasn't sure how I was going to actually get back all the people I was hired to find, but it made sense. "You. Show us the way out of this place. A back way."

"The back..."

"Don't," I said, showing her the cross.

"Fine, fine," she said, throwing her hands up and flinching from the cross. "Be that way."

We turned the corner of the hallway, passing a room service cart piled high with used plates. The sudden flash of white light and the sharp pain didn't have an immediately obvious source. I was on the floor, holding my now-bleeding nose and looking up when Mr. de Kay, his suit shredded, stepped into my field of vision.

"Hello, meatstick," Bellum crackled from the speaker.

FORTY

"Pretty clever for a meatstick," Bellum said, and it was tough to separate the mirth from the distortion in her voice. De Kay looked a little worse for wear, a few new stripes in his papery flesh revealing gray muscle and yellow bone. He had clocked me right in the nose. Guess he figured he didn't need a gun anymore.

Hell of it was, he was right.

Leona, a smug smile shining, moved to de Kay's side. "Go on," she said. "You can kill him."

"A meatstick getting onto Catalina Island, not once but twice," Bellum mused. "Resourceful."

"Look," I said, getting unsteadily to my feet and clutching the faucet of my nose. "I don't really have time for this. I have four cases I need to solve, so if you could just..."

De Kay grabbed my arm and threw me into a wall. The aches and bruises Prime-8 had put on me exploded all over again. I wished for Keyes to be there to break my fall. "Ow."

"I could use a resourceful meatstick like that," Bellum continued.

"Brains," de Kay whispered.

"I feel like you're not listening," I said, wincing.

De Kay and Leona were focused on me. They had completely forgotten about Hexene. Who could blame them? A witch without her magic was barely better than a human.

"I *am* listening," Bellum said. "I just don't care. You see, Mr. Moss, if I want you working for me, you're working for me. That's the end of the story."

"I don't care! Take this stupid place! You're welcome to it! Kill Kong while you're at it. Hell, knock out a wall or three and add an amusement park for the kids! Don't you get it? I! Don't! Give! A! Damn!"

I might have been getting through to them. Probably not. Monsters, especially powerful ones, gave as much of a hoot for humans as I gave for their plans. But they weren't looking at Hexene, who had picked up a platter from the serving cart, a nice heavy steel one, since they couldn't use silver anymore. Hexene raised that platter over her head and slammed it down on de Kay.

CLANG.

A blow to the noodle like that? That zombie should have been pushing daisies. Sure, Hexene was barely a hundred pounds soaking wet—which she was, in point of fact—and she was exhausted from climbing Kong's hotel, desk, and pyramid. Didn't matter. De Kay should have gotten the big goodbye then and there.

Not that clang of metal on metal. Or the mildly confused look on de Kay's face— managed, fascinatingly enough, without eyelids or lips. Or Hexene yelping in pain and dropping the platter onto the floor, then yelping again when it almost landed on her feet.

"Armored fedoras," Bellum said, and chuckled with all the warmth of a funeral director.

"Brains," de Kay agreed, taking off the hat to reveal a partly skinless skull with a few wisps of black hair clinging stubbornly to the flakes of flesh, then thumping the inside of his hat to show that, yes, it was in fact steel. He stuck it back on his head and twitched the brim to give it the same rakish angle. "Brains," he said again, in case I hadn't gotten the point.

"Now, if both of you would stand over there," Bellum said.

De Kay pulled the gun from his jacket and motioned. "Brains."

Hexene and I moved over to be covered by the pistol.

"Now move," Bellum said.

We did, the zombie and balam directing us to a doorway. Stairs led downward, where an exit awaited.

"I don't know what you're thinking," I said to Bellum. "I'm not working for you."

"You will. One way or the other. Either you agree in your present state or I have Mr. de Kay turn you. Once he eats your brains, you'll listen to the first thing a brain tells you."

It made a certain amount of sense.

"You can't leave Moss around," Leona said.

"I *can't*? Miss Pryde, if you suggest there's something I can't do again, you're going to have another talk with Mr. de Kay, and I promise you, this time it will go differently."

"Brains," de Kay said, and I swore I could detect some anger there.

We were at the door and de Kay prodded me in the back. I opened it. The rain was driving now, the trees bowing in the wind.

"Go on."

Hexene shuddered.

"Are you going to be all right?" I whispered to her.

"I think so."

"If you think you can't take it... tell me."

"And then?"

"And then I'll do something."

She knew what I was saying. I saw it in her eyes. "Do something," as in attack the zombie with the gun and get plugged for my trouble. Offering to trade my life for Hexene's. A stupid promise, sure, but I meant it. And I think she understood that, too.

"Get moving," Bellum said. "And can the chatter."

De Kay prodded me and we were outside in the rain. We made our way around the side of the casino, where the various plants and terraces gave a little bit of shelter. The waterspouts had multiplied and lightning was crackling from the sky continuously now. The thunder swallowed anything below a shout. It sounded like the Belgian forest in that horrible December of '44.

Hexene and I walked into the wind. She staggered and I held her, shielding her from as much of the rain as I could. She pressed her cheek into my chest.

"What I meant," Leona shouted, "is that Moss is dangerous! He knows too much!"

"He knows nothing about me," Bellum said. Unlike the rest of us, Bellum wasn't shouting. It sounded like she had merely increased the volume on de Kay's speaker. "He knows everything about Kong. That makes him dangerous to everyone *except* me."

"Eliminate him!" Leona screamed.

"I'll take him off the island," Bellum countered. "Signal one of my boats and take him back to the mainland. You'll never have to deal with him again."

Leona was silent and I pictured her seething. "Fine," she said, low enough that I could barely hear it over the wind and thunder.

They herded us down the paths of jungle foliage that looked about ready to be torn out by their roots, to the beach where

Pilar surfaced daily. I wondered if she was planning to swim back today. Could a giantess take a bolt of lightning? Was that like static shock to them?

Maybe time start worrying about myself. If they got me off the island, it was going to be hell getting back here, and there was no doubt in my mind that this was where I had to be. Added to that was Hexene. I couldn't leave her, not without her powers.

"Hey! Miss Bellum!"

"What is it, Mr. Moss?"

"What's going to happen to my friend here?"

"Your lady friend will not be harmed."

"I'm not his..."

"Not the time, Hexene."

She muttered something, but I lost it in a peal of thunder. "I got your word on that?"

"Unlike your word, mine is something I trade on. Ironclad, Mr. Moss. You can take it to the bank, and as long as you're talking about a Los Angeles branch, I mean that literally."

I tried not to shudder at that statement and chalked up the icy hand working its way up my spine to the inclement weather.

We stopped on the beach. De Kay reached into his coat and removed a mirror, trying to catch sunlight that wasn't there. Leona, shifting her weight back and forth, glanced back at the hotel. It was deserted outside, Kong either having returned to his pleasure palace or still up in his pyramid.

"Can you hurry up?" Leona grumbled.

"Watch your tone," Bellum said. "No, Mr. de Kay, I need you to..."

"Brains," de Kay snapped.

They were so focused on the mirror and Leona so intent on the hotel, they didn't see the bubbles. Hexene and I did, though. They were just off in the crashing surf, and they were getting closer. Leviathan maybe, coming close to shore? Wanting to have a look at the casino and be disappointed there was nowhere for a giant fish monster to stay?

What surfaced was not an animal but a small submarine. It was boxy and ugly, looking nothing like the few I'd seen in the service. It also had a clear section where an engine glowing with St. Elmo's fire crackled. The front porthole was red. Reminded me of someone. Just like a mad scientist: everything had to look like them.

"What the hell?" Bellum demanded.

"Brains," de Kay said, not having anything useful to add.

"What?" asked Leona, finally tearing her attention from the hotel.

The hatch opened and Prime-8 bounded out. His antennae were buzzing with a thread of lightning, the television screen of his face showing an angry line. His orange fur trailed behind him as he landed on the beach in a spray of sand and saltwater. De Kay whirled to point the gun at the new arrival, but he was too slow. The orangutron hit the zombie with a backhand from one leathery fist, sending the dapper enforcer sailing into some lava rocks. Armored fedora or no, de Kay did not get up, and the only sound came from the crackle-hiss of the speaker.

Prime-8 turned on Leona, who put up her hands. "Thank god you're here! He was kidnapping us!"

"Stand aside, Miss Pryde." The way Prime-8 said it was almost childlike, a strange cadence from a robot-headed ape-monster, but then, I wasn't certain what would be normal under those conditions.

"What? You saved us from the zombie."

"Don't bother, Leona," I said.

She frowned, turned back to Prime-8, and without missing

a beat, he dropped her to the sand with a single blow. I braced myself for the attack, but he zigged instead of zagging, picking Hexene up off the ground.

"Sorry, Mr. Moss," Prime-8 said, and with another powerful leap, was back on the hatch of the sub.

Hexene's struggles grew more frantic when she saw the water all around. "Nick!" she screamed, not that there was much either of us could do at the moment. I ran for her anyway, even as Prime-8 descended the ladder, closing the hatch behind him.

Right before it shut, my eyes met the screen of his face. "JJ?" I asked.

"Sorry, Mr. Moss," he repeated. This time, I caught it. That was the Brooks kid who had gone missing back in '52. My first case. My first failure.

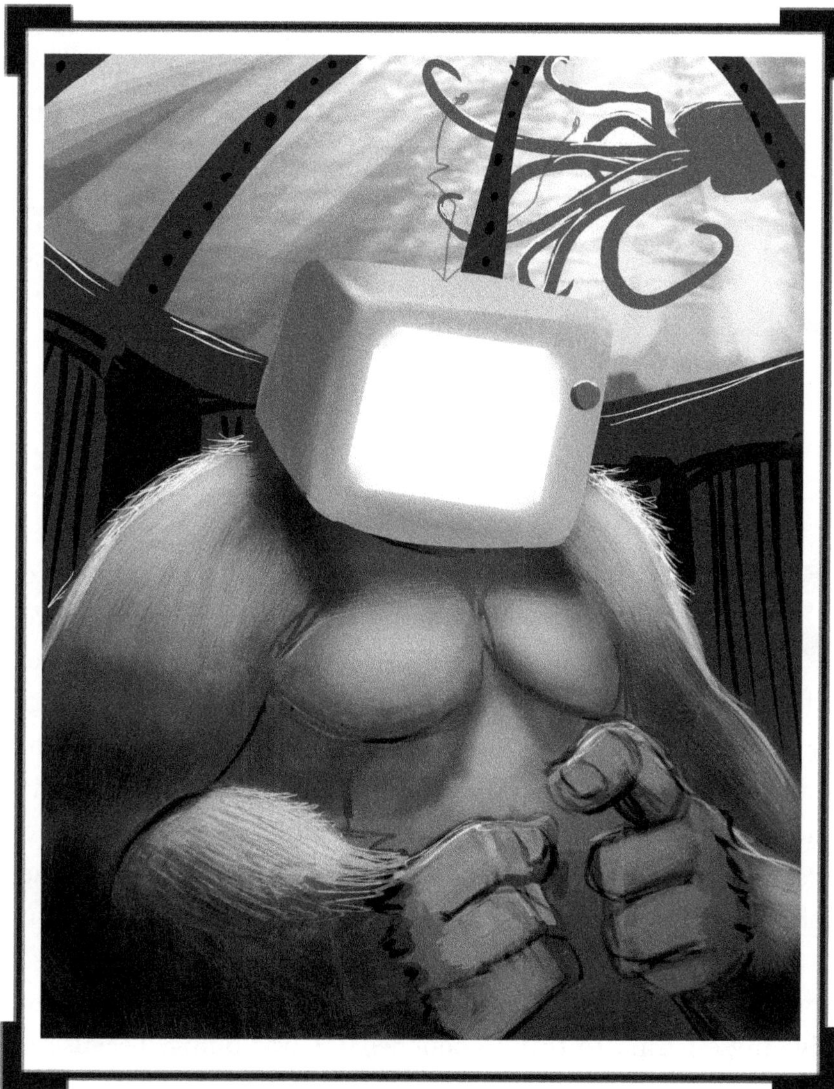

Prime-8

Forty-One

You can't really prepare for seeing the first person you'd ever failed showing up as a new kind of monster to abduct a friend in some kind of cockamamie submarine. All in all, I think I handled it pretty well. Wordless screaming, or impotent raging on the shore, or just a slackjawed gape into the storm off the coast, marveling at how cruel and specific the universe could be; all of these would have been expected reactions. What I did instead was sprint up the beach to the Isla Calavera casino.

I didn't check on Leona Pryde or Mr. de Kay, because frankly, they could lie there for all I cared. I didn't want to give myself time to think about what I was doing, because it was objectively insane.

By which I mean it made perfect sense at the time, since it was my only option to solve the case and rescue Hexene. It turned crazy only if I took a step back and realized what it was I was about to do. No way I'd do that, since I wanted to make certain I'd do it. And confront every last fear I'd ever had.

And it all came down to lights.

God bless Foote, that big, hairy, stinking monster. I was going to start a Christmas card list just to put him on it. He'd mentioned it, and I was too much on my rails to realize what he'd said. Now I understood what he had been saying, and I knew the way to get there. All it would take was the scariest thing I'd ever done.

I ran through the howling wind and punishing rain, pulling open the door to the casino. The gaming room was sparsely populated, but a few monsters glanced my way. I must have looked a fright, but even on my best days I can usually pass for a wolfman, and my present state only enhanced the illusion. Most of the monsters looked away almost immediately, the spins of the roulette wheel and the somersaulting dice carrying much more interest than a single waterlogged cop. The only one giving me a truly hard stare was one of the jaguar guards. He looked like what might happen if Michelangelo had ever seen an Apache, and he was already moving in my direction.

I sprinted for the entrance to Kong's chambers. That surprised the guard long enough that I could get into the hall and to the door before he was able to react.

That was right when I realized what a terrible idea this was. I was already committed, though, and threw open the door to Kong's throne room.

"...Kong says you are as petite and pretty as a porcelain doll." It was the wheedling voice of Lurkimer Closett, emanating from underneath Kong's throne and directed toward Jayne Doe, who was sitting in her chair on the arm of the throne, blushing and giving him an "oh, you."

Pilar was on her throne as well, carefully not watching the exchange between her supposed boyfriend and the tiny lady on the mini-throne. This humiliation had probably grown so common any outrage had long since rotted away.

Kong's eyes came up and met mine. First time I'd ever locked eyes with fear itself. First time I knew for a fact he really saw me. Saw right into me. Knew how scared I really was. It was nearly enough to send me to the same place I'd been on the pyramid. He looked annoyed, probably still seething over someone breaking into his pyramid. I should probably have thanked my lucky stars I was too small a thing for him to recognize, even after our run-in the previous day. And why not? I was a bug to be squashed, not a man to have a conversation with.

I started walking up to him, because I knew the instant I stopped moving, that would be it. No force on earth could get me to move under my own power again after that.

"The Mighty Kong wants to inform you that this is a private... you! It's you!"

Kong hooted again, the edge of anger in his mammoth voice. Pilar's mouth sagged open in fear. I couldn't blame her. I barely knew what I was doing, and she didn't have a prayer of figuring it out.

"He's the—"

I started to jog and cut Closett off before he could say anything else. "Great Kong, I was wondering if you ever had trouble with a vampire?"

"All-Powerful Kong, this is—"

Now Kong cut Closett off with a few grunts, the irritation expanding to encompass his obsequious translator.

Closett sighed and said, "The Regal Kong would like to inform you that, yes, he had trouble with a vampire once. Great One, he is the—"

"1952?" I was close enough to smell the ape-stink washing off Kong in waves, and it smelled almost exactly like Prime-8.

Kong nodded and grunted. Now the anger was being replaced with confusion.

"The Mighty Kong would like to say, yes, it was in 1952. He would now like to know who you are and why you are running at the throne, when you know he will crush you like an insect."

"My name is Nick Moss and I'm a private eye," I said, picking up speed, aiming right at the source of all my nightmares. He was above me now like nothing more than a skyscraper. "And I just need to borrow your bogeyman for a second."

Closett had time to squeal before I tackled him under the throne. I grabbed the wriggling bogeyman, getting a deep whiff of his scent, like toys and sugared cereal.

"Great Kong! This is him! This is the man who broke into your pyramid!"

Closett was underneath me, struggling with more arms than your average octopus. I grabbed handfuls of his hair and held onto his body with my legs.

Kong roared and his massive fingers curled under the throne.

Closett saw this, his glowing eyes perfectly round. "No! No, Masterful One! Don't do it!" I didn't blame the bogeyman: if Kong turned the chair over, that amount of light would kill Closett instantly.

Jayne Doe screamed, and that was when Kong's fingers vanished. Then his face appeared, mashed to the floor to peer under the dark throne at the intruder. His arm came next, reaching for me and Closett. I hauled the bogeyman on top of me, then rolled again and again, desperately tumbling away from the black fingers the size of my car. The tip of one brushed both of us and Closett howled again.

"Kublai! You can't kill the guests!" Pilar shouted.

Kong snarled.

"The Great Kong says he can do what he likes," Closett

shrieked. "Help me! Someone help me! The man has me!"

Kong growled and disappeared. The grunts and thumps said he was moving to the other side of the throne. I started rolling again, the bogeyman squirming and thrashing in his attempts to get away.

The massive face eclipsed the other side and the hand came again. Kong's finger touched us, and for a moment we were pinned, but as he tried to scrabble more fingers onto us, the weight gave and Closett and I rolled free.

"He drags me out of here, I'm not letting go," I growled to Closett. "We're both going into the light."

"No!" he screamed. "What did I ever do to you?"

"We're going to get dragged out, Closett. Unless you take me where I want to go. Got it?"

"Where do you want to—ahhh!" Kong had switched to the front of the throne and I jumped off the bogeyman, keeping my grip on his hair, dragging him literally kicking and screaming toward the back.

"Concentrate, Closett! You sense the places you can go, right? The closets and beds? Off the coast of the island. To the south. The sea floor. Can you feel it?"

I looked up and saw Kong's face, contorted in hatred. His hot breath washed over us, carrying the stench of rotting bananas. The hand blocked that soon after, reaching for the both of us.

"I can't keep away from him forever, Closett! Can you sense it or are we both dying?"

"I sense it! I can sense it!"

The hand got closer, ready to grab us.

"You'll be lucky if you even see the light!" I prodded. "He's going to crush us both!"

"NO!"

"Then take us there!"

It felt like a blink at first. A sudden darkness before a return to light. Yet there was no light. Not in the way I understood light, anyway. Somehow I could see. It was black all around, every side and above and below. It smelled like mothballs, old paper, dust, like the back of a closet or under a bed. It had the same feeling, too, of being surrounded and hidden, and yet, when I reached out, I touched nothing at all.

Lurkimer Closett struggled to get up. I only had the sense of him, and his eyes were the only light source. They had changed shape again, becoming almond-shaped and accented with slitted pupils. He seemed larger here somehow, and when he got up, those eyes loomed above me.

I could hear voices around me, echoing everywhere. They were wheedling whispers, but whatever they were actually saying, I had no idea. I knew that in this dark place, I was far from alone. And I was unarmed.

"That was a very mean thing to do," Closett said reproachfully.

"I know. Sorry about that. I needed to get where I was going, and you were the only way."

"You could have just asked."

"And you would have taken me?"

He was silent. "Well, no."

"The sooner you take me there, the sooner you never see me again."

"You promise?"

"Definitely."

"And you won't threaten me anymore?"

"Promise."

"All right. It's this way." Closett started to walk, and whatever fur I had been grabbing was a hand now. I didn't want to know how he did that. I would never see a bogeyman in the light, and I was grateful for it. "What did you want in the Great Kong's rooms, anyway?"

"I was looking for evidence he had made the orangutrons."

"There are more than one?"

"I don't think so. I think for whatever reason, Prime-8 is the only one."

"And you thought Kong made them?"

"I still do, but it was unintentional. Rather, he and Zzzolt created them, without ever knowing they'd done it." As we walked in the strange twilight place, we would occasionally pass a horizontal line of light at floor level, sometimes strong, sometimes weak. It took me a second to realize this was what a closed closet door looked like from the inside. Closett gave these a wide berth, hissing under his breath.

"Oh," Closett said after a moment. "Are you undercover?"

"What?"

"It's a strange cover. Meatstick, I mean. Your identification didn't say you were a wolfman, but you clearly are. Pretty obvious, since no meatstick could do what you're doing. Catalina *isn't* your jurisdiction, you know. And we're all paid up. You ask Sheriff Thorpe." He paused. "Here it is."

I peered into the darkness, unable to see much of anything. "Where?"

"Right here. Follow your nose, wolfman."

"Uh... of course. Sure." I looked where it seemed like he was indicating, but of course, it was pitch black, and I was in the company of a large monster and some glowing eyes.

"Wrong way," Closett said.

"Uh, sorry. Everything smells like mothballs in here."

His paw came down on my shoulder, forcing a grunt out of me. He was strong. Stronger in here, where it was good and dark. He redirected me the way he was indicating. I still didn't see anything, and the faint glow from his eyes didn't do much to illuminate it. "Right there."

He didn't let me go.

"Say..." he said, like it was something he had just come up with rather than a niggling doubt that he'd only just found the stones to mention, "You have a smell, too."

"Um... dog, I suppose. You know, they, uh, they tell you that when you change, you don't have to clean your suits more than normal, but as soon as you get wet, it's, uh... well, you know."

"You don't smell like a dog," Closett murmured. "You smell like a meatstick. A *scared* meatstick."

"Well, you know, I brace, uh, suspects from time to time, so it probably rubbed off."

He still wasn't letting go. "I don't think so. I think your ID was correct. I think you tried to snow me. A goddamn meatstick snowed me in front of my boss."

"Careful, Lurkimer. I might get angry, and then, you know. Grr."

"Go on."

"I *said* grr."

"No, go on. Change. Because I don't think you can. And if you can't, there's nothing to stop me from keeping you here, is there? Whaddya say, meatstick? You want to be a bogeyman?" He giggled. "Or maybe I'll just kill ya."

Just like a bogeyman. Coward until you're on his turf, then he's a big man. I felt like a kid, and I realized that's what his newfound stature was all about, looming over me in the dark. Big enough to be an adult to my size. I wanted to get angry, but it was fear coming over me now. I was a kid again, deathly still in my darkened room, praying the noises in my closet were my imagination and knowing they weren't.

"Yeah. There's the fear. Poor, poor meatstick. Got in a bit

over your head, did you? Well, those days are over. Where you're going, you won't be scared ever again."

He pulled me closer by the shoulder of the jacket. I knew I didn't have much time. If I was going to move, it had to be now. Of course, it's easy to think that. Harder to escape a monster when every instinct wants you to go as still as prey.

Harry Foote saved me. Not literally. His jacket. It was so loose that when Closett pulled on it, it went without me. I slipped out of it and ran smack into the door I couldn't see. I pushed aside the clothing hangers that were suddenly around me—or had they been there all along?—and shoved the door open. It was a steel-walled bedroom. I didn't see much more because I felt Closett coming up behind me. There were enough shadows in the room for him to survive. He'd get me.

I turned and punched, aiming for the one thing I could see perfectly: the pale glowing almonds of his eyes.

I popped him square in the left one, and even felt a little bit of give and the wetness of tears. Closett staggered backward, his eye going dark as he closed and covered it. "What was that for?" he demanded.

I jumped out of the closet and slammed the door. He could put the pieces together himself.

Forty-Two

I'll say this for mad scientists: they were great with the ambience. I was in a bedroom of some kind, and my guess was it belonged to Dr. Uriah Bluddengutz. I figured that because I couldn't imagine anyone else needing a room that big at the bottom of the ocean just to sleep in.

The closet spilled me out in what I initially thought was a corner, but once I saw that the room was dome-shaped, I realized there were no actual corners. I flinched when something moved in my peripheral vision. It was a mechanical arm, tipped with a pincer. It grabbed me by the shirt, hauled me to my feet, and started to primp me. I dodged aside and fled to the far side of the room. The arm had no idea I was gone and got to work on the space where I had been. It opened up the closet and attempted to drape a lab coat on nothing, succeeding in dropping it on the floor. I checked to see if Closett was in there waiting, but couldn't see anything past the hanging clothes.

I had a look around. The walls were steel, painted a soothing blue—almost the same shade as my house, so maybe there *were* coincidences every now and then—pimpled with heavy rivets. The dome arced up, seeming to disappear. It was a glass ceiling, or more likely some other mad scientist material the rest of us didn't know about yet. A few pale fish swam past the ceiling, lit by white beams from floodlights that were positioned out of sight.

Because he was a mad scientist, and thus, by definition insane, Bluddengutz had some odd ideas that surfaced in the decor of his room. There was what I think was intended as a bed. It was actually a pit in the center of the room filled with red Jell-O. A watermelon hung from the ceiling, punctured by a dozen wires. Another armature, this one partially disassembled, slumped by the "bed."

An archway led out into a hall. I followed that.

The air was chilly down here, and the walls were positively icy. They were all the same blue steel, though many windows looked out into the dark ocean. We were on the sea floor, probably around three hundred feet down, and very little light penetrated that far, even if the sun had been shining. The windows looked out onto a featureless marine desert, the lights picking out the occasional bizarre and nightmarish fish. How long before Bluddengutz got wise and enlarged those? Or was he still obsessed with his pigeons?

No, I reminded myself, he had much bigger goals, didn't he?

The undersea base felt both empty and endless. The bulk of it comprised these long hallways, entirely deserted. The only sounds were a distant thumping and the occasional ghostly whine, though the source of either was not clear. The smell was antiseptic, a bit like a hospital, but my brain added a salt tang to it just to make me feel better. I found rooms, though none as big as the first one I had fallen into.

Until I found the brig.

That's what it had to be. I turned the corner on one of the

hallways and emerged into a long room with cages all along one wall. In the last cell at the end, I thought I saw movement, and stepping into view, I found a young woman standing by her cot ready to fight. When she saw it was me—or, more accurately, someone she didn't know—her face relaxed. "Who are you?"

"You're Corrina Lacks," I said. It was her. Even in her shiny silver skirt and top, with the odd band they'd used to corral her curls, I recognized her.

"Who's asking?"

"My name is Nick Moss. I'm a detective. I've been hired to find you."

She heaved a great sigh of relief. "Thank god. There's a lever out there somewhere. I can't see it. The big robot-ape that snatched me pulls it whenever I'm being let out for exercise."

"Got it."

I found the lever near the door. There was no real security, and why would there be? Who else but the two monsters who lived on the base would ever be wandering around it? Besides, mad scientists were known for always overlooking one crucial thing, though the nature of the oversight varied. If this was it, then Bluddengutz was still in excellent shape for our upcoming showdown, and that had me worried.

I pulled the lever. The doors opened smoothly, making only a soft clang. Corrina came out of her cell. "All right, Mr. Moss. Let's go."

"Well, uh, it's not that simple actually."

"What do you mean, it's not that simple?"

"You're not the only, um, the only person I was looking for. I'm pretty sure the others are down here somewhere."

"They're not here."

"I can see that. Is there another brig?"

"How should I know?"

"You said they let you out."

"Yeah, there's a gymnasium." She gestured over her shoulder. "No brig over there. They have a pool."

"Oh, good." I glanced around, I guess because I thought Hexene, Aggie, and all the familiars would have suddenly appeared. They had not.

"Okay, so you get the other people you're looking for and we go, right?"

I didn't think it was time to tell her that technically speaking, we were completely trapped. That was not the kind of thing that was good for morale. Bluddengutz had to have a way out, and probably more than one. I'd just have to steal that. And, you know, hope for the best.

Yeah, I was going to keep Corrina in the dark for the time being.

"I don't suppose you know where they came from?" I asked her.

She shook her head.

"Great, we'll keep looking."

Which we did. The halls were beginning to curve around and go in the other direction. I guessed that meant we had rounded the far side of the undersea complex.

"Hey, mister," Corrina said. "How long have I been down here?"

"Couple days. Less than a week. Sorry it took so long, but, well..." I gestured. We were at the bottom of the ocean.

"Less than a week? Feels like forever. They never turn off the lights."

"Have you seen anyone else down here? Other than the orangutron?"

"Orangutron?"

"Uh... robot-ape."

"Yeah, there's a mad scientist. He doesn't talk to me or anything, but sometimes I'll see him go past, and then I hear him yelling at the... orangutron?"

I nodded. She had gotten the pronunciation right. "Yelling?"

"You know, mad scientist stuff. Calling him a minion, calling him stupid. A lot of the time, he's yelling at him to change me, but the orangutron doesn't want to do it. It's like he's scared."

I didn't want to tell her he was still a kid.

"What does the orangutron say?"

"Not much. Sometimes he... sometimes he calls the guy 'dad,' though."

"Dad?" Henry Brooks was topside and...

...oh.

There was the last little piece for me, clean and clear. Mystery solved, for all good it would do. I had answers, but what I needed were the five beings I was presently on the hunt for.

"What?" Corrina asked me, sounding worried. "You had a look."

"It's, uh, it's detective stuff."

"Oh, okay. Who hired you? Mama?"

"Uh, no. It doesn't really matter. I've been hired to find you and return you to your parents." I paused. "That's what you want, right? You're not going to lose your mind if I try to get you out of here?"

"You crazy? You found me in jail! Take me home, please."

"Sorry, it's just... there was one time I got hired to find a girl, about your age, and I found her in this martian's lair in San Berdoo and when I tried to get her out of there, she started hitting me. With a newspaper. Now, leaving aside the fact that I had no idea martians even got the paper, I was sort of flummoxed."

"What happened?"

"Well, I guess it wasn't so much a kidnapping as one of those, you know, human-monster relationships that you hear about in, um... you know, literature and so on." I coughed.

"Literature?"

"Well, not the kind *I* read, obviously. But you know, in this job, you, uh, you see things. And these two had a rather extensive collection of, um... paperbacks. And not the nice kind of paperback. You know the kind."

"I most certainly do not," she said, but the way she was blushing, she knew exactly what I was saying.

"Right, yeah. Don't worry about that. The point is, I'm not going to take anyone anywhere they don't want to go. I figure that's the monsters. They do that. I'm not a monster."

"You're what?"

"I'm not a monster. I'm human."

"Didn't you say you were a detective?"

"Yeah."

"You're not a werewolf?"

"No."

"Wolfman?"

"No."

"Invisible man?" She paused. "Dumb question."

"I'm human, Corrina."

"Didn't know there were human shamuses left in Los Angeles."

"I'm the last one."

Maybe in the world, and a good reason for that. She was quiet after the revelation that I didn't have a single special power to keep her safe, and good thing, too. I started to hear an insistent buzz coming from somewhere ahead. Unlike the other sounds of this undersea base, it had a definite source, and it was familiar, but only because of who I was. It was the sound of arcing electricity.

Yeah, I knew that sound better than I would have liked. Go up against enough mad scientists, robots, meat golems, and brainiacs and the sound gets as familiar as anything the Salem Sisters ever crooned. I followed the sound, and within a few twists and turns, I found its source.

The room was bigger than the bedroom. By a lot. It was a dome, too, though the ceiling was ribbed into spokes and the lights outside dyed the ocean red. The center of the room was a depression, ringed by a wide catwalk lined with machinery. Most important, however, were the people.

Dr. Uriah Bluddengutz was on the catwalk, scampering from console to console, tapping and laughing and muttering to himself. His brain crackled with energy, though that was not the sound I had heard. That came from the naked rope of bright blue lightning arcing from a pair of antennae in the center of the room.

Prime-8 was also on the catwalk, standing apart from the doctor, the line on his face a series of angry squiggles. He wrung his big simian hands as he watched. I had no way to know what was going on in his mind, but I hoped it was regret. That he saw what he was doing and knew it was wrong. That there was a little bit left of the boy Alice Brooks loved.

Hanging in the middle of the room, over the depression in the center, were two large birdcages and a cylindrical tank. The tank was full, the glass walls a dark red. Pilar's blood, harvested over the past couple months. The center birdcage held Aggie Brooks, crying softly in fear, her little hands gripping the bars. I hadn't seen her in three years, but I knew her. She still had the same upturned nose, the same pretty brown hair, the same big brown eyes. In the other cage, three creatures sat in an awkward heap. There was the snapping turtle at the base, the slimy salamander on top of him, and at the crown,

Escuerzo. Alone among everything in the room, the toad saw me immediately, giving me a saturnine look as if to say, "Oh. Wondering when *you'd* finally show."

And last, beneath Aggie Brooks was Hexene, strapped down to an operating table. She wasn't crying or fuming anymore. She was staring upward at Bluddengutz with cold hatred. If her powers suddenly returned to her, I had no doubt she would find some way to blow the mad scientist apart into bloody chunks.

I turned to Corrina. She was staring at the tableau with naked terror.

"Stay here," I whispered.

"You're going in there? You crazy?"

"Thought we'd established that." I tried a comforting smile. "Don't worry. I handle this kind of thing all the time."

She wanted to believe me. I saw that in her eyes.

Step one was going to be exactly what Hexene was after: her powers. Get her those and my job got much, much easier, while Bluddengutz got the worst day of his life. As for Prime-8... I had no idea.

I tiptoed into the room. Bluddengutz was overhead on the catwalk, his mutters having no real relationship to English as I understood it. Maybe that's what he was cackling about.

I got to Hexene's side. "Where's the lever? There's got to be a lever that releases this!" I whispered to her.

"What?" she asked.

I shushed her, but it was too late.

"Dad!" Prime-8 shouted. "It's Mr. Moss!"

Bluddengutz grabbed the railing and peered down at me. "Mr. Moss! So nice of you to join us!"

My cover blown, I didn't have much of a shot left. He didn't need to know that. "Let the witch, the girl, and the amphibians go, Bluddengutz."

He cackled. "I don't think so, Mr. Moss. Turtles are reptiles! But I should not expect a mere flatfoot to know the finer points of herpetology! Besides, you are only here to witness my final triumph!"

"Triumph? All I see is a terrorized girl." I gestured at Aggie. She was looking at me and I nodded slightly to her. She nodded back through her tears. I wanted to strangle Bluddengutz for doing that to her, but I had to keep my cool. I started sidling my way to the ladder up to the catwalk while I continued my summation. Best way to distract a mad scientist was to get them talking. They loved to talk. "Very impressive, 'doctor.' You're about as good as a schoolyard bully."

"You only say that because you cannot see the whole scope of things! You have only the tiniest view into a mind so powerful you could scarcely comprehend its greatness!" Bluddengutz stood by a circuit breaker. I knew that when he threw that switch, the game was over. I had to get to him before that happened.

While he tossed his head back and laughed, I took the time to scale the ladder.

"Dad!" Prime-8 took a step toward me.

"Stay where you are, my monstrous minion!" Bluddengutz held out a hand. "I am on the verge of becoming the ruler of the West Coast! And tomorrow... *the world!*"

"Yeah," I said, edging closer along the catwalk. "All you need is to do is create this new monster, right?"

"I have the familiars of the most powerful witches in the city! The power in just one of those creatures is incredible, and through my genius, I have acquired *all three*! Witches never relinquish them easily, and yet I have them! You should have seen what I went through just to get test subjects! But it never would have worked without a catalyst! I needed a witch to start the reaction, and you were kind enough to bring me one! You fool! You walked right into my trap!" He cackled.

I cursed inwardly. I should have insisted Hexene stay at home. She never would have gone for it, but I should have insisted anyway. Rather than give this monster the keys to his victory. "And now you're going to send it to kill Kublai Kong."

"Kublai Kong!" Bluddengutz spat. "An ape! A mockery! A fool! He could have everything, and yet all he wants is one pitiful island!"

I thought about telling him that Leona Pryde felt the same way, but chances were he wasn't going to team up with Sarah Bellum. Worse if he did.

"You hated him because he took over from you. He pushed you aside. And so you thought you needed a monster to destroy him, even though we were in the middle of the Night War."

"Yes! I would create something even more powerful! I would create... *MECHANIKONG!*"

"But you failed. You tried, and you ended up with an orangutron."

"I would have succeeded! But Kong's blood is weak! Don't you see? He sabotaged me *with his own blood! Does his craven nature know no bounds?*"

"And when you needed a subject to become your... um... mechanikong, you took your own son. Isn't that right, Mr. D'Agostino?"

It had been right there the whole time. JJ was a carrot top, like no one else in that family that I had seen. When JJ had been changed, he kept his coloring, producing an orange ape. Orange that was reflected in the streaks through Bluddengutz's white hair.

Bluddengutz had been nodding along, his huge eye somehow even bigger, and the lens flashing red light. His mouth was open, a bit of drool slithering from the corner. But when I said his name, the name of the man who had died on Omaha Beach, the man who had fathered JJ and Aggie, his entire mien changed. It was like I hit him in the face with a tall, frosty glass of sanity. He straightened up and the giant eye blinked for the first time I'd known him. "My son?" he asked hesitantly, like even he couldn't believe he could sink so low. "A man needs someone he can trust... no. Nothing like that. I don't have a son!" And he melted again, almost as quickly. "Kong robbed me of that! Don't you see? But now, with the giantess, and the power of the witches! And this girl! *She'll* obey me! *SHE HAS TO!*"

"First your son, and now your daughter? Is there anything left of you in there?"

He cackled, and I suppose that answered that.

"Where were you, John?" I asked him. "You hit the beach at Normandy in '44, then you're back here in '51. Where were you? We thought you were dead. *Alice* thought you were dead."

"I *was* dead! My colleague, Dr. Sutchensuch, found me in that hospital, clinging to life, and he took me to his lab in the Arizona desert!"

I knew the name and I knew the lab. It was the reason the southwest was still literally crawling with ants the size of Cadillacs.

"He put me back together, my genius finally uncaged from the prison of my skull!"

One mad scientist turns another. Bluddengutz spends seven years getting a brain that was aired out by a Kraut machine gun to work right—well, as "right" as it was going to—and he joins the war. Curiosity satisfied, for all the good it did me.

I turned my attention to Prime-8. "JJ!" That was John, Jr. John, as in D'Agostino. "You hear him? You hear what he wants to do to your kid sister?"

"I'm sorry, Mr. Moss. He's my dad!"

"And she's your *sister*! Come on, kid! You can't let this happen!"

Prime-8 was silent, and when he answered me, it was clear that's who he was. Not JJ. Not anymore. "Maybe when she changes I won't be so lonely."

I lunged for Bluddengutz, but he stumbled backward in time to avoid me. I couldn't get my hands on him, and it didn't matter, because now Prime-8 pushed past his father and grabbed me.

"I'm sorry, Mr. Moss," he said, and threw me off the catwalk, where I crashed into the floor. Above me, Bluddengutz cackled.

"My plan is complete! Count yourself lucky, Mr. Moss, to witness the ultimate change in the universe!"

He threw the switch.

Dr. Uriah Bluddengutz

Forty-Three

It's difficult to explain precisely what happened in the moment the mad scientist's plan came to fruition, mostly because I was still in pain from having been thrown into a steel-plate floor, and the amount of energy in the room made every inch of my body stand on end and sing opera. At least that's what it felt like.

What had been a rope of electricity thickened and forked until it was more like twin bolts fighting it out. The problem was, they were doing it through both cages and the tank of blood. Aggie was screaming, or at least she looked it, because the sound being ripped out of her wasn't even slightly human. The three familiars had levitated off the ground, each sheathed in an individual casing of lightning. The tank shattered. I flinched as glass showered me, but no blood came. It, too, was coated in electrical energy, snaking out to the center cage where Aggie was screaming. Or roaring. Or maybe the crackle-hiss of the blue death streaking from the machinery had found a new way to terrify.

Above me, Bluddengutz cackled maniacally. That I could hear perfectly. Prime-8 watched what was happening, the line on his television face perfectly flat.

I pushed myself to my feet and was somewhat startled when I didn't collapse instantly. Nothing broken. At least, nothing too important.

I ran to Hexene. She was staring at her familiar, her green eyes perfectly round, tears falling freely. Her mouth was open, but no sound came out. I flung the nearest switch and was relieved when her manacles popped open and she fell into my arms.

"Nick." She whispered it in my ear. I heard it over the bedlam, somehow. Like the despair with it somehow made it carry, so I wasn't really hearing, but feeling it instead.

I pulled her away. She reached for the cage where her toad was floating, his limbs outstretched, covered in a lattice of crackling energy.

And then with a pop, toad, salamander, and snapping turtle burst. Hexene screamed in agony and shuddered against me, the wracking sobs tearing through her. The bits of familiar flew through the lines of energy like they were riding pneumatic tubes of pure light, joining the blood flowing into and around Aggie Brooks.

Bluddengutz laughed louder. I wanted to punch him. No, I wanted to do a hell of a lot more than that.

The cages exploded, the metal falling to the ground and throwing blue sparks upward. Aggie and the blood and viscera covering her stayed just where they were, held aloft by the energy. Only it wasn't quite Aggie anymore. I could see her, barely, just peeks between gaps in the horrible fluid. She was getting bigger, for one thing, and her skin had turned green. I caught glimpses of bony spines bursting from her back. Her scream had definitely become a roar, and it was no longer my imagination. The howl reverberated around the room, amplifying the mad cackle of her father twice over.

She was bigger than me. Then bigger than Prime-8. The blood and pieces of the familiars flowed into her tissues. Her clothes ripped along seams and fell off her, revealing flabby green skin, almost amphibian, yet harder and more leathery, pitted and rippled. Beneath it, bone stretched and quivering muscles sprouted and grew. Claws ripped from her fingers and toes, curling and blackening. Her hair was down to a few strands, her jaw lengthening to a toothy muzzle, her eyes glowing red with agony. She roared again and I had to cover my ears, the sheer force of her fury sending me staggering backward.

She was bigger than a car now. A moment later, she was the size of a city bus. A tail pushed its way out of her, coated in the same blue energy. The spines on her back had become spade-shaped bony plates, and they strained against the catwalk. The metal screamed, broke. Bluddengutz cackled, backing away from his daughter.

Her hair was gone now. Her face wasn't human in the slightest. It had become something almost reptilian, yet graceful and terrible, too. She roared, and her teeth were as big as a baby's arm.

Her body smashed into the catwalk. Then into the wall. The steel was no longer screaming. It was making the kind of noise I thought was reserved for getting hit with artillery, only it wasn't a single sharp bang but a sustained howl made as something that was never supposed to bend was forced to. I backed off, Hexene limp in my arms. Prime-8 approached his father with a hand out, trying to draw him off, but Bluddengutz was in the midst of his mad scientist laughter. He couldn't be budged.

She was even bigger now. Too big for the room. I found that out when her head hit the ceiling, cracking the clear panels.

Seawater rushed in, raining around and over the monster that had been Aggie Brooks. Hexene was instantly out of her trance, screaming and hopping up into my arms. The water touched the machinery and it exploded. The lightning went out, but Aggie still grew. Another leak sprung in the dome's side. And another. The water was up to my ankles before I knew what happened.

"Dad! We have to get to the sub!" Prime-8 shouted.

"Yes! Yes, and direct my creation! *All of Los Angeles will tremble!*"

The two of them scampered out the other exit, leaving me across the room with a terrified witch in my arms and freezing seawater lapping at my knees while Aggie Brooks continued to break out of the underwater dome like she was hatching from a steel egg.

I sloshed through the water back to where Corrina was.

"Nick! Don't let it touch me!" Hexene shrieked.

"It's hard to hold on when you're wiggling."

"Let's see how you do in a room filling with acid!"

"Fair point."

"What's going on?" shouted Corrina as I sloshed by.

"We need to get out of here!" I shouted back.

"No kidding!"

Bluddengutz had a submarine, and he would be taking that. There had to be some other vehicle, in case the dome broke while Bluddengutz was home and the sub was gone on an errand. He was a *mad* scientist, not a stupid scientist.

"Follow me!"

I sloshed down the hall while Hexene climbed me like a terrified cat. "Why aren't you taller?" she screeched.

"I don't know!" I shouted back.

The water had reached my groin, which had a number of bad consequences. It was getting harder and harder to move through this stuff. Pretty soon, we'd be swimming, and that would be the end of Hexene. Corrina wasn't doing much better, and I was exhausted and beat up, not much more good myself.

We turned a corner. A ladder was set into the wall, leading up through a tube. Away from the water. I got to it, and Hexene needed no encouragement to scramble up. Corrina was next, and by the time I started up, the water had reached my belly.

I climbed. The sounds of Aggie's rebirth pains chased us through the halls, drowning even the racket of rushing water. I cursed myself. I'd found her, but too late. Same with Escuerzo, and Pilar didn't have an admirer after all. Just one mad scientist's vendetta against a monkey khan, destroying everything in sight. At least I'd found Corrina. Cold comfort, but it was something.

We emerged in a tube, just tall enough to stand in. Hexene was almost insensate from the fear, staring at the tube, her hands over her ears to drown out the horrible crashing. Corrina was on the other end at a hatch.

"I think I found something!" she called.

I grabbed Hexene, and she came bonelessly. Corrina was pulling on a wheel lock. A small window showed another room. I peered in and thought I could make out machinery. And it looked sealed. It was better than the alternative.

The rushing grew louder. Sounded like the hall below had flooded. I joined Corrina at the wheel lock and pulled.

Hexene screamed. Seawater was frothing in the tube we'd climbed up. In seconds, it would be over the lip.

I heaved. The wheel lock gave and the hatch opened. Hexene pushed past us and scampered over the lip into the room. Corrina was next and I followed, slamming it behind me.

We were in a small airlock, and one more door, this one open, led to a pod. It was big enough for one person to sit comfortably.

All three of us crammed inside without conversation. There

was a single seat, on which Corrina and I could sort of fit side-by-side, and I wondered if Hexene was still upset about my diminutive stature now. Hexene packed in behind us and hauled the door shut, turning the wheel lock.

"Now what?" she asked.

"Maybe this button does—" The rest was a surprised yell as something boomed at the hatch and we were suddenly rocketing upward like a cork. My ears popped and my eyes felt like they were ready to burst out of my skull. Through one of the portholes, I caught glimpses of what was happening below.

The booming traveled through the water, and the white wash of bubbles shot upward with every collapse of wall and beam. Aggie was huge, breaking out of the undersea base, then she was swimming to the surface, a massive creature maybe amphibian, maybe crocodilian, and maybe something that hadn't been seen on earth for millions of years. She flattened out, her powerful tail lashing back and forth as she surfaced.

She swept past the little metal globe the three of us were crammed in, the wake battering us. We sank, then rose, and Aggie was gone.

Our vessel broke the surface, and I opened the hatch at the top. The thunder boomed and lightning lit up the gray sky. I almost fell back into the vessel, but managed to pull my head and shoulders out. The rain drummed on my head.

And I saw Aggie, swimming hard for the mainland. They were *really* not going to like this.

Forty-Four

The *Merry Celestial* forged ahead just on top of the waves, its greenish-gray glow spilling out over the choppy,bleak water. I waved and shouted. "Over here! Here! See me!"

The vessel we were in was a globular pod, painted the same light blue as the interior of the base. On another day, it would have been well hidden in the Pacific. Here, it was the only thing that was blue that wasn't coming from the sky in giant crackling death-spears.

The ship was in the process of returning to the island. I couldn't imagine anyone actually wanting to gamble in this. Then again, I knew more of what was about to hit the mainland and figured anywhere but there was the place to be. I kept up the waving and shouting, perfectly willing to go hoarse. There was no way they would hear me. I was going to get left in the channel, and this time Serendipity wouldn't be there to help out. And this with Hexene ready to dissolve if she ever got dunked in the water that was all around us.

That made me scream louder.

The ship slid over the sea, waves crashing against its semi-translucent hull. The tattered sails billowed full and the rusted propellers, dripping with kelp, spun. The skeleton lashed to one of the blades seemed to wave with every turn. I was all but certain we were going to be stranded when several green lights shone from about six feet over the water. I winced and turned away. Then I realized what it was. The man in the antique diving suit, the ghost who walked over the waves.

He waved, and I waved back.

The ship reacted a moment later, coming about. The man in the diving suit ran alongside the ship with great, seemingly low strides, each one carrying him several yards. Ensign Pulverized was on the deck and he waved to me. I had never been happier to see a man missing half of his head.

The *Merry Celestial* came to rest right next to us.

"Moss! That you?" Pulverized called.

"Sure is!" I shouted back.

"What the hell are you doing out in this?"

"Long story!"

The man in the diving suit pulled ghostly ropes from the ship and guided the writhing forms over to our globe. One wrapped around me, and the other two snaked inside the vessel. Corrina screamed, and a moment later, both women joined me out in the rain.

"It's all right! This is the ferry to Catalina!" I called to them.

Corrina wasn't so certain, shivering helplessly in the cold. The ropes deposited us on the deck of the ship, then uncoiled. The ghostly crew gathered around.

"Lemme get you a blanket, miss," the pirate said to Corrina, wobbling off on his peg leg.

"What the hell are you doing out here?" Pulverized repeated.

"There was a mad scientist living on the sea floor." They all nodded, and I couldn't tell if that was because they knew, or if it was because of *course* there was a mad scientist living down there. "He was holding these two women captive."

"Where do you need to go now, my friend?" asked the captain, El Acerico. "For the wind is always at my back!"

"Uh... don't you have..." I glanced around the deck. It was free of passengers.

"No, my friend! The ship is at your disposal, especially after your heroic rescue of these two comely wenches."

"I'm not a wench," Hexene growled.

Corrina blushed. "Thank you, Mr..."

"I am El Acerico! Once the gentleman adventurer of the sea! Now a friend to all travelers."

"Uh... Captain... Acerico?" I asked. I checked. The island was closer than the mainland. "I need to get to the island. Immediately. And I probably need you to wait there for me."

"An adventure! Of course! TO THE ISLAND!" His crew sprang into action, the ship banking starboard for the harbor at the mouth of the skull. Lightning snapped and hissed, zapping the metal globe we'd come up in.

"Looks like we got to you just in time," Pulverized remarked.

"Yeah. I owe you one."

The pirate returned and wrapped Corrina in a tattered, glowing blanket. She didn't seem to mind. She took refuge against the forecastle and was shielded from the worst of the rain. I stayed on deck near Hexene, who huddled in the overhang by the captain's cabin. Other than the brief bit of fire at being called a wench, she had retreated to the gray place she had been when Escuerzo was taken. It was worse now. The toad was gone. He wasn't coming back. I didn't know what this meant for her, but did know this was not the time to ask. I had failed her, and all I could do was stand impotently next to her, hoping she would find a way to be okay.

As the *Merry Celestial* slid into port and the man in the diving suit helped the animate ropes tie onto the moorings, the doors of the Isla Calavera Casino opened and both of its giant denizens stepped out into the rain. Others were around their feet, but it was difficult to focus on anything that wasn't a giant gorilla or a fifty-foot blonde. They were staring at something beyond us. I looked over my shoulder and saw what they were watching.

Aggie Brooks had surfaced at the docks. Three martian tripods had closed in and were trying to cook her with their heat rays, but not doing much more than making her angry. Angrier. She opened her mouth, and even all the way across the channel, with the wind howling and the thunder booming, her squeal-roar carried. Some kind of energy—it looked blue, like a concentrated version of whatever had helped make her—shot from her mouth and hit one of the tripods. Orange blossomed from the top and it fell, trailing black smoke. I'd never seen one of those things taken out so easily.

I jumped off the boat, slipped down the gangway, and ran for Pilar and Kong. I had no idea how I was going to be understood. I didn't have the throne room's acoustics working for me, and I had none of Pilar's microphones.

Microphones.

I made it up the pier and aimed for the shore. The giants were still staring at the destruction of the city. Neither one moved a muscle. When I was in the roundabout in front of the hotel, I made out a few others, Jayne Doe and what looked like guests of the hotel, gathered around the giants to see the destruction happening twenty-two miles away.

I ran for the crowd. A few of the monsters saw me, but I was competing for attention with a giant, blue-fire-breathing dinosaur. Nick Moss wasn't going to win that fight, not unless

I had previously beaten them up. Closett, naturally, kept up his yelling.

Kong and Pilar stretched out above me, growing larger and larger as I got closer. Soon they were little more than a pair of knuckles and some shapely feet. I broke right—I'd rather run around Pilar than Kong—and good thing, too. That's when Kong saw me. This time, he recognized me.

Pilar shuffled aside—I just saw her feet moving away, and felt the hammering of her careful footsteps up through my body. Kong was almost on top of me. The doors of the casino were just ahead, and if I could...

The impact didn't throw me anywhere, but it came close. I glanced over my shoulder. Kong had slapped the ground, trying to trap me under his big, leathery hand. I jumped through the front door of the casino. The games were continuing, though the place looked populated with only the most serious career gamblers. I barely merited a look.

Onstage, Jungle Jim and the Hepcats were in the midst of a swinging performance of "That's Amore," while Jungle Jim himself conceived a whole litter of thought-children with a bug-eyed monster in the front row. I ran through the maze of tables, and right as the front doors boomed open and Kong roared a challenge, I hopped up onstage.

"Excuse me, Jungle Jim, I need to borrow this." I grabbed the microphone out of his hands. He was too stunned to stop me. I looked down into the audience, and now the bug-eyed monster was getting up, her tentacles writhing angrily.

"Sorry, folks," I said. "I'll return this to the very talented Jungle Jim in just a moment, but can we give the man a hand? Or a, you know, tentacle? Whatever you've got, slap 'em together!"

The applause started as a pitter-pat, and steadily increased until it was some respectable noise. Jungle Jim smiled and raised a hand, accepting what was due, though not without a little bewilderment.

"What the hell do you think you're doing?" whispered Jungle Jim. He'd dropped the Latin lover accent he sang with and sounded like someone from the Catskills.

"If I said saving the city, would you believe me?"

"No."

"Okay then. Um, just take five. One way or the other, I'll be done by then."

He glanced at the front of the casino, where Kong, Pilar, and the others had gathered. Kong fumed impotently—he couldn't get to me without crushing a bunch of gaming tables and his guests, which was very bad for business. Fortunately for him, he had security winding through the crowd in my direction.

"Um, hi. Mr. Kong and Miss O'Heaven. Good to see both of you here today... is it still... you know what? Doesn't matter. I know you saw what's happening on the mainland. They have no chance. They need you two. You have to stop what's happening."

Kong grunted a series of short bursts.

"The Mighty Kong," said Closett, his voice coming from one of the fake bushes nearby, "would like you to know he doesn't *have* to do anything. And I'm going to get you, Moss. If it's the last thing I do."

"I sleep with the light on, and I may be short, but I'm bigger than what you normally go after," I shot back at him. Into the microphone, I said, "Great Kong, I know you don't have to do anything. But you're a proud man... um... monkey. Ape. Person, proud person. The creature out there is a creation of Dr. Uriah Bluddengutz. The same guy who stole your blood."

Kong growled.

"The Incomparable Kong said, 'come again?'" Closett sounded reluctantly mollified.

"Back in '52, you had trouble with a vampire. Wasn't a vampire. It was Bluddengutz, stealing your blood to make a new monster. You've seen him around before, the orangutron. He tried again, and this time he was successful, only he used Miss O'Heaven's blood. It wasn't a vampire. It was a mad scientist." I said the last part to Pilar, and it was hard to miss how disappointed she looked.

Kong roared.

"The All-Powerful Kong would like to know how you know this."

"It's... uh... well, there was a lot of running, and screaming, and false leads and... detective reasons, okay? I know because of detective reasons. But the important part of this is that the monster is heading for the mainland, and she's going to destroy a lot unless you stop her. I'm not saying kill her, no one said kill, she's a scared little girl who just got turned into a fifty-foot dinosaur thing. Just stop her. Save some people."

Kong thought about it. He made a single sound. *Chuff.*

"The Mighty Kong says it's not his problem."

The one time I needed a giant gorilla to go ape and he wasn't having it. My heart sank. Aggie was going to destroy half the city until some other mad scientist killed her with whatever doomsday device he had percolating in his lair. Chances are, he'd take the other half of the city with her. We were dead.

Until Pilar pulled her dress up over her head and threw it aside, where it fluttered over three bug-eyed monsters, several balam, and a meat golem who had been half-asleep at the roulette table. Underneath the dress, she was in her famous leopard-print bikini. Her face was set, and she threw me a grim nod. She turned for the door.

Kong grabbed her upper arm and grunted directly in her face. She yanked the arm out of his grasp. "Maybe you're too scared to go, but I'm not," she said.

The ape's face went slack with surprise. I didn't think anyone else heard the faint quaver in her voice, but I did. Pilar was terrified. Wouldn't stop her. Not this time. She pushed through the door and was out into the rain.

Kong roared and punched the wall. The casino shook and dust rained from the ceiling. I handed the microphone back to Jungle Jim. "I'm really a big fan," I said, hopping off the stage.

The monkey khan boomed like thunder, picking up a poker table, scattering cards and chips like confetti and sending the monsters sitting around it sprawling. He hurled it into the wall, where it shattered.

Every eye was on Kong except the ones in my skull. He continued to throw his gargantuan tantrum in the foyer of the casino hotel while his guests and staff slowly backed away. Not me. I had places to be, and a ride out front. I ran down one of the side halls—I'd grown pretty familiar with the place over the last few days—and burst out the side exit. Pilar was on the beach, already gracefully diving into the ocean, cold and wind and lightning and waterspouts be damned. I sprinted for the *Merry Celestial.* Isla Calavera shook behind me as Kong continued his tantrum. He had no way of knowing how easy he was making life for Sarah Bellum and her mob, and I wasn't about to tell him. They could destroy each other for all I cared.

I ran back onto the ghost ship. "Where to?" asked the captain, his face alight and the ground around him bleeding centipedes.

"Follow that giantess."

Forty-Five

Pilar O'Heaven pulled herself into the Port of Los Angeles, water cascading off her geologic curves, and launched herself at the mammoth reptile presently tearing through Palos Verdes. The *Merry Celestial* streaked over the waves, wending between waterspouts and lightning crashes. I stood on her deck, clutching rigging that held me back, my face stinging from the salty wind.

When we were halfway across, Kong's barge wallowed into the channel behind us. The curtains on the dais flapped madly, and inside he was bellowing and beating his chest.

I pointed to a section of coastline that hadn't yet been demolished. "Can you bring me up there?"

"I can park you on the head of a specific crab if you want, my friend!" El Acerico called back, waving his arrow-perforated hand.

The ghost ship fluttered swiftly to the place I'd indicated. Pilar and Aggie were locked in battle now, the two monstrous beings grappling while Pilar did her best not to take one of those blasts to the face. Their ankles were lit by the orange of burning buildings, their heads by the blue flash of lightning. Police cars raced toward them, looking like toys ready to be smashed. How long before the Army showed up?

Other shapes came through the clouds and fog, the shafts of light showing little more than vaguely menacing forms, some geometric, others organic, and all elements of the bizarre in the City of Devils. These were the private citizens turning up to protect their city. With three tripods smashed and burning in Aggie's wake, there was little they could do. Still, something to be said for civic pride, no matter how misplaced.

Hexene joined me on the deck. She was shaking, holding her arms across her belly as though fighting off nausea. Corrina was where we had left her, huddled in her blanket but no worse for wear. The pirate lingered nearby whenever he wasn't taking care of the ship.

"I'm sorry, Hexene," I said.

"I know."

"I wish I could have found him earlier."

"I wish I could have found him at all."

Wasn't much to be said after that. I could tell myself there was no way to know Escuerzo had been taken as part of a mad scientist's revenge plot dating back to the Night War, but in retrospect, it was the only thing that made sense.

I really hate that about this job.

The ship ran aground on the same beach Escuerzo had been taken from. "Hexene? Corrina? This is our stop." I nodded to El Acerico. "Thanks for the lift."

"Godspeed, you mad bastard!"

I shook Pulverized's icy hand and dropped onto the sand. Hexene and Corrina followed me. I ran up the slope to the parking area. A mushroom of fire rose into the sky and turned black. A pair of phone booths stood by the side of the road. I stepped into one and called Serendipity. "Hello?" It was her this time. I was glad not to have to go through her crazy roommate.

"Ser, it's Nick."

"Nick! Where are you? Did you hear..."

"Yeah, I heard."

"Wait, does this have something..."

"Of course it has something to do with my case. Can you get that car and pick me up at Royal Palms ten minutes ago?"

"Sure. I'll be right there."

She hung up and I turned to both women, the ill Hexene and the frightened Corrina. "All right, I got us a ride."

"Are you taking me home?" Corrina asked.

"Sure am, but I need to deal with that thing first."

"Why?"

"Because she's killing people."

"Snatchers," Corrina spat. She pointed to the place where Pilar and Aggie battled. The monstrous reptile hurled Pilar away and raked the ground with blue fire, probably destroying a number of things I couldn't see. Pilar did not look so well. She was covered in cuts and scrapes, and her left eye was beginning to blacken and close.

Wasn't going to debate snatchers versus monsters with a girl who'd spent a week as a prisoner. Instead I went with the practical. "How long do you think it'll take before they get to a human neighborhood? And do you think the monsters are going to do anything to stop it then?"

Corrina fell silent. Hexene said nothing, keeping her arms crossed over her stomach in that way I found nervewracking. Waiting for Serendipity took forever. Hexene took shelter in the phone booth and huddled miserably in her wet clothes. I could only watch Pilar's losing effort against Aggie. Even with the occasional sally from the flying machines buzzing around the melee, Aggie could not be stopped. Bluddengutz had succeeded, after a fashion. He'd made an unstoppable monster. Not that she was listening to him.

Serendipity pulled up, splashing me with rainwater. If I had not already been soaked, I might have cared. Felt like weeks since I'd been dry and comfortable. I got in on the driver's side. "Scoot over." Serendipity did. Hexene and Corrina piled into the back.

"Hexene, you remember Serendipity. Corrina, this is Serendipity Sargasso, my secretary."

Ser flashed her terrifying smile. "Pleased to meet you."

"You sure do know a lot of monsters, Mr. Moss," Corrina said skeptically. I was pleased that she'd left the word "snatcher" by the side of the road.

"It's a living."

I floored it, the car fishtailing before straightening out. The rain splashed off of us, and through the windshield, the titanic battle continued. As we made the turn onto Gaffey Street, heading north, Kong's barge got close enough to land, and with a roar, he leapt off it. Good: reinforcements.

Kong, however, set about to prove that he was not above being petty. He loped at the combatants, and with a smack, put the back of his hand across Pilar's jaw. She had already been battered by Aggie and stumbled and fell, catching herself hard to avoid crushing a few houses by the seaside. That was when Aggie turned on Kong, I suspect because he was there.

I couldn't look anymore. I had to concentrate on driving. The streets were wet, and clogged with monsters. Some were the curious, out for a front seat of the three giants battling it out. Police and fire squads were everywhere, some of the cops in black-and-whites, every one of them covered in fur. Others were from the various sheriff's departments, wolves the size of ponies prowling around in yellow-eyed packs. The fire trucks were newfangled contraptions dreamed up by some mad scientist or another, looking more like tanks, and each one equipped with a giant glowing hamster running on a wheel. I dodged one of these while Serendipity gripped the seat.

"What the hell happened?" she finally asked me.

"He was coming right for us, so I thought I'd, you know, turn."

"With the giant monsters!"

"Oh. Kublai Kong had a feud with this mad scientist. Bluddengutz. Thought the feud was settled. Only this guy, he takes his two human kids who think he died in the war and turns them into monsters to kill Kong."

"Kill Kong? What are they doing *here?*"

"He's insane! He didn't have any way to control her! She went for the mainland. I think she's trying to get home, but is in so much pain and so scared, she's destroying everything in her path!"

"Uh-oh."

"Yeah, uh-oh."

"How did he do it?"

"The familiars of the Candlemas Coven and blood from Pilar O'Heaven."

"I'm so sorry," Ser said, leaning over the back of the seat.

Hexene muttered something.

"Okay, so I think I'm all up to date. Except... why is there a human girl in the backseat?"

"Oh, she was kidnapped as leverage. Bluddengutz wanted to draw Hexene off alone, so he grabbed Corrina. One of Hexene's, um, clients had a bit of a... well, you know... a crush. So Bluddengutz used her to get to him, and then Hexene."

"Gill-man?"

"What else?"

"I swear. They are so predictable sometimes."

"Bluddengutz had the poor bastard killed."

"Paolo's dead?" Corrina asked from the backseat.

"I'm sorry."

"Why?" she asked. "I told him to leave me alone and he wouldn't. At least Jaime won't do time for it."

"Oh. Well, all's well that ends well with that, I guess." I didn't mention that Jaime might still do the time despite being innocent. Being in a human gang, with a record like his, there were probably half a dozen cops who couldn't wait to get him off the street. If I wanted to keep that from happening, I had to make sure the right people went down for it. The monsters. Bluddengutz and Prime-8.

Poor JJ. He was lost, it looked like. Still, he was only fifteen. Maybe if he went down for this, spent a couple years in a reform school, he'd have a chance. Let his folks know he was still alive. Just a little hairier than they remembered. My usual disclaimer popped into my mind: Nine times out of ten, the best-case scenario is little Susie likes being a fish girl now.

I sailed into Watts, skidding out on the turn to Henry and Alice Brooks' street. The sun must have gone down, because the monsters were out and lurking. Or maybe they just didn't care. I'd believe either one. Especially now, with the world ending all around us. Seemed like the old laws scarcely mattered.

I swung the car into the Brooks driveway and got out of the car.

"Hey there, meatstick! Never got to finish our talk, hyuck, hyuck!" The Reverend Bobo Gigglesworth jumped from the shadows, his sharp teeth dripping blood and his breath stinking of death and cotton candy.

"Hey there, padre," I said, and decked him.

It was the hardest I'd ever hit someone. He wasn't expecting it. He was flat-footed, and considering the size of those shoes, that really meant something. My fist caught him square in the nose. And it honked. I nearly laughed at that. He keeled over right by the car, safely in dreamland. I cradled my fist as I jogged up the porch. The monsters in the neighborhood watched me intently, though none got any closer. Especially not after Serendipity got out of the car and fixed them with a fishy stare.

I hammered on the door. "Henry! Alice! It's Nick!"

The door opened. Henry held a bottle of makeup remover in one hand, and his wife was right behind with a sharpened stake. "Nick! Get in here, quick!"

"No, I need you to come with me!"

"You found Aggie?" Alice asked. The hope in her voice was heartbreaking.

"She's not what you remember, but yes. And she needs you right now. In fact, the whole city does."

"What?" Henry asked, confusion tinged with fear in his voice.

I glanced around. The monsters were beginning to get some courage back. Leveling a clown had an expiration date, I guessed. A zombie dragged a leg behind him up the lawn. A bug-eyed monster climbed over the fence and paused on the top. "Now, please, Henry."

He came out, bewildered. I grabbed him and hustled both of them to the car. Henry climbed in the back, Alice in the front. She screamed when she saw Serendipity and tried to shove the stake through her heart.

"Nick! Get her off me!" Ser shouted.

I started the car and snatched the stake from Alice. "Damn it, Alice! She's my secretary!"

"What's happening?" Alice screeched.

"I have to take you to your daughter."

Fire glittered off the raindrops pattering off the car. Aggie roared, and the windows shook. "What's that?" asked Alice.

"That'd be your daughter," I muttered, and instantly regretted it when Alice burst into tears. Ser tried to comfort the weeping woman and got shoved away for her troubles.

"What?! You said you'd save her!" Henry barked from the backseat.

"I know what I said," I mumbled, wishing that Aggie could find a way to step on only me, leaving the rest of the people in the car alive. "I didn't."

"Nick did his best," Serendipity said.

"No one's talking to you, snatcher!" Henry snapped.

"What happened?" Alice managed.

I explained as well as I could, running through the timeline of things, and included the identities of the other players.

"JJ is alive?" Henry asked, and there was a little hope in his voice.

"Alive, but changed. He's a monster now. And he killed at least one person, but yes, he's alive."

"Where is he?"

"You'll find him with Bluddengutz down there."

Alice sniffed. "And he's actually John?"

"Yeah, I think so."

"John died in '44. The first monsters didn't show up until '45," Henry said. "Problem in your theory right there."

"Oh, come on, Henry. You really think the first monsters simply popped up right when the war ended and just so happened to look like the ones in the pictures? They were around before that. Had to be. They were just hiding or something."

The car was silent, and neither of the monsters riding in it had anything to say about it.

"John *died*," Alice insisted.

I thought about the missing part of his skull. "Probably

looked that way to the Army docs at the time, but a mad scientist got his mitts on him and turned him. Missing half a head is just a challenge to them. Took him seven years and one of the biggest labs in the country, but he did it."

"Why JJ and Aggie?" she demanded.

"I don't know, Alice. Maybe he knew they were his kids somewhere deep down, and he wanted them close by. Maybe he was crazy, and that was the one part of him that felt like it was before. I wish I knew."

"He turned them for revenge."

"Yeah. But not on them. On the monkey khan."

We were close enough to see Pilar, Kong, and Aggie over the buildings, battling it out beneath the flash of lightning and the petals of fire. The streets were mostly clear, and I shimmied around stopped cars and took turns hard. The beings on the street appeared to be monsters. Maybe night had fallen. Who could tell? It felt like there wasn't going to be a sunrise, so maybe all bets were off.

We didn't have to drive very far. The swath of destruction had reached inland and was getting a little too close to Watts for my liking. I pulled the car to a stop at the makeshift barricade formed by police and fire vehicles. There were a few buildings in between us and them, plus what had once been Compton. Pilar was almost out of the fight, and Kong wasn't doing much better. Aggie was covered in small wounds, though she scarcely seemed to notice. She could probably go on stamping Los Angeles flat as long as she had a mind to.

I jumped out of the car, ignoring the uniformed wolfmen shouting at me, and pulled Alice with me. Serendipity and Henry followed and we ran between the cars while the cops yelled after us. It was only a few blocks to the battleground. Between the booming hits of the monsters pounding on each other, the high-pitched roar of the Aggie-beast, and the plethora of pops, zaps, and other noises from the assembled monsters, it was tough to hear myself think.

Beneath them, I saw the submarine that had taken Hexene down to the base at the bottom of the ocean. It was moving around on spidery legs, Bluddengutz poking out of the hatch, barking into a loudspeaker, trying to order his "monstrous minion" to attack what he wanted her to attack. Aggie was studiously ignoring him.

I stopped there, Henry and Alice grabbing hold of one another as they watched the fifty-foot reptile that had been their daughter rampaging over the city.

"Moss?" I heard the gravelly voice behind me, close enough to cut through the rest of the cacophony on the street and too familiar by half.

I turned. Moon and Garou, only recognizable by Moon's regrettable fashion sense. They were both wolfed, their faces covered in gray and brown fur respectively, their teeth poking sharply from lower jaws. Garou grabbed me without much preamble and slammed me into the side of a police cruiser. "Got you now, meatstick!"

"Let him go!" Serendipity screamed.

"Stand back, doll," Moon growled. "You don't want any part of this."

"We're bringing you in for Paolo del Mar's murder," Garou said, "And you're going to spill the whole thing." I found that I didn't have to fight panic down this time. I guess since I had spent the last couple days being terrified of Kong, my nightmares' nightmare, the idea of a wolfman about to throw me in the clink lacked a certain mystique.

"I didn't kill del Mar," I coughed. "But I know who did."

"Yeah, I bet you do."

"Moon! Your partner might be a sap, but you've got a brain in your head."

Garou slammed me into the car again. It hurt, but not like getting tossed into the bulkhead of an undersea base. Still, my legs gave out for a moment.

"Lou, let the man talk."

"So he can bullshit us?"

"Let's see if he does."

Garou spun me around and shoved me into the side of the car from a different angle. Behind me, the battle between the three giants continued. "Talk, you weasel-faced son of a bitch, and pray you convince my partner."

"Okay, it's like this. Paolo del Mar was a hex addict. He had a deal with a witch. A mad scientist wanted to get his mitts on the witch's familiar, so he could create... that." I jerked a thumb over my shoulder. I was pretty confident it hit the target, since Aggie would be tough to miss. "He got del Mar to set up the meeting by getting some leverage on him, and then he sent his minion, this half-ape, half-robot—called an orangutron, actually—to do the deed."

"You buying this goofy story?" Garou snarled. His teeth, jutting from his lower jaw, seemed bigger.

"You want to send me down for beating a gill-man to death with my bare hands?" I said. "Come on, Moon. You know you were just shaking the tree with me. Well, here's the fruit. You want me to come Downtown, I'll spill everything. I'll make your case for you, but you have to arrest the button men."

Moon looked me over. Even with the fur over his face and the bestial set to his jaw, intelligence glinted in his eyes. "All right, Moss. Finger the mug."

"They're in there."

"Under the monsters."

"Uh, yeah."

"There's a giant monster fight happening, Moss. Hard to make an arrest with that in the way."

I turned around as Aggie hit Kong with a blast of her blue energy. "Good point. You fellas have a bullhorn?"

"You want a bullhorn?"

"I think I can stop this. But she needs to hear."

Moon thought it over and eventually nodded. "Officer!" he called to one of the uniformed cops, who was holding a bullhorn. "Bring that here."

The officer handed it to Moon, who handed it to me. "All right, Moss. Do it."

I nodded, took the bullhorn, and regarded Aggie. I had no idea what I was going to say. I put my mouth up to the thing, and for a moment, all I could hear was my shallow breathing. Then I went with, "AGGIE? AGGIE BROOKS?"

The giant monster paused only for a moment. A gremlin flying machine fired a globe of acid that splashed and sizzled against Aggie's skin. She roared and knocked the thing out of the sky, where it hit the earth and exploded.

"AGGIE! IT'S NICK MOSS. I KNOW YOU REMEMBER ME."

Aggie stopped her rampage. This time, nothing prompted her to continue. I had her undivided attention, which, when coming from a fifty-foot-tall engine of death, was a little intimidating. She regarded me with her reptilian eyes, her massive mouth open, displaying teeth that could comfortably munch on cars without so much as breaking a filling. I tried to think of her not as a monster, but as the little girl who'd once given me a fried egg.

"YOUR PARENTS ARE HERE, AGGIE. THEY WANT TO TALK TO YOU."

Aggie cocked her head and inhaled. For a moment, I thought she was going to send a stream of her destructive energy to scorch everything around me. She didn't. I took that as a sign and handed the bullhorn to Henry.

"What am I supposed to say?" he asked. Tears glimmered in his eyes, but they wouldn't fall. Henry wasn't going to cry in front of a bunch of monsters.

"I don't know. Tell her you love her. Tell her that she's still your daughter."

"She's a giant snatcher!" Henry said. "That's not my daughter."

"The hell she isn't!" I nearly decked him so he could join the right Reverend Bobo Gigglesworth in counting sheep. "She's still the same girl you knew. Yeah, okay, she's fifty feet tall, and scaly, and maybe she breathes some stuff that might be atomic fire, but she's still Aggie. Now tell her you get that or so help me, Henry, you and I are going round for round."

It was Alice who took the bullhorn from me. Henry put his head in his hands.

"AGGIE? AGGIE, HONEY, IT'S MAMA."

Aggie made a noise that might have been a whine if it hadn't shaken every window in the area.

"I NEED YOU TO STOP DESTROYING THE CITY. YOUR FATHER AND I STILL LOVE YOU."

Aggie roared. There was no menace in it. It was more a plaintive cry.

"I KNOW YOU'RE A MONSTER NOW, BUT THAT DOESN'T MATTER. YOU'RE STILL OUR LITTLE GIRL. WE NEED YOU TO STOP WHAT YOU'RE DOING. NO ONE ELSE IS GOING TO HURT YOU."

Aggie considered. She glanced at her two opponents. Pilar had pulled herself to her feet, ready to fight if need be. She looked like a heavyweight on the wrong side of the worst beating in history, too dumb or stubborn to throw in the towel. Kong had long since given up, lying on his back in the rubble, swaths of his fur burned away entirely.

Aggie looked at the defenders of the city, waiting in the pregnant silence.

The giant reptilian head nodded.

"Ask her if she'll grab that vehicle under her for us," Moon rasped.

"What?" Alice asked.

Moon repeated himself.

"HONEY, THE POLICE WOULD LIKE YOU TO GRAB THAT THING."

Aggie growled in confusion.

"THE MOVING THING AT YOUR FEET. IT KIND OF LOOKS LIKE A BUG TO YOU, PROBABLY."

Aggie picked up Bluddengutz's vehicle. I imagined the mad scientist screaming orders at her. He could do that until he was blue in the face.

"THAT'S IT. THANK YOU, HONEY."

"What next, Nick?" Serendipity said, coming up next to me.

"I think I'd like to get home before all these monsters realize what I am."

Forty-Six

Three fifty-foot monsters and a burning city is a great distraction. Serendipity got me back to the car with no one the wiser, and we returned Corrina home first. Her mother came by the office the next day, calling me "son." It was nice to have returned someone in the same state they'd gone missing. I think it's Mrs. Lacks' intention to pay me in baked goods, and frankly that sounds fine by me, even if she's intent on destroying how my suits fit. Bud Thirst was just as happy, and he paid me what he owed, and promised me I would be his first call if his firm needed someone found. I didn't expect the call but thanked him all the same.

True to their word, Moon and Garou brought me downtown the next afternoon, and I laid everything out for them. Every last bit of it. Moon was happy enough to collar Prime-8 and Bluddengutz for the murder, even if Prime-8 was going to do his time in Juvenile Hall. I hoped Henry and Alice would go see the boy, maybe try to give him the childhood he'd missed out on being his father's warped experiment. Then again, they might not be welcome in the City of Devils anymore.

Aggie picked her parents up that night and left. I heard later they're living on one of the Channel Islands north of town. Aggie's still wanted for the whole destruction of the city thing, but apparently no one wants to go serve the warrant on her. She'll probably end up working that time off in the Army if she does it at all. Uncle Sam isn't one to waste a giant monster in the clink if she can protect us from the winter hags and werebears over in Mother Russia. Last I heard, Aggie was calling herself Dinah Sawyer.

As for the Bellum mob, I knew they weren't going to let my marker go. I was still waiting for the other shoe to drop. Sooner or later, I'd have a zombie at my door to collect on the favor I allegedly owed, and likely, they'd be wanting interest. Fortunately for me, they probably had bigger things to worry about at the moment. From everything I heard, the Los Angeles underworld wasn't quite as sewn up as Sarah Bellum would like. Goblins and zombies were getting dropped in the streets in what looked like mob hits.

The weather evened itself out after the storm ran its course. In some ways, we were lucky. The deluge kept the fires from spreading. Within a week, it was clear blue skies again. I guess the storms the Candlemas Coven were preventing all blew themselves out, and we were back to our normal weather now.

All of the Candlemas hexes were unraveling, no longer powered by the missing familiars. As for me, I found a twenty-dollar bill on the pavement in front of my office. Maybe the ripple of one of the bad-luck whammies Hexene put on me. Maybe a little overdue fortune. I didn't know. I'd rather she had her toad back.

A week or so after the case closed, I came home to find a familiar face waiting for me out front. Familiar in that it was the only face I knew that was made up of charcoal suspended in pink jelly. "Mr. Night Ranger! I trust that the inevitable specter of your meaningless solitary existence isn't troubling you this evening!"

"Not until just now. How are you, Keyes?"

Gelatin Keyes wobbled outside of the same car he had picked me up in the first time. "Miss Pilar O'Heaven would like you to join her at her home for dinner."

"Yeah, no problem. Let me get my toothbrush."

Keyes waved. I came out with my bag and got into the car.

"Plenty to drink back there, Mr. Night Ranger!"

"I'm fine, Keyes. What happened to you on the island?"

"Oh, I got lost, and I ate some tables and a few rooms, and then they froze me. And then I took the ferry home. One day I will be far too big!" He bubbled happily. "Say, what did the whale say when he bumped into the dolphin?"

"I don't know. What?"

"Nice belt!"

"Good one."

Pilar met me in the living room, where she was stretched out on the couch. She was covered in bandages and wrapped in her bathrobe. She looked bad, but she also looked happy. I found my jacket, ID, and everything else Percy Katz had confiscated waiting for me on the table. "I wanted to thank you, Mr. Moss."

"That's what the money's for," I said.

She smiled, then winced when that pulled on something. "Did you see the headline?"

Of course I had. Everyone had. Right on the front page of the *Los Angeles Minion.* THE CITY OF ANGELS' ANGEL, *Giantess Protects City.* They loved her. Everyone did now. Even if she hadn't protected much, she had gotten the credit. Of course she had, she was the monster. No one wanted to admit that a few kind words had done what a dinner-table-sized fist couldn't, especially when those words were from a human. The stain of HUMAC was off her. At least for the time being.

"I'm happy for you," I said, and I meant it.

"I left Kong. Don't know what I'm going to do, but I know it'll be something."

"Good."

"That's thanks to you."

I waved it off. "I didn't find your vampire."

"You found who was doing it. That's what I asked." Some color bloomed into her cheeks. "Besides, there are enough vampires calling now."

Pilar fed me and I bunked in her safe room while Keyes tried to get in.

I had spent the whole week thinking about Hexene, off and on. She was a witch, but one without powers. Not sure what that meant, really. But it kind of made any sort of commitment to the maiden thing seem pointless. I walked into her shop the following Friday, after spending my time screwing up every ounce of courage I had.

All the shelves in the shop were bare. Hexene came out of the back, not as gray as she had been, but far from the fiery woman I'd met only a few months ago.

"Nick?" Nicest greeting I'd gotten in a long time.

"Yeah, hi, Hexene. Listen, I was thinking... since you're not a... well, you know, I thought maybe you and I could..." and the courage failed me. Just ran right out the door. Good-for-nothing bastard. "What gives with the shop?"

"Oh. We're leaving."

"We?"

"The Candlemas Coven. We have to go."

I wanted some time to pull the icicle out of my heart. I didn't have it. "Go? Where? Why?"

"We're going to get our powers back."

"You can do that?"

She nodded. "It takes some doing… some convincing. There are tests. And other… concerns. We agreed. All three of us. We agreed."

I swallowed. "Or, you know, you could stay."

I think she knew what I was saying. The way she was looking at me, the way she pushed aside some of her red curls, the sadness in her big green eyes. "I… can't, Nick." She swallowed. "We agreed," she said again.

"Yeah, I know. Sorry, it was stupid." I watched my feet. "Good luck, Hexene."

"Thank you."

I went to the door and pulled it open. The bell rang. I paused. There was a lot I wanted to say to her, but I didn't have the words. I didn't even know exactly what I wanted to say. It was silly. She had things to do, and I was still only human.

I left her shop, and I didn't look back.

The next couple months I spent forgetting. Mira helped. Not because I was dating her. Because she and Sam Haine, my old admirer, got into a rather nasty dispute over the right to turn me, and my lawn became a nightly battle royale between doppelganger and pumpkinhead. Sam eventually won the right to annoy me nightly, but Mira was surprisingly tenacious.

It was late October, and I was putting the finishing touches on a case. I heard the outside door open, and before I had a chance to check with Serendipity, the door to my office opened, too.

It was Detective Phil Moon.

"Come to shake me down, Detective?" I asked him.

"I've come to hire you, Moss. Get your gear, you work for the Los Angeles Police Department now."

Nick Moss will return in:
WOLFMAN CONFIDENTIAL

Now Available

FROM CANDLEMARK & GLEAM

"Every conspiracy needs a guy like me.

Every conspiracy has one . . . me.

And now someone's trying to kill me.

When everyone has a motive, everyone is a suspect, and I don't even know who all the players are. It's a race against time to figure out who wants me dead, and why, and how to prevent all the underground conspiracies, aliens, cryptids, and things that go bump in the night from throwing the world into chaos while I'm at it.

Just another
normal day
at the office,
really."

Mr Blank by Justin Robinson

WHEREVER FINE BOOKS ARE SOLD

www.candlemarkandgleam.com

Dial M for Meatstick

BY

Cleave Hunter

Chapter One

All things being equal, it was a funny place to find a dead fella. In my line, the odd corpse isn't something to get the screaming meemies over, even if cleaning up after bodies ain't exactly on the menu. But when you find one sitting behind the wheel of your own jalopy with an acute case of glass poisoning, that's when you think you might be a patsy.

It didn't start that way. No, it started the way all of these things do: with a dame.

She crawled into my office like a warning I wasn't going to take. Her tentacles went all the way up to her fovea, where she had a string of oyster fruit wrapped around the stems, just asking to be undone. I thought about that choker a lot over the next few days, down to how much trouble I could have saved if I'd used it string myself up right then. Yeah, she was an eye of the crawling variety, just like me.

"Mr. Visionus?" she asked in a voice like syrup over a gas fire.

"Yeah, that's me," I said, folding some tentacles over others, and wondering how much trouble she was carrying in her ritzy handbag.

Her name was Chora, and she had come slithering down from Beverly Hills to my office Downtown. She told me her husband was making time, and here I was wondering what he thought he could be missing. Her getaway noodles kept fidgeting like she wanted to calm down with a coffin nail. Pegged her as a recent change, a dolly playing in the monster leagues. Made me want to buy what she was selling and ask for seconds. She doled this out while batting lashes that nearly got stuck in my ceiling fan.

"My husband turned me," she said, and it wasn't the oldest story in the book, but it was the most read these days. "If he's stepping out..." She trailed off, finishing with a shrug of her eight tentacles.

I named her my price and she agreed without trying to goblin me down. She slid over a calling card, and the number on it was a Madison exchange. Meant Hollywood, the world's crawling eye capital. The mister was a studio executive—weren't they all—at Universal, by the name of Scleros. She gave me the usual applesauce like she was reading from a script: late nights, strained talks. I checked them off in my head, and by the end of her rundown, I was sold. I'd catch him at it, snap a newsstand-ready still, and soon be dropping her money into my cornea, one whiskey at a time.

I took one look at the palooka they had working security on the Universal lot and decided to hang around outside the gate. No sense in getting a shiner trying to sneak in. I get hired for one thing, and that's my vision. I say it's 200/20 in the phone book ads, but that's guesswork. First crawling eye that needs glasses, and I'm a monkey khan's uncle. I picked Scleros up as soon as his Cadillac nosed onto Melrose Avenue. It was after nine, and most of the monsters in town were in South Los Angeles or Boyle Heights looking for love. At first, that's where I figured he was headed, to see if some hot-to-trot meatstick "accidentally" dropped a ward or two.

It can be a touchy situation with a new bride. Getting kids and stepping out looks like the same thing, especially to the freshly turned. That's all this was. Chora thought she was getting thrown over for some younger skirt, a bigger baby blue. Fact was, she was getting that kid she didn't even know she wanted. A fresh crawling eye, who'd need to learn all about six different new colors, and why we don't play with needles anymore.

I never had the urge for kids. Getting turned was the best thing for me, but I'm no proud papa. Give that to the other monsters out there, making the world better one turning at a time.

When Scleros went west, that's when I started wondering what his game might be. That sweet Chora was goofy with the green-eyed monster was one thing; that she might be right, well, it never plugged into my noggin. I followed him to the coast, and then north. The city was quiet out here. Nobody but us monsters. Something to be said for that.

He pulled into a Motel No-tell off the side of the road. The Sea Monster, complete with a winking leviathan on the buzzing neon sign. A Studebaker, a spectral charger, and a gremlin flivver were already parked there. Looked like the place was doing bang-up business, and judging by the pro-skirts lingering around the roadhouse up the way, three guesses as to why.

Scleros wasn't looking at the kitties. He headed for the front desk, bargained for a room from the sleepy devil behind the counter, and went to the second floor. Room 205. Good place for him to hole up, too. I couldn't stay pulled over without gluing all eyes to me, so I went up the road, came back and parked myself by the roadhouse, went inside, and took a seat where I could keep my eye clapped to that motel room door.

When the sea hag waitress stopped by, I ordered a dropper of beer. No real drinking when I was on the job.

Kept watching. The gremlin lurched out in an hour, tottered over to the roadhouse, and tucked into a dinner of cotton candy and jellybeans. The headless horseman made an appearance, taking a leisurely walk along the cliffs, but leaving his horse to paw the ground and snort fire.

I didn't think much of anything until a Ford coupe pulled into the parking lot. A young kid, maybe at the tail end of his teens got out. To say he looked like a meatstick doesn't mean much to most monsters, especially those who don't look much different most of the time. Your wolfmen, your doppelgangers, your mad scientists. We crawling eyes, we see more. Might as well have had a sign as big as the Sea Monster with the arrow pointing to him: Get yer meatstick here. Good-looking kid, too. Smooth skin, long limbs. Vampires must have been lining up for this one.

And here he was. Bait. Right out in front of me. In the best of times, meatsticks carry enough weapons to turn every monster they see into goo. This one was no exception. The bumps and bulges in his letterman's jacket might have been too small for most monsters to see, but not me. He was walking death, right out in the open. I pitied the first monster who tried to show him a better world.

The meatstick went into a room on the bottom floor. It had to be bristling with wards by now. I itched just thinking about the lines of sand he had to have up.

Didn't have too much time to reflect on it, as the rumble

of steel horses rattled the windows. Headlights flashed through windows as the rumbles got lower, then stopped. The door burst in a moment later. Phantoms. A whole choir of them. Wrapped in leather, probably packing gats and saps, kicking in the door like they owned the place and were keen to redecorate. Bunch of leatherboys was bad enough. A black eye really cuts into my business. But it was worse than that.

They had been pretty jake for clowns. I'd clocked them the instant I slithered in. Figured they'd be at their usual schtick, getting everyone to laugh until someone started to bleed. They had the whole shebang, white faces, the laughing mouths, and of course, the instruments of pain. They were at their corner table, eating their peanuts and candy, not bothering anybody. I was hoping to get out of there before they decided it was showtime.

When the phantoms barged in, the clowns turned. The phantoms stopped in their tracks. Clowns and phantoms mix like grease paint and varnish, like robots and gremlins, like vampires and werewolves. Everyone in the joint knew there was going to be a rumble. Monsters started clearing out as soon as the phantoms stepped away from the door.

"Look who ran away to join the circus," said the lead phantom, a plus-sized palooka with a face only a mummy could love.

The clowns got up to the honking of bicycle horns. The phantoms winced at the sudden discordant noise.

"Too much already?" said the lead clown asked, giggling with his pals.

Yeah, it wasn't my first Halloween. I got out of there before it really started, the phantoms belting out *La Traviata* while the clowns tried to drown them out with honking, screeching, and half-songs. The windows shattered two seconds after I skedaddled.

"I'm crawlin' here!" I shouted back at them, but they

couldn't hear me over the aria and the chicken sounds.

So much for waiting... but it didn't look like I had to wait much longer. Room 205 was standing wide open. No one was moving around inside, and it was quieter than a ghoul's grave on a rainy day. Looked like I was going to have to peek. Anybody in there, I could tell I had just misplaced some ice.

I slithered up the stairs, doing my best to ignore the unholy racket from the roadhouse. The wolves would be getting here soon, though how they planned to break that mess up was beyond me. Knocking a clown silly was nearly impossible, what with silly being their natural state and all.

The motel room was empty. The bed was made, with enough of a dent in the comforter to say someone had been sitting on it. The bathroom door was open, and past that, the bathroom window. Any other kind of monster would have missed the shadow falling past the window, but I'm a crawling eye.

I slithered to the window and pressed that big baby brown to the window. A shape ran down the narrow alley between the motel and the cliffside, heading for the smoky shadows of the roadhouse. A human shape.

I went back to the front, not wanting to explain to Scleros what I was doing in his motel room if he got back from wherever he was. Probably gawking at the brouhaha going on at the roadhouse. I needed to get back in my car and wait this thing out. Figure out what was next.

My car was waiting for me where I left it, and though the windows were humming from the phantoms singing, they hadn't shattered yet. The racket had turned into a brawl, with the sounds of hard fists honking onto clown noses. They could sort it out.

I opened the front door, and that's when I found Scleros, dead, slumped behind my steering wheel.

That's when I heard the first siren.

Fly, crawl, swim, or jump on over
to your local bookseller to pick up

DIAL M FOR MEATSTICK,

another fine Cleave Hunter
mystery that'll slay you
(unless you're already undead).

A Phantom Pen Publication

And now—

Fifty Feet of Trouble

A WORD FROM OUR SPONSORS...

Justin Robinson

Too hot at the circus?
Thirsty at the carnival?
Cool, man.

Just open up Bebop and -

POP, FIZZ, WOW!

The cotton-candy swirls of pink and blue
go round and round and never mix -
Something wild, man, something new,
And that's just one of Bebop's tricks!

Bebop Cola

Dig it. Drink it. Crazy, man.

SKULLS, SAND, AND RICHES GALORE!

Fabulous

ISLA CALAVERA

where screams come true

The gorgeous jewel of the Channel Islands! Only an hour from Los Angeles by boat or ten minutes' flight—or even less if your wingspan is big enough!—Isla Calavera Resort & Casino is your paradise getaway close to home! From the luxurious suites which cater to every shape of patron, to the fabulous spreads of our twelve five-star dining rooms, to the Floating Tables where every night fortunes are won on a single spin of the wheel, Isla Calavera Resort & Casino is truly the place where the joys of the hereafter come home to us here on earth!

CONTACT YOUR TRAVEL AGENT TODAY—OR JUST HOP ON OVER!

if you're TIRED of those rags you died in...

you can do better!

the very finest fashions of Paris, London, & Rome are now available in bespoke ectoplasm and soft Angora ghoul

HAUNT COUTURE

DESIGNED BY GHOSTS • MADE BY GHOSTS • WORN BY GHOSTS

TWILIGHT VISITOR

ENTERTAINMENT FOR GENTLEMONSTERS

50¢

New Issue Now on Stands
Featuring MISS JAYNE DOE
"The Girl Who Never Locks Her Doors"
In A Spellbinding Pictorial
Also: Interviews

ACKNOWLEDGEMENTS

As much as authors like to pretend otherwise, publishing a book is a team effort. As always, I want to thank my stellar publisher, Candlemark & Gleam. I also want to thank Kate Sullivan, who helps me out more than anyone I've met in this industry, and who continues to help me put out the best books I'm capable of.

For the second book in the City of Devils universe, I'd be remiss if I didn't thank the people whose books, movies, comic books, and everything else that inspired me to create this whole universe.

And that list is... wow. It's a long one. I've loved monsters since I can remember. The vast majority of my favorite books, comics, movies, anythings, have a monster in them. In a lot of ways, this series is an ongoing love letter to the creature features and noir that keep inspiring me.

So thank you. Thank you to Tod Browning, and Roger Corman, and Walter Mosley, and John Carpenter, and Stephen King, and Raymond Chandler, and literally everyone else who makes any kind of art with monsters or detectives. Thank you all. You make the world substantially better. For me, at least.

Photo by Leora Saul

About the Author

Much like film noir, Justin Robinson was born and raised in Los Angeles. He splits his time between editing comic books, writing prose, and wondering what that disgusting smell is. Degrees in Anthropology and History prepared him for unemployment, but an obsession with horror fiction and a laundry list of phobias provided a more attractive option. He is the author of nine novels in a variety of genres including detective, humor, urban fantasy, and horror. Most of them are pretty good.

Follow the Author Online

www.captainsupermarket.com

Twitter: @JustinSRobinson

Facebook: facebook.com/weirdnoirmaster

CPSIA information can be obtained
at www.ICGtesting.com
Printed in the USA
LVHW112318181218
601006LV00002B/265/P

9 781936 460717